Praise for Brad Leithauser's

# THE PROMISE OF
# ELSEWHERE

"Dazzling. . . . [A] keen-eyed comic work. . . . Leithauser, a poet, novelist, and MacArthur Fellow, recalls Stanley Elkin, Wilfrid Sheed, and Richard Ford in this complex anatomy of a midlife crisis and then some. An exceptional glimpse of the human comedy." —*Kirkus Reviews* (starred review)

"Like Andrew Sean Greer's Pulitzer Prize–winning *Less*, Leithauser's journey novel wonderfully mixes pathos and comedy, and Louie, as he struggles for a sense of value and self, is endearingly and wonderfully human at every moment." —*Booklist* (starred review)

"Charming and moving. . . . Leithauser's novel offers civilized comforts of beguiling characters, witty dialogue, and trenchant observations about modern life that enshrines the visceral pleasures of armchair travel." —*Publishers Weekly*

Brad Leithauser

# THE PROMISE OF
# ELSEWHERE

Brad Leithauser is a widely acclaimed novelist and poet and the recipient of numerous awards and honors, including a MacArthur Fellowship. He has served as *Time* magazine's theater critic. In 2005, he was inducted into the Order of the Falcon by the president of Iceland for his writings about Nordic literature. This is his seventeenth book. He is a professor in the Writing Seminars at Johns Hopkins University and divides his time between Baltimore and Amherst, Massachusetts.

Also by Brad Leithauser

# THE PROMISE OF

# ELSEWHERE

# THE PROMISE OF
# ELSEWHERE

## Brad Leithauser

VINTAGE BOOKS

A Division of Penguin Random House LLC

New York

FIRST VINTAGE BOOKS EDITION, FEBRUARY 2020

The Library of Congress has cataloged the Knopf edition as follows:
Names: Leithauser, Brad, author.
Title: The promise of elsewhere : a novel / by Brad Leithauser.
Description: First edition. | New York : Alfred A. Knopf, 2019.
Identifiers: LCCN 2018015741 (print) | LCCN 2018019293 (ebook)
Classification: LCC PS3562.E4623 (ebook) | LCC PS3562.E4623 P76 2019 (print) |
DDC 813/.54—dc23
LC record available at https://lccn.loc.gov/2018015741

Vintage Books Trade Paperback ISBN: 978-0-525-56412-6
eBook ISBN: 978-0-525-65504-6

Rome and London passport stamps © Victor Metelskiy/Shutterstock
Iceland and Greenland passport stamps © Marina Riley/Shutterstock
Book design by Betty Lew

www.vintagebooks.com

146122990

For Sheila McCormick—

*My fair traveler*

*Through climes & times*
*To the near & dear*

They will unite the spectrum, the floating red of wind-blown Italian rose petals, the floating blue of Greenland's icebergs, for in the Land of Colors without Objects, all is afloat and there is no land.

—The Art Student's War

Quant aux traits, aux traits de sa figure . . .
Ah! Sa figure était charmante!
Je la vois, belle, belle comme le jour où, courant après elle,
Je quittai comme un fou la maison paternelle
Et m'enfuis à travers les vallons et les bois!

—The Tales of Hoffmann

# AUTHOR'S NOTE

Lies have been told about the weather on the world's largest island at least since the arrival of its first lettered visitors. Distortion came naturally to Eirik the Red, the exiled Viking who arrived in about the year 982. Like some modern Sun Belt swindler who dubs the fetid swampland of his future real-estate development "Ocean Breeze," Eirik viewed its frozen, treeless shores and called it Greenland.

(Speaking of swindlers, the most powerful person on the planet as I write these words, in the summer of 2017, draws a few mentions in these pages. Honestly, it never occurred to me, during the years I wrote this novel, that a reality-TV-show huckster might become president. I leave these references intact as a reminder that, under the wrong circumstances, the court jester may become king—turning us all into fools.)

Actually, on my own visit to Greenland I was surprised by a couple of weeks of mild and complaisant sunniness, but this is not what my protagonist Louie Hake encounters. I'd justify any of my own distortions by declaring this novel a sort of fever dream. I'd like to think my Rome is a place that any American tourist, anyway, would recognize. That my London is bent out of reality but recognizably so. But that my northern Greenland is a few removes from real—a perception that any first-time visitor to this vastest of all islands, marveling and fretting that the unsinkable June sun never considers setting, is likely to share.

PART ONE

# Rome

*The first of your dreams discovers*

*a Mediterranean rose,*

*beckoning you toward its center*

*as the warm petals close . . .*

I<small>F AT LAST THEY ARE TO COME DOWN TO US—THE</small> Extraterrestrials—what better time than dusk, what better place than the American Midwest? It's midsummer and a small boy sits beside his father on their sagging back porch. The boy's name is Louie Hake and the father's name is Louie Hake as well, and so prickling-potent is the boy's sensation of kinship while the two of them hunch in the neighborhood twilight, it's like some internal scent lodged within the very bones of his head. Both wear khaki shorts. Both have blue-gray eyes.

Though the boy has some trouble pronouncing both *r*'s and *s*'s, he delights in childish wordplay, savoring in these quiet, seated moments a sweet male sensation of the two of them *drinking a beer*. The father's beer is a brown bottle of Stroh's, while the boy's beer is of course root beer, sipped from a Dixie cup.

The boy can hardly keep his eyes off the cup, which may be the oddest color he knows: a goofy, dancing, go-for-broke green greener than Nature herself. It's a color that conspires with the day's quivery orange dusk-light, converting the fizzing brown liquid into a minia-ture ebony pool. And when little Louie lifts to his lips the cup's waxy rim, here's another oddity: the drink plays him a sort of trick, an invis-ible prank. Again and again its leaping bubbles bring him to the intox-icating threshold of a sneeze.

The root beer is a *special treat*. For Louie the phrase is both fathom-less riddle and ceaseless obsession. The words confine him and they occasionally, capriciously, liberate him; the phrase holds in its jurisdiction some of the sharpest pleasures his body knows. Chocolate, butterscotch, licorice—all forbidden, except as *special treats.* Likewise the ebullient root beer exploding in his hand. Not normally permitted. Louie's stepmother believes that, just as chocolate impairs digestion, butterscotch induces headaches, and licorice interferes with sleep, too much soda pop stunts a boy's growth.

Louie is the shortest pupil—boy or girl—in Miss Davis's fourth-grade class at Hiawatha Elementary, three blocks from this bowed back porch. Vaguely, guiltily, he senses how his relative littleness distresses his parents, while not perceiving that something in his lisping and his sleight-of-hand quickness—a touch of the elfin in his sly-eyed glances—inspires an unease neither father nor stepmother will put into words. Of course the parents have no means of knowing that although Louie as an adult will face formidable physical problems, his stature won't be one. (Nor will he be effeminate.) Worries will dissolve, new worries materialize . . . In junior high school, while distracted by powerful waves of acne-spattering hormones, Louie will suddenly spring up to five feet eight inches—just an inch or so below average height for a male of his generation.

Mrs. Hake, who at five-nine will always have an overseeing inch's advantage on her stepson, believes that her husband stunted *his* growth with cigarettes, taken up on the gray, rakehell streets of Detroit at the age of twelve. She's a woman of firm views.

Mr. Hake no longer smokes, and little Louie has but one clear recollection of his father's cigarettes. This was at a family picnic at Detroit's Belle Isle. There, too, Louie had been sitting beside his father, and again both were wearing shorts. Reaching for a deviled egg with one hand, Mr. Hake allowed his cigarette-bearing other hand to graze his son's bare leg, just above the knee.

What immediately followed was a detonation: pain, indignation, *shock.* Really, there was nothing for little Louie to liken it to. Inside his head, the moment went rocketing upward, upward, as if into the open rings of outer space, there to circle and circle, becoming one of those named satellites you live your life beneath: the Day Daddy Burned My Leg.

Well, the little boy at the picnic—the burned and mistreated boy—wept and continued weeping, long after the pain subsided. He wept until he himself had to wonder why he didn't stop . . . When, occasionally, the child on the back porch recalls that other, earlier, smaller child, a slinking shame physically overtakes him: for he's big enough now to identify the internal kernel of malice in his infantile refusal to accept his father's horrified apologies. (The penitent man soon gave up smoking altogether.) This was another troubling riddle for young Louie: apparently, even in the midst of righteous tears, a person could be cruel. Yes, the wronged person, the hapless victim, could nonetheless be cruel . . .

Is any emotion more tenacious than shame? It brushes Louie as he sits beside his father on the back porch, and it infects him even when—worlds away, decades away, decades later, supine in a hotel room in Rome—he recollects that distant picnic, now so remote its diluted sunlight flickers, as in an old movie . . . While, from below, the foreign noises of Italian traffic carom and scuffle round the hotel room, and while, from above, an ad hoc flock of seagulls cries heartbrokenly for a missing sea, Louie Hake regrets those ancient tears, and it scarcely matters that his father has been dead for nearly eight years. Or perhaps his father's being dead and unreachable only intensifies the little boy's crime. Lost in the howling vortex of those tears, he'd refused to comfort the kindest man ever to greet the dawn.

It seems there are different Louies . . . Louie-the-boy, who believes in Extraterrestrials, sits on the back porch beside his father, and Louie-the-man, forty-three years old, who believes in journeys of redemption, lies in a towering overpriced hotel room in an unfashionable part of Rome, sleepless, thrashing through tides of futility and remorse. The two moments are parentheses, loosely enclosing nothing less than the sprawling conundrum of a life.

Or—or call it the two wings of a triptych, whose central panel has gone missing. After all, the fine arts are his vocation, his calling. And art by essence is an untrustworthy enterprise, the dozing adult Louie (professor Louie) senses, especially for someone of his own mysteriously blocked creativity. (*Surely* he's more imaginative than the hard evidence of his past suggests.) Still, if art's no solace and sanctuary, where is he to go? Where is his soul to go? Where on earth is the shore that might welcome him? He's dozing . . . Something in Louie wants Louie to sleep, so it can fully awaken. Where is his soul to go? Not religion—with all its strained, unreasoning demands. And not romantic love—for Louie knows by bitterest experience that love's a refuge more treacherous even than art.

On a warm summer day, in an orange dusk, son and father hunker on the back stoop, sipping drinks only slightly cooler than the flushed and vibrant air. Behind their narrow backs—both Louies are slender—lies an inviting vacancy. An empty house. The boy's stepmother and his big sister, Annabelle, who share a heavy tread, have marched off to the drugstore. The boy's stepmother, in particular, is an outsize and purposeful presence; even when he's upstairs and she's downstairs, her physical existence overtops his. She is imposing—she imposes herself. Though charitable enough toward living souls (she has never laid a finger on either stepchild, and Louie has seen backyard squirrels inch forward to filch a peanut from her tranquil palm), she is an exacting disciplinarian of the inorganic world. It's positively *scary* to see such righteous fury unleashed upon household appliances. Louie's father, grinning a half grin, calls these moments the Mother's Encounters with Objects. He makes a joke of it, but it can be truly *scary*, the house shuddering to her booming admonitions. Toasters, can openers, balky vacuum cleaner attachments, leaking faucets, fitful garbage disposals, fainting dehumidifiers, clattering electric fans—all cower and quail and sweat beneath the Mother's threats and coercions: "What do you imagine *you're* doing?" or "That's quite enough from *you*," or "Do you understand you are *test*ing my *pa*tience . . ." Or, most memorable of all, the Mother holding in one hand a new Christmas gift, a big fancy skull-sized alarm clock whose confusing dials weren't readily cooperating, and the woman crying at it, or to it, *Are you deaf? Are you deaf? Are you deaf?*

In truth, there's also profound reassurance in the Mother's banging, rattling presence, and on the sole occasion of her extended absence—a week away in Phoenix, caring for her baby brother, Uncle Jimmy, after he nearly died of a perforated appendix—a feckless and eerie silence infiltrated the Hake household. Life turned bewilderingly arbitrary. No compelling reason existed, without the Mother's monitoring eye, to comb your hair, or not to comb your hair. No reason to go to bed, no reason not to . . . Still, there was comfort—a sort of salmon-glow comfort, much like the tincturing of the sky as the two Louies survey the earth from the companionable vantage of the back porch—in these interludes when the house exhales a calm and clement emptiness.

The linking of color to feeling or mood or sound comes readily to Louie. Nearly a quarter century from now, when he has just turned thirty-three, a battery of tests and interviews will announce—the main point—that he's bipolar. But he will also informally learn what he has always known unthinkingly: his particular cerebral cortex traffics in synesthesia. For him, the integers have complementary colors, at least up to 9. (Why do others not see that 2 is sky blue, 3 is Kelly green, 4 a purplish brown, the subtlest of the number colors? Or 7 a pumpkiny orange, 8 a bruised red, 9 a glossy black? Are most people colorblind?)

Louie will eventually wonder whether his father, too, viewed the world synesthetically. It would explain a great deal. The man spent the whole of his working life at Universal Colorfast, which specialized in automotive paint.

It was a job whose nobleness Louie Senior never questioned. Armed with the colors of progress, he was helping to tint the American landscape wherever her rapidly expanding highway system extended. Cars more than any other feat of engineering were the future—a touchable, polishable future. An annual ritual arose with the new models: father would usher son into the swank, intimidating, gleaming, redolent dealer showrooms, an atmosphere so potent it locked up little Louie's tongue. Models kept changing, his father explained, some years looked more *stylish,* but each passing year meant improved paint: a future of finer, deeper, truer colors.

In fact, his father explained it to anybody who would listen: the fascinating thing about automotive paint is just how many ways it can go wrong. It bubbles, it blisters. It clouds and fades, cracks, scratches, chips, flakes. Your house stands still, it makes its peace with the plot it stands upon, but your car is always hurtling from one hostile terrain to the next. Your home has a home; your car has no home. It's attacked from without by pebbles and hailstorms, pounding sun and pounding rain, abrasive salts, flying grit. Sticky waves of pollen. Acidic bird droppings. Corrosive pollution, smoke. And it's attacked from within by rust and damp and leaching chemicals, ground frost, overheating engines . . .

Unlike most men, Louie Senior has a precise vision of the grail of his profession: perfect paint. After centuries of painstaking experimentation, after tireless trial and error, after endless mess and clinging clouds of stink and ever-mounting expense, somehow the first incomparable batch, a triumphal marriage of fixative and luster, would materialize: perfect paint.

It needn't last forever. No, perfect paint would have to endure, crisp and unmarred, only for an automobile's working life. And this was no jeweled mirage. This was a reachable goal. Here was a luminous vision of American junkyards whose exhausted vehicles—radiators exploded, engines fried, tires frayed, gaskets blown—sparkled like some virgin chassis borne on the slow, firm tide of the assembly line.

Not surprisingly, the front of the Hake house shows to the world a glistening surface; Mr. Hake repaints every third summer. And perhaps also not surprisingly, the gray back porch wears a dull and shabby coat. A man needs a place to relax. This porch is a harbor where, clad in white T-shirts, a father might sit with his nine-year-old son at day's end, taking stock, content to have nothing occur—while unknowingly awaiting an Extraterrestrial's arrival.

A young boy sits alongside his father on a back porch in the Detroit suburb of Fallen Hills, Michigan, and the same boy, some thirty-four years later, lies sprawled at dusk in the Eternal City. He has just this morning arrived in Rome. The phrase's ringing portentousness—Eternal City—inveigles Louie; it sings of the ranging grandeur of his pilgrimage. This is Step One on a tour of some of the world's most magnificent architecture. It's the trip of his life, or even—for Louie embraces an idiom of elevation—the Journey of His Life. In a sense he's become his own assistant, assigning himself tasks that he performs respectfully and scrupulously. *Take a mental snapshot of this.* Absolutely. *Give it a caption.* You got it. *Time to move on.* Right you are.

Louie has left behind a stupefying junkyard of wreckage, including a romantic life so laughably painful it will not bear inspection. Well, he won't inspect it. Instead, he will file in his brain, as in a series of notebooks, images of the earth's most sublime buildings. This very day, in all his jet-lagged bedraggledness, didn't he trundle himself off, aching back and all, to stand within the open enclosure of the Pantheon? Didn't he coin a phrase—"the most beautiful hemisphere in the Eastern Hemisphere"—which felt snappy and fun and auspicious? Louie has sometimes seen the Pantheon described, by critics with sizable reputations, as the world's most beautiful building, and perhaps the critics have it right. Or not. He'll decide for himself. By the end of this trip, he'll be able to compare it with the Blue Mosque in Istanbul and with the Taj Mahal in Agra and with Ginkakuji Temple in Kyoto. Such is his life's Journey.

Though Louie is a teacher—long term, life term—it has been ages since he felt extended pedagogical excitement. But he's feeling it now. Just a week or two ago, he emailed his department chair, crazy Leo Mattoon, proposing a new course for the spring semester: Four Masterpieces of World Architecture. The Pantheon, the Blue Mosque, the Taj Mahal, Ginkakuji Temple in Kyoto . . . He has now inspected one of the four, and he has found it good.

And unexpectedly, having launched himself on this odyssey, Louie is conducted into an adjacency of spirit with the nine-year-old boy who has dropped his skinny bottom on the top step of the back porch, the daydreamer who waits without knowing he's waiting—who is about to witness the most astounding sight of his life. Whether the adult Louie is today in Italy, wandering the ruins of Rome, or in the next few weeks is raptly investigating buildings in Turkey or India or Japan, what could possibly equal this humble backyard moment?

From a fading blue sky a creature descends and alights upon young Louie's knee—near the very spot where, five years before, his father's cigarette bit a nerve. All is forgiven. All is surpassed. The creature is essentially weightless. (There's only the faintest itchy kiss where its twitchy sentient ebony legs find purchase on Louie's skinny white leg.)

To call it an insect would be scientifically accurate but spiritually misleading. Species, genus, family, order—such distinctions no longer obtain. Oh, Louie has stared before, with burning boyish near-eyed intensity, at any number of bugs: at grasshoppers, with their plated, shoved-in, thuggish faces; at praying mantises, with their cutesy heart-shaped heads and elegantly elongated assassin's hands; at whiskery caterpillars whose miniature visages laughably reveal the drooping jowly humorlessness of walruses; at beetles so black no hole on earth could match their darkness. But nothing has adequately prepared him for the oddity and the exorbitance and the alien aristocratic ingenuity of the butterfly posed upon his knee. The thing is *huge,* and the duplicated, mirroring mosaics of its jeweled wings are an animate astonishment.

Father and son, who bear a close resemblance anyway, become twins. Interchangeably, with wet left-leaning slack mouths, they gape. The creature shivers its emerald-and-lavender-and-ivory wings. Clearly, it is no native of Michigan's dun tamed marshes and meadows and forests. This is a refugee from another planet.

In just a few moments, shortly after the otherworldly wings shimmer off into thin air and the light of day weakly regathers, Louie's father will group his wits and explain that the creature must be some sort of escapee: a runaway—a flyaway—from a zoo or a laboratory or a specialist's collection. And Louie will nod, gratefully. But such explanations are gray as the town sidewalks, dry as the backyard's wiry circles of brown grass where Ordie, the family dog, leaves his digestive diary.

For a few incandescent moments, Louie witnesses a variant reality. Some 127 million photoreceptors line the average human eye—an eighth of a billion entryways—and for Louie it's as though each has been potentiated. No other word can summon and reflect what the boy has glimpsed: *perfection.*

How much did he understand back then? To the fatigued man in Rome, whose back is throbbing after a cramped transatlantic flight, it seems the moment's ongoing significance has been grasped only recently.

At the close of day, most creatures must rest, and let's suppose the strangest, bravest of them all selects *your* naked leg for a way station— are you prepared? Are you really? How *could* the little boy understand that here was a moment he must spend the remainder of his days looking to replicate? The Journey of His Life is the bare, hopeful pursuit of an encore. One midsummer dusk, you behold a winged immortal, a god or goddess unsheathed, and naturally you must veer off in headlong pursuit, down Time's long maze of mirroring corridors. (And Time is your enemy. Time will darken your life's every image. At the close of day, at the close of day . . .) It was some eleven weeks ago, on March 27, 2014, that Louie Hake was officially diagnosed with AOFVD, adult-onset foveomacular vitelliform dystrophy, a disease with no known cure.

Even *before* the diagnosis, the situation was dire: it was no easy task being Louie Hake, with a career going nowhere and a second marriage avalanching toward divorce, a forty-three-year-old man apologetically childless and bipolar and inadequately bankrolled. Anyone looking at him might have supposed that the bullying gods above, having already dealt such severe blows, in fairness now would grant him a reprieve. Wrong. Here is another pitfall in his path, and this one is dank and black as the grave: evidently, he may be going blind.

·   ·   ·

THE ROOM HAS DIMMED WHEN LOUIE AWAKENS, BUT IT'S A long way from completely dark. The bathroom light is on. Louie hasn't slept in a fully darkened room in eleven weeks. Back home—his new and temporary home, a dreary railroad apartment he stumbled into after somehow getting finagled out of his beloved house—he installed a bedroom night-light a few days after receiving the diagnosis from the head of ophthalmology at Pioneer Hospital, blond and tanned and kind and unshakably tranquil Dr. Scott Dimiceli.

Before his appointments with Dimiceli, Louie had never heard of AOFVD, an acronym that resembled the random letters on an eye chart. And for a few minutes after the term first surfaced, it mightn't have signified anything too ghastly. It might have been like cataracts—a tamed scourge. Cataracts? These days, a laser scrubs your cornea in the morning, and in the evening you're lounging in a restaurant marveling at the candlelight flickering on the wineglasses. Unfortunately, AOFVD seems a different sort of malady.

Enough. It's time for dinner. Food will steady him. He's feeling needy and upended.

*And who wouldn't be?*

For Louie, the phrase has become a stubborn, haunting motif. He finds himself uttering aloud anxious self-assessments, to which it's the logical response: *And who wouldn't be?* I'm feeling a bit shaky. I'm acting a little impulsive. I'm disoriented. I guess I'm exhausted. *And who wouldn't be?*

It's like carrying a heavy pack all day and at nightfall discovering you can't remove it. You become your burden. You feel you're carrying *it*, but *it* won't let you go. It's carrying you—though not the weight. (*You're* asked to bear the weight.)

In one regard, weirdly, Dimiceli's diagnosis provided relief. After so much painful black comedy, here was, stark and simple, tragedy. And tragedy held out the potential for much-longed-for dignity. Having been a public laughingstock for months, Louie could almost look forward to playing catastrophic victim.

Five months ago, on January 27, his wife, Florence, was caught in flagrante delicto—the *delict* so wildly *flagrant* that not even close friends could discuss the matter without smirking. She was arrested under the Michigan Penal Code, section 750.338b, "gross indecency between male and female persons." And then cunning Florence somehow finessed Louie out of the house while making this appear his own inclination. Then she'd consulted a divorce lawyer. Then his lousy job had come under threat. Then he received Dimiceli's catastrophic diagnosis. And then he'd decided he needed serious psychotherapy, and started up with the very Waspy and buttoned-down Dr. Lawrence Douglas. (No Larry, he.) Of course Louie had dealt with therapists for years (ten years, ever since being diagnosed bipolar, though he prefers the old-fashioned term *manic-depressive,* as more descriptive and accurate), but he'd never really taken to therapy, or overcome a healthy midwestern prejudice against talking so much about yourself. For years he'd accepted therapy as the necessary prereq for access to his bipolarism meds. But when his personal life collapsed and his job turned dicey and he suddenly couldn't bear the company of various Schadenfreude-fueled friends, Louie crossed an internal barrier: he needed serious therapy. Three times a week. Hence the intensely intellectual Dr. Douglas, brow perpetually gnarled, his office presided over by a black-and-white photographic triumvirate: Charles Darwin and Franz Kafka and an unrecognizably young and hirsute Mahatma Gandhi, whose broad face, when you added in his jug-handle ears, was wider than it was long.

Shortly after Louie began seeing him, Dr. Douglas suffered a "cardio event" at a student film festival called Huge Heroes. Dr. Douglas, astoundingly enough, had ventured alone to a midnight showing of *The Incredible Hulk.* All therapy was canceled as the good doctor convalesced in Florida. And so Louie'd had nobody to talk with when he conceived the Journey of His Life.

Actually, when Dr. Douglas headed down to Florida, Louie felt worse than abandoned: betrayed. After a few weeks, while chaste Gandhi rolled over in his grave, Dr. Douglas posted a YouTube video of himself playing tennis with a bouncing-breasted red-haired girl wearing matching lime-green shorts and halter top. And where in hell was Louie to look for counsel?

Of course he could have talked to his sister, Annabelle. Annabelle was always there to talk to—poor, forever-husbandless Annabelle. Way back in childhood she'd elected herself his chief confidante, and this would never change. Nor would Annabelle ever stop talking . . .

But the job. It sometimes seemed to Louie that every misconceived and misaligned aspect of his life was manifested in his job. He taught in the Art History Department of Ann Arbor College. And this meant that whenever he met an "outside" academic—someone based any-where except Michigan—excruciating misunderstandings arose. It scarcely mattered how painstakingly Louie sought to clarify his cre-dentials. No, new acquaintances immediately assumed he taught at the University of Michigan. They thought he held a prestigious posi-tion. They thought he was a success story.

Not *that* Ann Arbor, I'm at the *other* Ann Arbor—that's what Louie longed to express. I'm an untenured fixture at a small, private, unsightly, poorly funded, disrespected, rudderless, self-loathing, self-congratulating liberal arts institution whose acronym is, suitably, AAC. Pronounced *ack*. That's where, for all my sins, I'm condemned to spend my professional life: Ack. *Ack.* ACK. *ACK.* But what are my sins?

He might additionally have mentioned—but at this point new acquaintances had already guessed as much—that he was paid far less munificently than professors at U of M. And further appended that while U of M professors taught two classes a semester, AAC instruc-tors taught *four.* And if anyone was still listening, Louie might have noted that while professors at U of M were expected to publish, and did so, instructors at AAC prided themselves on being representatives of a "teaching institution." And here, if he wasn't careful, Louie knew he was apt, like a drunkard urinating over a balcony railing, to lose all sense of target and delivery—he could go into a real rant. For he *resented* those U of M profs (the coddled, cocksure bastards), even as he *resented* his AAC colleagues for posing as teachers so devoted to pedagogy as to render outside publication—alas—impossible, even as he *resented* himself for publishing nothing in the twenty years since starting grad school.

But the students! Louie originally "specialized" in the history of painting, though lately he prefers to teach (when permitted to do so) architectural history. The shift was self-protective. When discussing any branch of art, Louie finds himself in much less danger of spouting inanities if restricting himself to big, touchable, earthbound objects in whose shelter someone might eat a burrito or retie his shoes. His lectures are held in prefab "modules" that leak when it rains, and you could only laugh to think what those ancient Greek masons, whose immortal marble edifices Louie is forever PowerPointing upon a lop-sided screen, would have made of American twenty-first-century "higher" education.

But paintings, architecture—what does the ostensible subject matter matter? Louie's true occupation, perforce, is the presentation of *extremely* rudimentary lessons in speaking and writing. He is at bottom an instructor of English comp. How could it be otherwise? There is no other self-respecting way to teach humanities at AAC—at any of the AACs distributed across the nation. In all Louie's years of heading a classroom, the most memorable remark he has ever heard was uttered by an undergrad responding to a Van Gogh self-portrait: "I really like, when he like, really like goes deep and stuff." Something to recall on your deathbed! But the remark was even better than that—or worse. For in order to offer his observation, the young man had *raised his hand.*

Though certainly no scholar—and hence almost Darwinianly doomed to enter a teaching institution—Louie truly loves books. He has a number of somewhat-valuable first editions, including some too-nice-to-open volumes of Ruskin. Though he reads mostly mysteries and popular history these days and makes no effort to keep up in "his field"—provided one could be identified—he still loves to caress hardcover volumes, to browse, to linger over a table of contents, to fall haphazardly upon a random and perhaps (who knows?) illuminating paragraph. And his students? What his counterparts at the rarefied University of Michigan don't yet grasp is that the latest generation of students regard books as Louie might regard a washboard or a mangle or a hand scythe: indispensable implements for an earlier generation, now happily obsolescent.

But it's time to clamber out of this Italian bed, whose proportions, like that of European typing paper, seem deliberately, designedly, ill coordinated.

Louie sees things a little differently, however, as he showers and shaves. The room's compactness—shower stall and sink and medicine cabinet folded in upon themselves—pleases him. He appreciates artfully husbanded space. Actually, Louie can be perhaps a little self-congratulatory in his penchant for tidy surfaces, moderate dimensions. He likes clean numbers, preferring the evens to the odds, wholes to fractions, rationals to irrationals, and so on, ever deeper inside that increasingly cluttered labyrinth in which his father, the engineering student, had felt himself a citizen as his son never could. When, a few years ago, Louie's narrow waist modestly ballooned from thirty to thirty-two inches, he'd regretted the change almost as much for the loss of a nifty physical symmetry (his thirty-thirty waist-to-inseam ratio) as for its hint of a middle-aged spread. He'd once planned a book on the American Impressionists (he was especially taken with John Henry Twachtman), whose foreword would advance an authorial credo. And though the book's text was never seriously commenced (nor the foreword, for that matter), he'd mentally reformulated many times a few sentences explaining his preference for the Frick over the Met, early Sinatra over late Sinatra, Fred Astaire over Gene Kelly (who muddied the aesthetics by looking sexy), Al Green over James Brown.

The truth is, Louie feels mostly unmoored in Europe, and finds himself sheepishly missing home. He's reluctant to confess this to his colleagues, a number of whom fly annually across the Atlantic. He doesn't envy them.

Even more embarrassing would be to confess how little, overall, he has ever enjoyed Continental dining. Dutch menus, Spanish menus, especially French menus—all dubious, all strewn with aggressive little ruses and booby traps. And the menus were only the beginning. What about all the confusions over tipping? The waiters' flourish-filled presentations of the third rate? The hauteur of the barefaced swindler? Unfortunately, it's the challenge of dinner—his first in Rome, and a solitary experience—Louic now faces.

So he dresses defensively. Dining in a city inarguably more worldly than he is, he'll at least go well outfitted. He's methodical in the tucking in of his alternating navy-blue-and-apple-green-pinstriped shirt, the cinching of his braided leather belt, the arranging of his appearance's one great glory: his thick ringlets. Though his hair has no color to speak of (old oatmeal color? cardboard color? dust-ball color?), it has lushness in bouncy abundance. (It seems his students have nicknamed him Professor Mop-Top.) His hair is a twin gift. The curls derive from his father—though Louie Senior's curls thinned with age. The thickness belongs to his not-quite-imaginable biological mother, a woman who died of non-Hodgkin's lymphoma before her second child, Louie Junior, turned two.

Taking his time, Louie arrives at what is typically the most difficult but pleasurable stage of dressing: the selection of a necktie. Members of AAC's Art History Department dress better than most of the faculty (no difficult task, given how frequently Louie's colleagues express their solidarity with the homeless by dressing like them), but even within his department he stands out as something of a dandy. He loves neckties, as had Louie Senior, who wore one every day except Saturday. Louie never appears in class without one. He loves it all: the pronounced colors, the sharp angularities of the designs in contrast with the soft-spoken slippery feel of the silk, the silk on silk of ties plaited over a silver rack on his closet door . . . Having always adored them, Louie in the last eleven weeks has grown positively doting. What would it be like to put on a necktie you couldn't see? To have a whole row of handsome neckties you couldn't see? One recent morning, he found himself standing at his closet—indecisive, still sleepy—stroking his ties with the marveling tenderness you might show the flesh of your lover's flank.

To Rome he has brought a wealth of silk: an even dozen ties, ranged atop his dresser. He has never understood why pleasure in color ought to be "gendered," as his colleagues would put it. Why does traditional male fashion offer so little allowance for colors playfully proclaiming joy in color? He selects a navy-blue tie with intricate little yellow dots. Only someone looking very closely would detect that the dots are miniature creatures—fireflies, hundreds of them. It's a process that has always enchanted Louie: the realization, as the plunging eye probes deeper, that geometric abstraction is in truth a chain of miniature replicas of some beloved worldly object—butterflies, tulips, hourglasses, sailing ships . . .

First taking a deep, reflective breath—a "mindful breath," as his occasional forays into yoga classes would have it—Louie ambles from the hotel lobby into a Roman street. This neighborhood, east and a little south of Trastevere, is one he doesn't know. The hotel was selected by his travel agent.

Louie can recall a time when the phrase "my travel agent" sported some cachet. Not long ago—but ages ago. Among the academics Louie lives too closely beside, travel is handled yourself, online. To visit an agency these days (as Louie discovered recently in Ann Arbor) is to ally yourself with the patently incompetent: the hard of hearing, the ditzy, the not fully literate.

And yet, all the same, he has reached Rome—the Eternal City. The damp air smells of car exhaust and pastry. It's cool, and breezy. He passes a woman's clothing store, where the tall, gunmetal-gray female mannequins—high cheekboned, high breasted—look down on him with an unnerving lunar disdain. He passes a *gioielleria,* a jewelry store, still open, and a closed *latteria,* and an *erborista,* which sells vitamins. Then another clothing store—this one for men—whose black mannequins, though androgynous and headless, are somehow postured to suggest a collusive homosexuality. Louie laughs and says aloud, "Perhaps I need a drink."

Louie actually isn't much for drink. He's fond of ritual, and enjoys at day's end producing a gimlet or his father's standby, a manhattan. But the hand that dispenses the spirits is a light hand.

It's much the same with food. Louie prides himself on not being one of those guys whose kitchen repertoire is limited to hamburgers and pancakes. He owns a Zojirushi Virtuoso bread maker and a Breville juicer. He delights in displays of culinary dexterity, whether in chic bistros or greasy diners. Florence used to joke that Louie loved everything about food except the eating of it. (She also once pointed out—loudly, at a departmental party—that it was only alcohol that kept Louie from being a big drinker. The woman did have a knack for put-downs. He reminds himself of this when he occasionally questions whether he's well rid of her.)

Still, it's dinnertime, and he must eat.

As an American dining in Europe, his chief responsibility is the steering clear of tourist traps. But nearly as imperative is avoiding voluble Americans congratulating themselves on avoiding tourist traps. His eye follows upward the wandering plummet of a drainage pipe and, attaining the roof, vaults into the heavens, where a pair of white birds go wheeling, bellies hoarding a pink flush mostly receded from the streets below. Gulls. Louie has been in Rome only once before, briefly, at the aching tail end of a college backpacking trip. Not surprisingly, he failed then to notice the city's gulls. Is he correct in thinking them louder and fiercer and more cynical sounding than gulls back home? To ask the question is to ruminate about objects that people routinely train themselves to identify, minutely, at a great distance—birds, trees, airplanes. In forty-plus years, though heretofore blessed with faultless twenty-twenty vision, he has never taught himself to identify any such group, and presumably never will . . . He pushes the thought away.

Another thought follows, vaguer still, though Louie senses he shouldn't push this one away. To the contrary, tantalizingly, it promises the good and desirable: some happy destination beyond or in addition to the restaurant he's seeking. And whatever it is, he must be open to it. As he approaches Viale Trastevere, with its impressively quiet new tram cars, it seems he's moving, step by step in his cordovan Bacco Bucci loafers, toward some solution, illumination. A momentous encounter, around this corner or the next.

When he rounds the next corner, the actual encounter coaxes a smile to his face . . . *This* isn't it, any more than if he'd come upon a statue of Venus or Minerva. In a cornice in the wall opposite, with a starburst of tea candles at her feet, a two-foot-tall effigy of the Virgin stands, flickering in the soft but vigilant light. She's a consolatory presence, but it isn't *Mary* he's seeking, not religion, maybe not even art. But what, then? Something, something. And this city of ancient mosaics is inlaid with its immanence.

Is there a finer place on earth for him tonight? *Surely* Rome holds more buried potential than any palm-treed tropical island, such as the one where his wife, his perhaps soon-to-be-ex-wife, now vacations. Florence and her lover Daryl have fled to Charlotte Amalie in the Virgin Islands. At home in his apartment in Ann Arbor, Louie looked up the Virgins in his old *New York Times* atlas. Flyspecks, really.

Florence and her lover have deliberately shrunk their world to a locale built of and upon grains of sand, which is their prerogative. Louie has pictured their situation a dozen times, a dozen million times . . . A cabana by the whispering shore. White beaches. A huge idle sun mindlessly tossing confetti on the bay. Life as some sort of goddamned celebration, but clearly, inarguably, celebrations demand to be earned. No doubt the ocean breezes create a lovely, thrilling plash through the overhanging palms, and likewise lovely the breakfast platters of fresh fruit presented to the two cooing *innamorati,* but how could such a scenario compare with what now so thrillingly surrounds and enfolds Louie: not just beauty, surpassing beauty, but the soaring mortar and brick marvels of antiquity. Here are acres and acres of encoded stone—an architect's riddle, an art historian's fantasia—

ensuring that every *passeggiata* is a foray through not just space but time. If the two lovebirds wish to turn their backs on such things, it's all right by Louie, who as he saunters along a cobblestone street lifts his arm as though in high-minded farewell, and observes that his hand is trembling—as happens occasionally when he has forgotten to eat. He must stop soon.

He's an art student again. Or at least reminded of what that was. In those heady days, maybe you contemplated a photo of the Golden Gate Bridge, or Taliesin West, or the Seattle Space Needle, and then one fateful future day you'd actually stroll upon the scene. There it was. It's what made the study of architecture the finest of all disciplines: in time, the structure on the page may arise before you, as real as your rib cage. You may even—the heart of art—enter it bodily, progressing from two dimensions into three. And one day you reach Rome, advancing from three dimensions into four, for this is deep history, the sort measured in millennia. And of *this* pleasure Florence and Daryl haven't an inkling.

Even so, there is a way—Louie is relearning—in which mischievous Rome plays the spoiler, thwarting your brightest touristic envisionings. For the visitor—for Louie, anyway—the city stubbornly resists seeming altogether real.

Here are two men engaged in argument. One is a grizzled aproned shopkeeper, standing in the doorway of his tiny shop, which sells tomatoes and smaller-than-American-sized heads of lettuce, and the other, having doffed his cap, baring his threadbare scalp, is a customer. The shopkeeper chops the air. The customer, hunching under the onslaught of words, looks both browbeaten and defiant, but why does the entire tableau resemble a stage set? It's all faintly preposterous. You might be sitting high in a box at the opera, surveying a milling crowd of miming villagers, Italians doing what they do best, playing Italians, while the overture swells.

Theatrical natives, theater-hungry tourists: here's a road leading to one variety of Rome. Is it jet lag, or is Louie penetrating into the mystical core of things when he sees that the aproned shopkeeper's

playing a shopkeeper? And the customer: how skillfully he imperson-
ates a cowed customer, stooping but not retreating, while—a brilliant
touch—wringing his cap.

The choice of where to dine resolves simply. Many people are eating outdoors, despite the evening's cool breeziness, but the look is
unappealing and anarchic to Louie's eye: he craves some semblance of
shelter. Louie strolls past what may be a hardware store *(ferramenta),*
and what ought to be a cell-phone store *(mobili)* but which turns out
to sell furniture, and he skirts what must be Santa Cecilia—not wanting, at this point, to muster any professorial assessment. He chances
upon a bistro with two quite pretty Italian women, his own age or a
little older, dominating a corner window. One is blond, one brunette.
A voice inside his head declares, *The women are so pretty here,* and
Louie obligingly follows the voice into the restaurant.

The proprietor is a bustling little goateed man who looks far more
Parisian than Roman; in every significant way (except that he wears
nothing on his head), he is sporting a beret. He doesn't seat Louie
where he'd hoped, adjoining the two women, but three tables away.
Between him and the beautifully dressed women (the unmistakably expensively dressed women) sits a party of four hefty folks, one
woman and three men. They are older than Louie—probably well into
their fifties—and must be Scandinavians; the darkest is what might be
called sandy-haired, and the fairest is tow-haired. They are Swedes,
Louie decides, and are, contrary to all your phlegmatic Nordic ste-
reotypes, loud and demonstrative. They are embroiled in argument.
The woman pushes a travel brochure at the man seated directly across
the table. He doesn't accept it. Louie can read the brochure's title, cool
white billowy italic letters a-sail across a cerulean sky: *The Seychelles—
Pick Paradise.* But why has this outsize Swedish quartet come to Rome
to argue about some tiny islands in the Indian Ocean?

Meanwhile, the two elegant women are sipping white wine. And
how is it possible, Louie marvels, that the pair of them announce their
distinctiveness—their Europeanness, their Italianness—in a motion
as rudimentary as the lifting of a wineglass? Yet they do. Their every

gesture proclaims a proud national identity. The brunette's arm is a ruddy tan, and the blonde's is a cream color warmed, in a marrying of restaurant light and street light, to a shimmery apricot. The complementary skin tones are lovely, the sight is more than lovely—the artfully tilted arms, the matching golden hemispheres of wine—and in Louie's head an all but audible click resounds: another mental snapshot. If, God forbid (God forbid), his eyesight's truly deserting him, he must preserve every truly beautiful sight. Until a few months ago, he'd scarcely given thought to his eyes; ironically, unlike so many people in their forties, he doesn't yet need reading glasses.

In his wallet he keeps a few Ativan tablets.

When the attacks of nervousness assault him as they have been recently, with some frequency, typically they begin in his stomach and lungingly seize his chest. Then Louie feels gripped, as if some giant from a fairy tale or cartoon has clutched him with an icy hand. He can wiggle and thrash, but escape's impossible; the giant's monumental fingers hold his body fast. Ativan helps. It relaxes the giant's grip. Given all the meds for his bipolarism, Louie's wary about adding to the mix. But Ativan helps. Lately, he's been tormented by a suspicion that it isn't merely his eyes that are failing—no, something's undermining him at a lower level, the deepest level. In the brainpan, in the buried headquarters of his thinking, something's playing havoc with the storage cabinets, jumbling files, discarding files . . . And Ativan helps with this particular nervousness (even while introducing the worry that it chemically contributes to the undermining).

Enough. He too must order wine. In college, he liked to drink— mostly beer. And later, gin with Lizzie, his first wife, born in Smethwick, a suburb of Birmingham, England. Though only four when the chemical company her father worked for transferred him to Saginaw, she enjoyed playing up her English heritage. A transplanted Brit reared in Michigan's Thumb, Lizzie would drink gin and tonic, or gin and 7Up, and Louie gladly played along. (His English wife—oh, he'd relished the circumstance of an English wife!) But something happened a decade or so ago, connected to but distinct from his diagnosis of bipolarism. His doctors urged avoidance of drink, given a daily regimen of pharmaceuticals, and he'd deferred. But more than that, alcohol's pleasures had evaporated. Or maybe he felt frightened?

Back in college, though, still in his teens, in a life as yet mostly unmarred by the quiet disfigurations of fear, it had seemed only appropriate to celebrate, frequently, loquaciously, the joyful discovery that Louie Hake was accepted as one of the guys. It wasn't that he'd been unpopular at Fallen Hills High—not as simple as that—but he certainly hadn't been one of the guys. They knew who they were, the guys who were the guys, and Louie wasn't one. But at Kalamazoo College he'd found his way into a warm fraternity and discovered what it felt like: to be one of the guys. Some of his frat brothers had even nicknamed him Hakey—an ugly sound that brought no end of private pleasure. *What a great deal:* to sit and smoke pot with your frat brothers. *What a great deal:* another beer with your frat brothers. He'd never had a brother—only a sister, poor eager underutilized Annabelle—and the more he smoked and drank with them, the better about himself he felt. It was the opposite of a vicious circle: a benign circle. Smoke and drink more, feel better; feel better, smoke and drink more . . . And years later, unexpectedly, while dapperly lounging in a bistro in Trastevere, Louie realizes how profoundly he *misses* his grungy, gregarious brothers and *misses* those days when he wouldn't have thought to worry about the fate of his eyes or his mental stability.

He misses the past and craves wine—the glow of the women's glasses beckons. When the Parisian proprietor comes by and bends with highly discreet solicitude, as though to inquire about details of Louie's sexual health, Louie says crisply, *Vino bianco.* A prompt question follows, in Italian, which Louie doesn't fully comprehend, though he nods knowingly. A minute or two later he discovers he has ordered an unexpectedly large carafe.

So be it—he'll accept this as a Latin hospitality gesture. The wine's a lovely color—the light this evening remains exquisite—and each sip's splash of fruit on his palate is an exploration of one vintage's individuated hue, one tingling and fortified point on the vinicultural spectrum. Within him, a sense of well-being swells and continues to swell, until Louie experiences a sensation unknown in the eleven weeks since Dr. Dimiceli's diagnosis, in the five months since his marriage fell apart: *Oh, he feels fine* . . . Naturally, Louie helps himself to more wine, and when he observes that the two beautiful soft-spoken Italian women have ordered raw oysters, he does the very same. *(When in Rome . . .)* Yes, Louie grandly orders *ostriche*—squelching a sudden absurd qualm (the millionth American tourist to suffer this qualm) that he may be ordering ostrich meat.

The restaurant has begun to fill with diners—welcome presences all. They're a distraction from the Swedes, whose vehemence runs unabated. Accusingly, the four of them keep pushing around the pamphlet. *Pick Paradise* . . . *Pick Paradise* . . . That's precisely what Florence and Darryl did. (No doubt Florence has bought herself a new bathing suit. Lemon yellow, probably. To show off the ancestral glory of her olive skin.) Louie downs more wine. Only when the oysters arrive, on a bed of ice smaller than what you'd expect in the States, does he recall that he has never really cared for raw oysters, or oysters generally, which to his skeptical midwestern palate taste too pungently of the seashore. And these are *raw*. It's only logical, sane and sanitary, to suppose that things salvaged from the ocean, those primitive creatures that never progressed to land, ought to be well cooked—if eaten at all. Louie doesn't much care for seafood, honestly, though he likes tuna-fish salad with pickle relish and also Corporal Admiral Goldbrick Fitzhugh's Extra Crisp Fish Fingers, a freezer staple in his new apartment.

And yet this Italian variety of oyster, when liberally doused with lemon and some sort of garlicky oil, then bundled down the throat without any chewing and immediately chased by white wine, is not half bad. He eats two of them, anyway. Another image to relish: a well-dressed American art historian in Rome, dining alone on white wine and raw oysters.

And then a startling revelation. The Swedes get up to leave, although their argument seems unresolved. A sonic vacuum ensues, soon filled by the two beautiful women seated at the corner's double window. One—the blonde—says, not at all loudly but with eerily delineated enunciation: "So then Frank proposes we sell the apartment on Riverside and move back to *Bridgeport,*" and the other replies, "Oh, you poor thing. Isn't that a man *all over*?" and the blonde says, "Nineteen years of marriage and does he know me *at all*?"

They are not Italians—they're New Yorkers. He had it all wrong . . . Louie's wine-loosened wits scramble for fresh coordinates. The brunette is divorced, say. The blonde's having marital troubles. They're old college roommates, come to Rome to see some sights but mostly to reconnect—which means to talk about men, the disappointing half of the species, and here Louie wishes he could saunter over, plant himself winningly at their table, and confirm wholeheartedly their catalog of disenchantments, though what Louie would focus upon isn't masculine insensitivity. No, what any female list of male shortcomings is apt to underestimate is the male's appetite for *pure evil,* the strain of behavior embodied by Florence's lover, the indescribably abhorrent Daryl Force, who apparently expects to be congratulated for hauling a confused woman away from her husband, her job, her community, her circle of third-grade students, this man beside whom Florence these days presumably sleeps naked in some cabana on some beach in the spectacularly misnamed Virgin Islands, offering up the nape of her neck for someone's nose, a theatrical stranger's nose, to sniff at dawn—and Louie at this juncture does recognize that the wine, in tandem with his jet lag, may have gone to his head.

The blonde is holding forth. Her voice has lifted. She has three children. They are ungrateful. It's something of a theme: the world's ingratitude. Then she's speaking of somebody else, and it takes Louie a moment to pin this down as a masseuse.

"So I had to fire her."

"She didn't relax you? You didn't like what she did?"

"It wasn't that. No, she was a lifesaver. Fixing my knee when I'd given up the tennis foursome."

"That's right."

"No, what it was was having no system. There was no system in her."

"What do you mean?" the brunette says. "Exactly."

"One day she'd concentrate on my arm. My *left* arm. Why? There didn't seem anything wrong with it. Or more wrong than my right arm. Next day, it's my *right leg*."

Is everyone here captivated by their conversation? Why has the place fallen so quiet?

The blonde sips from her wineglass. The outside light has faded, but the room's internal light has enriched to compensate. Everything glitters . . .

"There was no system, no order. And I mean, I don't need more disorder. Not *now*."

"Not now especially."

"So I decide to fire her. Of course first I have to wonder whether it's another emergence of the dreaded Control Freak. I can't tell you how Claudia's been on me. Jason and Delia, too, but *especially* Claudia, and I can't buy little Delia a birthday present without the whole family calling me an out-and-out control—"

"But what did you get her? For her birthday, I mean."

"See? See? You're doing it, too!" The blonde sips from her wineglass.

"Sorry. Sorry." And the brunette sips.

And Louie, the solitary diner, sips from *his* glass, suddenly acutely aware of how untouchably remote the two women are. And how dizzyingly desirable. They had been desirable as Italian signore, whose life adventures he couldn't begin to narrate, but more desirable yet as jaded Manhattanites whose tales he's keen to embroider.

. . . And whether you start in Italy or in New York City, the pitiful conclusion is so unquestionably, so dispiritingly, the same: they're unattainable beings. Oh, easy to satirize them, these two wealthy and attractive American women hoping to be mistaken for Italians. But beneath the satire lies an immovable bedrock truth: for all his tasteful neckties and the charm of his ringlets, neither woman would have the slightest interest in deepening any acquaintance with Louie Hake, an unpublished art historian at a third-rate midwestern college.

Socially, Louie is a free man these days, and he can imagine nothing more thrilling (while his soon-to-be ex copulates with Satan in the torrid Virgins) than to engineer some blazing Roman affair with the sort of New York woman who fires her "lifesaver" of a masseuse because she lacks a system. (Men may be the biggest fools Nature has yet invented, but Louie's prepared to *give anything* for such an affair.)

"So I decide to fire her, of course terrified the monster's emerging, Ms. Control Freak, but I run it past Winston, that's the other Winston, not the stock swindler who's playing golf in prison while Carol's left cleaning up the mess, but Winston Pudder, the new therapist, and he tells me I'm *not* being a control freak. He says it's healthy. Self-definition. So I fire her."

Night deepens, and the windows, growing introverted, occupy themselves with interior reflections. When the Parisian proprietor peremptorily materializes at his side, Louie orders the first thing his eye falls upon: *spaghetti alle vongole.* It's only a few seconds later—monsieur is still descending upon the kitchen—when Louie senses just how foolhardily he's behaving. More shells? Clams still in *clam-shells*?

Other voices compete for their share of the restaurant's sonic space, and the interchange of the two women is lost. Louie has brought nothing to read while awaiting his unsatisfactory entrée. Reading, too, in these past few months has become a complicated, treacherous, delicate business. In the background lies the sickening possibility—too scary for contemplation, actually—that he'll eventually forfeit the pleasure of books. (His online investigations tell him that AOFVD is "slow moving," though its eventual target is the fovea, the "sweet spot" of the retina where detail is absorbed—as when you sit down to read.) (And there's a further, utterly terrifying addendum from Dr. Dimiceli: given that a routine eye exam two years before turned up no retinal irregularities, Louie's disease may be moving more rapidly than usual.) The proper response to his diagnosis is patently apparent:

the classics—Louie must read the classics. Worthy books to complement this Journey of His Life. No more of those salacious memoirs and cheap histories and murder mysteries monopolizing his bedside table! He must matriculate at the School of Great Masterpieces. And so Louie commenced with *King Lear,* which probably was a mistake—in any event, he didn't finish it. For one thing (looking ahead in his heavily footnoted Penguin Classic), there was the blinding of Gloucester to look forward to ("Pluck out his eyes"). And Louie was struck by what was admittedly a pretty obvious point: just how much talking everybody did. Wasn't there something *unkingly* in how, let's face it, Lear never shut the hell up? And the play made the heath sound as dangerous as some alligator swamp, when it was really a level stretch of English countryside, destined in time to nurture snug little shops peddling knit bookmarks and elderflower marmalade and pastel tea cozies.

Admittedly, too, he hadn't given Shakespeare his all. Louie was terrifically distracted. Ever since his diagnosis, he'd become obsessively, excruciatingly attuned to every quirk and vagary in his vision: every floater, every blinked-away shadow, every wobble and wince of ocular strain. These days, when he picks up a book, he often isn't reading so much as monitoring visual irregularities. In other words, too concerned with seeing to see.

A sense of melancholy floats down, which the clanking arrival of the *spaghetti alle vongole* does nothing to lift. Louie immediately arrives at an elementary realization: no human food ought to clank. What other land creatures in the animal kingdom eat food that clanks? He has joined a diner's club whose indiscriminate members include pelicans, goats, wharf rats . . . Warily, he samples the broth, then one of the clams. The chef has done everything he reasonably could—Louie identifies in the broth tiny parsley flakes and minced garlic and flecks of red pepper—but still there's no disguising the organism's marine origins. It's Louie's own fault. After all, he has ordered *mollusks.* It's like saying to some enthusiastic apprentice chef, *Prepare for me the rodent of your choosing.*

Louie recalls a long-ago potluck dinner party with Florence. A table of eight, mostly academics. The hostess asking a marine biologist whether he'd prefer seafood chowder or chili. And the biologist calling out, "Nix to the chowder, sweetie, there's a *reason* our ancestors climbed out of the ocean!" And everybody, especially the hostess, laughing extendedly, while Louie quietly envied this gift he'd never possessed: the ability to unleash merriment at dinner parties.

Actually, Louie has thought often of this remark—specifically, how witless and at bottom *unfunny* it was. When asked the same question, Louie replied, politely, "Either one, they both sound good," and of course nobody even chuckled. (Laughter wasn't what he was aiming for.) But why wasn't politeness at least as valuable, socially speaking, as some hale-fellow, bumptious humorlessness? What was it about adult dinner parties that made them so *awful*? How and when did we all sign up for *this* ill-fitting world, embracing an unspoken social contract which stipulated, *If you say something that isn't witty, we'll all pretend it is*, and why was he himself so unsuited to it?

Wary about disappointing either proprietor or chef, Louie eats as much of the pasta as he can, then flips over most of the shells, disguising their intact innards. When he pushes the plate aside, the proprietor gracefully lifts it away. *"Merci,"* Louie says.

The French proprietor maintains his masquerade: *"Prego,"* he replies.

*"Très bon,"* Louie declares.

He takes it hard—almost as a shove to the chest—when the two women, in a whispery flurry of feminine communication, rise and depart. Is he merely imagining it, or do they leave behind a lustrous shimmer of perfume?

Suddenly Louie, too, yearns for departure. He regrets ordering coffee. (He hadn't intended to, but the proprietor had looked askance at his initial demurral.)

Louie sips his too-strong coffee. He does so while musing on this other obstacle with European dining: the difficulty of crafting an exit. What Americans seem just naturally to understand so much better than foreigners is that a meal is something you may wish to flee. (A meal is like a building: the responsible architect provides emergency exits.) Louie lingers, not wanting to linger.

Finally, calling his au revoirs to the *propriétaire,* Louie reinserts himself into the vast Roman night. A little too much wine. Louie knows the way back to the hotel, but he selects a shortcut, or what rightfully should be one. Before too long, the streets grow less familiar, and much darker. And shuttered. Louie now rediscovers something he'd forgotten about the Romans, that for all their broad and open gesticulations on the street, they prefer to live behind barricades.

Louie jumps when a scrawny cat, right beside his confused head, raucously meows. The creature is perched in a sort of sconce that should hold the effigy of a saint—not this disconsolate nocturnal hunter. A word flares in Louie's consciousness: *banditi.* But is the word Italian, or is it Spanish? At the moment, he can't say. The shuttered buildings climb imperviously toward a narrow isthmus of sky wherein, though the night seems cloudless, no stars shine.

Only now it dawns on Louie that he's carrying not only more money than is prudent but also his passport—and he is thoroughly lost. Lost in a lightless and deceptive foreign land. And a fear far older even than the streets of Rome grips his chest—until it becomes impossible to tell whether the thumpings of his overworked heart mark a reasonable, adult fear (*banditi,* mafiosi, foreign agents) or merely a child's ignorant terror of the dark.

TOO MUCH WINE? JET LAG? THE SEDUCTIVE STIRRINGS OF some weird early-onset midlife crisis? Maybe a display of rebelliousness, foolish but understandable, by a man whose wife recently showed him up as a public laughingstock? Or simply the strained response of somebody whose soul wants out?

Whatever, when Louie at the conclusion of his first long day in Rome finally found safety, bolting himself into his hotel room, in truth feeling quite raw and shaky, he did something utterly uncharacteristic:

he failed to fulfill his pre-bed med regimen. He took his trazodone (50 mg) but left untouched his lithium (600 mg). More than once he has heard his doctor refer to lithium as *the great stabilizer*. But was it also, Louie has often wondered, *the great stultifier?* Wasn't it perhaps a filter removing the highest, brightest frequencies—of sound, of color?

Throughout the restive night Louie was aware of a push-and-pull in his head, just inches below the tattered blanket of sleep. His mind, like some big sweating body much bigger than his own body, kept cumbersomely shifting positions—rolling over, rolling over. Meanwhile, under an unsettled sky, insomniac gulls bickered and jeered. (Their broad derision was catholic and inexhaustible.)

But the curious thing was how morning light ushered in ease and steadiness and appeasement. Louie does not wake feeling heavy. Or self-reproachful. Louie does not wake feeling that his old life must immediately be resumed and righted. No, Louie all but leaps from bed and tosses back the curtains. Below lies the bright bonanza of an outstretched Roman street, saturated in foreign sun. Louie's gaze sweeps up and down. PANE, he reads at one end, and FARMACIA at the other, and the coolly assembled reality of this alien tableau bolsters Louie's surging, surprising resolve: he will take his morning medication (300 mg of Wellbutrin, plus 0.75 microgram of Synthroid), but the lithium will remain in its phial.

The decision ought to feel monumental and terrifying. Never once in the ten years since being diagnosed manic-depressive has Louie shifted his medication without a doctor's say-so. But his brainy new shrink, who suffered his "cardio event" while watching *The Incredible Hulk,* is down in Florida chasing tennis balls and tennis babes, and Louie's new watchword can only be *self-reliance.*

Well, it's doable. And in the wake of his big decision, he experiences few of the dark swirling forebodings he might have expected. More comforting still, he experiences little of that airless, overbright excitement which spells trouble for a manic-depressive. He feels instead a strong, planted ease—an enthroned aplomb in harmony with those seated monarchs whose upthrust statues, like so many tent stakes, fasten the Eternal City to its rolling terrain. This is hardly impulsive; it is no snap decision. Rather, it's a steadily approached resolution. On his walk before dinner last night, it was already in the offing. He'd *known* something was nearing, cohering, and he almost pinned words to it then.

And if he's making a mistake, how catastrophic can it be? He isn't tossing away his meds. Or quitting a job. Or reinvesting his retirement savings in semiprecious metals. He can always retreat to his lithium if he starts feeling wobbly, or sad, or, heaven help us, even a little crazed.

What he's contriving is nothing but a highly monitored close-surveillance moratorium. On the street below, appealingly soignée, an elderly signora has appeared in white high heels. The air organizes itself around her. She stands before a closed pizzeria whose window says COTTO IN LEGNO, which must mean *selling by the slice*—literally, *cut in line*. The woman's salmon-colored sweater exactly matches the hue of the vest on the Jack Russell terrier she's walking, or promenading, and her amour propre is refined and inspiriting. But still more so is Louie's insight into his own enhanced powers of observation. Only a clear-sighted person could read the street so comprehensively. He's going to be all right. And whatever crises he must weather, he'll weather them himself, with nothing as guide but his original and still-intact (battered, but intact) brain.

As Louie sits, later that same morning, in a sunlit café not far from the Fontana di Trevi, under a Kelly-green awning (Kelly green—the color his brain synesthetically codes with the number 3), he utters a phrase that makes him laugh: "I'm moving on my own locomotion." Within him, progressively, confidence and competence are rallying, locomoting. He can't remember the last time he so savored a cup of coffee! It's a cappuccino, and the body of the heated hidden liquid, dozing underneath its duvet of foam, breathes a pleasure steeped in dreams.

Words can't keep up with this eased strain of exhilaration. Just now, he watched a beautiful red-haired girl bicycling helter-skelter down the street, firecracker tresses bouncing ecstatically upon the tops of her shoulders—*pop, pop, pop*—and you might say that he's caffeinating, carefully, in order to catch up with her. Isn't this what other people do, what everyone in history did before the murky dawn of the Pharmaceutical Age: make a physical/mental adjustment here, make a physical/mental adjustment there? Isn't it possible that Louie's reliance on medications has dulled his sensitivity to the good and bad, to all the little grievances and emoluments of his own body? And also possible that, if he remains self-vigilant, he can steer as others do, as the Italians in particular for millennia have steered themselves—a little caffeine here? A little alcohol there? Some coffee, some wine?

This morning, Louie finds himself good and hungry. He has already scarfed down a croissant. (Louie experimented with *crossanta* but the word turned out to be *cornetta*. Live and learn.) He orders another. The elderly waiter wears a kindly but agonized face—he's a bit of a raisin himself—while limping painfully. Louie wishes he could invite the fellow to sit down and, reversing roles, fetch *him* coffee. But there's no way to make the offer. It's the language barrier, or the class barrier, the life barrier . . .

As he's crunching on his second pastry (it isn't quite fresh; the morning's getting on), it occurs to Louie that the ancient Romans founded the greatest empire the world has ever seen without pharmaceuticals; they, too, steered by way of caffeine and alcohol, coffee and wine. And then it occurs to Louie that the Romans *didn't* have coffee, which came over from the New World—along with chocolate and corn and tomatoes. Or potatoes? Louie again laughs aloud. Who could think in orderly fashion on a morning of such tipsy loveliness?

(An unexpected, inundating memory arrives, happily having nothing to do with his wife, Florence. No, it's his first wife, Lizzie, he's recalling. In college, back when love was breaking over their heads, they drove one early summer morning toward a Lake Michigan picnic. They selected a secluded spot, a sunny tawny grassy promontory overlooking the lake, with nobody in sight. They ate deviled eggs and bologna sandwiches and split a pricey nine-dollar bottle of red wine, and then reclined on propped elbows, feet pointing to the blazing water far below, and Lizzie, giggling, announced, "They're all drunk," and Louie peered up and down the shore and, seeing no one, asked, "Who?" and Lizzie giggled again, and fluttered her hands euphorically, and declared, "*All* of them," and Louie saw she was right. (On this early summer afternoon, the dragonflies, the bees, the gnats, the birds—all were inebriated.))

And yet he *was* thinking clearly on his return to the Pantheon just an hour ago. Two visits, two days in a row. He was performing a sort of clinical before-and-after. A lithium-medicated Louie Hake visits the Pantheon; the next day, an emergingly lithium-free Louie visits same. Only yesterday he had confidently—okay, a little pompously—proclaimed to himself, *I'm staring into the eye of ancient Rome,* as he glanced up the dome into the open ring at the top, the oculus, where a thoughtless white cloudlet, shaped like a wine bottle, happened to be drifting. But this morning he required no such grandiloquence. There's a rare, purified strain of oxygen in today's air, and simple respiration is enough.

Yet there's a further component to his pleasure. Louie is additionally feeling giddy over an encounter outside the mighty Pantheon. Boldly interrupting two young Asian women who were taking selfies before the entryway, he'd asked them to snap his picture; he meant to have a photograph of himself posing before each of his Four World Masterpieces. (Wouldn't his students marvel at Professor Hake, the world traveler!) Giggling, the two women agreed, but just as he was arranging himself—folded arms, spine erect—one of them bounced forward in her orange-and-white saddle shoes. "In Singapore, I am hairdresser!" she cried, and she plunged her slender, dexterous hands through Louie's tousled locks. Of course this demanded a second picture: Louie and his Singaporean hairdresser, both smiling victoriously into the camera, the American man's arm tucked firmly around the Asian woman's waist. She was a fragrant, fine-boned creature, and he can still feel, in his buzzing fingertips, the delicate protuberances of her rib cage.

Lounging under his green awning, sipping a cappuccino, Louie recalls an article in maybe *Harper's* written by a commercial pilot who explained that for all the modern cockpit's multimillion-dollar techno-wizardry, we have no reliable substitute for *gut instinct*. Occasions arise when a pilot—a *prudent* pilot, taking full responsibility for his irreplaceable living cargo—must fly by his innards. The lesson was obvious . . . And Louie sips from his powerful coffee.

*You're making a huge mistake . . .* It's a suspicion Louie can't quite shelve, an inner voice all the more discouraging for its evenness, its know-it-all resignation. It admonishes him as he finishes his second croissant, and he'll hear it periodically in the days to come. And yet as time goes by (as solitary Louie successfully manages Rome for two days, then three, then four, five, six), his conviction securely grows that this is an expendable commentator. It's the bratty voice of that inner spoilsport inside everyone, who specializes in introducing gloom and doom to any celebration . . . Louie visits the Forum and the Colosseum and the Sistine Chapel and the Villa Sciarra and the Villa Borghese and the Gianicolo and the Palazzo Farnese and the Villa Orsini. On his seventh Italian night, in a surprisingly unpeopled square just blocks from the Piazza del Popolo, Louie successfully commandeers a personal harbor, dining outdoors in a lovely space of only six tables, islanded off from the world by a hedge of potted hibiscus, flowering in a rainbow's orderly, segmented hues: watermelon red, orange orange, lemon yellow. He begins with bruschetta and a glass of prosecco, and to sit in this mini-piazza whose surrounding buildings' stucco walls leave him feeling more at home than when he *is* at home (his new home, his grotesque Ann Arbor apartment), and to recall the distant evening when everything began to unravel and then reravel, when he arranged misery for himself by ordering raw *ostriche* and *spaghetti alle vongole,* when he lusted after a pair of glowing women who had brought their silliness all the way across the Atlantic in order to parade it in Rome, is to evoke a small and furtive figure less embarrassing than genuinely pitiable. Oh, Louie is feeling so much better! Only now does he recognize how *many* years he has spent feeling beleaguered and frightened. Only now does he perceive how he has allowed some firm and marvelous incarnation of himself to be eclipsed into near nonexistence.

Surely it's a sign of refortified mental health that in Rome he keeps revisiting his childhood in Fallen Hills, uncovering scenes he might well have forgotten. Why—he has often wondered—does his childhood normally feel so irrecoverable? Perhaps because some principal players are dead? His father died so young—sixty-two, of a heart attack, with Louie newly engaged to Florence. And deep in the background hovers a biological mother abducted from Louie's infancy. She's a creature known purely by photographs, though he must initially have entered the precincts of language with her, whose lovely, numinous name was Elvira, whose lovely nickname was Elvie. It's all coming back.

The scraped-raw, all-but-ineffable emptiness he sometimes feels within himself—is this something everybody experiences? Or is it a sensation peculiar to the child deprived of its mother before the age of lasting memory? (On the other hand, it sometimes seems he *does* remember her, the maternal Elvie, or anyway her voice, humming a lullaby—a lullaby just for *him,* for infant Louie as he's drifting into sleep.)

The great leap of speech, the freedom sprung from marrying vowel and consonant—surely it was first accomplished in order to address and gratify her: *Ma-ma.* But still, no conscious memories. And so few memories, really, of early childhood. When he first met Lizzie, Louie marveled, enviously, as she resurrected the menu at her fifth birthday party, or the names of siblings of third-grade classmates. His own past was blank!

Or so it has seemed. But perhaps the past wasn't, after all, so difficult to exhume. Here in Rome, city of perpetual excavation, something unprecedented is happening. His buried early years are shuddering, seismically, as with a reawakening reality. Louie has read somewhere of lost ships that, years after their sinking, will now and then, while sluggishly decomposing in their frigid underwater gloom, release some buoyant fragment and propel it skyward; to be buried doesn't mean you're gone. These days, it almost seems he might turn a corner—wandering through the tumbled ruins of the Forum—and encounter his earlier self, a boy wearing khaki shorts, eyeing the forty-three-year-old Louie interestedly and shyly and hopefully. They have a good deal in common, after all.

It's a sign of how much better he's feeling, how deeply he's savoring Rome, that he calmly plots a departure from it: a day trip to Orvieto. He can do this. He's no vulnerable soul who must fret about losing the essence of a city if it's abandoned for a day.

At midnight, however, Louie wakes in a different state: panting and trembling. He has barely escaped the savage bite of a nightmare. This one came slithering straight out of childhood, where maybe everything was *not* so benign as recent sunlit reminiscences suggest. Flat on his back, in this queer location—an Italian hotel room—he listens to his breathing slow and is returned to the Jupiter Theatre in downtown Fallen Hills.

As a boy Louie once saw a movie (a Tarzan movie?) in which our hero, loincloth clad, climbs and climbs a rickety ladder. Woven of reeds and stems, clearly not intended for any burden greater than a Pygmy's weight, the ladder plunges this way and that. Below, unthinkably, a black maw opens. Down there, pure appetite: huge unglimpsed jaws snap-snapping, snap-snapping with crisp crocodilian finality. And our hero, clambering frenziedly, his life bobbing like a flashlight, seeks one handhold after another. Up, up now, but *this* time what his frenzied fingers clutch, coiled upside down around the ladder, is a *snake*, a gloatingly fat, spotted, pink-tongued snake . . . And Louie lies panting in his hotel bed in Rome. His heart is rap-rapping. For more than thirty years, coiled in some sunless crevice of his brain, the spotted snake has attended him. His brain is wheeling. Snakes are easily negotiated symbols, you tell yourself, like Freud's cigar, and the hopeless, huffing panic occupies only a few moments; in mindful breaths, self-possession rises and reasserts itself. But while it seizes you—terror like this—you know in your bones that nothing in the world so effectively strips away irony and detachment and balance. It takes you apart, terror like this.

When Louie wakes fully, into the airy and sunny morning, a network of subsequent dreams has reburied his snake, his nightmare. It lies behind and below him. Or above him? Throwing a shadow over the streets? *Something* throws downcast shadows as he jumps into a cab headed for Roma Termini.

Louie identifies what he's feeling: fear, lingering fear. Something is coming back into memory that rarely comes back—those hellhole days, ten years ago, before he was diagnosed as bipolar. There was a stretch when he lost friends through aggressions that later looked inexplicable, and chased after women he knew were utterly wrong for him. He even, for the first and only time in his life, pitched into bitter arguments with his father. (Oh, he still feels guilty about those.)

Louie buys his ticket from a strikingly efficient and user-friendly machine and effortlessly locates his train. Everything slides forward as it's supposed to. Actually, he's disheartened by this evidence that nowadays in Italy, too—as in Germany and Switzerland, as in Belgium, Holland, France—the infrastructure functions. Which it so obviously *doesn't* in his native land. Befuddled, beleaguered, more than a little embarrassed, Americans these days naturally look to fellow incompetents for companionship, and it's painful to think the Italians have deserted us, and who would have thought the *Irish* would let us down?

*This is quite interesting,* Louie keeps telling himself, riding the funicular up from the train station to the ancient fortress town of Orvieto. But the air is close and sweaty and overcast. He's peering out into a haze where his eyes cannot settle, his gaze a struggling swimmer in a lusterless gray sea. The funicular is itself disappointing. Not knowing what to expect, Louie romantically concocted an image of swaying aerial transportation—like gondolas on a ski lift. Instead, with its crisp red-and-white exterior and its interior hand-pulls dangling from the ceiling, it reminds him of a bus, but worse: a bus on a track.

*Interesting,* Louie repeats while wandering Orvieto's dry, tan-brown, dusty, surprisingly unpacked streets. Overrun by tourists the town isn't. Admittedly, aided by his little map, he's sticking to side streets. He's saving for later the main thoroughfare, Via Cavour, and the Piazza del Popolo, which sounds crowded, and the town's most spectacular sight: the vast Duomo, the Cathedral of Orvieto, whose polychromatic façade Louie has occasionally encountered in art history books.

His probings around the town's peripheries confirm what he has read: Orvieto is a high, flat island, riding atoll-like upon an unseen mountain. Here and there, an opened vista discloses the terrain below, and you realize you're perched in an aerie, well above any marauders in the low valleys. But such security comes at a cost, and you're all the more exposed to the sun, which on this sweltering June day fairly crackles. Gazing over the pantiled rooftops, a subtle tessellated patchwork of tan and ocher and beige, Louie objectively recognizes an admirable accretion of beauty. But he isn't partaking in it.

After half an hour's wandering in side streets, with ten or fifteen minutes devoted to sifting through neckties in a crass souvenir shop, all the while deliberately avoiding the town's primary sites, Louie reaches the realization that, in the case of Orvieto, *interesting* is code for the distressingly familiar notion that a once-powerful, thriving culture went smash, and who is to say its inhabitants were any less intelligent or hopeful or industrious than, say, the people of Detroit? The ancient people of Orvieto, anyway, could speak Latin.

The day is heating up and the atmosphere keeps closing in— it seems Louie needs a little more air between him and the air. His guidebook informs him that many caves lie underfoot, and at one point last night's nightmare flashingly returns. Standing in the shadow of a souvenir shop, he closes his eyes against the heat and feels the low presence of a writhing nest of snakes. Louie needs a café. Another coffee. Perhaps another *cornetta.* No reason to hurry *anything;* he's here for pleasure, after all.

He stops at a bar and sits outdoors under a red-and-white-striped umbrella. Its frilled edge echoes the town's fondness for flowing cloth, for flags and gonfalons, swaths of color draped to brighten and dulcify the desiccated masonry. He drinks two caffe lattes, downing an Ativan with the second, and nibbles a roll filled with an alien yellow custard. It tastes good but, frustrated at being unable to identify its flavor, he abandons it.

Wherever he goes, Louie keeps stumbling upon unhappy associations. In the venerable Church of Sant'Andrea, where Pope Innocent III blessed the doomed Crusades, what strikes him most forcibly is how the Virgin's halo, a string of little lights, suggests a pinball machine. In the church-turned-museum of Sant'Agostino, the big-boned statue of Mary is so vast, and the annunciatory angel comparatively so small, that Louie recalls the heartbreaking end of his favorite children's book, *Peter Pan:* how, years after the great escapades with Hook and Smee and Tiger Lily, elfin Peter materializes once more, seeking to lure back to Neverland a Wendy grown too big to fly . . . Worse, though, somehow a *lot* worse, is a confrontation in a rundown little park with a crumbling, headless Venus. And yet the space above her lovely shoulders is not quite empty: where the divine head once floated, a curved rusty iron supporting rod remains, revealed through decapitation. The rod's a sort of metal spinal cord—as though Venus were mercilessly exposed as some windup automaton. The Goddess of Love? A robot.

Louie eventually finds his way to a scenic outlook on the town's western edge. He should have worn shorts instead of sweaty blue jeans; his swaddled crotch could hardly be wetter if he'd peed himself. On another day, the outspread fields and hills must sing of magnificence to any American traveler. But the heat and haze discourage all far-flung prospects; behind his sunglasses, Louie's eyes wince tears at the brightness and blindness. And maybe he's a little paranoid, but the mechanics of his vision seem to be malfunctioning today.

Still, as he stares into the void, Louie does see something clearly and afresh: he has been avoiding the Duomo because he isn't sure he possesses the psychological wherewithal, the aesthete's reserves, that any architectural masterpiece will naturally demand. He's hot, and sticky, and listless; he isn't himself, and he dreads the thought of what today's weakness portends as he girds himself for grander, stranger sights—the Blue Mosque, the Taj Mahal, Ginkaku-ji Temple.

Dread drives him underground. As he finally approaches the Duomo, not directly but from its southern flank (a colossal vertical plane of horizontal stripes), Louie spots an entrance to its cellar or crypt. He doesn't hesitate. He ducks in and immediately is engulfed by that odd, unsettling, motionless mineral odor, damp and dusty dry at once, that is the essence, the distinctive scent, of archaeology. It whispers of death, of course—or some nullity deader than death. Backward and forward, the sound of the word is the same: *dead*. Dead as in *dead*. Who would choose to live beside such a smell, to breathe its airless air? It's like volunteering to be a doctor, agreeing to live inside the sharp, warring stinks of a hospital. (The world abounds in noble vocations from which Louie's nose would debar him.)

Yet this isn't really any crypt or cellar. Broad, and immensely high ceilinged, it's much too vast for that. The hollowed space underneath this church is bigger than a good-sized church. A long corridor outstretches; he must be walking under the cathedral's apse. And yet for all its spaciousness, he feels intimations of claustrophobia, feels invisible megatons of sacred architecture straddled above him, cutting him off from the sky.

An hour or so later, still feeling cut off from the heavens, though now the sky is open overhead, he stands some thirty yards from the face of the Duomo. His guidebook informs him that this "unparalleled example of Siennese Gothic" is "one of the chief masterworks of the late Middle Ages." But it all seems so *busy*: the banded travertine and basalt, the soft arches and the aggressively acute angles of the three gables, the gold leaf, the "remarkable" sculptures by Lorenzo Maitani, who was responsible also for the design and who is definitely a name Louie should recognize, though maybe he doesn't. He has no knack for Italian names. He has occasionally entertained ugly fantasies concerning a televised spot quiz on Masters of Italian Art, and with each incorrect answer the studio audience applauds and hoots to see Professor Mop-Top unmasked.

He'd feel better about himself, anyway, if he could marshal any certainty as to whether or not he's standing before a masterpiece. And inside the Duomo at last, he's even worse off: the barred horizontal lines, which turn out to be painted, bathetically remind him of barbers' poles and convicts' stripes. He is, perhaps, unworthy—unworthy of Italy, no less.

Louie eventually finds his way to another café, this time for lunch, though he isn't hungry. He orders *un bicchero di vino bianco,* which seems a sensible idea now that he is not only registering but openly acknowledging that he's fending off the onset of a possibly dangerous depression, only partly concealed beneath a gnawing anxiety. He's a bit of a mess. He withdraws another Ativan tablet from his wallet and downs it with a swallow of wine. Most of the customers are clusters of lively Italians, but there's one other somber solitary diner, an impressively well-coiffed silver-haired man who Louie has concluded is American, partly because he's lugging around the same guidebook that Louie carries today, but mostly because he's wearing an unfortunate tan-and-navy-blue-horizontally-striped polo shirt whose logo is a flying stork from whose beak dangles not a diapered baby but a set of golf clubs. Louie has already noticed him a couple of times, dutifully and dolefully poking through the city's sites. His look of woeful displacement is encouraging and, hoisting his glass of white wine, Louie offers the old man a convivial nod.

LATER, ON THE RETURN TRAIN TO ROME, THEY WIND UP SITting across from each other. The old man has donned a pair of sparkling, silver-framed reading glasses. This meeting feels fated, and such is Louie's current mental state that virtually any show of fatedness seems heartening: there's solace in the sensation that, despite his having been blown thousands of miles from home, some gods somewhere are monitoring his progress and making adjustments accordingly. *Anything* except the chaos of pure happenstance, unplanned and unpredictable and unremarked.

As the train pulls out of Orvieto, Louie says to his companion, "American?"

"American," the man replies, decisively, and the two share a moment of appreciation at how well their conversation is progressing.

"My name's Louie," Louie says. "Louie Hake."

"And my name's Louie, too," the man declares. "Louie Koepplinger."

"Nice to meet you, Louie."

"Nice to meet *you*, Louie."

Laughter. The men shake hands.

"I'm actually a Louie Junior," Louie says. "My father's name was Louie."

For an instant it appears delightfully possible that this profound bond and pledge, this individual Louie link, might be further reinforced. But then Louie Koepplinger says, "My father's name was Isaac."

"That's a good old name," Louie says, which somehow comes out sounding inane.

This other Louie is a retired dentist from Philadelphia. It's his sixth day in Italy. He's currently free to travel wherever he wishes, having nobody to accommodate or report to; he has been a widower for eighteen months.

And he's almost certainly Jewish—given his father's name and the concentration of forbearing irony flaring in the small brown eyes on either side of the generous, quivery nose. Further confirmation comes with the eager deference he displays when Louie, offering up his own capsule autobiography, identifies himself as an art history professor. This other Louie shrugs off Louie's apologetic dismissal of Ann Arbor College as a poor, poor cousin to the University of Michigan. No, this other Louie will have none of it. He embraces his own good fortune in stumbling upon a fellow American of, clearly, enormous erudition. It's an unmerited assumption that our Louie finds most welcome.

"What is your—academic specialty?" this other Louie asks, serving up *academic* in reverential italics.

"I don't know about specialties, but I suppose I'm happiest teaching introductory architecture courses or nineteenth-century American painting."

And Louie replies, "So you were much better prepared than me to appreciate Orvieto."

"I didn't, though," Louie confesses. "Actually, it depressed me."

"*Me too,*" Louie confesses, and this conversation, so propitiously initiated, undergoes a further warming.

"I made the mistake of reading some of the history," the other Louie continues, with a weary bobbing of his head. Meanwhile, Louie has begun to study, with admiration, the man's hair, whose waves and spirals are held under stringent control by what appears to be lotion. He has the antiquated, amiable luster of some sporty toff in an old Brylcreem magazine ad. It's another thing the two Louies have in common, even if the spirit of their styling is altogether different: curly hair of a thickness most middle-aged men would kill for. "The endless warfare," the other Louie is saying. "If you read the landscape, it's telling you, *Here's a beautiful countryside, so let's start slaughtering each other over it.* It's the past. That's what's depressing."

"You've got it *exactly,*" Louie says.

"Maybe it's just timing. Maybe my timing isn't right . . ."

A pause opens like an abyss, into which Louie hastens to toss the bright coin of a hopeful comment: "Maybe we make our own timing." But here it is again, the stomach-pinching possibility that Louie's own journey may be misconceived—or embarked upon at the wrong moment. In any case, there's no not facing the possibility that the journey's introductory, Italian leg is unraveling ominously. Christ, this isn't what he'd pictured, slumped in his cheap-but-not-cheap-enough voluminous but unwelcoming new red armchair in his ugly, not-cheap-enough new bachelor's pad in Ann Arbor! Back then, the trip was meant as a spectacular refutation of Florence's decision to leave him, and of Life's decision to menace him with the loss of something so basic, so human a birthright, as his eyesight. When the idea first broke—the Journey of His Life—it uplifted him, levitated him right off the ill-bought armchair . . .

"Timing hasn't been my for-*tay,*" the other Louie opines.

"I know what you mean," Louie says. Outside, something all but boundless, nothing less than expansive Italia herself, is flipping her illustrated pages for any train passenger's readerly eye. Mile after mile, field succeeds field, and hill hill, all ultimately too rich and manifold for assimilation. A blur . . . And yet within the blur lies Louie's hardening suspicion that complaisant Italy is failing to put out for him. It's more than a week since he arrived in Fiumicino, bedraggled, upended, with a raw heart that openly declared, *Make me yours,* and Italy apparently is planning—with an aloof smiling charm that forestalls the necessity of any outright dismissal—to rebuff its distressed suitor.

"It isn't the past itself that depresses me," Louie begins, and though aware as the words issue from his mouth that they must emerge as arrant nonsense, he considers this still a point powerfully worth attempting: "It's only the *actual* past that depresses me. Reality—the way things in fact turned out. In history. I mean, look at the Romans."

"That's just what I did," the other Louie lugubriously concurs. "These last days. Look at the Romans, and their joy in watching wild animals tear their fellow human beings apart, limb from limb. That's family entertainment? It makes you question human nature. I tell you, you paid me a hundred dollars I wouldn't set foot in that Colosseum again."

"Hard to wrap your head around," Louie replies.

"A kid today? He sees his cat accidentally run over by a car? Well, we send him off for a year of therapy. For his so-called PTSD. It makes you wonder."

"It does," Louie says. It does.

"And the graffiti. Everywhere. You noticed all the graffiti."

"I've tried to ignore it," Louie says. It's no easy task. He rode recently on a train on whose lower windows some graffiti artist had spray-painted a broad expunging black band.

"What does it tell you about human nature?" the other Louie inquires. "Let's say you're born in Rome, one of the most beautiful cities in the world . . ."

"For my money, the *most* beautiful," Louie says.

"Quite possibly," Louie concedes. "Okay, and what do you do if you're one of the fortunate, fortunate few, you're actually born in the world's most beautiful city? What do you do? You vandalize it. Honestly, it makes you question human nature."

Louie has no immediate answer. Lord knows, critics keep sentimentalizing graffiti—so-called street art. But painting the train windows black surely isn't art. Art is intended to make you see, whereas this street artist was intending to blind you. Which meant he was art's enemy. The notion is inescapable: artists can be art's enemy. Louie says, "It must be hard, traveling alone. Losing your wife."

"That's it exactly," Louie agrees. "Two weeks ago today, I turned sixty-seven. I retired at sixty-five. Ruthie—that was my wife's name, her legal name, not a nickname, Ruthie—was always pushing this retirement thing. She's always saying, *We're comfortable, Louie,* and tell you the honest truth, she was right. There were no children, we were just the two of us, and I was a good investor, if you'll permit me saying."

Louie nods; he would.

"It was Ruthie's refrain: 'My entire life, Louie, I'm dreaming of seeing the world. Louie, let's go *see the world.'* And you know what? We coulda. It's a fact a man must face: he coulda done it. But I don't know what it was, I had this rigid conception: a man does not retire before sixty-five. Why was I so rigid? Why was I so rigid? I mean, I ask you, what the hell? I ask you, Is this some eleventh commandment Moses brings down on a tablet—*Never retire till you're sixty-five*? Goddammit, why did I keep saying, 'Hold your horses, Ruthie.' *Why was I so rigid*? And instead of waiting for me to come round, what did she do? Well—life. It's what life does. It's where it goes. We all know it—why can't we see it? Ruthie passed on. Of an embolism. In her thigh. Which went to her brain."

"I'm so sorry."

"And I appreciate that."

In the sunny, shuddering air of the train compartment, needy glance joins consoling glance. It's where life goes, it's how it goes. Louie feels a powerful kinship with this other set of eyes: quick, dark, collusive eyes that flatter Louie with their assumption of a shared understanding of the nature of pain. The two men do understand. The other Louie's glance speaks forthrightly of common male shortcomings, the alliance born of our endless miscalculations, our serial bankruptcies, a perpetual falling short of the situation's emotional demands, and Louie finds himself struggling hard not to open the most pitiful story he knows: his life story.

He takes a deep breath.

"I'm divorcing," he says. "My wife left me flat. Five months ago. She was in an amateur theater production. Very amateur, I'm afraid, since she left me for the director."

"I'm sorry to hear that. They say the course of true love—"

Louie interrupts, bitterly: "I'm not sure how true it ever was."

A pause follows. "I sympathize. But it might not always be like this. Things change. You're young. Things improve. Before they don't. I thought I was alone forever, when Ruthie died, but then a lady friend came my way."

Maybe the admission intends a cheering message: *Life moves on.* Or maybe it's meant as scrupulous disclaimer: *Don't offer me more sympathy than I deserve.* Scant comfort, either way . . . The other Louie continues, "Barbara, a very attractive woman. A patient, and not even fifty. She was only forty-nine, though she did have some gingivitis. And incipient periodontitis. Still, I mean a woman *in her forties*! I tell you something, I'm having to worry about things I thought were long behind me." Behind the flashing lenses of his silver-framed glasses Louie winks. Or blinks. Could he possibly be referring to birth control? Sexual malfunction? Or—more likely—is Louie's lonesome imagination turning prurient? "She was going to accompany me to Italy," Louie says.

Louie pounces eagerly: "She left you?"

"Well. Let's say she found greener pastures," Louie concludes.

This humble admission is all Louie requires. No longer will he withhold his tale of woe. "My wife's name is Florence," he begins again.

Outside the train windows, history hums its broken melodies to the disciplined historian whom Louie might have become. The train has presumably passed from hilly Umbria into flatter Lazio, upon whose minutely tended fields an inexhaustible and indulgent Mediterranean sun has deposited bars of purest gold. Meanwhile, Louie Hake launches into the comic disaster of his romantic life.

"My wife, Florence, she was arrested in January for a violation of section 750.338b of the Michigan Penal Code, or 'gross indecency between male and female persons.'"

"I'm sorry to hear that," Louie Koepplinger replies, but his eyes flash with an avid feral gleam, as what man's eyes would not? He's keen for more. The whole world can't get enough of this stuff; it's what keeps newspapers alive, radio, cable TV. It's the meat we lust after, and this is a particular bloodlust Louie can actually satisfy.

"It was in the local paper. Everybody knows. I step on the campus, or wander into a bookstore, everybody knows. Whisper, whisper. You sound like a classic paranoid—*They're all whispering about me*—but then you realize the classic paranoid's better off than you: *he's* got the benefit of being delusional. Lucky him. *You* step into a grocery store, it's whisper, whisper, 'There's the guy whose wife's arrested for indecent behavior.'"

"Yes . . ."

"Sexual congress in an automobile. In a Honda Odyssey. As a good Detroit boy, I've always distrusted Japanese cars, and here's my worst fears confirmed. Florence was with the director, whose fucking name, excuse me, is Daryl Force. Very amateur theatricals."

Louie feels he's being witty, but his companion looks discomfited, and when this other, elderly Louie repeats, "I'm sorry to hear that," the appetitive gleam has dimmed from his eyes. He's heard enough.

But Louie hasn't *said* enough: "I don't think the cop would've pressed charges if it hadn't been a *church* parking lot."

"Probably not."

"The company, the theater company, the so-called Pyrographic Theatre Company, rehearsed in a Presbyterian church. Where a local Boy Scout troop holds its meetings. They were spotted by an eagle-eyed scout." Louie pauses to let the joke sink in. "I'm sure the officer's feeling here's young people to protect. You see: the two of them chose *the wrong parking lot*. The wrong parking lot! I mean how goddamn dumb can—"

"Yes . . ."

"The play was a comedy. It was originally *The Importance of Being Earnest*. By Oscar Wilde?"

"I've seen it. I did theater myself. In college. I sang the role of Major-General Stanley in *The Pirates of Penzance*."

"I never could get up on a stage," Louie discloses. "Although recently I guess I was thrust upon one. My wife joins an amateur theatrical company, and I wind up in a play. It's called *A Man You Can Laugh At*."

Again, Louie's looking for some deserved acknowledgment of the wit and self-possession he's exhibiting. But in his companion's dark and empathetic gaze he detects, instead, a recoiling alarm. To an outsider, Louie's outbursts must sound manic—or just plain mad. Still, Louie goes on:

"I say *originally* the play was *The Importance of Being Earnest*. But the director, Daryl, he kept making huge alterations. Eventually, he moves the entire play out of England, for one thing. Sets it in Iowa. Maybe he did it because Florence, I'm sorry to say, committed real linguistic atrocities with her English accent. I have a bad ear for accents, but even I winced to hear her. That's the irony. Maybe the most painful irony of all. It bothered me like crazy, it *bothered* me, it kept me *up at night,* worrying some audience'd be hooting at poor Florence. And her doing it unneces*sar*ily. I found it so painful, I don't know, I just found it so, so painful, her volun*teer*ing to do it, to make a travesty of all of England, and English history, and the theater of Shakespeare and Shaw and—and all the other greats. Maybe I'm overly sensitive to public embarrassment. I ask myself. Certainly that's possible. But I found the prospect excruciating—like watching some prim schoolmarm yanking off her clothes under hypnosis, or barking like a dog when the hypnotist says, 'Bark.' It broke my heart, Florence's not seeing just how truly and deeply atrocious an actress she was. I wanted to protect her, you understand. There's the irony: I wanted to protect her."

"It's hard to hear ourselves."

"Florence is a very bright woman, don't get me wrong—she once considered getting a PhD in sociology—but she couldn't hear herself."

"I was never much for foreign languages," Louie acknowledges. "I studied three different foreign languages, and the other night, when I couldn't sleep, I couldn't think of the word for happiness in any of them."

"Was French one of them?" Louie asks. *"Bonheur."*

"French wasn't one," Louie notes unhappily.

"Was Italian one? *Felicità?"*

"Italian," Louie unhappily observes, "wasn't either."

Louie would continue pursuing *happiness,* but right at the moment can't summon another specimen. So he says, "Eventually, the director, Daryl, he made so many changes, he changed the title, too: it became *The Impertinence of Being Earnest."*

"That's sorta clever," Louie declares, then adds, evidently in response to Louie's scowl of indignation, "though not Oscar Wilde."

"Certainly *not."*

A pause. What Louie has just told Louie is as good as a lie, a case of Louie's even now trying to protect Florence from his—Louie's—scorn. That's the irony. The change in name had been *her* inspiration, and maybe it was *sorta clever.* But what embarrassed Louie then, and embarrasses and enrages him now, was the flushed thrill infusing the receptive pores of Florence's olive-skinned fine long neck—her skin erotically charged, he later would understand—as she all but squealed, or yipped, the news that theater director Daryl Force had *accepted the name change.*

Louie goes on: "I keep saying Florence moved out, but that's not strictly accurate. *I* moved out. She kept the house, I took an apartment. I'm not sure why. I keep thinking I got outmaneuvered."

"Typically, it's the man who moves out. In these cases."

"She somehow convinced me I'd always fantasized about some bachelor pad. But *was* it my fantasy? I ask you. And *if* so, how in the world did she know fantasies of mine even I didn't know?" Louie could go on—perhaps about his grad-student neighbors in the apartment above, who, though seemingly polar opposites (she a dark and short Korean pursuing gender studies, he a pale and lanky Polish paleobotanist), are alike in issuing peremptory and slangy and graphically pointed directives during fornication. Truly hellish—the new apartment.

"Hard to tell with these things. I think back on my marriage, and it looks so rosy, but then I recall Ruthie once going four days without speaking to me. She was not a woman with an even temper."

Another alliance-strengthening silence. The two men have in common this, too: inscrutable women at the pivot of their lives. "There were these rehearsals," Louie goes on. "At first it seemed so sweet. Positively jolly. Lovely to see Florence revved up. Believe it or not, Florence can be shy . . . The director, Daryl, who naturally I thought was gay, and it does seem snaky and dishonest his *not* being gay, at least he should've had the simple courage and decency to come out publicly, as straight, I mean—anyway, he was cutting scenes, adding scenes, and Florence found it so exciting, coming home all chatter, chatter, chatter. Why *couldn't* Oscar Wilde be moved to Iowa?"

"A college professor of mine once said it's how you know Shakespeare's a genius: you can set his plays anywhere."

"She's in the Virgin Islands now. With Daryl. I'm convinced they chose their destination purely for its painful irony."

"I can't believe that," Louie says, fair-mindedly. The lenses of his glasses shake, side to side. His hair doesn't move when he shakes his head.

"Okay. Maybe not. Anyway, they've been there *weeks*. His sister owns an actual place down there. I got an email from Florence—though we're *not* really in contact—and she tells me she's getting badly needed rest. After the, you know, the arrest. Section 750.338b of the Michigan Penal Code. Your average gross indecency between male and female persons. Resting? You can imagine what I imagine is Virgin rest!"

Again, Louie observes an uneasy flicker in his companion's gaze. It's probably time to back off, but Louie finds he hasn't concluded. "Obviously, they wouldn't take her back at school. Florence teaches third grade. Imagine. Imagine the pleased parents: *Our kid's teacher was arrested for gross indecency.*"

From the protective tightening of his eyelids, you might suppose the other Louie's about to shutter this conversation, but instead he advances a tender, indelicate admission of his own: "Actually, Ruthie wasn't my first love. I'll tell you another thing: I was no virgin when I married her."

"I'm sure you weren't," Louie replies. Though comradely in intention, the words emerge with all sorts of silly, roguish overtones. Louie offers a modification: "I mean, if you look at it the way the world actually *is*."

"I had a lady friend, a very lovely lady friend. Her name was Sheila Patrice Ogden. But my family—nobody—they didn't approve. Of her background. Sheila Patrice was—"

It is bold Louie who steps forward as decorous Louie falters. "A Gentile?" he gently inquires.

A pause. Then, "Yes. Yes, she was," Louie matter-of-factly confirms. Yet he seems grateful to have this bridge expeditiously crossed. "Oh, it all worked out in the end. She married a Mr. McCormick. A contractor. Very successful. *Very* successful, and I'm not talking just financial: the man's a real community spark plug. And I married Ruthie. So everything works out."

That the older man is choosing to open up his life like this is hugely endearing. Louie says: "Can we have dinner tonight? When we get back to Rome?"

Louie says, "I have some old patients. A man and wife. They used to live in Philly; now they live here. They're having me to dinner."

"Tomorrow night?" Louie presses.

"You're going to get the wrong idea about me. I assure you I am no social butterfly, but tomorrow I'm meeting a fellow dentist and his wife. We're going to some operatic recital. I don't know why. I don't care for the grand opera," Louie confesses. "I never got past Gilbert and Sullivan if you want the truth. *I am the very model of a—*"

"I never got as *far* as Gilbert and Sullivan," Louie likewise confesses. "I mean I've been to opera, to the Met, in New York, *The Tales of Hoffmann*, but it's the whole premise I can't swallow. What does it have to do with me? Somebody onstage wants a glass of wine, or is asking for directions. Okay, you want wine, or directions. But why *sing*? Isn't that distracting? Wouldn't that make it much less likely you'd get what you wanted?"

"But the next night," the other Louie goes on, "if you're still in Rome, I'd love to have dinner. And since I keep meeting up with folks who insist on treating, let's say this time you'll be my guest."

And here in smiling Italy, gregarious but ultimately retractive Italy, it seems Louie until now hasn't ascertained the depths of his hunger for some personal, focused human amiability. If nowhere near tears, he's nonetheless aware of a stinging in his eyes as he replies, "Oh, I'd like that very much!"

THAT NIGHT LOUIE AWAKENS A LITTLE AFTER MIDNIGHT TO find, below his waist, his hand clasping himself in a state of challenging arousal. *Why was I so rigid?* an antic, bantering voice echoes, and he follows the voice, for he may be on the trail of something brightly witty ... But it leads him instead to Louie Koepplinger, the dentist from Philadelphia. It's one of the questions the other Louie had asked so touchingly. Why so rigid? Why deny Ruthie her lifelong dream of the world?

Louie means to have the world.

Outdoors, big meteorologic rumblings roll across the open gray amphitheater of the Roman night sky. Lying under an Italian darkness, in a dreamy state, he recalls last night's dream of a rope ladder and a snake, and recalls something else, such an obvious point, yet elusive until now. A couple of days ago, on a trip to a new museum salvaged from an old power plant, Centrale Montemartini, he'd stood in front of a vast and ancient stone bowl, large enough to bathe an infant in. The museum described the bowl as "bean shaped." This puzzled him and made him loiter; it looked perfectly round.

But that wasn't the point. The point was that, as he'd contemplated its shape, he felt a frigid breath upon his neck: the arrival of something insidious and creepy. Good Lord! The bowl's scaly handles were carved snakes! Reaching out to grab a handle? You'd grab a snake. And that, of course, was where his dream had originated.

*That* was the key, *that* was what had transported his imagination to a childhood Saturday matinee at the Jupiter Theater in Fallen Hills: an ancient Roman bowl in an archaeological museum. This was the key, and how heartening to locate the genesis of the nightmare . . . Dreams really *can* be unlocked, à la Freud. (Louie has long been intending to embark on *The Interpretation of Dreams*.) And if, at bottom, a person's demons are comprehensible, they are conquerable.

Another Roman lightning flash, another insight. Beginning now, he needs to reexamine his life. Needs to rethink it, refine it. Just the way the other Louie's so calmly rethinking. Too flustered, too self-preoccupied, he has been coming at things too narrowly. It isn't enough to be brooding constantly about Florence—though of course he is. She's always there. (He might *appear* to be lecturing on Albert Bierstadt, or eating beef fried rice out of a greasy cardboard carton, or staring at a photograph of a lost Siamese cat on an AAC bulletin board. But in fact he's having an ongoing discussion/argument. Sometimes he'll find himself gloating triumphantly, no doubt to the bewilderment of those around him, who don't realize he has just bested Florence with some deft riposte.) But thinking of her constantly—it isn't enough. He has been seeing things through smudged sunglasses.

He needs to examine the world from her viewpoint. In her eyes, what's his *primary* fault? So many things he'd mismanaged, but the *primary* fault? Until recently, he'd thought his shortcomings more likable than not. He was woolly-headed; he was timid; he was unforthcoming. Okay. Point taken. And he had no friends. Now, *this* accusation did genuinely disturb him. Florence was implying he wasn't likable, but Louie knew that people liked him. What was somehow lacking was the capacity, or maybe just the inclination, to convert warm intentions into invitations. Perhaps it would have helped if his bipolarism hadn't discouraged casual drinking. (Louie sometimes overhears, with envy, male colleagues in the hallways exchanging impromptu invitations: "Say, what about a beer?" or "Time for a quick one?") Perhaps he'd have more friends had he gone oftener to the gym, but he dislikes gyms. Without exception they smell of bullying—they return him to those dreaded junior-high phys-ed wrestling matches where you wound up with someone's precociously hairy armpit straddling your face.

Perhaps it would have helped to teach at some prouder institution. AAC's flagrant third-rateness instilled among faculty a shared identity as losers, fostering the competitive self-pity losers substitute for a healthy intimacy. It was a game Louie couldn't play with the relish his colleagues brought to it. ("You think *that's* ignorant. Wait till you hear what one of *my* students said . . .")

Yet people like him. His students, particularly, like him. Teacher evaluations confirm his likability. Louie can go to any computer on the planet and within a minute assemble a cyber-stack of testimonials: he's bright, he's funny, he knows his stuff, he's understanding and inspirational, he's good, he's funny . . . And he's *hot*. He has encountered this one with some frequency: numerous girls have looked to the head of the classroom and, observing an unprepossessing and not-quite-tall-enough but stylish and mop-topped fortyish professor of art history, have discerned, potentially, behind the talk of American Luminism, or the Rise of the Skyscraper, a male of ardent sexual gusto.

Actually, it wasn't only girls. There were the hapless boys, too, though not usually the flamboyantly and precociously "queer." Louie's male tagalongs were typically the coming-out-slowly boys, not especially good-looking, who enrolled in American Nineteenth-Century Landscape or Fundamentals of Architecture less from any rooted interest than from a vulnerable yearning for entrée into some less jeering and more rarefied world. Louie liked these kids. Years ago, there was a boy from Muskegon, Bradford Doerr, still a teenager, still pimply faced, quite bright and chattery, who'd dogged him everywhere. Initially, Bradford got almost everything wrong: he thought Venice and Venezia were two different places; he sounded *Caravaggio* with a hard *g*; he pronounced the last syllable of *Renaissance* to rhyme with *underpants*. And when Louie, ten years after Bradford's graduation, ran into him by chance on the Mall in DC, he met a shaved-headed multiple-earringed dude from Miami who was impressively suave— but far less appealing.

(In fact, Louie now recalls, the encounter had haunted him for days. The conversation dragged, and when Bradford at last brought up AAC, he did so with puckery-mouthed embarrassment; clearly, he was disclaiming any affiliation with so unglamorous an institution. Okay, Louie had no great stake in AAC's eminence—but Bradford also made apparent his conviction of having outgrown Louie, his old teacher and mentor, and what self-respecting fine arts professor could bear to be outgrown by somebody for whom, not so long ago, *Renaissance* had rhymed with *underpants*?)

*You have no friends*, Florence would say. *But Florence*, he'd reply, *we socialize frequently*. And she'd reply: *Those are my friends. You met them all through me.*

Maybe . . .

And there was: *You don't give me any space*. And: *You eavesdrop on my phone calls*. And: *You're hurt if I go out with one of my girlfriends*.

Had this been his biggest fault: *too dependent*? Was it simple, really—he'd failed to make for himself a full life? Failed to make the friends he ought to make, failed to launch the scholarly career he'd envisioned, and failed to sire children, though open to the idea—still perhaps open. But it turned him so anxious, all this doting talk of *babies*—and everybody willfully ignoring how these adorable creatures are really naked animals howling like dictators from the minute they vacate the womb. And later, after you've somehow effortfully raised them and gotten them out of the house, they return to say, *I'm miserable, and it's all your fault* . . . Of course the real change in his thinking came with the diagnosis of bipolarism. Sometimes he'd envision a little boy, his own child, an upright youngster with an old-fashioned fifties flattop haircut, standing beside him at the bathroom sink, and father explaining to son, "Now this is lithium, I take six hundred milligrams of this a day for bipolarism. And this is Wellbutrin, I take three hundred milligrams as a check against depression. And this is Synthroid, which counters side effects from the lithium. And this . . ." How could he subject such a sweet little boy to such a bitter prospect?

Or he was *too demanding*? For he'd longed after Florence indiscriminately—longed to make her friends his own friends, her siblings his siblings, her skinny olive-skinned flat-busted soft-bellied sweet-smelling body his playground and freehold. Jesus, she'd come home from work and immediately stiffen at the hand around her waist, the pat on her firm bottom, the squeeze on her upper arm. *Louie, let me get a drink first.* Or, *Louie, let me just check the mail.* He spent too long cooped up in the house, in bondage, wound in the chains of interlocked papers on his desk, and when at last Florence came home he exhibited the loosed excitement of a puppy whose owner has belatedly returned. He'd be doggily breathing on her, bouncing against her, wanting to lick her face . . .

Was it any wonder she was always pleading that her period had started, or was about to, or she had what might be a urinary tract infection, she had a headache, her stomach was queasy, her knee hurt? How had she put up with him as long as she had?

One night they attended a cocktail party at the home of an old high-school friend of Louie's (yes, he *did* have friends), now an extremely powerful attorney. Chet Miskinis had successfully defended General Motors in some wrongful-death suits. He'd even had his picture in the

*New York Times.* Chet and Amber lived out in Grosse Pointe Shores, right on Lake Saint Clair, so if you had a good arm you could probably pitch a baseball into the water from the terrace where everyone stood guzzling drinks. And Chet during dinner referred to Louie's *uxorious* relationship with Florence, and everybody laughed, and after a pause Florence said, "I'm not sure I know what the word means," and everybody laughed again. But no one bothered to define it. And a quieted Florence had evidently deduced that the word held sophisticated, racy, even thrillingly scandalous overtones, for to her pensive face came a look of crestfallen disillusionment when, back home in scruffy Ann Arbor, she'd sat down and consulted an online dictionary. *"Excessively submissive or devoted to one's wife,"* she reported, glancing up from her computer. "Is that all?"

Is that all? Excessively submissive or devoted to one's wife—should he plead guilty? And was this an offense duly punishable with exposure as a cuckolded buffoon under section 750.338b of the Michigan Penal Code?

In the darkness, the skies of Rome again rumble, grumble—more minatory this time around. The malcontented gods, in eternal disagreement . . . Louie Hake is a victim. No, Louie Hake is an insignificant obstinate ass, who could not read the heavenly signals, who has brought his own doom down upon himself and deserves no pity. Louie Hake is a well-meaning manic-depressive, recently diagnosed with a potentially blinding retinal disorder. Hake is an artist without a medium. Hake is a bright man so full of rage and indignation he sometimes can't think straight.

But it seems there's an exit from this routine of miserable thrashing upon the bed in his high hotel room, where all night long evil gulls chuckle over end-of-world conspiracies. The exit lies in the twisting string of his recent thinking. He needs to rewind, unravel . . .

And then he has it, the link in place: the chain goes from uxoriousness to doglike devotion, from doglike devotion to dogs generally. The two of them once owned a mini-dachshund, beloved Gator, christened by clever Florence: *He looks like a little brown-black alligator.*

And when gluttonous Gator one day choked to death, the two of them wept inconsolably. And each, independently, composed a little verse tribute to their vanished housemate. In retrospect, both poems were doubtless laughable. Mercifully, Louie can't remember a single phrase of his own. But he does recall Florence's valedictory lines: *We'll see you later / Dear imitation alligator.*

Literary merit is hardly the point. No, the point is that Florence clung to him, weeping and weeping, and Louie, while also weeping, served as a bulwark: he radiated solace. So drenched with her tears was the sleeve of his white shirt that it stuck to his overheated flesh. If not an actual child's death, this was the tragedy, no less real, of a symbolic child's death. And his own beloved Florence had come as supplicant, beseeching forgiveness.

Hadn't *she* left the mortal hunk of brisket in a trash bag where Gator must find it? And Louie's job had been absolution—*We all make mistakes*—and this image remains heartening, like Florence's weeping. For this was one of those rare occasions when the woman's tears sprang from the elusive fountainhead of her being. Oh, if he could only find some way to tunnel regularly to that place and encounter her there, soul to soul! She could hardly stand upright, beneath such sorrow. She clutched him for support, which he provided.

And, unexpectedly, those recollected tears elicit tears of his own, and Louie finds himself weeping a little into his pillow. Then Louie sits up and wipes his eyes, and his breathing dramatically slows, for he has made another, an amazing, a blazing discovery: he has it in his heart to forgive Florence.

Yes, he can truly grant her what he has so often pledged: absolute, unshadowed forgiveness. What's past is past. The shape of her pain precisely complements his; the two of them can, harmoniously, refit themselves. Over the years, he has been impossible—defensive, dependent, *smothering*—and the breadth of this realization opens up his chest: Louie breathes deeply, inhaling the scents and the sounds and the splendors of the Eternal City.

Louie swings his legs over the side of his bed. His heart is bounding like a rabbit's. There's no light but the glow from the bathroom. Fully formed, ingeniously contrived, tomorrow's itinerary has arrived. In every detail the plan seems so faultless, surely he must have been concocting it long before it surfaced.

Tomorrow, he will take the train to Florence. He will email Florence *from* Florence. He'll seek out some Internet café and compose a long resounding letter expressing his inextinguishable love and newfound forgiveness, his regretful understanding of the ways he once limited and constrained her. His will be the simple eloquence of pain-purchased wisdom. Years ago, Gator's body having been discovered in front of the fireplace, blunt and inert and weighty as some fallen log, he watched Florence weep her eyes out over a symbolic child's death. What joys, then, an actual child might bring! He will overcome his every anxiety, every tremulous trepidation. Tomorrow, he will write to Florence suggesting they conceive a child.

Clarity breaks as drunkenness might—in rhythmic, powerful waves. But the difference is this is clarity. That's what's so astounding: there's nothing quite like having *clarity* break over you . . . He has no need to experience the Blue Mosque, or the Taj Mahal, the hillside temples of Kyoto. If Florence will grant him another chance, he could depart for Ann Arbor tomorrow. The so-called Journey of His Life has been a necessary pilgrimage, but one whose aim wasn't as heretofore envisioned. He needn't voyage any farther. Or compile any mental scrapbook of the world's wonders. The goal has always been to isolate an emotional lucidity; and to attain by means of lucidity an emotional calm; and with calmness, charity; and with charity, a final renunciation of all spite and resentment. He will return home all but purified.

People change, they do, and he, Louie Hake, engineered this trip expressly to undergo change. He is no longer who Florence thinks he is. He has no friends? Why, he made a friend just today, on a train, traveling from Orvieto to Rome. He and his friend are planning to have dinner two nights from now. And this, too, might be something to include in tomorrow's letter, a phrase casually inserted into one of the middle paragraphs: *My friend Louie . . .*

AND THERE HE SITS, HIS FRIEND LOUIE, AT A TABLE BY THE doors to the kitchen, drink gamely uplifted. He's a smaller, older-looking gentleman than he was in Louie's recollection.

Louie, like Louie, is wearing a necktie. "Sorry to be late," Louie offers, a little breathlessly, and takes the seat opposite his friend.

"Perhaps my directions were faulty."

"Not at all," Louie evenhandedly points out. "I got waylaid by the marvels of this marvelous city."

Louie expects easy assent, yet his companion's nod looks grudging. On this issue of lateness (it occurs to Louie), the former dentist has had his fill of ingratiating apologies.

Surprisingly—doubly surprisingly—this other Louie appears to be drinking a martini. Two gray olives doze at the bottom of the glass. Louie wouldn't have taken Louie for a martini drinker. And he has often heard that genuine American cocktails are unknown in Italy.

A heavyset waiter with proportionally plump ears and bristling eyebrows materializes at his shoulder, and Louie impulsively says, with more confidence in his Italian than in his judgment, "*Il stesso per me.*" He has never liked martinis. He prefers drinks that make some minimal effort to disguise their raw intentions.

"I've been to Florence since I saw you last," Louie begins.

"I've been meaning to go. Just haven't mustered the energy."

"It's an energizing city," Louie pronounces. "I found it liberating."

"Liberation." Louie sighs, as if according the term long-overdue consideration. He goes on, "Your trip agreed with you, my friend. You've got much better color than when I saw you last."

"Yeah, I went to Florence and I saw some of the city but not much, because actually I spent more than three hours in an Internet café. I wrote my wife. You remember, her name is Florence."

"I do remember."

"It was—it was the most intense letter of my life! Three hours! I honestly didn't move for *three hours*. I don't mind telling you at one point I could hardly see the computer screen, that's how hard I was crying."

"I think it's something specific about Italy. Normal people like you and me, it makes us overemotional. Scientists in fifty years will discover the water here makes you overemotional. Look at the people in the streets. Arguing as a way of life. I can't believe it's good for the stomach."

"I told her I wanted to start over with her. Florence. I honestly think this trip has done me amazing amounts of good! Sometimes you have to get away, in order to think clearly . . ." Louie runs a hand through his hair, which, it occurs to him, he hasn't combed today. "I was putting all the blame on her, and sure, she deserves lots, but what about me? You maybe wouldn't guess it, but I can be hell to live with!"

Louie pauses to permit a polite objection. When none follows, he scrambles on: "You've got to start with yourself! Fix yourself before fixing anybody else. First, figure out what *you* must atone for."

"Atonement? None of us can go forward without it. All the great religions—"

"It's amazing how much you can be at fault without seeing your own faults. You know? Especially if you don't want to see them, and who does? Who does?" The repeated question echoes in the quiet restaurant. It seems Louie has consumed his martini; the glass in his hand is empty.

He is of course talking much too much, much too fast. This reminds him of Gator, that doted-upon little long-dead dachshund whose liquid brown eyes brimmed more soulfully than all but a few human gazes. Gator threw himself into everything, yanking his leash with truly uncanny—given his compact body—force and ardor. He'd lunge forward, choke himself against his collar, lunge forward, choke himself, lunge forward . . . It's like, Louie somewhere senses, his own lunge and choke, lunge and choke, while something as supersized and grown-up as Common Sense keeps yanking back on his leash. But his thoughts are getting away. Or if not his thoughts, the words pursuing those thoughts: he's running to catch up with himself.

It isn't easy, but Louie does stanch his flow of talk. He nods at the waiter, ratifying the notion of a second martini, before realizing that the other Louie, whose stare momentarily tightens, evidently plans to halt at one. Louie says, "Tell me about meeting your wife," and with a few focused questions, he rights the conversational balance. He can even relax a little, as his companion chronicles the bare-bones novel of his life.

Louie Koepplinger was born in Newark, New Jersey, in 1947. His father owned a neighborhood hardware store, and he has sometimes wondered whether his fondness for dentistry's fine gadgetry was traceable to his father's shop. He attended Rutgers, both as undergraduate and as dental student. It was in dental school that he first fell in love.

"I mentioned her before."

"Sheila Patrice," Louie supplies.

For just a moment, the man's face clouds at an outsider's volunteering the intimacy of the young lady's name. Then his narrow features open up, generously: he's grateful for Louie's attentiveness.

"Yes, the very lovely Sheila Patrice Ogden. You know, it's peculiar, this trip, but I'm thinking of her constantly. I'm thinking about Ruthie, of course, but that's expectable, forty-one years of marriage. But why does a trip to Orvieto leave me mooning about the time I took pretty Sheila Patrice Ogden to Atlantic City and we ate T-bone steaks at a restaurant right over the water? Why do I go to Orvieto and find I'm thinking about a relationship that ended forty-five years ago?"

"Well, for one thing," Louie replies, "Orvieto is built on ruins."

The dentist tips his martini glass toward Louie, in a mock-solemn show of appreciation. It's one of the man's most appealing aspects—his eagerness to credit the acumen of his newfound friend, the professor.

"My plan was to make her Sheila Patrice Koepplinger. I remember thinking, What an unusual name. She'd be one of a kind in the whole world: Sheila Patrice Koepplinger."

"You had family opposition."

"I had cowardice. That's what I had." After this bold remark, the old man dabs rather daintily at his mouth with his napkin. "No one could honestly have stopped us. No, we stopped ourselves. This was America, this was 1969. Young folks were doing all sorts of wacky things"— though with this old fogy's choice of *wacky* to describe *young folks,* it's obvious that Louie Koepplinger, even back then, wasn't among them.

The two men study their menus. "Nice restaurant," Louie says. "Howdja find it?"

"A recommendation," Louie says. "Actually, the owner's from Philly. It's supposed to be somewhat American-style."

"Smart," Louie says.

The Italian descriptions are ornate and mostly impenetrable, but the English translations, couched in parentheses, are appealingly no-nonsense: cheese ravioli, veal stew, fried fish.

When conversation reopens, the dentist chooses to deepen its intimacy. He says, "I suppose I've had three great love affairs in my life. Technically. Three what you'd call actual affairs. As a married man, I did not play the field. I suppose three sounds meager to you in your sophisticated world, Professor. Sounds like a small number?"

"I'm not sure about sophisticated. And I don't honestly know what small or large means when we're dealing with a subject—" But this subject's so vast, Louie fails to assemble his words. The dentist takes advantage of the pause:

"I don't mean to ask highly personal questions. I don't suppose I want highly personal answers. All I'm trying to do is to describe this peculiar . . . *business,* how Italy's working on my head. It's got me all higgledy-piggledy. That was a word Sheila Patrice would use: higgledy-piggledy. That really tickled me. It seemed, I don't know, Irish. Goyish. Anyway, not the way we talked in my house."

"Lizzie, my first wife, used all these Briticisms. And Florence—"

"I've mentioned already I had a lady friend since Ruthie passed away. She—"

"She found greener pastures."

"Exactly." And another grateful nod for Louie's attentiveness. "We were planning to travel to Rome together. As a couple. Barbara has Italian roots."

"So does Florence. She's half Italian, half Greek. She's quite dark. People think of *olive skinned* as a poetic exaggeration, but in reality—"

"And when I decided to make the trip anyway, on my own, having been abandoned, I figured I'd be mooning over Barbara. But you know what? She's hardly in my head."

"I keep thinking it clarifies a person's thinking," Louie says. "Being here. My email yesterday? I've never put so much emotion and attention into anything I wrote. Ever. And I'm a writer. At least in theory. I have a good start on a book about nineteenth-century American landscape painting."

"Oh, I've been thinking about my wife, naturally. Which just makes me feel guilty." The dentist, who has been using his martini glass more as stage prop than source of refreshment, now takes a substantial swallow. "But mostly I've been thinking about days like the day I took Sheila Patrice to Atlantic City and a restaurant right over the water. You can't believe how *classy* that looked to two kids like us. Young people. You know, we were two young people in love, which means we had everything, though maybe we didn't know we had everything. But we lacked courage. And that's why I'm in Europe: to show myself I still got some guts."

"I'm not sure I'm tracking the gist here." This is a pet phrase, something Louie often says to his students. "I'm not sure I'm following—"

"After Barbara left me, I was frightened about doing this trip alone. I don't mind telling you, Louie, I was a *frightened man*. Frightened. What was I scared of? Melancholy, I suppose, because that's my black dog. You know the phrase? Winston Churchill—"

"It's funny, but *black dog* for me suggests something else. We had this dachshund, this wonderful little creature named Gator, and Gator would—"

"I think Winston Churchill popularized the phrase. In any case—but am I sounding self-pitying?"

"They're very serious," Louie replies, consciously restraining himself once more. He pauses. "Bouts of depression. *Very* serious once you're inside one." And the entire ten-year history of a manic-depressive's diagnosis, the watchful, fretful business of never going overnight *anywhere* without the telltale rattle of pills in your private pharmacy, and his recent heady and hell-for-leather decision to do a moratorium on lithium—oh, Louie could bend the man's ear! But he won't. And this ability to curb his tongue, with so much language thronging inside him, is a heartening portent. His own word for how he's feeling tonight is *manicky,* and yet he's *managing.* He sips from his drink.

"So I come at last to Europe," the dentist observes. "The Old World. On my own. And I do some proper sightseeing. Even if I never get to Florence."

"Next time," Louie says.

"No. Oh no. No next time. You see, Louie, it's my last trip across the Atlantic."

Though tranquilly delivered, the announcement devastates Louie; Mr. Koepplinger might as well be saying, *I'm heading home to die.*

"But life has so many chapters!" Louie protests.

"Chapters? Oh, please understand, no complaints from yours truly about the so-called book of my life." Louie shakes his head. "My maternal grandfather lived his whole life within ten miles of his farm in Poland. Ten miles, one valley, and one man's whole life . . . And me? I've seen Big Ben. I've seen the Arch in St. Louis. I've seen the Golden Gate Bridge, the Grand Canyon, the pyramid at Teotihuacán. That's in Mexico."

"Yes," Louie says.

"But I guess I wasn't prepared for Rome. It's just too much past. Maybe that's why I'm living in the past? Perky little Sheila Patrice, the very lovely Sheila Patrice Ogden, bright as a tack. A new tack in your good old neighborhood hardware store, back in the day when there were good old neighborhood hardware stores, instead of these—"

"Goliaths," Louie helpfully supplies.

"And she and I having dinner one evening right over the Atlantic. Eating steak on top of an entire *ocean,* for Christ's sake, like our own front yard."

And now Louie can't help but leap in. "But to go forward, you first hafta go back! Into the past! I've been recirculating everything, *everything,* in my head . . . As I told you, I wrote Florence yesterday. I've been recirculating every moment of our lives together. And not just that! I've been thinking about Lizzie, my first wife, who had serious self-esteem problems, though maybe back then *I* had such big self-esteem problems, I couldn't recognize hers. And other women I dated. In college. Puppy love. When I was nineteen I was absolutely mad about this Vietnamese woman who lived down the block, married to a doctor, a surgeon. They were about to move to Omaha. I gave her tennis lessons. She was unhappy. Maybe she had the black dog? Her English was far from perfect and some of her errors *tickled* me. I remember once her talking about gray days making her gloomy and she said, 'I am depressing when it rains.' God, I *loved* that! 'I am depressing when it rains.' How could you not be half in love with her? That whole summer, she was the sun and moon to me."

"What Sheila Patrice and I had?" Louie says. "It wasn't puppy love." He declares this a little indignantly.

"Oh, I'm not saying!" Louie breaks in. "And have you got in touch with her? She still around? Just maybe, Louie"—Louie shakes his head sagely—"just maybe, right now, this very moment, Sheila Patrice is doing what you're doing: reminiscing about Atlantic City and T-bone steaks right over the water."

"You can't dwell in the past," the dentist says, and this pronouncement disconcerts Louie even more than the other one a few minutes ago, which he can't at the moment recall. "That's why I won't come back to Rome."

"But open, you hafta keep it *open*! Otherwise it's—it's all amnesia. Life. And nothing gets built. Rome never gets built. It fails to become even a ruin: *Rome never gets built.*" The line he's seeking to draw is subtle—a gossamer distinction—and rather than proceed further, maybe producing only greater obfuscation, Louie reiterates: "If we don't keep the past open, Rome never gets built." He goes on: "Life has to be—"

And here he has begun a sentence as well as any sentence possibly *can* begin. He's on the threshold of declaring a bold existential credo, of making some utterance that will surprise him, surpass him, succor him. But all his stammering words are getting in the way of his thoughts . . .

He backtracks. "Veronique. Her name was Veronique. The Vietnamese woman. I was totally *mad* about her. Of course we were never lovers, or anything like that—but maybe a *little* like that? Or more than a little, at least in my mind . . . I kissed her once. Well, actually much more than once—I suppose I mean on one occasion. In her kitchen. We'd never touched before. Well, that's not exactly true. She once patted my head. But people always did that when I was a kid. It was the curls. The ringlets." Louie pauses. "But I daresay, Louie, given *your* hair, you received your share of head patting as a kid."

And the old man (oh, how endearing it is!) steadily, proudly blushes. "It's true," he concedes in a near whisper.

"Anyway, Mrs. Gantry and I were both sweating—I'd just given her a tennis lesson. I think the sweating had a lot to do with it. Otherwise, I can't believe I'da done it. I'm very shy, Louie. And shyer back then. But she was standing closer than people normally stand, and I made some nervous remark about the morning's rain, and she said, 'I'm depressing when it rains,' and—"

And the living moment comes railroading back, with a packed, linear force it hasn't possessed in more than twenty years. Though Louie's talking quickly, his words can't keep pace. What he would like to express is that it was precisely this artless remark of hers, murmuring of distant exile and vulnerability, that emboldened him to step forward and press his boyish lips to her lovely, grown-up, error-riddled mouth.

Fortunately, a waiter materializes. Louie initially resents the interruption. But a moment later he appreciates this opportunity to calm down and redirect the conversation. He needs to return to earth. He's flying . . .

The dentist orders prosciutto and melon, to be followed by "spaghetti with meatballs" *(tagliarini d'estate da una ricetta di una fidanzata scomparsa),* and Louie, though tempted by the "meat lasagna" *(le lasagne della matrigna Elisabetta da una ricetta delle Colline Perdute),* orders exactly the same thing. He asks his friend how he likes Philadelphia, and the dentist accepts the question as intended—not as specific inquiry but as general invitation to expatiate on life. Somehow the dentist winds up resurrecting the modest hardware store in Morristown, and Louie winds up speaking of *his* father, that *other* other Louie, Mr. Louis Hake, a temperate soul dreaming a capacious dream of automotive paint.

"And my father used to say if he hadn't become an engineer for Universal Colorfast, he'd've been a high-school Latin teacher. He just loved it. He called himself the *pater familias,* and he'd roam around the house depositing Latin phrases: *De gustibus non disputandum* and *Ars longa, vita brevis* and—"

And? Nothing follows. An embarrassed Louie says, "Really there were *lots* of them. But at the moment I don't remember mostly. Louie, do you think maybe it's why I started my round-the-world journey in Rome—to get in touch with my father?"

The question turns oddly repercussive. It sounds initially like something you'd say to give an impression of being psychologically astute. But as the words echo, it occurs to Louie that the question may *be* psychologically astute. Isn't it possible, on his Journey, he's genuinely learning things?

Again, Louie tips his glass at Louie, acknowledging his intellect.

The two men talk about this and that, as two friends will. The other Louie *does* order a second martini, which prompts Louie to order a Chianti. Their prosciutto and melon arrive. None of the three principal colors appetizingly posed before Louie are one-word colors; it would take calculated, complex phrases to do justice to the blushing peachy orange of the melon's crisp moist flesh, or to the terra-cotta dried-blood pinky red of the prosciutto (in whose liberal ribbon of white fat, if you look closely enough, microscopic rainbows of organic opalescence dance), or to the gold-candlelight-enfolding garnet of the wine—and this, too, must be remembered. In the wake of Dimiceli's diagnosis, Louie must recall not just his Pantheon moments and Palatine Hill moments and Villa Borghese moments, but humble vignettes, too. Like tonight. A quiet yet festive dinner in Rome, with a newfound friend . . .

"If I understood your point about Veronique—do I have the name right?"

"*Veronique*," Louie eagerly echoes. To utter or to hear the name—it's thrilling.

The other Louie says, "You're saying somebody doesn't have to be your physical partner—your lover—to haunt your imagination. And that is so true, my friend. I think of a lovely lady I knew, Amanda Peerman. The most memorable patient of my entire career: Amanda Peerman of Ozark, Missouri. She was a very attractive and fashionable lady, but actually that wasn't so unusual: I had more than my share of patients who were attractive, high-fashion ladies. In fact, Ruthie used to tease me about it—how many attractive, high-fashion ladies were my patients. She said I must be secretly advertising in fashion magazines." Louie gives this one a happy, extended chuckle that trails off into another sigh. "But Mrs. Peerman was something else: she had the most amazing teeth, the most flawless dentition, I've ever seen."

"Well, you oughta know," Louie says. Though true enough, the remark sounds dopey. In order to say something further, Louie says, "My teeth could definitely be whiter."

Louie falls respectfully silent, and Louie goes on:

"Say you're a dentist. Just imagine. And day after day you peer into strangers' mouths. Thousands of mouths over the years, and can I make one more boast?"

"I wasn't aware you'd made any."

"Well, I have, and here's another: I have a terrific memory for mouths. I suppose many dentists do, but I *really* do. I mean if there was only a competition—*Do You Know This Mouth?*—I might just win. Or come damn close."

"Funny you mention weird imaginary competitions. I'm constantly inventing—"

"I've seriously wondered about this very thing. If you presented me with many, many open mouths, photographs of open mouths, and asked me whose they were, how many could I identify? And the answer is, Plenty. I'd honestly like to do the competition. To be a contestant on *Do You Know This Mouth?*"

"I'd bet on you to win," Louie says. It feels good, saying so. He is fonder of Louie than can be easily expressed.

"Now, let's say you've carefully examined thousands of mouths. That's your job: examining mouths. And one day? One day this mouth wanders in, you find yourself staring it right in the mouth: perfection. How can a man not fall prey to perfection?"

The question is so wonderful that Louie acknowledges it by saying nothing for once. He speaks his gratefulness through his eyes; the two men study each other.

"After a while I learned I couldn't even bring up Mrs. Peerman's name around Ruthie. Ruthie didn't want to hear it. Not even the name. She was tired of hearing about perfection. Ruthie had an overbite, actually. And a capped upper-left bicuspid. And a chipped incisor. I remember one time her saying to me, 'It's just her *goddamned teeth,* Louie,' which wasn't like Ruthie. Generally, she wasn't one for cussing."

"One of the reasons I should've figured out Florence had taken up with Daryl is she started saying *bloody.* Calling people who irritated her *so bloody goddamned—*"

"But I tell you perfection's a complicated thing, Louie. If you're speaking dentally. I mean there's straight, there's white, and of course these things we more or less take for granted today, what with orthodontics and all the new teeth whiteners, but Mrs. Peerman's teeth were not just naturally straight and extremely white. That's just the start. She didn't have a cavity, it goes without saying, but I'm also talking about ratios, proportions, these little hidden symmetries, this perfect expanding arch from incisors to canines to premolars to molars. Crowns in balance, the bite absolutely even all around. Almost like an experiment, I'd insert some what we call articulating paper, it's a sort of dental carbon—"

"It's the tap, tap, tap paper," Louie says. "Tap your teeth together."

"That's right. I'd insert some tap, tap, tap paper into Mrs. Peerman's mouth, and she'd tap, tap, tap, and the occlusion would come out absolutely even. The whole way round. She was like something out of a manual, but *this is someone's actual mouth*. And the gums—Louie, sweet Jesus, you wouldn't have believed her gums! Again, it's right out of the manual: glossy pink, firm, not a blemish. You're wondering about recession, measured from the cementoenamel junction to the gumline?" The dentist pauses a moment, as if waiting to hear Louie confirm that he had indeed been wondering about this very thing. He goes on: "There's no recession! And pocketing—you're wondering about pocketing? You can have gaps of up to three millimeters and still be considered a healthy mouth, but you weren't finding even two-millimeter gaps in Mrs. Peerman's gums. When she first comes to my office, she's a woman of forty-five, and she opens her mouth and whaddaya know? Now she's twenty. It's the darndest thing you ever saw. Because mouths don't lie. Ask any dentist: mouths don't lie. Maybe you get plastic surgery on your eyes, your breasts, your chin, and everything about you becomes artifice, but not the real inside of your mouth. Mouths can't help it: they tell the truth. And Amanda's mouth said, *I am the mouth of a girl . . .*"

"That's really quite something," Louie says.

"And when she smiled? Louie, I can confirm it, there's no *natural* smile more beautiful in the whole darned history of the world! The lower edges of the upper teeth exactly following the curve of the lower lip. And when she smiled wide? The whole of the anterior upper teeth exposed, but only tiny triangles of those perfect gums. I'd spent four years in dental school, I'd been out practicing some twenty years already, and only on the day when Mrs. Peerman wanders into my office does my whole career make sense. Because I *needed* all that preparation. Damn it, I *needed* every year of training to appreciate the miracle before me. Someone like you? My friend, there's simply no way you could appreciate."

"I'm sure I couldn't."

"You went and looked in her mouth? You might say, *Great set of teeth,* but you'd have no idea. No way in hell."

"I'm sure that's right."

"I mean, this is Michelangelo painting the Sistine Chapel. This is Michael Jordan charging down the basketball court."

Now it's the other Louie's turn to catch his breath in a state of pink-cheeked embarrassment. His eyes are aglow. With one monitoring hand he lightly tap, tap, taps at his silver pompadour. With the other he drains the remains of his martini and signals to the waiter. *"Uno Chianti,"* he says. Then he says, "You can see why Mrs. Peerman became a forbidden topic around Ruthie," and he laughs joyously.

Conversation takes a placid and pleasing turn over plates of spaghetti. Both pasta and sauce are delicious, quite as good as anything you might get in Philadelphia. And it turns out the two men have another thing in common: a single sibling who happens to be an unmarried older sister.

Louie says, "You know, I brought no computer on this trip. And no phone. Nobody I meet can believe it—especially young people. *I* think there's something extraordinary in traveling round the world looking at architectural sights. And *they* think what's amazing is no computer or phone. Honestly, you'd think I was traveling without money, or shoes, or a toothbrush.

"And why do I have no computer? It's all because of Annabelle," Louie says. "Or mostly Annabelle—I also worried it might get stolen. But mostly Annabelle. And she's definitely why I have no international phone. Because I knew she'd bombard me. It'd be like I never left the States. Annabelle works in an animal shelter in Livonia, Michigan. She complains she's underpaid, and I'm sympathetic, but maybe she isn't underpaid, given how she spends most of her working day telephoning me. Oh, Annabelle's a bit of a lost soul, I'm afraid. She'll call and say, 'The cocker spaniel's got diarrhea.' Or 'The big Siamese isn't eating, Louie.' God bless her, she honestly thinks I keep this whole big rotating cast of animal-shelter animals in my head."

"She sounds like a very compassionate woman."

The other Louie has touched a nerve, and Louie replies with a pointed fierceness. "Annabelle? She's got the biggest heart in the whole goddamn world." He adds, more gently, "But you know? I needed the distance. You know? She can email. Hotels have business centers, or I go to Internet cafés. How am I going to get any distance if I don't have any distance?"

"It's a valid point," Louie says.

"And you know, I think she was hurt I'd take this trip at all. I think she wanted to come along. But Annabelle would've defeated the entire purpose. I adore my sister, but to make this trip with Annabelle was the very last thing—"

"It would no longer be your trip."

"You've got it! Annabelle's this big woman and—and it can be too much! She can be—too much. There can be something a little smothering about her, actually."

"My sister, too, she's a big woman." *Big* presumably doesn't need to be quite so big to this other Louie, who is a couple of inches shorter than Louie. He's a neat, small man with large, hairy, trustworthy-looking hands. Good dentist's hands, with the strength to apportion pain professionally.

"Her name's Marcie," the older Louie goes on, "and she worked twenty-seven years for Gordon-Goddu Electric. That's a small company in Wilmington, Delaware. Marcie worked as chief assistant to Mr. Goddu, and I can tell you she practically ran the place. Twenty-seven years, no problem, Marcie's positively thriving, the company's doing fabulous. Then she retires, and bang, she doesn't know how to get through the day. This was five years ago. She'd turned sixty-five and you know what? She's never learned how to get through the day. Really that simple. So she starts making little trips to Atlantic City. She likes to play the slots, and I don't think anything of it."

Louie senses where this is going and nods. Louie nods back.

"Then one day I get a call; Marcie's in tears. Absolute hysterics. It turns out she's been losing money. Big money. How much? Marcie doesn't know. Big money. How much, *how much*? Here's this woman basically running a company twenty-seven years, while Jay Goddu's out golfing in Boca Raton, and now she's got *no clue* how much of her own savings she's burned through."

The older Louie pauses, drains the last of his Chianti. The younger Louie still has an inch or so of liquid in his glass. In this race through drink (is it a race?) the veteran Louie has pulled ahead.

And has done so without exposing a wobble of inebriation. Louie's head is tipping a little, but this other Louie shows an armored finesse. Having sliced up his spaghetti into inch-long segments, he has consumed most of it without spilling onto the white tablecloth a single strand, a drop of sauce. Around Louie's plate, by contrast, there's a shameful broken web of orange-red filaments.

"Well, to the best of my ability," the other Louie continues, "calculating the sums after the fact, I figure Marcie's out over a hundred thousand dollars. In less than three months. Or just over three months. One hundred sixty-two thousand dollars, to the best of my ability."

"Oh my God," Louie says. "Jesus. That's serious."

"Serious? You bet. Serious? Marcie's made a hash of her retirement nest egg, and maybe this helps explain why, a couple years later, when *I'm* approaching sixty-five, I tremble with fear whenever Ruthie gets after me about seeing the world. I honestly think my sister put the fear of God into me."

"That's only natural," Louie says. "I mean, it's a scary story." Louie has been aware for some time now of American voices at a table behind him. A man's resonant voice rises, speaking with almost eerie appositeness: "She tells me she doesn't feel like herself. I say okay. I say, 'Okay, then who do you feel like?'" Male and female laughter follow. Louie says, "So what happens next? To Marcie?"

"Next? Next, Marcie starts talking about moving in with me and

Ruthie. This wasn't strictly necessary, financially. I mean, Marcie's dented her nest egg, but still . . . Moving in? You see, she's feeling lost. Isn't that your word? About your sister? Lost?"

"I might've."

"Lost soul? Well, I'da taken Marcie in, I suppose. But Ruthie's adamant. And she's right. Marcie's this big woman, as I say, and there can be something—something—"

"I know precisely what you mean," Louie says. The two men exchange glances—collusive, sly, underdog glances. "And what happens next?"

"Next? Meds. We get Marcy on meds. And soon she's right as rain. Happy as popcorn. Simple as that. A few days, she's right back being Marcie. Only"—Louie adds—"a version of Marcie that's some one hundred sixty-two thousand dollars poorer than the previous Marcie."

"Wow. That's a real story."

"The reason I bring it up? It's that afterward I come up with the Three-Month Rule. At some point in our lives, I figure we're each entitled to three months of nuttiness. Right off the deep end. Stark raving. Behaving like it's no tomorrow."

"I'll agree with you there!" Louie says.

"So when you talk about your wife—"

"My wife?"

"Florence, isn't it?"

"Yes, Florence. But I'm not sure I'm tracking the—"

"Maybe once in her life she goes off the deep end. It's what I call the Three-Month Rule."

"Well, actually, this is more than three months," Louie accurately points out. "I mean, since she started up the affair with Daryl."

"I'm not sure the rule means an absolute fixed mathematical number."

"But it *is* less than three months," Louie continues, brightening with this realization, "since Florence *really* went crazy and left Michigan for the Virgin Islands. So maybe what you're saying pertains here."

"It's just an observation," Louie modestly volunteers, and with those precise dentist's hands of his brings triumphantly to his mouth, without spillage, a final towering forkful of chopped-up spaghetti.

"Actually, I *like* this," Louie replies. "I really do! I mean, maybe I invented the Three-Month Rule without knowing it? I mean, why else did I write Florence yesterday, proposing we get back together? Maybe it's just new meds she needs, and just like Marcie, she'll be right as rain!"

And now another topic opens—opens dizzyingly. To Louie it's like thrusting your head out the window in a skyscraper and peering down toward the unthinkably distant but much too near and real and unforgiving concrete sidewalks below. This is all the result of drink, maybe—this lurching, off-balance sensation—but is he really going to detail for the dentist how he was diagnosed bipolar ten years ago and only recently has tinkered with his meds? (Meanwhile, another vista opens, in some sunlit alter-place: he and Florence together again, a sunny domestic future before them, seated at the old kitchen table, both taking prebreakfast meds and getting along famously. But the question emerging from Louie's mouth has nothing to do with any of this.)

"Now that you're retired, do you ever see Mrs. Peerman?"

There's a wincing in the dentist's eyes—not simply in the flesh around his eyes but seemingly in the eyeballs themselves. Something awful is about to spring.

"She's dead," Louie announces. "I'm afraid she died. Mrs. Peerman. In a terrible accident. In a terrible fluke accident."

"I'm so, so sorry to hear that," Louie murmurs.

"Early one Sunday. Six years ago November. After a storm. Amanda was out in her garden, and there was a downed power line. Maybe she didn't see it, because of the fallen leaves. In any case, Amanda Peerman was electrocuted. Like some death-row criminal."

"How horrible. How simply horrible," Louie says.

"And that's that. One moment it's early Sunday morning and you're out surveying your garden. It's early Sunday morning. The next, you're stretched out, flat-out dead. For anyone to gawk at."

"Really *hor*rible," Louie says.

"Still, I've often wondered what the electric current did to her teeth. I suppose it blackened them."

"*Really* horrible."

"Or cracked them. Anyway, that's it. Cracked, blackened, it's all over. What may well be the most perfect set of teeth in the whole evolutionary history of humanity is *gone,* just like that."

"Maybe not completely *gone?*" Louie says. "Not in today's world? Things—these days they're recovered. All the time—it's all recoverable. You know, DNA."

The dentist will have none of this. Now that it's squarely before him, he's going to look unblinkingly at all the world's squandered beauty and reckless indifference to beauty. "DNA? What are we going to do, Louie, dig her up for her teeth? No, I mean, *that's that.* Besides," he adds, though perhaps nothing need be added, "there's no skull to dig up. Mrs. Peerman was cremated."

The response is wrung from Louie's chest: "Such a horrible *loss . . .*"

"Exactly. And *that's that,*" Louie pronounces. "One Sunday morning, while you're having your coffee, the Sistine Chapel goes up in smoke."

HE WAKES INTO AN EXPANSIVE BUT NARROW HEADACHE. HIS head is fissured and the fissure runs deep. Easily explained as a simple hangover. But in the new territory he has entered, easy explanations no longer obtain, and maybe he's suffering from medication withdrawal. Or allergies. Or, hell, it's a witch's spell, it's a time traveler's vertigo, it's subliminal geoseismic activity. The fissure threatens to widen, and he soon learns how unwise it is to move his skull from side to side at customary speed.

An hour or so later, Louie trudges out into the street to discover that his corneas are hopelessly smudged. Even hard rubbing at his eyelids with the back of his hands fails to clear them. He shuffles down Viale Trastevere, vaguely heading for the Pantheon. Breathing this morning is a thick and begriming activity, and things must worsen as the day heats up. Today will be a real scorcher.

What he's searching for is a message from home—but where exactly is home? An unexpected memory of the old family house in Fallen Hills came flooding back in the shower this morning. Christmas, years ago—ages ago. One blazing, unforgettable gift lies under the tree, indeed the most thrilling gift anyone ever gave anyone: a homemade cardboard castle. Its mead-hall walls boast rows of banners, and here the *pater,* the painstaking wizard whose neighborhood nickname is Mr. Paint, has outdone himself. Peer in and see for yourself. Each banner radiant as a gemstone. Literally, it took little Louie's breath away. A spiritual bequest, from father to son. Call it little Louie's first exposure to a Masterpiece of World Architecture.

Such recollections leave Louie guilt stricken, as though he chronically shortchanged his father, and yet throughout the man's setback-riddled tenure as *pater familias* he exuded a steady, equanimous, ample contentment with his lot. His prime regret, no doubt, was the non-arrival of grandchildren—the family name evaporating in the loins of a spinster daughter, a chary son. But such disappointments went unspoken. Louie recalls, and it makes his head pound, that two days ago he wrote Florence broaching the idea of children. To an outsider, the offer might sound generous, but she would see it for what it was: a spasm of pure craziness. Louie mutely calls upon the old Roman gods to lift the city's unbreathable air, to remove his head from their vise. Definitely, traffic this morning is louder, fiercer. The heat's riling everybody.

His endless letter to Florence—when can he expect a reply? Not today, probably, but maybe. Of course there's no knowing how often those adorable thespian lovebirds haul themselves out of bed to do anything so pedestrian as check email . . . The trouble with his endless letter, Louie now perceives, is that he plunked down all his capital on a single spin of life's roulette wheel. And what if the wheel spins and slows and stops and he's a loser—a loser in life's Game of Love? What's next? What else can he offer Florence? (Florence was the very first person he wrote after Dr. Dimiceli's diagnosis. And, silly boy, sentimental boy, he'd honestly believed—*in sickness and in health*—that his yelp of fear and bewilderment and despair must fetch her back home.)

He's feeling nostalgic—which is literally homesickness, or so he once learned in some vanished lecture hall. But he's effectively home-less now that Florence somehow appropriated the house, and then what did the woman do but jet off for an open-ended stay in the Vir-gins? Empty is the domicile where until recently two people, a mar-ried couple, the Hakes, peaceably cohabited. The far-flung weirdness of it all (wife vacationing in Eden with Satan, outcast husband wan-dering Rome alone, while beyond the horizon, off in the mappings of an unreckonable East, a faint metallic humming, as of a vast gently drummed gong, sounds from Turkey, India, Japan) hurts Louie's head so much he must sit down. He needs to eat something—anything. Why does so much food in Rome—even the nonnative food, the theoretically generic and dependable food—taste somewhat off? Why would Pepperidge Farm Goldfish, or a packet of Heinz ketchup, or McDonald's Chicken McNuggets taste different in Italy?

Louie finds a little bar, mostly a stand-up place, though a couple of tables create a harbor in one corner. There's a stack of croissants on the counter, and he orders one. Actually, to his surprise, he orders a pair—holding up two fingers—and a cappuccino. Will Florence have written?

Louie's life is propelling toward some murky resolution, and no preparation or propitiation can now count for much. In the end, one meaningful reality obtains: the heart of the woman who has shamed him, the woman he adores. His fate will bloom as mail from cyber-space, having first rooted and sprouted in the warm, sandy soil of a tropical paradise.

Caffeinated, croissanted, Louie drags himself across the mud-green Tiber. His shirt's soaked right through. By the Largo di Torre Argen-tina, where buses and tramlines clamorously converge, he locates an Internet café. Café World View. Reasonably auspicious name. His Delta Visa card buys him time on a Dell computer. He logs on with an ad hoc username and password.

Louie feels prepared for a blow, but when it hits it hits far more viciously than anything he can handle.

Louie takes the blow right in the face.

Louie is far too overwhelmed for coherent thought, for lucid memories, but somewhere in his brain's recesses he's once more standing on the packed-dirt playground of Hiawatha Elementary, having suffered the first blow of his life that left him feeling his face had collapsed. Shamefully, his assailant was not only a girl but the smallest girl in the class, Katie Kunin. Katie had been shoved during tag. Actually, she'd been shoved by *him*, and a large share in his shame was that Katie was armed with righteousness. Little Katie's tiny fist struck him dead flat straight on the nose. Little Katie and her miniature fist smote him. (The old-fashioned word was appropriate.) It couldn't have been much of a blow, but its perfect centeredness was an icy spike to the brain, and Louie had responded the only way his body could: he'd squatted in the playground dirt and in a few violent heaves threw up his lunch. Is any emotion more tenacious than shame? For days, weeks—forever—afterward, he slunk the hallways of Hiawatha in quivering ignominy, the one boy in school history permanently to sully the playground . . .

This new blow in a sequence of such blows comes from an unexpected angle—from Florence's lover, the nightmare-born Daryl—but it swings round to hit him again dead straight in the face. Smiting him.

Daryl's message is buried in a stack of twenty-four new emails. Louie doesn't detect it at first; he's deliberately, calmly taking his time, cleaning up loose ends.

There's a message from Annabelle. And another. And two more, one called "PSSS" (she must mean *PPPS*), and another called "PSSSS." She's in her summer doldrums, more mentally footloose than usual. Her automatic garage door has been increasingly slow to open, which may be the battery in the remote. Some insect pest is feasting off the leaves of her beloved hibiscus. She recently picked up a never-before-used Swiffer Sweeper in the free box of her local library. Out to dinner on Friday with a girlfriend, she felt sick afterward because of the shrimp cocktail. Or maybe the blackened tuna, which was raw in the middle, and if she wanted raw tuna they would have eaten Japanese.

There is also a letter from a student who graduated a year ago, sweet Robby Townsend, who morosely and a little accusatorily reports that a degree in art history from Ann Arbor College opens precious few doors in a job search. And there is a letter from another and very adorable student, Claire Cheever, who graduated a few years ago and echoes Robby's conclusion.

Louie almost erases Daryl's message unread. It issued from Pyrographictheatre@yahoo.com, and for a few moments Louie's brain refuses—quite reasonably—to recognize the name of Daryl's asinine amateur theater company.

Another moment of disorientation follows on opening the letter. The contents are clear enough. Still, Louie has trouble piecing together that (1) it's from Daryl, and (2) it was sent from the Virgin Islands, and (3) Daryl is with Florence, and (4) the pair has no immediate plans to separate. But it's worse than that.

Dear Louie,

I hope this finds you well. Your trip abroad sounds very lyrical and I'm sure you'll have many adventures to make you the envy of your colleagues at AAC when (and if!) you finally return.

I'm writing for Florence, who doesn't think she ought to answer your email right now, and I agree. But she didn't want you waiting for a reply in limbo, and I agree with that, too. So I'm writing to wish you well from the both of us in all your far-flung adventures abroad. You're taking an edgy path, and everyone admires that!

Florence has been through hell, which you know as well as anyone. It's taken its toll. She has lost a job that she was absolutely devoted to. To say nothing of all the gossip and small-minded and dehumanizing treatment. And she has had to deal with something you and I will never have to deal with (hopefully), the disappointment and confusion of 27 third-grade elementary students.

I'm happy to say she's getting a much needed rest (and I am too). As it happens, my sister owns a condo here on the island of St. Croix which is vacant at the moment, so we are able to stay with privacy and no great expense. Florence wanted me to make it clear that we are hardly "living it up"! It's all pretty mundane, which is fine with us. A little sun, good no-frills ordinary food, reading, long sunset walks on the beach. I really think this is exactly what Florence needs. She's not herself, but I'm prepared to see it through until she is.

As for me, I'm working on Shakespeare's *Twelfth Night*. I'm reversing all the usual conventions about "updating" the "Bard." I'm planning to do it in period costume and modern language!

Avanti (as they say out there,
where you are lucky enough to be!),
Daryl

Louie reads this initially in a clumsy, hopping sort of way—like the dance of a barefoot sunbather traversing a stretch of scorching beach. The second time, he reads with an eye for its greatest outrages, pausing with satisfaction over the news that Daryl Force is busily rewriting Shakespeare. It's on the third reading that he zeroes in on the phrase ("So I'm writing to wish you well from the both of us") that delivers the blow that collapses his face. Both of us? The *both of us*? *The* both of us? Louie thrusts himself to his feet, tipping over his chair behind him. It thumps and clatters. People look up. People are staring at him.

Louie paces thrice around the little Internet café, in a tight circle, rapidly, running a hand through his hair with tearing motions, as you might rip apart a head of lettuce, then rights his chair and refocuses on the computer screen. The inside of his stomach is sweating profusely into itself. He finishes Daryl's letter. Then reads it a fourth time. And a fifth.

Then Louie outspreads his legs and plunges his head between his knees, and there's no saying how long he remains like that, eyes closed, while most of his body's blood pools between his ears. There's a thick coursing *flush-flush-flush* at the top of his upside-down head, which hangs not so many inches over the floor.

Louie sits up. He fishes an Ativan from his wallet. By sheer force of will, he swallows the pill without a drop of water. "He is a *bad writer*," he announces, aloud, at some volume, which does make him feel better. Louie considers. Lowering his voice only somewhat, he continues, "Anyone who believes in true standards that make life meaningful and significant, in the possibility of art and grace, in any final aesthetic accounting vaster than all of us, must agree that Daryl Force is an *execrable writer*," which leaves him feeling better still. But Time has lost its bearings and Louie couldn't honestly say how long it is before he returns to the screen, banishes Daryl's letter with a finger flourish, and finds himself once more surveying his inbox. Another letter from Daryl awaits, silently and colossally there.

Open it? Or boomerang it back, unglanced at, attaching for good measure the lewdest, grossest obscenities he can string together? Proceeding with almost the only thing left him—simple mindless defiance—Louie chooses to delete it unopened.

Or means to. But his mouse hand mutinies.

His mouse hand has other ideas. It clicks open the letter. It's as though his brain is functioning under a new operating system, where causation collapses and familiar input commands yield unexpected output consequences.

A new message materializes, and this one, too, bewilders Louie. Once again the words are clear enough. It's from Florence. But not writing from her own email account—rather, from the Pyrographic Theatre address. In the letter's first sentence she identifies herself as the writer, but Louie nonetheless struggles to field this information. He pictures her typing in the second-floor study in Ann Arbor. But

Florence currently resides on a tropical sandy shore, thousands of miles from Ann Arbor, dispatching a message to him in Rome, to him in an Internet café where he has humiliated himself by tipping over his chair.

Hi Louie, this is Florence and I'm sorry if you were hurt Daryl wrote instead of me but I just didn't know what to say. I feel so faraway from everything, Louie. My career is in ruins and I don't honestly know if I can go back to Ann Arbor. I think of myself always as a positive person but it's all the snickering I can't bear. People don't care if what they do tries to turn you into a misenthrope, but that's what all the snickering does.

But I don't want to be a misenthrope, I want to grow. And believe it or not, that's what I think is happening. I really believe something good will come out of all this and I won't hate all the snickering people who are so smallminded and dehumanizing if I can grow right past them. There's something dirty in what they do, and believe me, that's where the *real* dirt lies. But in the end it's up to me to overcome, and I think I'm growing. It's very simple here, just a lot of water and sun and good no-frills ordinary food and time for your thoughts.

I'm sure if I reread this letter people might say it's all about ME, but that's not why I'm writing. I'm writing about YOU, Louie, I'm concerned. I'm not sure you sound too good. You say your off your meds and doing fine but I wonder. I'm on 80 mg of Prozac at the moment, which is a lot, but when I tried cutting back to 50 I wound up crying so much there wasn't any point, so I guess about 80 is about right. For the moment. And I want to apologize for something else. Up until all this I don't think I really understood your need for medication, the bipolar issue and all. I think I was dismissive. And impatient. And I'm sorry. I'm sorry for so many things, Louie, but I'd ask you to ask whether you honestly think these last few years either one of us was GROWING. You've always been very understanding, so I figure maybe you agree with me now.

Love,

Florence

But if Daryl is an *execrable writer,* what is Louie to make of this? Maybe the tropical sun has steamed the woman's brains right out of her ears? Or she and Daryl were both somewhat unhinged to begin with, and the stress of Paradise, the pressure of all those pleasures, nudged them into full-blown lunacy? In every sentence there's something to worry about, argue with, rage about. It's such a *pitiful* letter, incorporating so many words and phrases borrowed from that *execrable* writer Daryl Force—and Louie begins to feel, once more, embarrassed on Florence's behalf. Has he really been married for nearly eight years to a woman who never spotted the *anthro* in *misanthrope*? Has he been kidding himself? When he informs people that Florence seriously considered pursuing a PhD in sociology, whom is he talking about? And whom has he been trying to fool?

*Why couldn't she bother to proofread one of the most important letters of her life?*

Surely Florence can't be recycling all this sixties rubbish? This tired, stunted New Agey *growth*? And if your goal is growth, why tie your fate to that jackass of jackasses, the "edgy" Founding Artistic Director of the Pyrographic Theatre Company?

Yet even while Louie's debating (even while some professor inside him is stridently berating some dim-witted student inside him), he recognizes that Florence's typos and grammatical mistakes and stylistic infelicities are peripheral. The catastrophe lies directly before him, almost too vast and proximate to examine: the sickening, scary actuality of his own terminal *rejection.* What other word applies? How else to read Florence's letter but as a stinging rejection of everything he, her husband, represents and embodies? Florence has spent years beside him, she knows better than anyone the true composition of Louie Hake (she knows his wariness, and his gentleness and hopefulness, his fears of fatherhood, his timorous soul's love of outsize gestures), and she has concluded she'd rather spend her days with the knuckleheaded artistic director of the Pyrographic Theatre Company.

Louie clicks clear of the screen, collects a meaningless receipt, and wanders dumbfoundedly into Rome's unforgiving stone streets. Everything's hitting him in the face. There's nothing intervening between the world and his face, and the world, like some merciless pinpoint boxer, is capitalizing on this. He walks awhile, getting peppered by blows. With some sense of being ironic, perhaps quite witty, Louie mutters a refrain: "My wife is *growing* . . . My wife is *growing* . . ." And inside his head the phrase mushrooms skyward, lofty as palm trees. He is approaching the Tiber, with a pale wedge of the Colosseum looming through the heat haze. Its sloped shape calls up a shipwreck. *My wife is growing . . . My wife is growing . . .*

The words slowly reassemble, becoming antic and mirthful, evoking some laughable fifties sci-fi horror flick—monstrous radioactive freaks, car-sized termites, kittens towering over horses. *Growing, growing . . .* Eventually Louie stumbles into a shadowy café, to be greeted warmly by a stranger in an ugly, ill-fitting, powder-blue sport coat who is leaning gracelessly against the long bar. It's dismaying, yet also endearing, that this man must be an American tourist. "Top of the morning!" he exclaims. Louie certainly isn't about to argue the time of day. "Top of the morning," he replies.

The man is sixtyish, bald, round, quite red faced, Louie's height, with thick glasses whose lenses render his eyes insectivally large. He's friendly. He's a friendly face, far from home, seeking a friendly face. He says, "I secured a fifteen-minute get-out-of-jail card from both the wife and the tour group. They're inspecting a church. Did you know Italy is full of churches?"

"Somebody once told me that. I can't remember who."

"So I'm using my fifteen-minute pass cleverly and productively. I'm having a double whiskey."

"And I am, too," Louie posits.

Of all the various improbable remarks he has found himself uttering in Italy, a disproportionate share have proved to be serendipitously well judged. Louie feels a little better, suddenly. Behind the bar, at the other end, the lanky bartender is chatting up two young American women. One has stringy pale blond hair and is a little round, and the other has bushy dirty-blond hair and is quite round. They might well be Louie's students, though each is wearing a sky-blue Johns Hopkins University T-shirt—which means, in Louie's mind, they go to a "real school." He calls to the bartender, "Whiskey. *Dobbia.*" He's not sure this latter word is strictly correct, and the bartender holds up an index finger: one moment. He must first conclude an anecdote.

The bartender's English, though stiff, proves remarkably resourceful. Louie eavesdrops. "In the south, near Naples, the farmers do the crossbreed. They breed together the olive tree and the red pepper tree, so you grow the stuff olives that no one needs to stuff."

"That's incredible," the paler blonde says.

"It *is* incredible." The bartender nods, with considerable gravity. "I tell you, the Italians are an amazing race . . ."

"Vince Colley," the man with the immense eyes says in an uncertain voice, almost as if asking Louie whether Vince Colley is *his* name. The man extends his hand.

"Louie Hake." They shake hands warmly.

Louie's whiskey arrives in a banged-up but serviceable square glass. It confronts him with a problem: he has a general aversion both to the raw taste of straight whiskey and to, beyond this, its aesthetic aims: Why would any beverage try *on its surface* to be nasty and unappealing? But apparently, given the state he's in, he could swill a beaker of motor oil without flinching. The first sip, the second sip, ease down the back of the throat.

"You're with a tour group," Louie identifies.

"Very much a group. A parish group from outside Pittsburgh."

"First time in Europe?"

"Guilty. I plead guilty as charged." Vince nods once, twice, deeply as if culpably, then drains his whiskey. "Personally, I felt no need or inclination to visit Rome." He stares at Louie challengingly, as though expecting disagreement. "I take the place's existence on faith. I needed no corroboration."

Given how broadly they magnify his jumpy eyes, the lenses of his glasses are not large enough. The effect is unsettling—eyeballs like creatures locked in cages too small for them. Louie nods in sympathy.

Vince falls moodily silent, and again Louie tunes in to the two young women and the Roman bartender, who is not strictly hand-some—he looks as though he once badly broke his nose—but who apparently exudes Mediterranean charisma. The two women, anyway, hang on his elaborate words: "I tell you, it will revolutionize automobile travel. Two amazing things coming from the same little-famous city of Modena! Number one, the birth of Luciano Pavarotti, greatest singer in all history of the world. Number two, the invention of the drive-through urinal. Never will automobile travel be the same. I tell you, the Italians are an amazing race."

The larger of the two women protests: "It doesn't seem fair, if girls can't use them." She giggles. She's charmed; she's having fun.

Again with great gravity: "I tell you, they are working hard for that . . ."

Then Vince uncorks a slow but seemingly unstoppable soliloquy: "The trip's a birthday gift for wife Sally, who turned fifty-three just yesterday. A few months ago, she starts ragging me about seeing the dome of Saint Peter's. I propose Vegas, as anybody would. I propose Miami. Sally's exactly my age, believe it or not we were in the same first-grade class, and in our school pageant, believe it or not, I played a troll and she played a pixie." Could this red-faced man with the blood-shot eyes and the considerable gut and the wispy white hair really be only fifty-three? Is this what Louie can look forward to in a decade?

Vince goes on: "And fifteen years after this memorable first-grade theatrical production? The troll marries the enchanted pixie. How's that for a story?"

"That's incredible," Louie says.

"It is incredible. Vince Colley marries Sally O'Brien in the Church of Our Lady of the Elms in Mount Judge, Pennsylvania, there to live happily ever after. Which, despite a few bumps and lumps, is what we've done. No reason to leave town. I don't *like* travel. I'm *unmoved* by travel." Vince pauses to check whether Louie has caught up with his witticism. Apparently satisfied, he goes on: "But one day the pixie decides the dome of Saint Peter's must be seen, and she won't take no for an answer. How's that for a story?"

Louie replies, "I think it's an excellent story."

The oversize eyes refocus; Louie is now fixed with an appraising look. "I consider myself a decent Catholic. If tomorrow they tell Vince Colley it's back to fish on Fridays, he's all for Friday fish fries. And no bellyaching. A real Catholic, you agree to the package. But going to see Saint Peter's? *I don't need to.* Far as I'm concerned, it's like saying, 'I must see heaven before I'm willing to die.' *I don't need to.* Far as I'm concerned, one day you're told to die, you die. No setting conditions, buddy. You listen, and do what you're told."

"That's sort of exactly what I'm beginning to think," Louie says. "Maybe you don't need to *see everything*. Maybe the *real* travel is more internal—"

"And right this minute? I'm listening. And what do I hear this time? I hear another voice inside me. What it's saying?" Vince tilts his head, as if hearkening to a distant birdcall. "It's saying, 'Order another whiskey, Vince, old boy.' Is this a good idea? Maybe not, especially before lunch. But I'm respectful, I listen." He signals to the talkative bartender, who is wearing black pants that shimmer and pucker like leather but don't seem to be leather. "The same," Vince calls, and adds, presumably in a stab at Italian, *"Exacto."*

And Louie only now ascertains his companion's role on the parish group tour: he's the perennial class clown, keeping them in stitches while holding forth with an often-replenished glass in hand. If there's something a little rehearsed about the man's free-spilling monologues, Vince is all the more, rather than all the less, endearing for this practiced air: you have to admire anybody who can skillfully negotiate, with enormous bonhomie and eloquence and dignity, his public need to get well and truly shit-faced before lunch.

"*You* tell me: Do I have to memorize names of a thousand years of popes? Isn't this God's job? *You* tell me: How much assistance does he need from Vince Colley?"

Together, Louie Hake and Vince Colley ponder the question. Meanwhile, Vince must wait for his whiskey. The bartender has again held up his index finger. Finishing another anecdote.

"You have seen how hard the job to make clean the streets of Rome? Until now, impossible. Because so many cobblestones, and the cigarette butts fall between. But the scientists of genetics in the North, in Milano, they are breeding up the pigeons that eat the cigarette butts."

"That's incredible."

"I tell you, the Italian people are an amazing race. But there is one problem. You smoke? The two of you smoke?"

"*She* does," the slimmer one says. And giggles.

"What brand? What brand you smoke?"

"Newports."

"Ah. Menthols." The bartender shakes his head lugubriously. He scowls. "The pigeons cannot eat the menthol filters. Can you change? Can you switch the brand?"

"I suppose I *could* . . ."

An immediate smile lights up the bartender's face. "Ah. Then you make the streets beautiful! Already you two American girls, you make the streets beautiful."

Vince at last gets his whiskey and sips from it greedily. Not surprisingly, he turns out to be a lawyer. In a two-man firm. Louie asks who his typical clients are.

"My answer: 'Criminals.' Your reply: 'How exciting.' My answer: 'Buddy, you've seen too many movies.' Because my clients? Some *very bad people.* Some clients are okay people. A few are better-than-okay people. And what's the one thing in common? One, they're poor, and two, they're all getting screwed, big time." Vince throws down the rest of his second double whiskey just as Louie is finishing his first. "But I'm a bleeding-heart old-fashioned liberal, and you're a stockbroker and a Republican, and you don't agree about the screwing they're taking. 'String 'em up. Suffer the poor to come to the gallows' is what you say."

"But I'm not a stockbroker or a Republican," Louie replies, and realizes that Vince is a good deal drunker than he has been supposing.

"You said you were a stockbroker," Vince insists.

"I said nothing of the sort. And I'm not a Republican."

"You at least said you were a stockbroker," Vince repeats, but with fading certainty, and Louie unexpectedly feels an ache of pity. Vince, too, is looking to go home.

"No, I didn't," Louie murmurs.

"But I thought—"

"No." Louie adds lightly: "So far I've told you nothing about myself. I'm an invisible man."

"Invisible. I see." Vince ponders, recognizes that he has stumbled into a lame witticism, repeats, "Invisible, I see," and laughs heartily. Louie tardily joins him. A boozy pause—open to generous reevaluation on both sides—ensues. Louie's newest friend declares, in what you'd swear was a totally sober voice, "You've been excellent company, but you know what, Danny? I better hoof it. It's a subpoena: the group calls."

"My name's Louie . . ." And Louie doesn't want Vince to leave. "You talk about listening?" Louie says. "Well, listen to yourself. Listen to your own heart."

"Listen to my heart? Listen to *my heart*?" Vince-the-lawyer has, happily, found his closing remarks for the judge and jury. "I ask you, had I followed such a wild practice as learned counsel now so recklessly proposes, would I have ended up in Rome? Would I have taken communion in Saint Peter's?" As he makes his dramatic passage to the door, shoulders thrown back, Vince gives Louie's triceps a fraternal squeeze. He adds a farewell shot: "If I'd listened to my heart, buddy, this conversation wouldn't exist."

Almost immediately, it becomes clear that Vince's departure has punched a hole in Louie's day.

It seems the only suitable response is to order another double whiskey, in Vince's honor, but Louie's grasp of Italian, too, has departed. *Is the word for double dubio?* Louie doubts it. Or *duppia?* Or even *dopio?* Or—hell—is he just spinning out variations on *dope?*

In any case, there's no flagging down the bartender, who is still at it: "Puglia, the very south, where I am from, is where are born the world's greatest inventors of all."

Louie doesn't know how to say *double* in *la bella lingua*—a shortcoming somehow connected to a hideous, a cataclysmic accusation: *Your Journey's a failure, buddy, and you best get on home.*

But how? How could he *bear* to reveal to Florence, in her condo in Paradise, that his life's bankrupt?

"You drink Coca-Cola? Well, now the scientists are inventing a soft drink that for the carbonating uses not carbon dioxide but carbon *monoxide.*"

Could he possibly, just possibly, conceal his return from Florence? Would it be feasible, back in Ann Arbor, in his dreary apartment, to fool her into thinking that his Journey is ongoing?

A bold, irresistibly bold, scenario is hatching . . . Why couldn't he send Florence one shimmering and inventive dispatch after another? Hasn't he always yearned to be a creative writer? And what more delightful creative task than to sit in Ann Arbor composing a glorious blog of fabricated adventures set in Turkey and India and Japan? Hasn't the whole genre of travel writing always been, à la Marco Polo, more invention than reportage? Mightn't Louie's original Journey evolve into a more marvelous journey still—a rich and rolling cast of characters, setbacks, and triumphs, an unfolding plot nuanced as any novel? He needn't actually travel to Asia to play Scheherazade.

"The bubbles are stronger, more *frizzante,* and the gas kills all the bad bacterias in your stomach. Very energy drink! Next time you come to Rome, I make you a special drink?"

But this prospect of returning to Ann Arbor raises a complication. (There's always a complication . . .) And it's a big complication: Annabelle. It would be insupportable, wouldn't it? Once she found out he'd returned, how could he possibly bear all her cooing sympathy, all her kindhearted and badgering inquiries? Annabelle would absolutely bury him under concern and solicitude. Unless . . .

"Really?"

"Tonight when I am finish with the bar, I meet one of you, either one of you, you get the choosing, at the Irish pub. I give you the true Italian experience."

Unless of course he could conceal his return from Annabelle, too.

But even as Louie's piecing this out, seeking to make his big sister temporarily disappear, Annabelle materializes: her solid shoulders and oversized head, and all the unshakable devotion in her crinkly brown pop eyes—and Louie grasps his plan's absolute lunacy. It's possible, just possible, to imagine hoodwinking Florence in some spectacular style, but Annabelle's another matter. Annabelle brings him back to earth. (It's what Annabelle does: she brings a person to earth.) Is he *really* going to sit in his musty Ann Arbor apartment and fabricate for Annabelle tales of his visits to the Blue Mosque, the Taj Mahal, the ancient hillside temples of Kyoto? How long before she sniffs him out?

But if the Ann Arbor scenario is impossible, what *is* he to do?

It seems no matter how hard and fast he dodges, his life keeps catching up with him. It's like some horrible junior-high-school social disaster. You're pursued by a would-be friend who dogs your every step—a fat, huffing, asthmatic, hopelessly uncool, hopelessly loyal friend. *Would you quit following me?* you bellow in exasperation; *Dammit, go away!* you cry, but in fact you're being followed by your own life.

And his life's unworkable: simple as that. He can't move forward, can't return home. Fate straddles a person's life, imposing inflexible labors and demands, and at the moment, absurdly, Louie's only even remotely conceivable pathway is to search the streets of Rome for a different bar (with a taciturn bartender) and a second whiskey. One task at a time . . . He will catch up, quantity-wise anyway, with Vince; he owes it to Vince. And after that—who knows? The rest of his day needs filling up, the rest of his life needs filling up, but it may be a task too large for him.

Louie pays his check and walks awhile and peers into a café that entices him by looking more raggedy and shadowy than most. A staggered hodgepodge of half-empty bottles creates a second disorder in the mirror behind the bar. Louie enters and finds himself a seat at a small, unsteady wooden table with a faux-marble linoleum top that has peeled away from its metal rim. A pack of matches lies wedged under one of the table's claw feet, but without much stabilizing effect. And yet, complicating everything, someone has painted a mural here, on the opposite wall.

Predictably, it's the fruit of a flamingly incompetent hand, maladroit and childish—and yet . . . Well, there's something *lovely* about it, and painfully unattainable. It's a landscaped Eden: a dark-haired man, seen from behind, sprawled in a hammock atop a high slope, a wineglass in one dangling hand, gazing out and down upon what may well be Umbrian hills, where grapes grow and lambs wander, and where the eye meets what it has always sought: home.

A quite handsome, tall and slim, and very bored-looking waiter, who can't be more than twenty, shuffles toward Louie. Louie means to say, in Italian, *a double whiskey,* but what emerges from his mouth is nonsensical, though understandable: *"Uno due weeskey."*

The kid is bored, and, having nothing else to do, makes a sarcastic show of incomprehension. *"Uno?"* he says, and holds out one finger. *"Due?"* he says, extending two fingers.

"Double whiskey," Louie says, and the kid merely shuffles off, with a gliding frictionless poise that American kids never display while shuffling, and Louie apprehends that if Florence were here she might find the boy extremely attractive. Upon which, a resolve comes firm to Louie's consciousness: he'll leave Italy (all of it: Rome, Florence, the hills of Umbria) tomorrow. He'll cut his losses.

What was he *thinking* in supposing he could head from Italy to Turkey? His Italian, though obviously never anything to boast about, has been revealed as painfully feeble—yet infinitely better than his Turkish. What does he know of Turkey or Turkish? Nothing. He has a pocket Turkish dictionary but hasn't yet learned *toilet* or *food* or *wine* or *medicine* or *beauty.* Is *mosque* Turkish? Is *coffee,* as in *Turkish coffee*?

What sort of modern pilgrim blunders into a land not knowing the word for toilet? Or beauty? As Louie perches at his rickety table, an image of orderly collapse rolls through his head—as when the plaster gives way around an overburdened screw, and a bookshelf bracket rips scarringly from the wall, and, in strict sequence, a long succession of volumes slumps thumpingly to the floor. And Louie slumps over his peeling linoleum table.

This time around, the whiskey—reverting to its essential nature—tastes thoroughly viperish, but even so, Louie swigs hard, followed by a swallow of tepid water. Would it be possible to go home in a larger, national sense? Why not New York? Hole up for a while? Breathe a language he understands? Free himself from the burdens of the foreigner? (But there's always a complication, and the truth is New York usually unnerves Louie, who's already feeling quite nervous.)

And then a genuine, doable idea arrives: fly back to Michigan but stop in Ann Arbor to pick up his car. Then head north—toward tranquility and clarity and spaciousness. It's the obvious direction for any true Detroit boy. A couple of hours outside the city, reliably, the air turns blue and crisp and pristine . . .

Louie sips more whiskey and recalls the famous Hake family vacation up to Lake Superior in the summer of '79. It was one more activity the Hakes collectively weren't much good at—family vacations—but the *pater*, ever tinkering, kept trying to reinvent them. In this case, they wound up in a modest rented cottage right on the water. Louie was eight, Annabelle ten.

The trip was even more problem-beset than usual. The long drive north was not only unending but blinded and scary. A downpour pursued them, cutting visibility down to near nothing. They were crossing the Mackinaw Bridge before its towering gray struts misted into view.

Then, a few days later, when the rain finally halted, the woods and the cottage swarmed with bugs recognizing no border between woods and cottage. Life's securest boundaries had disappeared. The bedrooms were the lairs of countless spiders, and hard-partying mice rummaged the cupboards.

So: another chapter in those dismal, lovable Hake annals in which the *pater* was slapped down for good intentions. While everyone else complained, he laughed and joked and commiserated. And nobody quite realized he'd suffered one more setback.

Yet this particular family pilgrimage wasn't wholly a failure, for it left Louie with one of the loveliest memories of his father.

One morning the two of them rose on tiptoe before dawn for some lake fishing. What they were hoping to catch, with their bamboo fishing poles and worms for bait, was anybody's guess; they came back empty-handed.

It was a befogged morning, whose low chill crawled in under Louie's jacket and sweatshirt and T-shirt and coldly gripped the young boy's shivering, narrow, hairless chest. His father rowed out a good distance, leaving the shore-bound womenfolk behind, and there the two men of the family sat, alone upon a lake that was an ocean—a gray ocean under a gray sky.

With the arrival of dawn, the sun commenced a probing through the mist, and soon father and son were gazing spellbound into a pink-and-gold crucible out on the ocean's rim. Rosy aureate shafts erupted, bringing to both Louies, irresistibly, broad smiles teetering on the lip of laughter. After all, what *is* more hilariously improbable than the light of a new day? Wonderment of this sort strips the years from any adult, and the powerful man with the oars in his artist's hands, the great mysterious alchemist of vehicular paint, momentarily was banished. Louie's father's breathy voice was a child's, one child addressing another: "Jeez, it's so many colors we'll never capture."

Sitting at a shaky table in a rathole bar in Rome, Louie mutters the phrases under his breath: *So many colors . . . We'll never capture . . .* And the burning whiskey inside him, filtered through pain and desperate confusion, seeps into his vision as scalding tears. Prisms break all over creation as Louie wipes each eye with the back of his hand. He needs to leave this bar, his whiskey one more unfinished task.

Louie takes again to the Roman streets. A white segment of the monument to Vittorio Emmanuele heaves up unexpectedly; he'd thought he was farther east, or maybe north. What stands right before his eyes isn't altogether stable—he has consumed too much drink, too early in the day—and the penumbra of his vision has turned edgeless and runny as a dropped egg. It occurs to him to head to the Pantheon—the city's most beautiful structure. And a monument to durability, in a modern world whose tables are stabilized with matchbooks.

Louie's lower back pains him—and perhaps has long been pain-ing him. It's the foreign mattress maybe, or the stress of his existence. The hot, exhausted air is running out of everyday components, includ-ing oxygen. They are pumping in carbon monoxide instead. Nearby, unseen, a little dog barks viciously, bitingly. Louie doesn't turn round to see; instead, he wills the creature out of existence. He's waiting for the alcohol to subside, but an internal river is in spate, still cresting, still cresting; Louie feels dizzy and shamble-footed as he makes his way across the dusty town.

Olive-skinned Florence in a new lemon-yellow bathing suit is strolling on a sunset beach hand in hand with the director of *The Impertinence of Being Earnest,* Daryl Force, who grew up as Danny Fricker. It would be hard to make this up. Yet it's the truth. The devil was once christened Daniel Fricker. It all ought to be dismissible on the grounds of sheer ludicrousness. If this world were a better and saner place, certain phenomena would never eventuate. God would impose on the cosmos some kind of Universal Ludicrousness Filter, a celestial Pop-Up Blocker, and certain too-dopey-for-words improb-abilities simply wouldn't materialize on Earth's screen. Daryl Force is one such phenomenon. He'd be deleted before appearing. Blip.

Louie, trudging along, pursues the idea. You push a button—and Daryl Force disappears. Louie tests it again, he pushes it again—and Daryl promptly, satisfyingly disappears into a void. It's simple. Behind the game lies an amazing revelation: Daryl Force isn't real—he's a made-up character. You push a button and he's gone. Simple. You push a button . . . And Danny Fricker? Though Danny may seem a little realer than Daryl (presumably Danny had a mother), he likewise doesn't exist. And even Florence is fading . . . Blip. Blip. It's a breathtaking pliable chain of contingencies at whose chilly terminus lies the suspicion that Louie Hake, too—not fully real.

Oh, but this isn't quite correct either, for if the Louie Hake wandering tipsily through the Eternal City one June morning in 2014 isn't fully real, the wooden rowboat, full of splinters, that once ferried him across the surface of Lake Superior nonetheless is real. And realer still the man rowing the boat. And realer still the dawn lights breaking over the oceanic lake. And realer still the insights that ultimately outlast the lights: *All those colors we'll never capture . . .* And *Ars longa, vita brevis.*

Louie keeps walking, and therein lies the rub, the difficulty, the small stubborn paradoxical problem that is managing somehow to spoil everything: objects keep resurfacing after you hit the Delete button. Why can't he, for good and all, dismiss Daryl Force, or section 750.338b, or AOFVD, or a wife who is AWOL but *growing*?

Louie's wanderings lead him, unexpectedly, into the open arena of the Piazza Navona. Oh. Here he is. His back's hurting more than ever, and he makes his way, limping a little, to an open café table.

Two tables over, a youngish mother sits with her young son. She looks unhappy, and very fatigued, which isn't surprising, since the boy radiates an air of indefatigable mental energy. They're Brits. *Mummy,* he calls her. Very few American children of his age would enunciate so plainly. "Mummy," he says, "how do we *know* they're treating Van properly? They *say* they're treating him properly, but how do we *know*? Is it *fair* for us to be here, when we don't know how they're treating Van?"

But who is Van? Have they left a younger brother behind?

"They're very nice people," the mother says. "You remember, darling, we checked on that. I let you speak to all of them. And you remember how fond they all were of him."

"But what if they're secretly mean? *Secretly* mean. He wouldn't be able to tell us. I think we ought to go home."

"Darling, your mummy needs a vacation. She never has a vacation."

Louie doesn't want to snoop, but the mother-son tableau irresistibly draws him in. Recently he maybe hasn't always focused sharply on the outside world, but now he's focusing. He steals another glance at the youngish mother. Indeed she needs a vacation. Worn and melancholy. Flickers of gray in her brown upswept hair. The little boy with the sharp gaze and piercing voice is in fact a strikingly handsome, lustrous little boy. Shiny brown hair, polished white teeth, glistening black eyes a face calling for a master portraitist. Sargent might have done him justice.

"What if they don't let him out? What if they *say* they will, but they don't?"

"He'll be out three times a day at least."

"What if they're only *saying*?"

"They'll give him walks. There will be other dogs to play with. I'm sure he already has all sorts of friends. You know what? I'll bet right this minute Van's lying on a grassy field with some of his dog friends . . ."

The boy ponders the image for a short interval of intense concentration. Then his expression alters. He looks soothed and placated. Yet the concentration regathers—his features are wonderfully transparent—for he has located another problem: "The man in the shop, he called me beautiful."

"I don't think he said that exactly, darling."

"He did. *Yes, he did.* He said I was beautiful like my mother."

And a smile comes to the woman's face. "I think he was figuring out a way to pay your mother a compliment."

Again the boy fiercely ponders. "He was *flirting* with you," he accuses.

The mother laughs—a gurgled, beguiling sound—and aching Louie, catching another glance, apprehends that she is indeed beautiful, like her son. "Oh, it's just the way they are. These Italian men. It's silly but sweet, it doesn't mean anything. He was a boy, really. Trying out his paces. He wasn't really flirting with the old English widow, I can tell you."

And among all the other little revelations and curiosity-feeders this conversation has provided, now arrives just the thing Louie has spent this crazy, overheated day searching for. *True* inspiration comes Louie's way. He doesn't need to cancel his trip. No, the Journey of His Life can proceed, roughly as planned. He merely requires some psychological R & R, and he needn't go back to the States for it. He just needs someplace less alien and impenetrable than Rome, someplace where he can understand what he hears and speak and be understood. Not a return home—but a return to his home language.

A detour to olde England, merrie England of the daffodilled hills, cool and northerly, languidly outspread England of the English-speaking English. And for just a few days. A few days in London, a metropolis with plenty of its own architectural marvels. He'll enrich his Journey visually, and also he'll rest and speak to whomever he wishes. And then resume his trip as originally planned, on to Istanbul, rejuvenated.

Louie rises from the bench on a new wash of hope. His head's swimming, but the waters are clarifying. He's moving out of the murk. He is seeing his life . . .

He needs a travel agent. He *knows* the word for travel agent in Italian, or normally he does, but the drink has roiled the currents of his memory. Louie begins walking with no obvious destination, looking for a storefront whose sign he cannot formulate.

He passes a *gioielleria*, a *ferramenta*. He successfully skirts the siren call of an entire roomful of headless but quite buxom naked mannequins. It occurs to Louie that the word in Italian for travel or voyage is *viejo* and that he must be looking for a *bureau de viejo*. But then it occurs to him that *viejo* isn't *voyage* but *old,* in Spanish anyway. And a *bureau de viejo* would be, if it were anything (in fact it is nothing), some committee on aging. His head is reeling as he begins to sing, under his breath. It's a song his father-in-law, his first father-in-law, his English ex-father-in-law, occasionally sang: "While we have Jack upon the sea, and Tommy on the land we needn't fret." While his head goes round, the melody is as fixed as a compass needle. Or a lamppost. Louie leans against it as he walks forward.

# PART TWO

# London

IMMIGRATION OFFICER

\* LONDON \*

JUN 2018

HEATHROW

*The second rose is English;*
*its old garden is a place*
*where stalks have been cut back,*
*grey autumn shows its face . . .*

TWELVE YEARS HAVE ELAPSED SINCE LOUIE'S LAST VISIT to England, an interval frequently disturbed by rumors of troubling developments, unrecognizable alterations. Newspaper articles, magazines, television shows, as well as various colleagues and friends, all report dramatic improvements in England's quality of life. Food is better, service is better, transportation's more efficient, hotels more comfortable . . .

It's a huge relief, then, to wind up ensconced in the Mulder Arms, only a ten-minute walk from the British Museum, and to find everything unflappably third-rate. To judge from one hotel, anyway, London's gentle, tenacious drowse continues unabated. Louie loves England wholeheartedly. Didn't he, the first time around, marry an English girl? He shuffles down to breakfast at the Mulder Arms and thinks, *Nobody still eats like this!* And yet they do. Each morning, the Germans, Spaniards, Japanese, and—heaven help them—homegrown Brits who make up the hotel's clientele assemble in orderly fashion for a "traditional English breakfast." At the Mulder Arms—in this land where the circulation of the blood was first charted—you can feel your arteries clogging while you dine.

Today, Louie eats most of it. (It would take a very sharp-toothed garbage disposal to masticate the bacon's toughest ridge of gristle.) He washes down his meal with three cups of tepid tea, all drawn from the same Tetley bag. He's prepared to testify that his paper napkin was previously used and refolded. And he's feeling so much better: so much more at home.

The color of the bacon, or Canadian bacon, or ham—the meat—is an underlying gray, though flashings of a hot lipstick pink kiss the grease-wet surface. Beside it, on the avocado-colored plastic plate, a fried tomato looks not ladled but tossed into position. And there are baked beans indifferently wandering around inside a sweet, ever-expanding pool. Louie is particularly delighted to see toast coolers, a phrase whose provenance belongs to Lizzie. And how delightful that long-ago morning when she coined it! This was during their maiden voyage—honeymoon voyage—to England. At that fateful first breakfast Louie caustically noted that his toast was stone cold. And Lizzie replied, *Louie, this is England.* On this side of the Atlantic, evidently, the kitchen staff yanked the bread fresh from the toaster and slotted it into an evenly spaced wire rack—a toast cooler—designed to chill the bread quickly and uniformly. No unexpected, disconcerting pockets of warmth for guests at *this* hotel. And Louie saw the humor, and abruptly ceased complaining. And the newlyweds passed four beatific days in London.

He's feeling so much better. He's still savoring yesterday's pilgrimage to the British Museum (his second visit of this trip, and no less marvelous than his first) and to the National Gallery (ditto, and ditto), and today he plans a return to the Tate Modern. Or not. Louie's flexible. Flexibility is of the essence. Everything's growing clearer and sharper, and there's a keen irony to this. The English are forever musing about *muddle,* but Louie in the five days since flying into Heathrow has come increasingly to appreciate that Italy was where he'd muddled himself. He cringes, even now, to think of his demented letter to Florence. Start a family? Start a *family? Start* a family? Talk about putting the cart before the horse! Before any such step could be taken, Florence would first have to part ways with the Founding Artistic Director of the Pyrographic Theatre Company, preferably by way of a butcher knife, and then come slinking home from her tropical paradise, and Louie move back into the house, dignifiedly, and a long, reasoned process of resettlement begin . . .

No, the muddle engulfed him in Rome, where he wandered the

streets in pursuit of double whiskeys while pursued by too many colors. The colors, he ascertains now, posed a huge and an un-understood problem. Almost from his arrival at Fiumicino Airport, the gorgeous Italian palettes had started messing with his head. All those flaking, voluptuous golds and bronzes and russets and siennas and ochers and apricots and umbers, the whole sunned chromatics of a sunken civilization, crumbling palaces and free-spent sumptuosity—all too much! How much easier to think persuasively in shrouded London, where even the church bells, or so Louie's synesthetic imagination determines, toll *grey, grey, grey,* rather than, as in Rome, *gold, gold, gold.*

London agrees with him, and London celebrates one of his personality's unremarked merits. It turns out Louie has long been praiseworthy for a virtue he didn't fully realize he possesses. For he has nobly remained faithful to an England few Americans know how to prize, a country neither quaint nor twee nor fey. And despite all those unsettling rumors of changes for the better, England has remained loyal to him.

Admittedly, the city's façades have grown unrecognizable. Block after block, nothing looks the same. Within a stone's throw of the Mulder Arms lie restaurants offering tapas or rillettes or sea urchin sushi that twelve years ago were contentedly peddling the remains of last week's steak-and-kidney pie. But the old dowdiness that isn't a quaint, cloying, marketable dowdiness—rather, the deep-down true English dowdiness inseparable from decency and a commonsensical sanity— perdures. Which is why the Brits, at least theoretically, are able to appreciate Louie Hake as his countrymen cannot.

He's so damned *glad* to be here. Good Lord, London still has phone booths! And—good Lord again!—he overheard a woman postal clerk (when Louie found himself, guiltily, mailing Annabelle a scarf from the National Gallery) actually utter the phrase "you shouldn't have done." Obviously, the Brits are keeping alive recondite verb constructions for which, these days, nobody at AAC even has a name. (Five years ago, under woeful budget cuts imposed by a sadistic, incurably anti-intellectual administration, Louie's college abandoned

its Linguistics Department—along with classes in Italian and Ger-
man.) Meanwhile, this past spring, the most popular course in AAC's
English Department was Thirteen Ways of Learning from the Flint-
stones, taught by a young Turk, or turncoat, whose Berkeley PhD in
medieval studies had failed, nationwide, to yield a job in his field.

Louie's thankful for the clarity instilled by English air and English
scenery; he'd utilized every bit of it in smoothing Annabelle's feathers,
who flew into something like squawking hysteria on learning of his
London detour. He was forcing her to—to redo her entire refrigerator!

Though this sounded like a joke, only a heartless person could
treat it as a joke.

By nature something of a town crier, Annabelle adores magnets,
Post-its, cutouts, bulletin boards. Her dual refrigerator doors serve
as an ever-rotating gallery. The current exhibition, a blockbuster, features Louie's travels. His pilgrimage is chronicled in a dense, sinuous,
raggle-taggle line of photographs, drawings, somber balloon-shaped
paragraphs of explanatory text. ("Istanbul was once known as Con-
stantinople. It is the only world capital lying in two different continents: Asia and Europe.")

And when Annabelle goes looking for orange juice, or a spoon-
ful of potato salad—well, she must confront the Journey of His Life.
Louie commands what museum designers would call the axial view;
he simply could not be more central to Annabelle's home. The Journey commences with an image of the Colosseum, afire in an exploded
sunset, and concludes with a vast stone Buddha whose hooded eyes
contemplate the human predicament from within the world's largest
wooden structure. (Another of her informative captions.)

Arrival and departure times are festively noted. (Exclamation
points abound.) His projected arrival in Istanbul (June 22) is celebrated
by a reproduction of a yellowed postcard of a steamship chugging
earnestly through the Bosporus Strait. His flight to Delhi (July 1) is
marked by a luminous, moon-limned Taj Mahal. Above and below the
ambitious chain of his travels Annabelle has placed additional fanciful
captions and images: a children's book illustration of a swan-necked

Trojan horse, a recipe for meatless goat curry, a newspaper headline announcing the factory recall of 240,000 Toyotas, a photograph of a quizzical-looking Gandhi in spectacles and loincloth. (This is the reassuringly desiccated-looking, hairless Mahatma—not the eerily hirsute and vibrant young barrister who, along with Darwin and Kafka, presides over Dr. Douglas's office walls.)

How *could* he have failed to remark that his abrupt London sortie would necessitate the overhaul of Annabelle's refrigerator art? To neglect her emotional investment in his Journey was callous and cruel. Louie felt ashamed—as the expensive silk scarf testified. If he scarcely needs Annabelle, he mustn't forget how embracingly she needs him.

He sometimes forgets that he isn't altogether a free agent. Her unblinking devotion comes at a price; his abrupt change of plans calls for lengthy reparations. Annabelle is so fragile and volatile, and shifts of schedule, in particular, disquiet her. Fortunately, these last few days Louie has had the city of London to fortify his patience. In proposing a new détente, he has been indulgent and generous. Daily since his arrival he has bombarded her with emails and calls.

And he has brought her round. In the end she has come to appreciate the wisdom of his amended itinerary. She has come to espouse his vision.

All's right with the world, and Professor Mop-Top, the ever-surprising Louie Hake, once more is at large in the England of Constable and Turner and Burne-Jones. It's hardly surprising that everybody else was wrong and he was right about the city: London remains London. What *has* surprised him is the degree to which Lizzie's hovering spirit tracks his every step. How many times, and when, did they visit London? He'd had to do some reminiscing before arriving at the details. Three times he'd brought his Lizzie to her native land. The first occasion was their honeymoon, of course, back in '94. Then the summer of '98, in a simple, privileged pursuit of pleasure. And then 2000, when, surprisingly, his woebegone application for a competitive AAC Faculty Fellowship met approval, despite his glaring failure to publish. (Delighted with the supplemental three thousand dollars, Louie had also felt chagrined on being selected—further confirmation of his colleagues' mediocrity.)

Three trips. Time enough to create a palimpsest, a richness of repetition and variation. Return journeys had allowed them—the two of them, the young married midwestern couple—to revisit memorable restaurants and used bookstores and tea shops and a favorite bench in Regent's Park under a spectacular horse chestnut tree. And each trip had culminated in the National Gallery with Hobbema's *Avenue at Middelharnis,* a big canvas whose tiny central figure, strolling evenly through a palisade of pruned, spindly poplars, has come to embody in Louie's imagination the sheer enchantment of venturing anywhere, the promise of somewhere *else:* an idle walk, a local errand, a journey round the world. And each trip culminated with Louie's taking Lizzie's hand as they stood before it (Hobbema's pint-sized rambler forever approaching the two of them) and declaring, "Isn't it *lovely?*"

She was always his precious English maiden, wherever they were, but never more so—flourishingly, bloomingly so—than in London. It was terribly touching, Lizzie's clinging to ancestral ties; and terribly appealing, her laughter at herself for doing precisely this. Okay, hers was a contrived identity. Okay, she was a gawky girl from Saginaw for whom enrollment at Kalamazoo College had constituted a rash adventure—all the way across the broad, flat belly of Michigan. She was an international relations major, a good and dutiful but not passionate student, fitfully driven to the library out of compunctions about squandering her father's money. Hazel-eyed, narrow chested, a little broad-hipped, she was happy and lively and popular, and, though much pursued (frat boys, athletes, computer nerds, clear- and yet crazy-eyed born-agains), Lizzie Sedgwick in her four years at Kalamazoo had had only one serious boyfriend, the somewhat-hard-to-categorize Louie Hake. And she managed to graduate without the barest notion of what should follow. "I'll get a job in some office," Lizzie breezily would chant while her sorority sisters were knocking off premed prereqs or cramming for the LSAT, padding CVs, investigating grad schools.

Well, after graduation Lizzie's father procured for her just the job she'd envisioned: working public relations for Dow Chemical in an office in dour Midland. And Lizzie had *loathed* it. Louie, meanwhile, off in cosmopolitan Ann Arbor for his first year of grad school, glimpsed a future of freewheeling and giddy prospects. He would secure a PhD in art history, and afterward who was to say he mightn't wind up a professor in Chapel Hill or Charlottesville, Austin or Chicago or Ithaca? Or maybe beach up at a museum in Seattle or San Francisco or San Diego?

For Louie, it was an era of thriving hurly-burly, even as Lizzie increasingly resented the world's turning into an interrogating police team, demanding she document her credentials and life plans. Under this steady, faceless pressure, it grew apparent to her that she and Louie Hake must marry. And her Louie—after many delays, and calls for further discussion, and further calls for further discussion—acquiesced.

A good decision, really. Happy, really, perhaps the happiest days of his life so far, of his life in sum: the opening years of his first marriage. Lizzie found herself a new and satisfactory job, with U of M's development office. Meanwhile, Louie daily savored a sensation never experienced before, and perhaps never to be granted again: a feeling of the planet's loose, cornucopian accessibility, all of its artful plunder outspread at eye level and almost at hand's reach. His professional bailiwick was meant to be nothing less than the boundless playing fields of human visual creativity: the thirty-thousand-year cavalcade archived in Janson's reassuringly mountainous *History of Art.* Surely there lay, within that glorious procession and panoply, some rich niche meant to be Louie Hake's own. He saw a future. Never would it have occurred to him back then—wouldn't occur for years—that he might turn out to be, as a writer, someone with nothing substantial and assembled to say. Never occurred to him that what was substantial within him might doggedly resist regimenting itself into paragraphs. Or, maybe, that he was afflicted with admirable but crippling moral scruples alien to most of his fellow grad students, who, posing as scholars with substantial things to say, would advance to burgeoning careers. Or—maybe—that he was merely unfocused and lazy.

He was less than two years entered into married life when Lizzie surprised him with an announcement of a fully formed intention of applying to law school. And surprised him a second time by acing her LSAT. (He'd known she was bright, but neither one of them saw her as a whiz at standardized tests.) And back then it appeared everything might keep opening up. Lizzie won admission to her first-choice law school, U of M. In the future, she would fly as his legal eagle, while he, earthbound, suavely patrolled the world's finest museums. They were a couple blessed with shimmering prospects.

But Lizzie disliked her first year of law school, and found truly hateful her job as a summer associate for a small firm in Troy, handling mostly medical malpractice. In mid-August, only a few days before the start of a second round of legal education, Lizzie announced, in a tone brooking no discussion, her abandonment of the law. And she'd returned to her job in the U of M development office, while Louie stayed quiet. Partly because he didn't know what to say. And partly because of inklings of his own unfitness for grad school.

His thesis adviser was an elderly, myopic, unapologetically flatulent Yorkshireman, twice a widower—Cambridge-educated, dry-as-dust Professor Jerome Pangborn, who nearly thirty years before had edited a single book, *The Art of Art Study*. Casting around for a thesis topic, Louie originally homed in on John Singer Sargent, a master portraitist and arguably America's finest draftsman. But the deeper Louie's immersion in Sargent scholarship, the less tractable the subject appeared. Sargent had hobnobbed with too many people, most of them off-puttingly aristocratic and posh, and his wanderings turned out to be (at least to an ill-traveled Michigan boy) mind-numbing: Venice, Paris, Montana, Florida, Corfu, the Middle East. Each of Sargent's significant portraits called for a few months of research: Robert Louis Stevenson and Henry James and Vernon Lee, Teddy Roosevelt and John D. Rockefeller . . .

And there was—bigger still—the enigma of Sargent's sexuality. At the outset, it hadn't seemed obvious that Sargent must be gay. Lots of good-looking men as models, admittedly. But gorgeous women as well. Okay, a connoisseur of attractiveness—nothing untoward in that. Yet it seemed most new Sargent criticism—a busy field—was devoted to investigating his alleged homosexuality. In Pangborn's office one day Louie remarked, somewhat petulantly, "I wouldn't think sexual orientation plays much role when you paint a potted plant." And old Pangborn, who in three years as Louie's academic adviser had never uttered a truly memorable or surprising observation, now said, remarkably: "I should have thought"—and proceeded to clear his throat, so painstakingly that Louie was left wondering whether a continuation would follow—"have thought it would infiltrate, well, everything." And in that instant Louie discerned, in a wash of belated dismay, that dry-as-dust Pangborn, though twice a widower, was a deeply closeted highly severe old queer. The exchange brought a blush not to Pangborn's face but to Louie's, who devoted the remainder of the conference, and much of his next few conferences, to cleansing himself from any imputations of homophobia.

Louie eventually dropped Sargent for Frederic Church, who admittedly lacked Sargent's uncanny, majestic knack for being able to position himself anywhere, fix a standpoint, and rapidly transmit an assured perspective. Church sometimes stumbled, as Sargent so rarely stumbled, and yet he struck Louie as ultimately the more affecting painter. A less-sure hand, but a bigger heart. Was any American landscape more beautiful than Church's *El Rio de Luz*? And what about his iceberg paintings? Louie would gladly trade away ten of Bierstadt's Yosemites for one Church iceberg painting—of which there were too few. Too few of those floating uninhabited palaces seized in their timeless heyday, sprawling and dissolving, disporting their gorgeous, gelid palettes under an arctic sun . . .

In the end, though, Church's life also came to seem unworkably centrifugal, with too many travels (South America, the Middle East, even the north Atlantic, pursuing icebergs born in unthinkable Greenland), and too many tangled expense accounts and health issues. At which point Louie settled on American trompe l'oeil, on John F. Peto and William Harnett, all those beguiling canvases that discount any need of travel, any reality beyond the flotsam and jetsam of the artist's studio: envelopes, stamps, photographs, keys, horseshoes, claim tickets, newspaper clippings. It was Emily Dickinson's credo: let the artist brood indoors and the world come to him. Peto never once left the United States; maybe he never left his atelier. Here was somebody Louie could handle.

But Louie had been slow, even so, to amass an acceptable thesis. Ten years in grad school, while steadily adjuncting at pitiful AAC. (He never would have believed, back then, that AAC was to be his dismal destiny.) Ten years in grad school, to produce something he wasn't altogether sure his adviser, old Pangborn, who with each passing year grew more bullyingly deaf, actually read in its entirety. It hadn't helped Louie's output that at one point in those ten years he detonated a bomb in his marriage.

Louie is having second thoughts while finishing his third cup of tepid tea. Maybe not the Tate Modern this morning. Instead, the Natural History Museum? The Tate probably means a more complicated Tube trip, but that isn't the issue. He has enjoyed reading a book on its crowded, clanking cars, thumbing through a used paperback picked up on a whim in a little shop off Charing Cross Road: *The Boorish American's Guide to London,* by a John Chapman Dwyer.

Privately printed, the book makes lively, opinionated reading, even if, alas, it isn't boorish enough. Louie had hoped for a real curmudgeon's rant. But Dwyer, for all his posturing indignation and splattering profanity, is manifestly besotted with his adopted city.

No, the book's true value lies in its off-the-wall reverse dependability. None of Dwyer's overblown, polysyllabic judgments can be taken at face value. At his urging, Louie caught a quick chicken-and-rice lunch at an Indian restaurant in Covent Garden ("a bastion of individuality among an army of establishments designed to hoodwink us all into believing that India's one billion–plus people consume the same half-dozen dishes every day") and found it reasonably tasty but largely indistinguishable from London's other modest Indian take-out-or-eat-heres, then visited a little fish-and-chips place in Fitzrovia ("none of your brummagem, the usual inevitable inedible swimming-in-grease gray slop-shop, but an aquamarine oasis in a block of unforgivably tarted-up Victorian storefronts") and received two breaded, bloated trapezoids aswim in, yes, cloudy grease. (They hadn't tasted all that bad, though.) Warming to the task, Louie followed the Boorish American to a South Bank Cajun restaurant, "a lagniappe for lackluster Londoners, and a place Louisianans might visit with pride," where he consumed a mound of comfortingly warm but stringy pork and a hill of overpeppered "dirty rice." Louie was enjoying the business of mentally writing strenuous rebuttals. He was composing a *Captious American's Reply to a Boorish American*.

It's a cool, uneven, skittery day—flocks of fleecy clouds wandering undecidedly over London town—as Louie emerges from South Kensington Station with the handsomest of his Rome purchases, an oxblood leather travel journal/portfolio, tucked under his arm. The Natural History Museum is only blocks away, but he detects a more urgent summons. Frankly, he's had enough of the Mulder Arms's complimentary breakfasts. Surely he can find something genuinely appetizing—something nontraditionally English—near South Ken.

He heads south, away from the museum, and soon makes his way into a French, or Frenchy, place, the Café Domat, where customers are drinking coffee outdoors and indoors. Louie decides to dine in. Lovely, streamlined, fattening pastries bask in a glittering vitrine of competitive self-indulgence. He orders a cappuccino and a *brioche aux pépites de chocolat*.

Louie knows he's hopelessly bad at distinguishing English accents, but his best guess is that the guy seated two tables back, hunched passionately over his cell phone, is a Scot. In any event, what he's saying is splendidly entertaining.

He's tall, with long, thinning black hair in criminal need of a shampoo. He's wearing a gray plaid suit and a blue-and-white-striped tie whose loosened knot falls between the second and third buttons of his black pinstriped shirt. He looks as if he's been up all night.

He's talking to his wife, or girlfriend. Either way, he's in a boatload of trouble.

"I agree, love. I absolutely agree. You're dead-on right," he says. "Only it's the opposite. I agree with everything you're saying, only it's the opposite, love."

Louie could sit here all day. His cappuccino is better than what was typically served in Italy, though predictably not as good as what you'd find in Ann Arbor at Roa's Deli, where the beans might have been roasted that morning. There's a weird logic to this, something about an object's improving the farther you wander from its source. Somebody who ought to know once advised him that Chinese food is inedible in Hong Kong.

"No one's questioning your logic. *I'm* not questioning your logic. I'm just saying it's the opposite. Your logic's perfect, love, it absolutely is, but you need to put a negative sign in front."

Louie bites into his brioche, which presents a marvelous marriage of crunch and chewiness.

"Listen, love, it's how I make a living: asking does somebody's logic add up. Their numbers—do their numbers add up? And your logic *does*. It checks out. Only it's the reverse. You've got to flip it. You got to flip it."

The terminal consonants are swallowed in the throat: *flih-puh*. Louie tears into another bite of pastry. He has a particular weakness for male monologues of self-exculpation.

"You've done everything all absolutely impeccable, love, truly impeccable logic, but now you just have to insert the minus sign. Everything you're saying is tight and right, but you need to flip it. Everything you're saying about me is true, only it's the opposite."

The guy runs a long, bony hand through his long, lank hair.

Louie is captivated. His amusement transports him a considerable distance. He's off—he's elsewhere. Long ago, as a boy, he once saw a silent movie whose hero folded his overcoat atop a huge rectangular block of ice, straddled it as you might a horse, and rode it down the vast valley of a golf course, mutely guffawing the whole way. Louie now is guffawing the whole way, and when inside his head his own personal ice block abruptly skids to a grassy halt, depositing him before a familiar stand of handsome birches on a breezy bluff over sunning Lake Michigan, a warm and perfect spot for a lovers' picnic, today's mission is revealed: he must contact Lizzie.

He needs to explore, having perhaps only recently become capable of exploring, precisely why his first marriage foundered. In 1994, Louie Hake and his new bride, Lizzie-not-yet-fully-Hake, née Sedgwick, arrived in London. They were buzzing along in a state of shared connubial rapture. What went wrong?

Vividly he recalls that young woman—his Saginaw girl, his very own Lizoliz—giggling and pointing and kicking up her feet as they crossed Kensington Gardens on a day when the cumulus banks over London looked too dense and ponderous to budge. The clouds had seemingly settled in for good and all, like a superior ring of mountains. Louie opens his portfolio. Time to begin. Scribble now, transcribe later into a computer.

If he had his laptop, he could determine just when they last communicated. A year? Two? He knows for certain he hasn't written since everything crashed with Florence in January—hasn't had the heart to. But surely he answered Lizzie when she wrote so movingly, a couple of years back, letting him know she and Justin had parted ways. "Dear Lizzie, I'm sitting in a surprisingly stylish French café in London absorbing a little caffeine before heading to the natural history museum we both love so much and thinking of one time walking with you in Kensington Gardens when the clouds looked so heavy it was like they were permanent fixtures." It's a hopeless clunker of a sentence, but he can smooth it out in the email version. Or not. Louie brightens to the realization that nothing he might possibly say to Lizzie could ever match the nonsensicality, the bold bald-faced asininity, of what the greasy-haired Scot is dishing up:

"Love, stop. I'm *not* being controlling, so *just stop*. I'm not being controlling, so you just do what I'm telling you. I'm being the opposite of controlling. I'm saying go with it, your thinking's spot on, but first you flip it. Nobody's controlling anybody. It's the power of logic, love."

Louie continues writing. He finishes a page, turns it over. Here, too, is the power of logic. He realizes he's composing more than a draft letter. He's creating something like a journal entry. Memory's floodgates have opened, wide, and he's creating page after page for and about Lizzie—mostly reflections on their three trips to England.

Their honeymoon ended in a puzzle. After five blissful days in London, they took a train to Birmingham to visit some little-known Sedgwicks. Birmingham was a great letdown, actually, for all the newlyweds' reluctance to say so. They'd been prepared to be made much of (the prodigal daughter, returning with a wedding band on her finger), or perhaps to be slightly resented for her father's New World prosperity. Instead, they'd encountered a wan sufferance, an unspoken and vaguely insulting, *You honestly have nothing better to do than come back here, where we're all quietly resigned to a belief that life was always meant to be dismal?* Lizzie's aunt Charlotte had agreed to put them up, but she had a bad knee and spent her days in front of her telly, which she addressed like a fretful immobilized spouse. ("Now I'll be right back. Just checking on those carrots.") She'd given Louie warmish cans of Guinness, and he'd lacked the nerve, quite, to tell her how little he enjoyed them. There were some sad-sack cousins, and an uncle who continued to smoke cigarettes, unfiltered cigarettes, though he'd had a laryngectomy.

Why chronicle all this? *What's it for?* Louie doesn't know, but he sits in the Café Domat for two unbroken hours over a second brioche and a second cappuccino—not stopping before accumulating twenty-two handwritten pages. Lizzie choking on a shrimp tail in an Italian restaurant in Soho. Lizzie's nervous hiccups in the Tower of London. Lizzie at Wigmore Hall, startling neighboring concertgoers by cackling when a mincing countertenor hit his first note. Lizzie admiring the erect-postured man (presumably mad) in Hyde Park who pledged,

"I shall stand right here until all illusory differences disappear." The Chelsea bakery with the numerous burned loaves in their display window. The guy with the word AMSTURDAM tattooed on the back of his neck like a dirty collar. (They'd debated whether the misspelling was intentional.) The little girl on the double-decker bus sucking not her own but her dolly's thumb. Louie resurrects all this and more. And when he has assembled his twenty-two pages, he stands up and strides purposefully toward the Natural History Museum.

Even lovelier in reality than in his recollection is the big public entryway. Its vast doors, the brick arches nested within arches, beckon him irresistibly inward. His guidebook cites this as one of London's finest examples of the Romanesque, but what Louie identifies with thrilling starkness isn't the links between this and the magnificent city he has recently departed, or fled. It's the difference that counts. This is something new. It's not really Roman. And it's not some indrawn cabinet of curiosities. It's an outward "cathedral to nature." They were creating something novel up here: a new, mutant, northern species of beauty. The relief carvings, the sculptures. Here's a new palette—a new Polaris. The whole terra-cotta edifice is just so, so beautiful! He strides into the cathedral-sized atrium and his heart lifts—soars.

Louie doesn't want to study the exhibits, not even the dinosaurs (despite his enduring boyish love of dinosaurs). No, to look too closely wouldn't be right—not today. He has delivered himself to this site not to burrow inward but to branch outward. He has been hungering for just this sensation of updraw, of overhead excavated expansiveness . . .

He'd forgotten about the wonderful (the admirable and beautiful) ceiling-tile panels in the Grand Hall: all those intricate depictions of flora and fauna, their fine particulars pitched at a height too great for any onlooker on the marble floor below to distinguish. In this, too—in its fidelity to minutiae discernible to God's eyes alone—the museum is a cathedral.

For nearly two hours Louie wanders buoyantly, taking in almost no solid scientific information, hardly stooping to examine the specifics of any exhibition (Creepy Crawlies, Fossil Marine Reptiles, Our

Place in Evolution). He's out for contours today, broader shapes. He watches with special amusement all the racing, squirmy little boys, a number of them outfitted in old-fashioned navy-blue wool shorts, heedlessly battering their way through the interactive displays: yanking dials and lifting lids and pounding at levers, mostly without even a glimpse toward the pop-up information thus provided. Learning? Forget education. Theirs is the raw, primeval pleasure of yanking, lifting, pounding, and today Louie's something of a boy himself, restlessly focused elsewhere, everywhere. He's seeking a feel for the way the building's space opens and closes, the way the light falls and scatters; for the human flow and flux, which is to say the museum's circulatory system, since this is a living place.

Then an internal buzzer sounds, with something of a school bell's liberating authority. It's time to depart, and Louie exits with the same assured steps he deployed in leaving the café. He marches up Exhibition Street. Though he doesn't know where he's headed, he enjoys a sensation of advancing toward it resolutely.

An old adage surfaces, and since he can't identify its source, he'd willingly claim it as his own: *Happy the man who has no destination, for he will arrive there* . . . Louie zigzags toward Knightsbridge and Hyde Park, and after a good deal of tramping winds up in Mayfair. In a little shop off Curzon Street he stops to examine the overpriced neckties. The shop's mirrors remind him that his need for a haircut is turning dangerous; given his long windblown curls, there is a treacherous point where a carefree casualness turns into clownishness. (Once, a few years ago, watching some friends' slightly out-of-focus home movie of a Halloween party he'd attended without a costume, Louie for a split second had wondered who was the little fellow in the too-big sport coat and circus fright wig.) He congratulates himself on purchasing none of the neckties. He drifts into a couple of antiques stores. He discovers that he isn't so far from the Boorish American's "little jewel of darkest Italy." The restaurant, called Caponata, is "Sicilian owned and run," but Louie's waitress turns out to be a blonde woozily tall Lithuanian who's leaving in two months for grad school at

Carnegie Mellon, where she plans to pursue robotics. The cook, who refuses to be confined to the kitchen, is a blue-eyed Viking with a hotheaded red beard.

Louie settles on spaghetti Bolognese and, after a moment's hesitation, a glass of Chianti. It's the first alcohol ordered since shoring up in England. But after this morning's two cappuccinos, he's probably over-caffeinated. The wine may be steadying; he needs to remind himself to monitor himself. This is no time for overconfidence.

The spaghetti turns out to be gluey, but in a mostly comforting way. Again, weirdly, the Boorish American hasn't disappointed him—only misled him. This is stick-to-the-ribs food, and stick to everything else (tongue, gullet, esophagus) on its torpid descent. The Chianti tastes sharp—spiny—and Louie orders a second glass of wine (this time a Cabernet Sauvignon) to dilute the prickliness. The light within the restaurant changes, darkens: an invisible sun has slid behind an invisible cloud. A faint but nonetheless disturbing presentiment of sadness touches Louie—the first such visitation in days. His afternoon is yawning before him, and no plan beckons. Of course he could write to Lizzie. He realizes, over his second glass of wine, that he's illogically feeling he *has*—has written, as though, through this morning's extravagant unpacking of memories, they've somehow communicated, telepathically.

Actually, it's probably an excellent time to write, when he's feeling more than usually balanced and measured. No more of the crusading dementia of his letter to Florence. (Over time, he grows more and more rather than less and less incredulous: starting a family *with Florence*?)

Yes, he'll write Lizzie this afternoon. And poke around in tiny antiques stores and used-book stores and art galleries, and maybe he'll buy himself a necktie. But he'll repose here for an interlude, in Caponata, London's "dark heart of Sicily," watching as a blond Lithuanian giantess, committed to a future wherein she will command squadrons of robots, briskly and mechanically goes about busing tables.

The sky has had a makeover by the time Louie, having concluded his meal with a sweetened double decaf espresso, flows back out into the London streets. Gray clouds, sliding. A backdrop of pale bleached-blue sky. He feels bucked up, as his father used to say, and soon finds his way to an Internet café. He has accumulated some twenty-seven messages since yesterday, but nothing of import. No hysterical string of inquiries from Annabelle, whom he talked to twice yesterday. Louie begins a letter to Lizzie:

> Greetings from London, a city I think you remember! Of course we were here three times. I've been in England some five days now. How I got here is quite a complicated story, actually.
>
> I don't know whether you know that Florence and I have separated. She is involved with someone else but I'll spare you the details. I moved out four months ago but it seems longer. The separation looks permanent.
>
> But how did I arrive in England? I don't know if you know I was left some money—intended purely for me—when my dad died in 2006. This was 18k back then, though it has appreciated somewhat. The pater didn't know Florence all that long but he always liked her a great deal—at least I think he did (you remember how quiet he could be!)—but he worried about me, esp'ly the bipolarism, and I think he wanted to make sure some funds were there that only I could tap into.
>
> Well, I'm tapping into them. I haven't until now. A couple of times I've thought about getting a really decent car, but that didn't seem to fit the spirit of the gift. Maybe I'm doing the wrong thing now and I should be leaving the money alone, but I came up with an idea of a sort of pilgrimage, really, and I felt confident that this *was* what Dad meant the money for. At some level this trip is dedicated to the pater. Eight years after his death, I feel I'm traveling w/ his blessing.
>
> I'm traveling around the world. I don't think I like

paintings any less now than I did in the old days, when we were newlyweds and I was a grad student, but it's definitely true I don't like *teaching* about painting as much as I used to. The kids don't care, and I find this truly paralyzing and disheartening. I mean in Detroit we've got one of the world's great art museums (a big Bruegel! A Bellini! A Titian! Some amazing Rembrandts!) and I send my students down there and the paintings fail to move. I don't mean the paintings fail to move *them,* though it's true enough. I mean, the actual Rembrandt portrait is static—it doesn't move the way TV would move or a video game or even their phones—and so they don't see the point. They relate better to buildings, maybe because you can actually go touch them, and some of them offer cafés and singles' nights, and I guess this is why I've come to prefer teaching architecture. As I write this paragraph, I can hear you teasing me in the old way about my being pedantic but honestly this does explain why I'm in London really: I'm on a round-the-world tour of amazing architectural sites.

Louie is writing very fast. In the Café Domat he did not play himself out, scribbling twenty-two pages mostly about Lizzie, and mostly addressed to Lizzie. More quickly than his hands can dispatch them, the words are catapulting upward in his head. But at this point he pauses. Wasn't his account of his father's bequest somewhat partial and maybe misleading?

Perhaps it's true that Florence finessed him out of the house. Okay, Louie has groused about this, but mostly he's accepting. Okay, too, if she keeps nearly all the furniture. (He surprises himself with how little he cares, at this stage of his marriage's dissolution, about his old belongings.) But the *pater*'s legacy is another matter. Louie will be damned if he'll let Florence get her hands on a red cent. And now he's spending the money before any claims on it might be laid.

No, the *pater* hadn't been very forthcoming about his aims for the eighteen thousand dollars. Perhaps he'd meant it as an emergency medical fund. But Louie has come around to a solacing belief that this particular nest egg was meant to hatch a different *rara avis,* bent on a different, idiosyncratic flight. The money allowed Louie to conceive and embark upon just the pilgrimage he has launched. Each of us has a journey. You might say that Florence, too, has undertaken a pilgrimage, hers beginning with the Pyrographic Theatre Company and an *Impertinence of Being Earnest* outsourced to Iowa, followed by an open-ended lay-by in the Caribbean. Whispering palm trees, long barefoot walks on the beach. Crass—all so amazingly goddamned crass! And sometimes Louie wants to puke at the thought, but there are other moments when he feels no resentment. Florence is showing confusion, and he's sorry for that, just as he's sorry for the various confusions his own pilgrimage has already manifested. Mistakes get made. *Everything happens for a reason* is one of Louie's least favorite popular sayings, a phrase to mollify the luckless and to excuse the lazy, and yet he'll concede that in Rome everything *had* to spin out of control before he could begin righting his life in London.

> I'm going to go to Turkey (almost definitely) and India and Japan (definitely)! And then I shall return home looking a good deal wiser, you can bet, and maybe a tiny bit grayer, and I'll find a new apartment and I'll find a new life though I'm not sure how *new* my life can be so long as I'm teaching at dreary AAC, whose halls I suppose I'll haunt till I'm a hundred.
>
> I find myself worrying about something, actually. I remember when you wrote when you and Justin split up and maybe you were taking the dissolution of a second marriage even harder than a first. And I spent a lot of time writing you, trying to express all my sympathy and support, but now I suddenly find myself worrying whether I actually mailed it. I'm being OCD, I guess, but I have this very guilty suspicion

that maybe I let you down. If I did, dearest Lizzie, let me apologize even at this late date. Forgive, forgive an unsteady man. I failed you in so many ways, and now I hate to think maybe I failed you in a way I haven't quite understood.

It's only one step from here—from the issue of illogical thinking—to the topic of forgoing his lithium. Louie gives his next sentence a good deal of thought:

I've had a shift in medication to more "natural," alternative medication—and the results seem most encouraging. Despite everything I've been through in the past few months (and there is more to tell! I assure you) I think I'm holding up pretty well.

Is he being witty in referring to caffeine and alcohol as alternative medication—or merely deceptive? There isn't time to mull this over. The writing advances with scurrying rapidity, and Louie uncharacteristically does not stop to proofread before hitting the Send button:

You have been constantly in my mind these past days especially our three trips to England. I remember those as such blissful loving times, to be cherished forever and I hope that's how you recall them! Lizzie, all sorts of things have intervened of course but I do think each of us has to hold onto the memories where life truly was happy and truly meaningful. It's memory alone that keeps them that way—that continues to make them meaningful and real.

Love,
Louie

Maybe it's the wine's aftereffects, but Louie's feeling exhausted—contented but exhausted. It's an altogether different sensation from what he experienced when dispatching his vast apologia to Florence.

It makes him squirm, makes his groin clench and grind, to recall that letter—but he's pretty certain he'll regret nothing about writing Lizzie.

Back to the Mulder Arms and a nap? Naps are risky for the traveler battling disorientation and endless jet lag. Better, probably, just to stay up. Today he has covered many miles of London streets. On the other hand, these are *London* streets, and what urban experience could be more exciting and charming? He makes his way into Fitzrovia, saunters up Great Portland Street, then plunges down a side street to a little art gallery in whose window hang a number of glass spheres, one of which, tinted a Chinese red, recalls a favorite childhood Christmas ornament. Inside, though, the place doesn't feel very festive.

There's an exhibition by a young British painter/collagist Louie has never heard of, Stew Rimes, born in Lancashire in 1982, whose work has already been acquired by the Tate Modern. There are eighteen new canvases. The show is called *Opside Down,* and all the canvases (apparently portraits of either Stew's homely, mole-speckled father or his homely, mole-speckled girlfriend) are hung upside down or are intended to look that way, Louie isn't certain which. There are projecting horizontal mirrors bracketed to the tops of the frames, so that a stooping viewer can examine the upside-down painting in right-side-up fashion, but Louie's lower back is twinging, and he doesn't actually make his way through all eighteen. He retreats to Oxford Street, congratulating himself on having largely switched his academic "specialty" from painting to architecture, where the percentage of work deliberately constructed upside down remains negligible.

Louie eventually winds up at the half-price-theater-ticket booth in Leicester Square. He has the good sense, for all his fatigue, to dismiss outright the only Shakespeare available: *Julius Caesar.* A tragedy? In period costume? (Maybe, he speculates, he ought to hold off on all Shakespeare until the eagerly awaited, convention-smashing emergence of dramaturge Daryl Force's *Twelfth Night.*)

He's drawn to a farce, *I Mean It Stop Right Now.* He's inclined toward it partly because he has found extremely fetching the posters, glimpsed all around town, of a soubrette, apparently unaware of the depth of her décolletage, stooping to pick up a fallen flower in what may be a men's bathroom. But a different poster on the ticket booth describes it as TIRELESS, NONSTOP FUN, which sounds fatiguing. As Louie stands half in and half out of the customers' queue, there's a moment, which he recognizes isn't fully logical, when he concludes that the problem with tragedy is that it openly conducts you where you don't wish to go, and the trouble with comedy is that it pretends not to be conducting you where you don't wish to go. Theater in a nutshell . . . In the end, he steps out of the queue.

Though he isn't really hungry, Louie decides to have dinner. *The Boorish American* has this to say about Leicester Square: "Hungry? Forget it. Begin a healthful fast."

Rebelliously, Louie chooses to eat nearby. He enters a Chinese restaurant, Lucky Ducky, in whose window a string of grilled ducks hangs upside down. Or opside down, as the painter/collagist Stew Rimes (b. 1982, Lancashire) would have it. Louie generally avoids all fowl that isn't chicken, but he feels drawn to the highly artificial, somewhat-crude, yet ultimately beautiful sheen of the ducks' flanks: a smoked ruby red that is fiery, cheap, and lavish. As a boy, he'd loved blazing-red candy apples (provided the apple was crisp). What the hell, he thinks, and orders half a duck and some chicken fried rice. When the food arrives, more quickly than he would have wished, he has no appetite, and so he orders a bottle of Tsingtao for assistance.

Louie takes stock. How is he doing? Various internal subsystems are functioning satisfactorily. Good digestion, pulse steady, sinuses clear. He's breathing more easily since going off lithium. Bad shoulder (left) and bad knee (right), both achy but holding up. Still, he's tired. He has walked and walked. Into the memory file titled "London 2014" he has inserted a prodigious number of images. But can he keep it up? Can he truly negotiate Istanbul and Agra and Kyoto? And what is he proving, exactly? Louie feels a touch of vertigo. Again, for a fleeting moment, the Journey of His Life trembles like a rope bridge underfoot. Would it have made better sense to stay at home?

The duck doesn't taste enough like chicken, and to make things worse, he can't find any white meat—perhaps he got the dark meat half of the duck. The chicken in the chicken fried rice is also mostly dark meat, and Louie arrays the humble frayed gray-brown fragments along the plate's scalloped rim, positioning them like hunkering mini-spectators around the amphitheater of the oval dish. The rice itself tastes fine, though, and there's lots of it. Louie stretches out the meal, and at its close he drinks a few gallons of jasmine tea. Finally, having gained in Lucky Ducky a fair amount of weight—maybe twenty pounds—he reenters a much-too-teeming, much-too-erotically-galvanized Leicester Square. He'd forgotten this about London: how you're often left wondering whether the woman you're furtively eyeing is a prostitute. He fails to understand the city's sartorial code. Or fails to understand England and the English. There's a predatorily tarty look on the streets apparently unconnected to prostitution. Putting one foot after the other, Louie makes his way toward the Mulder Arms. He finds it comforting that tomorrow's breakfast will be what it always is. Without brushing his teeth (an uncharacteristic delinquency), Louie Hake falls into bed and as though passing out from drink (while sober as a judge) he falls headlong into a colorless void.

THE MORNING IS DIFFERENT, THOUGH. AN INNER VOICE AN-nounces that he's himself again. Another voice immediately inquires what this means. He says to them both, aloud, *Oh hell, don't start,* and shuffles down to breakfast. He skips the bacon/ham entirely, as well as the baked beans—takes only a few nibbles from another shabbily abused tomato and the white of his egg. One cup of inferior tea is plenty, and Louie's off, he's out of there—bound toward a whimsical destination.

He didn't realize the weather had shifted. It's drizzling. Though these are cool halfhearted sprinkles, they've unleashed an explosion of prophylactic devices: blazing rain slickers, huge versicolor umbrellas, modest black umbrellas, knit caps, galoshes. Does everyone know something he doesn't know? A fast-approaching hurricane? Judgment

Day? Traffic along Guilford Street has taken on a progressive whoosh-
ing sound that suggests an accelerated pace, though in fact everything
has retarded. Should he go back for an umbrella? Louie decides to
chance it.

His destination this morning is a site he hadn't originally scheduled:
the Charles Dickens Museum. Dickens's life and work present another
topic he would hate to encounter in a televised quiz show before a studio audience of his disillusioned, headshaking students. Louie *knows*
he finished *A Tale of Two Cities* (back in advanced English in twelfth
grade at Fallen Hills High) and feels fairly confident of having completed *Oliver Twist;* in any case he saw *Oliver!,* the movie musical. He'd
like to claim he's read *A Christmas Carol,* but he may be confusing the
book with the old Alastair Sim movie. (Lizzie, who coveted rituals,
used to arrange an annual viewing, accompanied by generous serv-
ings of her mother's Christmas pudding, which, time-consuming and
difficult and expensive to make, was inedible. Year after year, though,
Louie put on a good show of feeling otherwise.)

A tourist brochure picked up in the hotel lobby touts Dickens as
"the world's most beloved novelist." Could this be true? It might well
be. Louie has painfully struck out with Shakespeare—*Lear* turned
out to be a downer—but he must reengage with the classics, and why
not formally recommence with the world's best-loved novelist? It's
something else on his calendar today: Buy *David Copperfield* or *Great
Expectations,* whichever weighs less.

Louie makes his way to 48 Doughty Street. The young man behind
the cash register, perhaps predictably, has polished his singularities
of gesture and tone. ("You are"—surveying Louie up and down—
"a-lo-o-one?") If somehow a resurrected Dickens were to materialize, he wouldn't have to look far from home for oddball inspiration.
In a city that abounds in outrageous hair—polychromatic Mohawks,
knee-length dreadlocks, starched dangerous-looking spikes that suggest a stegosaurus's spinal plates—the guy manages to look hirsutely
eccentric. He has closely shaved his head and face, save for two sizable
patches in front of his ears: he sports a sturdy pair of muttonchops.

And though he has the unlined face of a boy, his muttonchops (dyed?) are an antiquated pewter gray. "Welcome to the ho-ome of the novelist," he intones.

The novelist's ho-ome?

The place is great fun, actually, and less crowded than you'd suppose on a drizzly morning perfect for indoor sightseeing. It's a dark and narrow Georgian row house in brown brick. It turns out Dickens resided here for only two years, though an eventful stretch: he wrote *Oliver Twist* in it and welcomed two daughters to this world. Later, expanding with his success, Dickens moved to grander quarters, but this is his only surviving London residence. The rooms are small. Four floors. The furnishings are predictably unappealing. They're mostly of a particular rococo branch of Victorianism that Louie has always regarded as some sort of pervasive hoax—comprehending furniture makers and drapery manufacturers and silversmiths and ceramicists and picture framers and knickknack producers, all colluding to create interiors that nobody *liked*. Surely, these furnishings weren't designed to be judged as pretty or not pretty, comfortable or uncomfortable— rather, the intention was to look busy and padded and prosperously flatulent.

In the museum gift shop, Louie buys a copy of *Great Expectations* (lengthy, but three hundred pages shorter than *David Copperfield*). Having its bulk under his arm feels like validation as he marches back outside; Charles Dickens shall be his companion as he peregrinates through London. The rain has halted. He consults *The Boorish American* and discovers that only blocks away is Simon and Paul's, which is, "notwithstanding an otiose waitstaff," London's "only deli that would not embarrass a real New Yorker."

The place is already getting crowded, though it's not yet noon, and Louie is asked to share a table that seats four. Two of the chairs are empty. Diagonally across sits a largish, prettyish young woman eating what looks like a Reuben sandwich and drinking what looks like a chocolate shake. Louie orders the lox-and-bagel plate and a cup of coffee. Not wanting to make his tablemate self-conscious, he opens his volume of Dickens. He is only a few pages in—the child narrator has just encountered a man in shackles, in desperate need of "wittles," which Louie soon determines must be vittles—when the woman speaks.

"That's a funny title," she says with an unmistakably American accent. East Coast? One of *The Boorish American*'s real New Yorkers?

"I think it refers to the hero's hopes. He has great expectations of coming into a fortune."

"I meant the other book," she says.

"Oh. That." Louie laughs. "Well, I picked it up used. I've enjoyed it these last few days, partly because it gets *everything* wrong. You're an American."

"From Hampden. Maybe you don't know where that is?"

"Connecticut?"

"No. Part of Baltimore."

"I sort of know where it is. It's near the university?"

"There are lots of universities," she says.

"True enough."

He might answer that there are lots of Hampdens, or Hamdens, but Louie humbly accepts her correction. Academic prisoners like him—a lifer at AAC—have no business sounding elevated when speaking of educational institutions. "I suppose I meant Johns Hopkins," he says. "But you're right, lots of good universities in Baltimore."

"Right. Right near Hopkins."

"My name is Louie Hake," Louie says. "I teach art history at a little college in Michigan you've never heard of."

"I'm Shelley Pfister, but I'm not supposed to be. Not now . . ."

"You're not?"

"Not anymore."

"I'm not sure I follow—"

"I'm supposed to be Shelley Hornebeck. I'm supposed to be on my honeymoon. Right this minute. This is Day Four of my honeymoon."

Her glance—large and comely dark brown eyes aglitter—is seemingly less embittered than wondering and needy, and Louie feels a trifle self-conscious. Is this how he, too, comes across—desperate to broach intimate topics with strangers?

Apparently, she's primed to spill a tale of romantic woe and mortification, but is he prepared to hear it? Her acquisitive eyes draw him in, and Louie feels his heart go skimming toward her in light jolts, like a flung stone bouncing flatly across the surface of a lake. At the same time, he feels wary. He says, "How's the sandwich? My book here with the funny title says this is the only decent New York–style deli in London."

"*This* place is in your book?"

"Yes. But as I say, the author's completely bonkers."

"Oh, this place isn't Jewish. Not really. But it's what I was hungry for."

"You're Jewish." Again, he meets her with a statement.

"Just a half. Three-eighths, actually. Totally unpracticing. But I'm Jewish enough to know this isn't a real deli. It's just what I was hungry for. Maybe I was looking for comfort food?" And once more her dark eyes are publishing an invitation: Does he, or doesn't he, wish to enter her story—which is to say, her life?

Louie replies, "So London is where you decided to go instead of your honeymoon?"

"No," Shelley says. "I'm *on* my honeymoon. This is it. I'm *on* it."

"I'm not sure I— Your husband, is he here?"

"But I don't *have* a husband. That's why I'm Shelley Pfister. Instead of Shelley Hornebeck."

Louie stays in pursuit: "But you're on your honeymoon?"

"Who says a woman has to have a husband to be on a honeymoon?"

"That's a good question," Louie says, which is all he can think of to say, since he's still somewhat confused.

Fortunately, his lox plate arrives. The bagel turns out to be smaller than your average American bagel, but he's okay with that. It's also a uniform chewy consistency—no contrast in texture between crust and innards—which is less okay but not unexpected. He's glad anyway that the cream cheese isn't an inch thick, as it would be in New York.

The salmon is that old Mercurochrome orange, which, in the States anyway, seems on the way out as food coloring—like the scarlet and evergreen pistachios of his childhood.

"How's your bagel?" Shelley asks him.

"Oh, it's fine," Louie replies. "I mean not *good*. But fine."

He hadn't intended this as a witticism, but Shelley treats it as one, and Louie is grateful for her smile.

"You're welcome to some of my Reuben. I'll never finish it all."

"Honestly," Louie says. "This is fine." Food fortifies him, and he says, forthrightly embracing her situation and her name, "But I'm still confused, Shelley. Are you, or are you not, on your honeymoon?"

"Well, I'm *on* it," Shelley says. "I wasn't pulling out just because Frank did. If he pulls out, maybe isn't that all the more reason I should'na?"

"I suppose that's one way to look at it."

Shelley isn't much of a storyteller—perhaps a deliberately incompetent storyteller, reveling in her narrative's helter-skelter flow—but gradually Louie straightens things out. Mrs. Hornebeck, the woman once seemingly fated to become Shelley's mother-in-law, owns a travel agency, and she'd arranged for everything to be "absolutely first class" for Shelley and Frank, her only child. A first-class hotel, reservations at first-class restaurants, various vouchers and prepaid attractions. When Frank bailed out, only seventeen days before the actual ceremony, Mrs. Hornebeck literally cried in Shelley's arms. They cried in each other's arms. Wailing Mrs. Hornebeck diagnosed her son as a "complete idiot."

And when Shelley proposed a solo trip, so that Mrs. Hornebeck's planning wouldn't go entirely to waste, her mother-in-law-to-have-been applauded the girl's maverick spirit. According to Shelley, Mrs. Hornebeck at one point even expressed the hope that Shelley might chance to meet "some really nice London guy who isn't a complete idiot." And at this juncture does Shelley possibly pause, fractionally, to give Louie an appraising look?

Having protested that she could never finish it, Shelley has eaten all of her sandwich, and consumed her chocolate shake, and, unless he's mistaken, she's eyeing the remaining third of his bagel—Louie having pushed the plate aside. Shelley has spilled a minuscule drop of Thousand Island dressing on her white blouse, just above where her jilted heart must beat, and Louie debates whether or not to mention it.

He's also debating whether to confess anything of his own tangled romantic past, about which he's recently been too unguarded with strangers. Louie hesitates. Shelley orders coffee. He tells her that he, too, applauds her decision to embark on a solo honeymoon, though he isn't certain he does. Or isn't certain until, in response, she smiles brilliantly, and Louie recognizes the depth of his yearning for this woman's approval. And with this realization comes a now-familiar need to dilate on his own pilgrimage, and perhaps even say something about his marriages. It appears that two unattached people with big stories to tell have serendipitously collided . . . Instead of explaining his Journey, Louie asks what she has seen of the city.

"Well, the Tower of London." Shelley undergoes a cute, deeply histrionic shudder. "Never again."

"I know what you mean," Louie says.

"Executing them wasn't enough? They had to throw them in prison first?"

"That is actually the way it's usually—"

"Oh, and the National Gallery."

"Well. Now you're talking. You're talking to an art professor." Louie pitches forward. "What's the very favorite thing you saw?"

Shelley halts, bites down with her slightly overlapping upper front teeth on her plump lower lip. For one dismaying instant it appears she'll prove unequal to this minimal task. Is she unable to recollect, by either title or artist, a single object in the National Gallery? And of course Louie is immediately transported back to the AAC Student Union, where he has witnessed so many such abrupt mental bankruptcies and so often has felt, as now, that in requesting routine information he somehow risks coming across as pedant and bully. It's a great relief, on both sides, when Shelley triumphantly conjures up a name and image. "Leonardo!" she cries. "The Madonna with Child."

"*The Virgin of the Rocks*," Louie supplies. "It's an amazingly beautiful painting."

"It may be my favorite painting ever. Though it is so dark."

"Dark?"

"I think she has the kindest face I ever saw," Shelley says.

"And I think you may be right."

Yet this other, this still-more-arresting face—the brown-eyed one studying him over the rim of a coffee cup in Simon and Paul's Deli—is itself notably kind. And surely the face gazing back at her is comparably so, for Louie feels such gratitude for the woman's presence, for her freshness, her warm compulsion to talk . . .

"I like the way Mary's sitting on her lap."

A moment of confusion. "Oh," Louie says. "Oh, you mean the Leonardo *cartoon*. It's not a painting."

"This wasn't a cartoon," Shelley says doubtfully.

"Actually, it's sort of a technical term."

Shelley continues to puzzle. "A technical cartoon?"

"And where else?" Louie says. "Have you seen the Changing of the Guard?"

"No. Should I? Too touristy, I figured."

"Probably too touristy. Have you seen Big Ben?"

"Isn't it just a clock?"

"I suppose so." The fine arts professor Louie Hake of Ann Arbor College, who once taught a course called Symbol and Symbolic Landscape, a dozen or so years ago, back when he was getting divorced and flirting with a spiffier pedagogical vocabulary, adds, "Most Londoners would probably say it does more than tell time."

"You know," Shelley Pfister says, "I have two tickets to Madame Tussauds. Have you been to Madame Tussauds? Would you like to be my guest?"

*Too touristy,* an inner voice proclaims. But it's the same old killjoy who has been stubbornly popping up inside his head ever since he left America a couple of weeks ago. Louie effectively steps forward, cutting off the SOB, and declares, "Love to, Shelley. Love to go to Madame Tussauds with you."

THEY SPEND THE AFTERNOON TOGETHER. MUCH OF THEIR conversation focuses on Frank. He is a complete bastard, in addition to being a complete idiot, but also truly lovable, which is the problem. He's terrified of commitment, which is typically male, but his terror goes deeper: it goes back to his father, who abandoned Frank and his mother when Frank was only nine, and who might as well be dead, having left the country, basically, by emigrating out to La Jolla, California, where he started a new family with a new son, naming him Franklin if you can believe it, as if there was something the matter with the original Frank and he needed to be replaced.

Satisfied as he mostly is with his handling of things in these last few not-always-easy weeks, Louie must concede a recurring problem with curbing intimate disclosures. But there's no such problem today. He's in control. Perhaps because being with Shelley feels like being with a student (though she's in fact twenty-nine; she's a grown-up woman), he reposes inside a comfortable, decorous reserve. He's certainly in no hurry to recount some of the topsy-turvy developments of his last weeks, months.

Still, after Madame Tussauds (which more than he'd readily admit had thrilled Louie, who'd experienced a genuine spinal *frisson* in the Chamber of Horrors), while the two of them luxuriate over snacks and glasses of wine in a Lebanese place called Cedar Palace off of Portobello Road, he opens up somewhat. He tells her that his wife left him for an amateur theater director. And that the two lovebirds flew to the Virgin Islands, with no return date in sight. But he does not cite section 750.338b of the Michigan Penal Code, which is probably a good thing. He may be clearheaded today, but he's also emotional. When he mentions how Florence was relieved of her job as a teacher of third graders, unshed tears burn his eyelids. Poor Florence! Or is it poor Louie? And Shelley reaches over the tabletop with a heartwarming efficiency and briskly pats his hand. "There's more to the story," Louie says, and stops.

But it seems there's more to her story, too: the tale keeps subdividing. When Shelley looks back now on what went wrong, she sees how tremendously important the fitness issue was. Frank's in amazing shape. He can bicycle fifty miles in a day. He once swam across Lake Massapick, which Louie has never heard of but which sounds immense. "He's completely tireless," Shelley says, and a flicker of lubricity, perhaps, whets the luscious luster of her dark eyes. Louie's own gaze drops away.

He says, "Did you have clues beforehand? Indications he might balk at the wedding?"

Shelley pauses. "Enough about Frank."

"Fair enough."

But she goes on. Frank is a troubled sleeper. Frank can't stay in bed, even on weekends. Sometimes he dreams he's fighting—not an argument, *fighting*—with his father.

In addition to their glasses of white wine, they've ordered hummus and tabbouleh, one of the few foreign salads Louie genuinely likes, provided the parsley isn't too dry—or wet. Or scratchy. The dishes come with pita bread. Shelley's evidently keen on carbs; the bread bowl has been stripped to a lonely sliver. "So tell me more about your job," Louie says. She works in the accounts department of her uncle's thriving auto-body shop.

"Not much to tell, really. Uncle Garvin pays me more than I'm worth. He doesn't have any kids and he likes having me around. He's got these terrible ulcers. He used to drink like a fish, but then he stopped, but he didn't really stop, only we're not supposed to know he didn't stop, only he knows *I* know he didn't and keeps a bottle in his desk drawer."

The money issue has frankly been puzzling Louie. Shelley has been taking cabs all over the city, and her engagement ring—she still sports an engagement ring—flashes a chunky diamond. She dresses well, or at least expensively. (On one trip or another to the ladies' room she must have noticed the Thousand Island stain, which has mostly been removed.)

Like Mrs. Hornebeck, Uncle Garvin considers Frank a "complete idiot." But he has gone a step further. He vows, "If he ever steps into my shop again, I'll have his legs broken."

Of course Uncle Garvin is joking. He's a very gentle man. But he talks tough, which is how people in his business tend to talk, according to Shelley. They're dealing all the time with smashups, drunk drivers, blood-spattered interiors—you name it.

Whatever Shelley's accent is (maybe straight-up Baltimorese: she pronounces *town* in two syllables, and *very* as though it rhymes with *curry*), Louie enjoys listening to it. Though individual pronunciations are those of a gangster's moll *(whatcha, couldja)*, the timbre of her voice is clemency itself. They have each finished a glass of wine, and Louie's fearful she's about to propose a sundering of the ways. It's only 5:45, not really dinnertime, especially for people who have been snacking. The threat of another solitary evening overhangs.

Shelley notices his eyes on the empty wineglasses. She says, "Shall we double down?"

"Hm?"

"Have another?" Her wide smile exposes her gums. Her teeth are quite white and, except for the overlapping upper two front teeth, straight. Dr. Koepplinger would have approved.

"Only if you'll finish off that last piece of bread. It's going stale."

Shelley smiles again, plucks up the bread, scoops upon it the last of the hummus, which makes a sizable mound. "It's terrible, terrible," she says. "How much I've been eating in London. You're seeing me not the way I am, believe me."

"You're on your honeymoon," Louie says. "You're entitled."

Louie means this good-humoredly, but Shelley looks pained, and what she next says startles him, particularly since he was just now appreciating her smile: "Jever consider having your teeth whitened?"

"Can't say I have," Louie replies, which isn't true. "Are they that bad?"

"Not at all. I'm asking 'cause isn't it sort of customary after a marriage falls apart to make some physical self-improvement gesture? You know, get a new haircut, buy a new wardrobe, not that that would make sense for you, Louie. I keep noticing how well the colors of your tie and your sport coat go together. You obviously know how to dress."

"Thank you."

"And you have amazing hair."

"Thanks. I'm in dire need of a haircut."

"I like it."

"In Rome, I guess it was just two weeks ago though it seems longer, I asked these two young Asian women to take my picture in front of the Pantheon, and at the last minute one of them comes rushing forward and arranges my hair before the picture's taken. 'I cut hair in Singapore,' she tells me."

"I like it," Shelley repeats.

Louie feels an awakened tingling along his left forearm—the one he wove around the hairdresser's waist. "I found out my students call me Professor Mop-Top."

"Cu-ute," Shelley says, and it isn't clear whether she's referring to the nickname or to Louie himself. Again an exchange of glances, charged by a mutual sensation that each succeeding gaze is penetrating a little further into the other's. "So what sort of self-improvement gesture are you thinking of making, Shelley?"

"Maybe some liposuction?" She giggles. In a reflex of gallantry, Louie begins offering up reassurances about unnecessary procedures, slimness as a modern, unhealthy fetish, the Rubens and Renoir ample feminine ideal, etc., but she lifts her hand in traffic-cop fashion. "Oh, I know it's not a suitable weight-loss technique. It's only for body sculpting."

In this quiet, shadowy restaurant her remark grants his imagination free license to travel over the amplitude of her freshly bared limbs. What sort of sculpting is she envisioning? Seated, she looks less plump than she is. She has a relatively narrow face, and the breadth of her hips had surprised him when, back in Simon and Paul's, she first stood. She's also taller than she looks when sitting down; she's his height anyway. Over the course of the last few hours he has had some additional opportunities for assessment. Standing in the queue at Madame Tussauds, he briefly took her arm, and found it fleshy above the elbow. She has large hands and quite large feet.

Second glasses of wine arrive, guaranteeing him company for some time yet. "Well, here we are," he says.

"What do you weigh, Louie?" she asks him.

"What do I weigh?"

"What do you weigh?"

"A hundred fifty-two," he tells her.

"I was afraid you'd say that . . ."

"You were afraid I'd say a hundred fifty-two?"

"I was afraid you'd say something less than me. Frank's just the same. Weighs less. And he's taller than you."

"Well," Louie begins but stops. He doesn't know what to say.

"Don't start talking about different body types. I hate that! Like I'm born to be fat. I actually have fine bones. High-school graduation, I weighed a hundred twenty-seven."

"I wasn't going to start talking about body types," Louie says. This time when he smiles, he's aware that his teeth need whitening. Still, she smiles back. She says, "You're a funny one, Louie."

"Am I?" Louie says. "Funny like sweet? Or more funny like weird?"

"It's funny like sweet-weird."

"Am I?" Louie says. "Well, I'm in a funny place in my life . . ."

And abruptly, all of it—his upended existence—opens before him: Florence's *gross indecency* and his gathering certainty that it isn't Florence but Lizzie he longs to reconcile with and his crazy behavior in Rome and his veering detour to Florence. There's bipolarism and abandoned meds and that other diagnosis, which surprisingly seems most of the time ignorable, though in reality it's more comprehensive than anything, it's the pursuer darkening his dreams, the hooded blackness following him across the surface of the planet. "This is a highly livable condition," or so Dr. Dimiceli, head of ophthalmology at Pioneer Hospital, had described AOFVD on that day when the diagnosis fell like some sort of blinding blade.

. . . In his memory, deep in Louie's memory, that blade is a link to a lasting childhood revelation. In his bedroom in Fallen Hills he was lying one midsummer day while sunlight in the big birch outside his window dapple-danced alike over his body and the caramel-colored wide-wale corduroy bedspread he lay upon. He was wearing a powder-blue T-shirt and bottle-green pajama bottoms. He must have been about twelve. He has never forgotten the day. The playful sun was the frothy gold of the melted butter you pour on popcorn, and he was reading a book about famous explorers when he stumbled upon an extended account of Aztec human sacrifice. Back then, he was still so young that he'd never heard of such a procedure, maybe; certainly, he'd never pondered it or, you might say, seen the world's evilness unveiled. Oh, that boy on the caramel-colored corduroy bedspread was, for the last time in his life, an innocent. But a blade goes up, it catches fire in the brazen Mexican sunlight, and the varied congregated people of this earth are stranger than anything a boy can imagine. They will conceive and organize and execute far queerer and scarier practices than a boy can conceive of. A blade goes up, and the slashing arc of the fatal deed is powered not by malice or hatred but by a conviction that plucking out your squirming heart from its rooted home, while a sweating, attentive audience looks on appreciatively, is the right and proper thing to do. Everyone on the planet wishes for something, and the executioner wishes for a sharper blade . . .

*It makes you question human nature.*

Clearly, his energies must now be focused on keeping Shelley beside him. He could open up about the Journey of His Life, but he's beginning to fear he's talking himself out on the subject, generating too many words, and words—at least casual words—are the enemy of that intimate vision that prompted his travels. Instead, he says, "Forgive my asking, don't tell me anything you don't want to, but was there someone else? Did Frank find someone else?"

Shelley spaces out the words: "There's. Nobody. Else. Naturally, it's everybody asking. And you know what I think? It'd be easier if there was. Honestly! Then I'd say, *Damn the little bitch, she went after my Frank.* Or, like, *The slut just turned his head.* But if there's nobody else, then I've got to face it: Frank, he's just saying he doesn't want me for his wife."

With extraordinary neatness and rapidity, a single teardrop forms at each of the outer crooks of her eyes and slips down her cheeks. One of them plops onto her tan paper placemat. Also neatly and rapidly, Louie reaches over and takes her hand. Their fingers interlace, right up to the needy knucklebones. "Maybe you're a funny one, too, Shelley."

"What it is? It's the nights I really dread here." Her voice is trembling. "It's one thing, honeymooning alone in the daytime. But it's another thing, nights."

"I dread the nights, too," Louie says.

"Louie, will you have dinner with me?"

The question elates him, even as he experiences a few misgivings about Shelley's again seizing the initiative. Shouldn't *he* be doing so—not merely as the man, for whatever that's worth these days, but as the older and more worldly party? Again, Louie undergoes a faintly illicit, stirring sensation that he's negotiating with one of his students—and letting her guide him by the hand. "I'd love to have dinner with you," he says.

"And you have to let me treat."

"Now, that's something I really can't allow," Louie says.

"You have to let me treat, else I'm *rescinding* the offer."

Shelley accompanies this with a mock-stubborn outthrust of her chin, followed by a very winsome quarter-tilting of her head. Her watered eyes sparkle. She is—Louie's beginning to realize—quite an adroit flirt.

"I'll let you buy me dinner tonight," he reconsiders, "but only if you let me buy you lunch or dinner tomorrow." He's showing his own mock stubbornness. "C'we call it a deal, Miss Shelley?"

IT TURNS OUT THAT MRS. HORNEBECK, SHELLEY'S NEAR mother-in-law, weeks ago made a dinner reservation for tonight at a place near Piccadilly Circus called the Daily Retreat. Of course the reservation was originally intended for bride Shelley and husband Frank the Complete Idiot, who these days is holed up in his Baltimore apartment letting his phone go unanswered, not that anybody's doing much to reach him. The reservation is still valid. As guest, though, Shelley will be taking Louie Hake, a surrogate groom, for her next-to-last honeymoon dinner. She's returning to Baltimore the day after tomorrow, in the morning.

Shelley wants to change clothes at her hotel, the Excelsior Palace in Chelsea. Louie proposes that he meanwhile head back to the Mulder Arms to do the same thing. Shelley tells him not to be ridiculous, he's already wearing a fancy sport coat and a beautiful tie, if he gets any more dressed up, he'll embarrass her. But they decide to separate, and he deposits her into a cab. They'll meet at nine at the Daily Retreat, which sounds as though it belongs in LA rather than London. Louie finds his way to an Internet café. All day long, he has been wondering whether Lizzie could have written.

Seventeen new emails line up before him. Only one matters. She's done it—already gotten back to him.

Dear Louie,

It was so good to hear from you! I'm so sorry to hear about you and Florence. I really am. Maybe things can be patched back together? I know this must be very hard for you, and I'm thinking about you and praying for you.

My own experience is that things don't necessarily get any easier the second time around. Maybe harder in a way? When you and I split up, I was very, very hurt, and very, very angry, but I guess I could tell myself it was just bad luck—that you and I simply were not "meant" for each other, or maybe you really weren't ready for marriage as young as we did.

Even now, these many years later, the words hit hard. Louie longs to defend himself. He wants—patiently, lovingly—to hammer it out once more with his Lizoliz. After all, wasn't it possible they really *were* "meant" for each other, only under different, maturer circumstances? Wasn't it possible that, back then, as people in their twenties, they hadn't yet acquired the wisdom, or amassed the basic life experience, needed to overcome obstacles that only *looked* insurmountable?

First off, I want to reassure you. In your letter you were worrying you never wrote when Justin and I split up. But of *course* you did—a really beautiful letter, Louie, full of sympathy and kindness. I think probably you remember now.

He wants to think he remembers—but does he? What did the letter say? Somewhere, he has retained a copy, but his filing cabinets lie thousands of miles away, like his computer, and nothing of the letter's tone or phrasing is coming back.

But anyway, the second time around, when Justin and I split up, I could no longer convince myself I was the victim of bad luck. *Two* failed marriages, and me still in my *thirties*? Louie, I began to feel I was somehow getting what I deserved. Wasn't it inevitable? Wasn't I doomed in love (it's the kind of phrases I was thinking in). I was certainly looking for peace in all the wrong places.

But wasn't that precisely the problem—Lizzie's treating every setback as evidence of her own personal shortcomings? And isn't there something profoundly heartening in their independently reaching this revelation? Lizzie understands so much better now her tendency to blame herself unfairly, *Louie* understands it better, and the air tingles with the enthralling prospect of a resurrected relationship, this one rooted in freedom and clarity and emotional justice.

> I don't know all the circumstances, but I gather that this time isn't your fault, Louie, and certainly not all your fault (it rarely is).
>
> I was touched to hear you were back in London and went back to look at some of the sights we saw. I came upon some pictures recently, and I was struck by how young we look. I guess I mean struck by how young I look (you probably look the same). Did you know I've started dyeing my hair? I think maybe this is divine justice for all my gloating, me taking *way* too much pleasure throughout my thirties in having no gray, unlike most of my friends, then one day waking up in my forties and overnight half my head is GRAY. I'm not kidding!

Meanwhile, he himself has gone gray at the temples. Maybe Lizzie knows this? Maybe she's being coy? Surely she has Googled him? His "candid" on the AAC departmental website is recent. He actually likes the image—the animated art professor pointing urgently toward an invisible blackboard, cropped for the photo—but it doesn't hide the steady advance of time. Professor Hake is thinking, and he's graying.

For years, it turns out, he has been yearning to receive this very letter from his Lizzie. It's immensely satisfying to place side by side two images: the young, promising, romantic couple they were and the mature, dynamic, romantic couple they might become. Lizzie dyes her hair, and Louie's waist has ballooned from a spare thirty inches to a trim glutton's thirty-two, yet there is something timeless and indefeasible in their bond.

He's more than tired, he's bleary-eyed tired, and probably he shouldn't have had that second glass of wine. It's almost eight. He's due at a restaurant called the Daily Retreat in just over an hour. The distance he must travel is more than geographical. He has penetrated deep into the past, and at the moment Shelley Pfister, with whom he spent most of the day, is a remote and superficial presence.

Louie, I don't want to intrude anywhere not my business, but when you talk about all the money you're spending, it worries me. And I worry even more when you talk about changing your medication, natural medications, etc. Don't get me wrong, I'm all in favor of finding ways to reduce the meds or get off them (it took me years to realize I was marooned on the Island of Prozac, which is a pretty bleak place, I can tell you. I'm in a better place now). But you have to be careful. Are you being careful?

Marooned? The Island of Prozac? Well, the islands of modern life. Tropical islands, psychotropical islands, and Louie Hake and Wife Number One and Wife Number Two all castaways among them.

But hasn't Lizzie, in that startlingly intuitive way of hers, struck to the elusive nub of things? She gets it. He's seeking a way out, but she's right, he must be *careful,* and there was a point in Rome—a number of points—where he was tipping forward, headlong, in some spectacular ass-over-teakettle fashion. (Is the phrase a Briticism? It ought to be.)

But now he's righting things, building self-confidence, and nobody could gainsay his progress. Hasn't he so thoroughly charmed a pretty young honeymooner that she has invited him as her dinner guest?

I can't believe you're going to Turkey and India and Japan! I've only been to three countries, Canada and England and France (all with you—I never added another one). I hope you make out all right with the food, Louie. (You remember the trouble in Lyons!)

And how sweet of her to remember the ghastly little Lyonnais den of evil, where at one point the waiter, as if to illustrate that the Aztecs had little on the French in terms of barbarized civilizations, attempted to foist on him the sautéed brain of an animal—all the while jabbering excitedly and unintelligibly.

I guess I didn't tell you Aunt Charlotte died three months ago. I hadn't seen her in years. You remember how odd she was when we visited Birmingham—watching soccer all the time, drinking Guinness, which she kept offering you though you obviously disliked it. Anyway, believe it or not she died watching TV—watching soccer!

Do keep me updated on your travels. Like I say, I worry about you, Louie. You're in my prayers. I think at heart you're really a Michigan boy, and those places sound so far away!

Love,
Lizzie

It's turning late—only forty minutes to get to Piccadilly Circus—but it isn't merely the press of time empowering Louie's sensation that his reply must be written in one go, swoopingly, without revision or reworking, without forethought or hindsight. Her letter has challenged aspects of his essential character, and any failure to address her with corresponding directness and probity would disserve both of them.

My dear Lizoliz,

There's an odd openness to things at the moment. I'm trying to let my days take their own unique shape, which I suppose is a somewhat pompous and professorial way of saying I'm trying not to close myself off to adventure.

Pleasure radiates through Louie's chest as he surveys the magic of that sterling last phrase: *trying not to close myself off to adventure.*

The oddest thing happened today. I met a young woman from Baltimore on her honeymoon—alone! She's a jilted bride. Her husband-to-be called off the wedding seventeen days before the ceremony, and she decided to go on her honeymoon anyway.

Outspread before him, Shelley's tale ramifies, while Louie briefly stalls. It isn't that he fears Lizzie would misunderstand. To the contrary, here's a story that would tickle her. But Shelley's tale is simply too hectic and nuanced for the little rented computer screen, and he's going to be late for the Daily Retreat, and this anecdote about his honeymoon dinner date maybe sounds too much of a piece with his recent crazy zigzagging. Louie recalls Lizzie saying, twice in her brief letter, that she's worried about him. He erases his second paragraph and plunges on.

I'm wondering, frankly, whether you can ever forgive me. I'm wondering, frankly, about things like wrong turns and redemption. I suppose the issue is whether I've actually learned something of meaning in my life. I like to think I have. Or I'm learning. These are difficult days, to tell the truth.

I worry about Annabelle. She gets so involved with the animals at the animal shelter, and so involved with what I'm doing—and in both cases I think she needs more of a life of her own. I often think she's got the biggest heart of anyone I know, and this ought to be sufficient. This ought to guarantee glorious success, and what is *wrong* with people, with society and life, that having the world's biggest heart guarantees you nothing? If this world had its priorities straight, statues would be erected to the kindest people, for in the whole history of civilization, what achievement is more impressive than human empathy?

Speaking of the world, I really am hopeful that this trip of mine will bring me some clarity I've maybe been looking for for a long time, too, without knowing it. Not to sound grandiose, but I look upon it as a pilgrimage.

Here in London I keep thinking of a day with big beautiful heavy white clouds and you and I in Kensington Gardens (remember?). You were sort of kicking your feet up (those famously mismatched two-different-sizes feet of yours) and you were wearing blue Keds with red laces (remember?). We both remarked on how solid the clouds looked—as if you could walk right on them. And there was something so beautifully appropriate when we came upon the Peter Pan statue: up above Peter this long white bridge was floating, this skywalk to Neverland. (Remember?)

I'm also dealing with health issues I haven't told you about. Nothing catastrophic, but a bit upsetting and unnerving.

Louie pauses once more, scrutinizing this last sentence with vulnerable eyes, whose retinas are imperiled. Is he, in the tone he's taking, yielding to the sort of taciturn macho foolishness he's usually quite good at resisting? He expunges the sentence, substituting something better, and moves on.

Nothing life-threatening, but no less upsetting and unnerving for that. One day I look around and I have no parents and I have no children and my job is an embarrassment, which wouldn't be so bad except that I realize I'm never going to have a better one and my second marriage is collapsing in an excruciatingly mortifying fashion, which is maybe exactly what I deserve, and then you throw in serious health problems and I do have to ask myself what are the really important relationships in my life, and I recall our time together and I value it so much even as I want so much even now to make it so much better. I'm writing this in a really rushed way, which I suppose is a way of ensuring later that I can use my hurry as an excuse for having said things I actually very much want to say. I have a dinner engagement with someone I really, really shouldn't be late for (it's a long story and I think you will like it), so I'll cut this short but not without first saying again how sorry I am and hoping you'll write back and tell me how you are really doing and what you are really thinking.

My love,
Louie

Louie hits Send. After which, life turns very efficient. He collects his receipt, confirms the continuing presence of his wallet and hotel key card in his pants' pockets, steps out of the Internet café, immediately locates a cab. Even so, he'll be late. He begins explaining laboriously to the cabbie, who wears a turban, that he is headed to a restaurant named the Daily Retreat, when the cabbie cuts him off. No need, the address.

Is it a tourist trap? That a turbaned cabbie with wobbly English would immediately know the location of the Daily Retreat seems highly inauspicious.

LOUIE ARRIVES THIRTEEN MINUTES LATE. SHELLEY IS AL-ready seated. He has various apologies on his lips, but none is demanded. The warmth of her greeting is simultaneously flattering and disquieting. "Louie!" she cries. He stoops for her cheek, and she swings her face so that his kiss falls into the plush limbo between upper lip and base of nose. Her relief in seeing him is palpable, and understandable. She's been terrified of being stood up: a bride twice jilted before the honeymoon's complete.

Shelley's wearing an unflattering, low-cut, shiny, teal-colored dress that looks like a prom dress. Her bare shoulders are broad and white and fleshy. A fist-sized blossom shape, spun of what looks like yellow satin ribbon, overhangs her left breast. The dress makes her look fatter than she is—or perhaps precisely as fat as she is. Her too-bright lipstick is vermilion. The warmth of her smile is endearing. Her drink, served in a martini glass, is a bright pink—she is a study in bright colors. "I'm having a cosmopolitan!" she announces gaily.

"Then so am I," Louie tells her, taking his seat.

"Here we are!" Shelley says.

"Nowhere but here," Louie replies.

But where are they? The restaurant is cavernous, low-ceilinged and deep. Its distinctive visual details (waiters and waitresses in black shirts and slacks and glossy aquamarine patent-leather belts, a voluminous tropical-fish tank in the center of the room, a vast heavy-handed clock on one wall that might oversee a good-sized railway station) don't suggest any coherent stylistic whole. The cuisine is "fusion"—dependably, a sign of a cowardly unwillingness to take a culinary stand.

He's handed a menu and is alarmed to read, first thing, that the Daily Retreat recommends a four-course prix fixe dinner, including a glass of prosecco, for seventy pounds—well over a hundred dollars. "You must let me pay half the bill," he says.

"I simply wouldn't dream of such a thing!"

Shelley's pronouncement arrives in a gliding mezzo-soprano terminating in a cluster of low giggles—and though their acquaintance dates back only a few hours, Louie knows this is neither an authentic voice nor authentic mirth, even if she is enjoying herself. Shelley's being grand. She's like a young girl imitating the movies—a borrowed, cut-rate version of sophisticated repartee. It's endearing. Shelley is playing hostess, and yearning to make this evening a success.

She asks to hear more about his job, and Louie resurrects AAC—the classrooms located in modules with leaking roofs ("The joke among the faculty is we're really trailer-park trash"), the drinking fountain outside the Fine Arts Department office that four different chairmen have vowed to fix, the student who once immortally remarked, of Vincent van Gogh, "I really like, when he like, really like goes deep and stuff." But as he amplifies, it grows clear that Shelley resembles the other Louie—the one who found Orvieto so depressing—in resisting any vision of a Louie Hake assigned to some rinky-dink, outpost institution. She's having dinner tonight with a dapper art professor from

Ann Arbor, Michigan, an adventurer scouting the globe for legendary architecture, and what a glittery story this will make in Baltimore and Garvin's Auto Body!

The drinks are delicious, and the glasses are drained perhaps sooner than they ought to be. Signaling to a waiter with an outflung, boneless wave of her wrist, and without first consulting Louie, Shelley orders a second round.

Louie asks to hear more about Uncle Garvin.

"Well, he smokes cigars. Big ones. His whole office stinks like a brewery. Well, not a brewery but maybe a cigar shop. I told you, he talks very tough, all day bark, bark, bark into the phone, every other word a cuss. But on the sly he's a big donor to the Hampden Pediatric Hospital. He's very hush-hush on the subject. They wanted him part of this big evening honoring big charity donors, but he begged off. He wrote them another check, but he begged off."

Louie says, "He sounds like quite the admirable guy."

"He lost his only child. Before I was born. A little boy, Garvin Junior. Only two years old. It was spinal meningitis."

"So you're something of a surrogate child to him," Louie postulates.

"Symbolic you mean?"

"Maybe that's a better term for it," Louie says.

"Don't think the idea's not occurring to me. He calls me Shell-gal." Her laugh this time—airy and chiming and childlike—signals genuine mirth.

And with these few conversational strokes, Uncle Garvin in his stinking office in a Baltimore auto-body shop comes pungently alive. He's a gruff, good-hearted man—a broken-hearted man. He stubs out his cigars on his dinner plate, he hawks and spits on the street, he slams down his telephone, and he has never recovered from the death of his diminutive namesake. And Uncle Garvin is but one such vivid figure. Louie's daylong encounter with Shelley has introduced a constellated firmament of rich, overarching lives: Frank's mother in her travel agency, painstakingly planning the doomed honeymoon; and Frank's deadbeat father out in La Jolla, raising a second Frank;

and Frank himself, the fitness freak, the lovable complete idiot, listening month after month to wedding plans as he felt the muscles in his legs contracting with the urge to flee . . . The pretty woman sitting across from Louie in her teal dress, exposing too much bosom perhaps, flashes an encouraging gummy smile. (Shelley's cleavage runs deep, in a fashion Louie isn't used to; Florence often would joke—not fully a joke—about getting breast-enhancement surgery.) Her second drink has injected a becoming flush into Shelley's youthful, unlined features, and Louie's flattered, he's roiled. It's like being invited to a holiday party of some stranger's extended family, entering an elastic web of warm and confusing and subtle connections that embrace and titillate your perplexities.

"It was so kind of you to invite me to dinner," Louie says.

"Where would I be if I hadn't run into you, Louie? Can you imagine being in this place alone?"

Louie can't, partly because he can't place this place. Just now, with otherworldly self-possession, an elongated black woman so gorgeous he honestly thought she must be some variety of international supermodel went sashaying past their table, seriously undermining his suspicion that this is, to any savvy London eye, a simple tourist trap.

Shelley's pronouncement is so decisive—"We need to try the fixed-price menu!"—that Louie instantly concurs. When the waiter comes, a poltergeist or ventriloquist leaps into Louie's throat: he winds up ordering duck pâté, truffled eggplant pasta, a garden salad with fresh figs, and molasses *pot de crème*. Mysteriously victorious, having extracted his ruinous order from Louie, the waiter in his black outfit and gleaming aquamarine belt weightlessly drifts away.

In immediate retrospect, the only one of Louie's four choices that doesn't seem highly dubious and risky is the garden salad, which sounds merely redundant. He considers launching into an account of some of the problems he's had when dining out in Europe, but instead he asks about Frank.

One of Frank's problems is his simply not getting it through his idiot's head that other people don't have his energy. Tell him you're tired after working all day, he thinks you're being lazy. In *his* universe, plain everyday fatigue is a moral failing.

"Maybe it's being young," Louie says. "When I got into my forties, I realized I didn't have the energy I used to. When I think about this trip of mine, you know, this round-the-world journey, I sometimes wonder whether my energy reserves are up to—"

"But all his friends say the same thing! They're his age, but can they keep up? No fricking way! Frank's a total machine. That's what they say: Frank's a total machine. No, if *they* bicycle twenty miles, they're a little tuckered out, can you blame them?"

"Energy's a wonderful—"

"Or eating. Frank can go all day on one simple single handful of pumpkin seeds and raisins. But does that mean the rest of us can?"

"Obviously not. Given everything I'm eating today. A four-course dinner . . ."

"Oh, you're just like Frank. A hundred and fifty-two. Didn't you say you weighed a hundred and fifty-two?"

"Well, yes, but over the years my weight has steadily—"

"Oh, you sound just like Frank! He'll be like 'I'm full,' and I'm like 'You've had half a sandwich,' and he's like 'Well, it's a very big sandwich.' I mean, as if that *matters.*"

"Well, I suppose I do sound like him if he's saying American portions have gone haywire. You come to Europe—"

"He thinks everybody can be like him!" Shelley's on a real tear. "Ride your bike ten miles. Munch a dozen Beer Nuts. Ride another ten miles. You know he put me on a diet? With a whatchacall? A flowchart? I mean he printed it out. With a big title and everything: SHELLEY'S DIET. I was supposed to lose five pounds from New Year's to Valentine's Day. And another five by Tax Day, that's April fifteenth. And another ten by the wedding. He prints it out, with a picture of me taken on New Year's, and another from New Year's two years ago, when I was skinnier, and he puts it on *my* refrigerator."

"That sounds a little insulting," Louie says.

"A *little*?"

Louie corrects himself. "*Very* insulting."

"Just ask any girl. Just ask *any girl* how she'd like her boyfriend making a flowchart for up on her fridge with a photo of her on New Year's with the camera angle giving her a double chin. You go ahead. Just ask her."

She glares defiantly but expectantly—as though she honestly envisions Louie's rising from his chair to inquire of some woman at an adjoining table how perhaps she'd like it if . . .

"That's incredibly insulting," Louie says.

"You're telling me?" Shelley's still glaring.

"I'm agreeing with you," Louie says. "Very insensitive."

"*Right.* You see, that's the whole nutshell. You see, I'm very sensitive."

"And Frank's not?"

"Totally not. He's *in*sensitive." Shelley pauses, reconsiders. "Well, you know, not really in a horrible way. Just mostly a guy way. What do you expect? It's different. Guys. He thinks if he can get by on a handful of Beer Nuts and raisins, the rest of us can, too. Everybody thinks you can do what they can do," Shelley says.

"It's a funny kind of arrogance," Louie determines. "A paradox."

Sudden uncertainty clouds Shelley's gaze. "I'm not sure that's what Frank meant," she says. "You're the professor," she says.

Their glasses of prosecco arrive, along with a breadbasket. Its contents are enfolded in a pumpkin-colored napkin, which Shelley, betranced, parts with the look of a child at a birthday party steadily peeling the wrapping from a gift. She says, "They're *different*." She places a slice of what looks like whole-grain bread and a tawny, glossy dinner roll on her bread plate. Louie selects a slice of the whole-grain for himself. The squinting countenance Shelley immediately lowers on him all but phrases a request, and Louie accordingly selects a dinner roll, so his plate mirrors hers. Shelley nods at him, satisfied.

Louie lifts his champagne glass and proposes a toast. "To the resilient bride," he proclaims, wondering even as the adjective emerges whether he's being too professorial.

But Shelley's reply is perfect: "To the resourceful teacher."

They butter their rolls and start eating. "After this, I'm going to have one glass of wine," Shelley says. "White wine."

"Me too," Louie says.

"Frank won't drink hard liquor. He says it's too hard to measure—too hard to figure just how much you're drinking."

"Maybe that makes sense," Louie says.

"He calls it machine maintenance," Shelley says. "He's totally cool with this notion of your body as a machine."

"It does make perfect sense," Louie says.

"Of course it's got compensations. I mean romantically." Shelley, having finished her second cosmopolitan, angles her empty glass toward Louie, as though requesting a refill. "You get me?" He does, but she repeats herself anyway. "Being with someone who's a total machine—it's got compensations."

The look in Shelley's dark liquid eyes is sly and mischievous and perhaps coquettish—though how exactly Louie is meant to take the news that Frank is a "total machine" isn't absolutely plain. He clears his throat and says, "He sounds like quite a character."

It has compensations, but evidently it's also a little exhausting. "Have you ever tried keeping up, you know, romantically—with a total machine?" she asks.

"Well, I'd actually like to think I'm actually quite—I mean on *that* score anyway." He concludes: "Well, it's complicated, isn't it." And clarifies: "The human body."

Well, yes. And as it turns out, it isn't really the Complete Idiot's fault that he's a complete idiot. His father's an ex-marine who used to beat Frank with a belt even after Frank entered his teens. Frank is dyslexic, but this wasn't diagnosed until high school, so he had to endure years of thinking he was an out-and-out dummy when he was actually suffering from an untreated medical condition. And Shelley has begun to cry.

Louie places his hand atop hers, as though to pat it reassuringly, but soon their fingers intermesh.

"I don't know what I'm *doing* coming here," Shelley declares. "On my honeymoon alone."

The warmth of a female hand is enlivening—liberating and expansionary. Louie's language enters a new domain: "You're on a pilgrimage, my dear. Do you see how it is? We're each launched on a private pilgrimage."

"Maybe nothing like that for me," Shelley says. "Nothing so big. It's the simple truth, I just didn't wanna be laughed at, Louie. Didn't wanna be staying home and people *laughing*. Saying, 'That's the one, she's the girl whose fiancé dumped her at the altar.'"

"Oh well, hell, Shelley, I know about that," Louie says. He could truly advise her, if she'd listen. "Just ask me. I mean I know about that, what it's like feeling everybody *smirking*."

Firm conviction somehow turns his voice shaky. He's on the verge of making another impassioned speech, this one concerning the revelation, born in these disastrous last few months, that no human connection runs deeper than the one forever linking souls once trapped and held in a public scandal. Everyone thinks they understand deep humiliation, but they don't. To inhabit the charged center of a real scandal—the sort that strangers buzz about—is something else again. Louie used to enjoy it when some errant Hollywood royalty, or a Republican politician, met his disgrace under exploding spotlights—Hugh Grant arrested for public sex with a street prostitute, or Senator Larry "Wide Stance" Craig nabbed in an airport men's room. But nowadays that sort of glaring publicity, whatever its target, and however deserved the ridicule might be, conveys associations of such profound misery, there's no joy for Louie in any such downfall. "And the desperation of it," he continues. "The needing to run from it."

"I just hadda get out of Hampden. And I had these tickets. And I wanted to show Frank maybe I could do something *bold*. On my own. He's always teasing me about being such a fraidy-cat. I suppose I am."

"Well, Shelley, I think it took real courage, coming here on your own. You may not like the word *pilgrimage,* but I think we're both showing—"

"I'm certainly a fraidy-cat about driving over bridges, or chipmunks, or eating oysters. Things like that."

"Well, things like *that*—I suppose most people are cowards."

"Frank once offered me twenty dollars to eat a single raw oyster, and of course then I had to do it."

"Can you guess what I ordered in Rome a couple of weeks ago?"

"Except I couldn't. You know, actually *eat* one. Not with it wide open that way, sort of like this great big watery eye staring up at me, full of tears. I mean, who wants to eat a crying eye?"

"Not me," Louie says. "That's always been exactly what I don't want to do."

"Actually, I don't mind chipmunks if they're standing still. But they never are. I honestly think I could pick up a dead one. Provided, you know, it was definitely dead."

Their appetizers arrive. Louie stares at his in glazed befuddlement, having momentarily forgotten his blundering order. It's duck pâté, arriving as a gray parallelogram served with triangular slices of toast, a massive pink-gray onion, and a couple of halved pickles claiming to be cornichons, though half again as large as any cornichon Louie has ever eaten. Shelley—whose tears have evaporated—has been served cheese ravioli in wild mushroom sauce, or maybe mushroom ravioli in wild cheese sauce. "How is it?" he asks.

"Yummy," she says. "Super yummy. How's yours?"

"*Good,*" Louie fires back. In fact, surprisingly, it's pretty tasty. Fortunately, the pâté isn't very flavorful (flavor being a problem with any nonchicken fowl), and if the toast isn't warm, at least it's crisp—unlike toast in the Mulder Arms, which is neither. As a boy, known as quite a picky eater, Louie surprised his stepmother by developing a taste for Oscar Mayer liver sausage, if served with a crunchy iceberg lettuce leaf and French's mustard on white bread with crusts removed. Tonight, ordering the pâté, he'd known what he was doing.

"Louie," Shelley says, "tell me about your wife. And what went wrong."

"Happy to," Louie says, though he isn't. He's done a pretty thorough job, these last few days, of banishing Florence from his brain, and the task of exhuming the whole sorry saga feels onerous. Still, he respins the tale, this time with greater specificity—though again avoiding section 750.338b. Some of the finer points seem lost on Shelley, who apparently is unfamiliar with Oscar Wilde and misses the preposterousness of an Iowan *Importance of Being Earnest*. Other aspects of his story, though, are surprisingly accessible. Not only has she heard of the Virgin Islands, but her uncle Garvin sometimes vacations in Charlotte Amalie. And has promised to take her.

"Email me from there," Louie says. "Think of me: a guy who corresponds with women in the Virgins."

Shelley mops up the last of her mushroom sauce, or cheese sauce, with the last of her dinner roll. Delicious though it is, Louie is finding his own appetizer too rich, and he pushes the plate aside with one whittled trapezoid of pâté remaining. He follows Shelley's example and orders a Chardonnay, whose puckery tartness is refreshing.

"Actually," Louie says, "I feel funny talking so personally about Florence." He pauses. He appreciates Shelley's lack of immediate reassurance. She merely stares at him, interested and sympathetic. Louie says something he knows he is volunteering only under the influence of two cosmopolitans and a little wine: "I don't know why, but it's like you're one of my students, and I honestly don't talk to my students about my personal life. I mean, why am I talking intimately about my marriage? Is it because you're on your honeymoon?"

There's a winsome skew logic to Shelley's response: "If you can't talk to me intimately when I'm on my honeymoon, when can you?"

"Okay." Louie sips again. "O-kay." He might almost be in a shrink's office, rather than in a Californian London restaurant, when he replies, "I mean, what roles are we playing here? Are you my Romantic Counselor?"

"Sure I am, Louie," Shelley croons, and her limpid eyes have picked up every stray light-lick in this dark room: "I'm Shelley Pfister, your Romantic Counselor."

"Well, in that case, Counselor," Louie says, embroiling himself yet more deeply, "let me tell you about my first wife, Lizzie."

Some of this information, too, was supplied earlier in the day, though it seems a week since he first met Shelley Pfister in Simon and Paul's. Louie dredges it all up, amplifying and embellishing: Lizzie's birth here in England; her childhood in Michigan's flat Thumb; their meeting in college, at Kalamazoo; their semi-separation afterward, when he headed off to Ann Arbor and grad school and Lizzie took an office job in Midland; their marriage in '94, when both were twenty-three; Lizzie's decision to apply to law school; their year as grad students in Ann Arbor, with Louie casting about for a thesis topic and Lizzie beginning to despise anything connected with the law . . . While Louie chronicles these milestones, he fears he lacks Shelley's full attention. She seems preoccupied. She seems in fact distracted by his pâté. Or is he being overly sensitive? Is this paranoia: to be suspecting he's in competition with some discarded chopped liver, and he isn't winning?

Everything clarifies when another black-wrapped waiter-in-mourning comes to remove their appetizers, his motions respectful and lugubrious, as if the plates bore bodies of the fallen. "Louie, you going to eat that?" Shelley interposes.

"Oh, please." He nudges the plate toward her.

"I did just want to taste it . . ." And on her brow a crease of anxiety dissolves. She has been worrying that some rare English delicacy would elude her forever.

"Oh, Louie, this is so really *good*!"

Louie with recovered dignity resumes his narration. Lizzie's flight from law school and return to employment in U of M's development office. Her dawning wish for a child. His own wish not to conceive of conceiving until his career was in place. His feeling stuck. Her feeling stuck. Her growing resentful silence, his restlessness . . . "She was unhappy and I let her down."

"How did you let her down, Louie?"

After a pause, deliberately ignoring the more spectacular ways he let Lizzie down, Louie says, "I didn't give her enough support. She had low self-esteem, and I didn't help with that."

Shelley's reply shouldn't be unexpected, but even so it flummoxes him: "What do you mean, low self-esteem?"

It's no easy thing to describe, actually. "Well," Louie says. "There was no reason for it. Here she is, this extremely intelligent young woman, and very pretty, but she lacks confidence, and I failed to help. You know, the fact is she hated her own body."

"What woman doesn't?" Shelley says.

Louie says, "How do you mean?"

"It's breeded right into you, Louie. The whole thing's telling you your body's wrong."

"What do you mean, the whole thing?"

Shelley pauses to consider, and a faraway look suffuses her face. Her slightly squinting eyes grow focused but remote, as though peering out across panoramic tracts at something on the horizon. Then she returns to him, proclaiming with etched bitterness: "The whole world. Society." She adds, virulently, "*Every* TV show, *every* magazine, *every* billboard, the whole thing's telling you your body's wrong."

Just then, their second courses arrive. Louie's truffled eggplant pasta actually looks appealing. He loves the jade-green hue that sautéed eggplant sometimes assumes. The small cubes have been stirred right into the pasta. Louie has been worrying that his eggplant would come at him nakedly, so to speak; he doesn't like looking at the seeds. Something brighter green than the eggplant and airier has been liberally strewn atop—parsley or cilantro. Shelley has ordered meat lasagna. "The plate is so *big*," she says, which is an indirect form of fretting that the portion's too small. Her lasagna is a compact steaming red block on a black-and-mustard-yellow plate. Moving warily, exuding skepticism, Shelley inserts a tentative forkful into her glossy vermilion mouth.

"How is it?" Louie asks, and Shelley pauses theatrically. Her face acquires a glow, again like a child's at a party. "Honestly, Louie," she announces, "this may be the greatest lasagna I've ever eaten! Honestly. Here, have a bite."

"Oh, I've got plenty of food," Louie protests.

"Butja gotta," Shelley says. She extends a steaming fork toward him and waggles it. "Louie," she adds in her other, hostessy tone, "you have to *sample*."

Louie obligingly drops his lower jaw, and Shelley slips the hovering, laden utensil into his mouth. "Now, that's just delicious," Louie declares. It is. But extremely rich—as if soaked in heavy cream. He says, "It took me a while to understand—that Lizzie didn't like her body. I mean, I thought she was *so pretty*. She'd wander round the kitchen in these fire-engine-red boxers and a sleeveless T-shirt, or in the basement looking for some Halloween decorations in these crazy khaki shorts with about fifty pockets, and I'd think, *So pretty*. But things bothered her nobody else would ever even notice. I mean, one of her feet was a size larger than the other. Did I care? No one'd ever even notice, but boy, it bothered the hell out of Lizzie. She described them as freakish. *Freakish!* And sometimes she'd perspire heavily. Did I care?" To utter this question not once but twice heartens Louie. Isn't it undeniable that on at least a couple of issues he'd been truly decent? "She mostly wouldn't wear white, on account of the sweating. Well, didn't that leave a whole spectrum of colors?"

"The whole thing is designed to make you hate your body," Shelley says. "I mean, if you're a woman. The whole thing."

"I'm sure there's something in that." Somewhat to his surprise, Louie realizes that if Society is culpable in this regard, he himself may be innocent. He may be, for once, on the side of the Good Guys. "It's like it's coming at you with a flowchart, isn't it? Placed on your refrigerator. Saying, 'By God, you better reach *this* weight by *this* date.'"

Louie is expecting further approbation. But Shelley's face shows a thoughtful, wavering expression. She says, "I let him down."

"Who?" Louie says.

So obvious is the answer, Shelley simply ignores the question. "I told him I'd lose five pounds by Valentine's, and I only lost three. I told him I'd lose another five by Tax Day, and I only lost one more, so already I'm six behind the goal. Six behind what I promised. And I told him I'd lose ten more by the wedding, twenty in all, but everything's making me so *jittery,* and I don't seem able to stop, and I don't lose *anything* those last few months—in fact, I probably gain back a couple."

"That's understandable."

"And now I'm left asking myself: Shell-gal, what have you done? What have you done? Would your whole, whole life have been different if you'd laid off the Doritos?"

"That's really quite a question," Louie says. It is. It's a haunting, an immense, question: an inquiry for our times. "I mean, you can't have your life run by a flowchart on your fridge," Louie adds, but even while speaking by fiat he's undergoing stubborn twinges of guilt. He's wondering: Is he being a hypocrite? Because a different perspective is coalescing within. He's seeing things through other eyes—Frank's, who, having anxiously watched his girlfriend gain ten pounds a year for the last two years, from New Year's to New Year's to New Year's, might have started conjecturing about where this trend would take the two of them after, say, a decade or two. Shelley has finished every morsel of her lasagna, and she's begun, unless Louie is sorely mistaken, longingly regarding his eggplant pasta. The *whole thing* that Shelley keeps referring to—Society—indeed may have forged a world where most women hate their bodies, but it's also a world where most people, women and men both, can't or simply won't quit stuffing themselves to bursting, and Frank the marathon bicyclist might well have been thinking, as he went whizzing along, his lean legs rhythmically lifting and plunging, that he didn't want to stop permanently among them.

Louie says, "By the time I was your age, I was already moving toward divorce, and here *you* are, not even getting married. I tell you, you're way ahead of the game."

Admittedly, his logic's muddy, but Louie trusts it will distill if he keeps talking—that given enough words, an idea will emerge. He says, "And now I'm wondering if I had it right the first time. If Lizzie was the *one*. And me just too young to know—to deal maturely. So what I'm saying"—Louie says, relishing a familiar professorial sensation of belatedly rounding toward some apt homiletic conclusion—"is that things play out over time. In six months, Frank may be mentally somewhere else. *You* may be somewhere else. You see, things play out over time."

He reaches across the tabletop and again links fingers. He stares into the woman's eyes. She stares into his. The day's other acts of hand-holding were shows of consolation or approval, but this pulses to a different drum. What is the rhythm? Louie isn't sure, but he suddenly feels good about everything. Shelley has wrapped a pale gray shawl over her shoulders, and in the restaurant's candlelight she looks alluringly pretty.

"I feel weird rattling on like this, all my romantic confusions," Louie says. "But then I say, Why not? Aren't you my Romantic Counselor?"

Shelley purrs, "Sure . . . sure . . ." Then flatly adds: "But this *is* weird."

"This is *weird*," Louie echoes.

"As I say," Louie says, "it may be a question of maturity. Frankly, Frank sounds immature to me. In my opinion."

"Oh *no*," Shelley protests, "Frank's mature. Very mature." She adds, "Except emotionly."

"Precisely," Louie says.

"Emotionly, he has some growing up to do."

It's time to move along, and Louie talks about Annabelle, whom he hasn't heard from in ages—more than twenty-four hours. He's trying to be funny, of course, but Shelley misses the joke. This Michigan woman older even than Louie, working for an animal shelter—what's her connection to Frank and the abandoned wedding? Any topic's relevance is in direct proportion to its distance from Frank and the abandoned wedding. Louie talks about his stepmother, Betty, who shortly after his father's death did such a peculiar thing. She moved to Ari-

zona. She flew out to play housekeeper for her two brothers, temporarily, and then permanently, thereby vanishing from the lives of her
two stepchildren. There was nothing hostile or punitive in the move.
Rather, it was as though, having responsibly seen her adult duties to
completion (husband laid to earth, stepchildren launched into the
outer world), she could finally return to her true, her original family.
As for the children she'd raised for so many years, the unspoken message was: *I am not your mother.* And Louie would have to agree. Any
mother he might acquire in this world must be found elsewhere.

Shelley listens politely but inattentively. Louie then turns, a little
desperate for subject matter, to the "other Louie," hoping to evoke the
poignancy of that superbly coiffed silver-haired man so haunted by
the hunt for perfection, by Mrs. Amanda Peerman and the dream of
flawless dentition. Likewise (on this subject of various Louies), there
was once one who chased the grail of perfect paint—and the unanswered question lurking here is: What is the perfect perfection that
defines the ideal world of that other other other Louie who is himself?
Meanwhile, Shelley's face is again asking: *Why are you telling me this?*

Then Shelley says something surprising. She says, "I feel like I was
a virgin when I first went to bed with Frank."

"You were a virgin when you and Frank first went to bed?"

"Not sexually. But I feel like I was. Do you know what I mean?"

"Sure," Louie says. "Sort of."

"So you could almost say I was a virgin bride."

"Well . . . ," Louie says.

"That's what I was offering. And I ask you, where's he going to get
another virgin bride? Given how slutty and disgusting they all are."

"It's a good question," Louie says.

"He isn't even thinking," Shelley says.

"Evidently."

Louie's garden salad arrives. In the middle lies a small mound of
odd, gray, translucent, disturbing, saclike objects that look like fetal
mice. Then Louie recollects, through a couple of cosmopolitans and
some prosecco and a glass of wine, that his salad comes with macer-

ated fresh figs. *Macerated*—do they have the right word? It sounds like a synonym for pre-chewed. Shelley on the other hand has ordered potato-and-wild-mushroom croquettes. These are accompanied by two copper mini-tureens, one holding a peach-colored sauce and the other an emerald sauce.

"I guess these are for pouring, but I'm wondering about dipping," Shelley says.

"I don't think it matters."

Shelley tries slicing a croquette with a fork, but the crisp brown crust simply collapses and ruptures, and the pale interior squirts out the side. She picks up the croquette. "You think anyone in here minds fingers?"

"I don't think this is a finger-minding place."

"You've gotta try one of these," Shelley says. "They're super scrumptious."

"I'm getting full," Louie says. "And dessert's coming."

There is something endearing and cheering—and just a little dismaying—in how gleefully Shelley vacillates between her two sauces. She hesitates, deliberates, redeliberates, tries one corner of a croquette in one sauce, the other in the other. When the last bite's been consumed, Shelley says, "God when I get back to Baltimore I'm going on a *strict* diet, I mean it, you don't think I'm gonna, but I'm gonna."

"Honey, I'm not doubting you."

"God, Louie, it's so sad. It's so goddamned sad."

"You mean—"

"Life."

"Well, exactly," Louie says. "Life. Exactly. That's the key, isn't it? But it also isn't. I think you have to think about flipping your thinking around. It's like changing a negative sign to a positive sign. You flip it, and then you say, 'Whoa, well, here we are. The two of us. We're having dinner, we're in London, the food is good, the conversation is good, or so I'd like to think, and'"—he takes her hand—"'we're holding hands.'"

"God, Louie, I don't know what I'd done without you . . ."

Desserts arrive (Louie's *pot de crème,* Shelley's steamy bourbon bread pudding), and they eat one-handedly, fingers intertwined. A sense of ease reigns. Wisely, simultaneously, when asked by a passing waiter about Chardonnay rerefills, they demur. Louie talks some more about growing up in Fallen Hills, Shelley about Hampden. Meanwhile, in the little private chapel that the tabletop in the Daily Retreat has become, to the comforting organ strains of a shared blood pulse, lean male palm takes plump female palm as his wedded wife.

Eventually, they clamber into a taxi together, though their hotels lie in contrary directions. They're still holding hands. What God has joined . . . "Tell me about your hotel," Louie says.

"Oh, it's all first class," Shelley says. "Absolutely first. Frank's mother saw to that. It's a Sterling Gall operation."

"A what? Who?" He adds: "Operation?"

"Sterling Gall."

"Who the hell's Sterling Gall?"

"Well, *I* don't know," Shelley says, but her tone suggests that *Louie* ought to. "I guess he's this big huge deal. He owns all these London hotels. He's like some English Donald Trump."

So automatic is Louie's reply, it scarcely grazes his lips. "God, how depressing . . ."

Shelley's tone shifts, turns a bit reedy: "What do you mean?"

Louie retreats a little. "Well, I don't know," he says. "It's just—well—Trump. I mean, how depressing can you get?"

Shelley deliberates for a moment. "Louie," she says, "are you pretentious?"

The question is so unadorned, so earnest—so *un*pretentious—that Louie has no immediate response. Finally he says, "Maybe I am, but I'm just thinking how horrible, truly ghastly, ghastly *horrible,* it would be to wake up one morning and discover you were Donald Trump. Worse than Gregor Samsa. I mean to be absolutely synonymous not *just* with blind crassness and greed but with this—this sort of big-farting, microphoned asininity. And then you think how much *more* horrible it would be to wake up and realize you were just some little British little Trump wannabe."

And Shelley says, "I didn't realize it before now, but you know, Louie, you've got a nasty side."

Louie laughs. "Maybe not *so* nasty. But I am cultivating it."

Outside their taxi, blocks of office buildings flicker by on sliding panels. London itself intricately encircles the two displaced Americans, colossal concentric ring upon ring. Whenever he leaves Ann Arbor for some metropolis—Paris, New York, Houston, Cleveland, it doesn't matter which—it's often the office buildings that most stir and affect Louie, particularly at night. Not the compact yet soaring Eiffel Tower, or a glimpse of a spotlit Statue of Liberty, or the glowing dome of the Capitol, but the cheap anonymous glass boxes, the seemingly random distributions of lights where people are working late. A lifetime in academia has left Louie with multiple misgivings about never having held a real job. He wonders about paths not taken. Even back at the start, a fresh college graduate, he was never going to become a coal miner in Appalachia, or a cowhand in Wyoming, or for that matter a spot-welder in Detroit, but he plausibly might have wound up in a glass box, laboring for some corporate counterpart to his father's Universal Colorfast. It's all imaginable, some modest office on the sixteenth floor, the twenty-seventh floor, sweating at midnight over the Billingsgate merger, the Singapore account . . . Shelley says, "Wouldja have one more drink? At the hotel? I want to share the view. There's a bar at the very top."

"I shouldn't. But just one," Louie says. He says, "So I'll be seeing you tomorrow?"

"Of course," Shelley says.

"What do you want to do? Whatcha want to see? Just tell me whatcha wanna see and I'll be your trusty guide."

"I don't know, Louie."

"Well, wouldja like me to plan your day? F'you want, I'll plan your whole day."

"That's what I want, Louie," Shelley says. "Plan my whole day."

The words reverberate, truly; they set up an ambitious low hum down there in his crotch, as if Shelley has uttered some shameless, wanton proposition. Her request emerges as one of the most carnally enthralling invitations Louie has ever heard: *Plan my whole day.* No suitable response exists except to kiss her at last, time and again. At one point he stops and says, "I'm French-kissing my Romantic Counselor," and the two giggle into each other's faces, kiss again. They wind up kissing all the way to the Excelsior Palace, where a penthouse bar awaits.

"YOUR FEET'LL BE OKAY?"

"My feet?"

"It'll be a fair amount of walking."

"Oh, these are great. Super comfy."

Shelley's legs are crossed. She dangles an ankle to show off what are actually quite attractive tan-and-red woven sandals. Louie has already noticed the bigness of her feet, but her ankles' slender shapeliness comes as a surprise. They're seated side by side on a new train that looks less like a train than a subway car. Her toenails are polished bubble-gum pink. The sandals look deliciously overstuffed. She's quite a captivating sight this morning.

They're on the 9:25 express to Cambridge, having met at 9:00 at King's Cross. Shelley's wearing cuffed khaki slacks, a white cotton turtleneck, a plaid windbreaker. She looks sporty and scrubbed, and the joy he'd felt as she came solidly bouncing toward him across the station was hearteningly unambivalent.

He'd admired the cool, chaste set of her cheek as they kissed, her wordlessly communicating a wish to overlook all that frenzied necking in last night's taxi. Those had been hot, pulsing, sloppy, tooth-tapping, lovely kisses. But this was a new morning, and intricate proprieties have blossomed overnight. Louie's amenable. Whatever approach she wants, it's all fine, all playable. Here is a boon, a pure bounty: on his vacation, a graying forty-three-year-old Louie Hake winds up sight-seeing with a pretty girl who is still—for another month yet—in her twenties. And the skittish English sun is shining boldly, racily.

He admires, too, her mature directness in confronting his tangled personal issues. She says, "Ja look at your email, Louie?" And when he says, "I had eighteen emails," she says, "Anything important?" And when he says, "What do you mean important?" she says, sweetly zeroing in, "Anything from Florence? Or Lizzie?"

"No, nothing more from Florence," Louie says. "Though I'm not expecting anything. And sort of hoping I *don't*. Don't get anything. I wrote her such a nutty crazy letter, I'm praying things'll just calm down. I'm hoping she'll ignore me."

"And Lizzie?" Shelley presses.

"No, nothing yet, though I'd like to hear from *her*."

"To hear what, Louie? What is it you want?"

What is it he wants?

Their train bundles along. It takes longer these days to tug free of London's exurbs into farmers' fields and traditional countryside. Meanwhile, he reveals to Shelley the contents of his lightweight nylon sack: two water bottles and two chocolate croissants. "Yum," she says, and adds, "Aren't you the clever professor . . ."

The sky is full of loose, baggy clouds that Constable might have painted, silver-gray, silky gray. In Italy, on a sweat-thickened afternoon that now seems quite faraway, Louie rode a train back from Florence to Rome through landscapes Raphael might have painted.

What is it he wants? Louie's grateful for her question. Though a stranger, or a relative stranger, Shelley is (he must keep in mind) offering almost the finest gift a stranger can offer you: a heartfelt interest in the twists and turnings of your life. It's the highest of compliments: a patient and painstaking listener.

According her question the solemnity it deserves, then, Louie takes his time. He sips from his water bottle and says, "When this trip's all over, and I'm back in the States, I guess I'd like to sit down with

Lizzie, talk things over. Explore our possibilities, the various connections that maybe once didn't seem so important but are. It takes so many years to puzzle things out. You're so young, Shelley," Louie says. "Hell, you're younger than the age I was when Lizzie and I came here the last time. Twelve years ago. Just imagine sitting down with Frank twelve years from now. Imagine twelve years ago. You were what—seventeen?"

"I really *was* a virgin."

Louie winces at the stridency of her laughter, which doesn't sound like her—which sounds peculiarly middle-aged: the barroom bray of some aging gal showing the world she still knows how to have a good time.

The train thumps and clatters. Cambridge announces its imminent arrival through a scatter of "tech centers." Cambridge was never a town he knew well, and he hasn't seen it in a dozen years, but he knows it well enough, surely, to guide Shelley Pfister around. The two of them climb into a taxi outside the station, and Louie says, "To the gate of Saint John's, please." But traffic clogs, then slows to a near standstill, and Louie asks to be let out. They disembark before a closed restaurant whose name, Louie is a little distressed to see, is Oenothèque. It bills itself as "a bit better bistro." He remembers Cambridge as a town where a diner's choices divided between roast beef and plaice.

"O-enothèque," Shelley says, sounding the initial vowel. "Means wine, right?"

"Exactly," Louie says. "We'll have some with lunch. Remember, I'm taking you to lunch."

They wander onto the beautiful grounds of Emmanuel College, and Shelley gives him a sharp nudge on spotting somebody in an academic gown. She could be pointing out a mandrill or a peacock at the zoo: glimpsed through Shelley's eyes, the stooped frizzily white-haired bespectacled don is an exotic and likable and faintly preposterous creature.

Shelley's a tonic presence. While her taste is catholic, it's also irresistibly effusive—everything is "amazing" and "awesome." If he pauses to examine, so far, his elaborate Journey, Louie must concede that all too many bright and promising sightseeing ventures have turned weighty and dutiful. But not today. Shelley has never seen anything like this! Louie, having some familiarity with the architectural brand, in a sense knew Cambridge before ever arriving here. He'd seen Collegiate Gothic both at Michigan State and the U of M Law School, where Lizzie spent her one disillusioning year. But Shelley standing before King's College might just as well be contemplating minarets, ziggurats, torii. She is beholding the Blue Mosque and the Taj Mahal and Ginkakuji all in the same morning.

The chapel of King's is open to visitors, but the grounds are closed. Brief conversation with a porter reveals that many, or most, of the colleges are closed to the public today—closed for May Balls, for end-of-term activities, perhaps for the pleasure of asserting their own exclusivity.

Rubens has never been a touchstone of Louie's, but the *Adoration of the Magi* altarpiece, its golden palette rotating around the luxurious drape of a Magus's cardinal-orange robe, is a beautiful thing. (He'd had a professor at U of M, the gay, gangly, celebrated Matthew Burdon, who claimed that Rubens was a small principality bordering on Flanders, since no individual could have produced so many gigantic canvases; and charming Matthew was denied tenure and—so Louie last heard—entered his father's home insulation business in Omaha.)

Well, Louie has stories that might amuse Shelley and others that would leave her clueless, and it's the mark of a pedant not to note the difference, but Louie does. It turns out Shelley never finished college. She did a year and a half at Towson State, but saw no point in squandering her parents' money when she "wasn't all that into studying." She speaks wistfully of going back for her degree. To Louie's jaded academic ear this sounds sentimental—though probably it's just the flipside of the sentimentalizing he'd extend to the employees of an auto-body shop.

He has been leading Shelley in a broad semicircle, whose terminus is to be the Fitzwilliam Museum, even as he frets that its dusty galleries might strike her as precious and rarefied. But quite the opposite, it turns out. Everything at the Fitzwilliam is "awesome" and "amazing." He doesn't know when he last so enjoyed a museum. He's seeing art through a new pair of eyes. *Now that's just amazing . . .* The amazing Edward Lear *Temple of Apollo*, Ruisdael's amazing view of Amsterdam, the amazing Rembrandt. *This is so awesome . . .* The awesome Egyptian sarcophagi, the bust of Hadrian's male lover, the erotic Roman vases.

"Didn't they actually invent all of that?" Shelley asks, mischief in her eyes. "The Romans?"

"All of what?" Louie asks innocently, extending his own mischief.

"The gay stuff."

"I'm not sure about *invent . . .*" He hears a voice, the wily, seductive Roman bartender: *The Italians are an amazing race.* "Maybe you mean *perfected*?"

At another point Shelley says, of a Poussin, "That's a lovely red," and Louie says, "You can probably thank a ton of Mexican beetles for that," and Shelley says, "Mexican beetles?"

"They brought a fresh red to the painter's palette. Cochineal. That's the name of the color: cochineal. Jillions of these crushed-up beetles. The Spanish conquistadores went in search of gold and found something better: a brand-new red." And Louie, in the midst of his teacherly exhilaration, is brushed by that special poignancy attached to a lost vocation: the notion that had things broken a little differently, he'd have ended up a respected professor in a respected university.

"I never realized there was so much to see in a museum," Shelley says. She says, "You're the best guide of all, Louie."

And perhaps the best guy? His blood, circulating closer to his skin than usual, bubbles with pleasure. The forty-five minutes allotted to the museum turn into an hour and a half. Suddenly, two o'clock approaches, and he has no plans for lunch. Louie takes Shelley by the arm and leads her into the first pub they encounter, called the Stolen Hour. They're led to a wooden booth the welcoming color of caramel corn.

Shelley says she might want a salad and Louie explains what a ploughman's lunch is and Shelley (perhaps demonstrating that she doesn't always choose the most caloric item on the menu) says, *Perfect.* Louie settles on shepherd's pie for himself, partly to introduce her to another typical pub meal. He says, "Beer often goes best with this food, but I promised wine, so I'm happy with wine," and Shelley votes for beer.

Straightforward enough, it would seem. But conveying their order to their tall and scrawny waitress is a challenge. She's a mere kid— maybe still in her teens—whose long lank black hair drapes half her face, Veronica Lake–style. She's blanched and bleary eyed—at least her one exposed eye is. From her pierced nostril depends a toy of a toy: the smallest marble Louie has ever seen. It's a purple cat's-eye. Louie asks for two pints of bitter, a ploughman's lunch, and a shepherd's pie, and she peers at him as though he were speaking an impenetrable dialect. A pause extends. The cat's-eye trembles. Louie gamely repeats the order, and she wanders off without volunteering any sign of comprehension.

"Is she on drugs?" Shelley wonders.

"She may be. Or she's studying theater. It's a big theater scene in Cambridge."

"When did your wife get interested in theater, Louie?"

"My wife?" Louie has to think for a moment. "Well, I don't know if the Pyrographic Theatre Company qualifies as theater. It is self-*expression.*"

"We don't have to go into it . . ."

Again Louie is struck by the maturity of Shelley's tone. She makes his own voice echo as petty and carping. "Do you like theater?" he asks her.

"I saw *The Lion King* in New York." This time, though Louie has a moment to prepare, her words nettle him: "It was deeply awesome."

"I'll bet."

"And Frank and I saw *The Streetcar Named Desire*. Jever see it?"

"A couple of times."

"You know what Frank said about it?" Shelley chuckles appreciatively. And although Louie is primed to dismiss the Idiot utterly, Frank's quoted observation emerges as weirdly, paradoxically trenchant: "He said, 'I wish they'd settled their arguments before we got to the theater.'"

Professor Hake can't quite help himself. "Actually, there's something pretty astute in that," he observes. "About the fundamental nature of theater," he observes. "You see, I mean, the play *can* begin at any point."

Their beers have arrived, and Shelley sips deeply. "Oh, he's a complete idiot," she says.

"Well, let's just say he made a terrible mistake about the wedding."

"But there's nothing wrong with loving a complete idiot," Shelley says, and over the wet rim of her uplifted glass her wet eyes glisten.

"Maybe there's nothing wrong with loving anybody," Louie says, not having anything else to say.

"That's just so right, Louie," Shelley says.

Score another point for Professor Hake. If she had a pen in hand, she might jot down his observation.

Meanwhile, Louie obliquely studies the young waitress. Her jet-black, presumably dyed hair has been carefully pinned so that her right eye is never revealed. What a thing to do: to give up binocular vision and make yourself a sort of Cyclops (though a Cyclops with a child's purple marble dangling from your septum). Louie recalls an AAC student, Ira Havira, whose face *bristled*. Louie regards himself as youthful, and yet this particular impulse that his students find irresistible (*I'd pay good money to have someone shove metal rods through various spots on my body that are particularly sensitive*) leaves him feeling old and baffled.

Shelley revels in her ploughman's lunch. "It's amazing cheese. Is this real English cheddar?"

"I suppose so."

"It tastes different," she says. "Better."

Still, the arrival of his shepherd's pie, steaming briskly under its crisped golden crust of potato, captivates her. So avid is Shelley's gaze as Louie delicately pricks it with his fork that he feels it only polite to offer her the initial bite.

"No, no, no," she protests. "You first."

So Louie takes the first bite, but he gives her the second, the third, the fourth. "That is also so amazing," Shelley says. She really does have an easy, beautiful smile.

"You always know just what to order," Shelley says, scarcely knowing how her words must tickle him. He isn't about to confide Florence's constant complaint: *You'd rather sit at the kids' table.* In truth, Florence had no idea how accurate this was. He concealed from her, concealed from everybody, how at dinner parties, pretending to seek a bathroom, he'd swing past wherever the children had eaten and filch an inch of hot dog, a ketchup-softened fish finger, a couple of ruptured tortellini. Meanwhile, the adults would be dining on some recipe pulled from the *New York Times:* pork loin with pumpkin-seed coulis, scallops with fig reduction, beet-and-quinoa loaf. But why, when no one was compelling them to do so, *why* did so-called grown-ups subject themselves to stuff like that? Why *reduce* figs when with surprisingly little effort you could eliminate them altogether?

In Louie's middle-class America, laden with well-stocked pantries, food oughtn't to be a problem—yet for him it always was. He'd been hurt when Florence ridiculed his childish palate. But, to be honest, he'd been disturbed, too, at Lizzie's treating him like an invalid, as if his "food requirements" were fatal allergies.

Louie and Shelley drink their beer, eat their lunches. They trade plates, trade back. Casually. Louie is neither child nor invalid. He's a forty-three-year-old man dining with an attractive new date, picking his way skillfully through one cuisine after another. Conversation has a warm, unforced, trustingly undirected feeling, as though they've known each other for a couple of years rather than a couple of days. Louie's talk drifts from Annabelle to Fallen Hills and that haunting image of his stepmother one Christmas morning, holding up her big new alarm clock in her big fist and demanding of it, *Are you deaf? Are you deaf?*

"That sounds crazy," Shelley says.

"Well, in a way it is. I wrote about her in a paper in college."

"You wrote about your *stepmother*?"

"In an anthropology course. I was a freshman and I'd come upon a new idea—new to me—called magical thinking. It doesn't mean maybe what it sounds like. It's a technical term. It's very common in so-called primitive societies, where you think inanimate things think. And you think your thinking can influence inanimate things. So if you talk to a river, you can keep it from flooding. Or you talk to the ground to prevent earthquakes. And suddenly I realized it: this was my stepmother to a T. I once saw her open the fridge and a Granny Smith apple fell onto the floor, and she swore at it and said, 'Okay, you love the floor so much, you can just *stay* there.' Do you see what I'm saying? The woman was *punishing* it, punishing an *apple*. She was always threatening toasters and electric can openers and windshield wipers. And it was all so *exciting*," Louie rattles on. "Here was an anthropology course, but it was telling me not about some remote tribe in South America or New Guinea but the household I grew up in! Do you see what I'm saying? Even anthropology, the study of mankind, was *relevant*. Books could explain your life. I sometimes think this was the moment I became an academic." Louie stops himself from appending, *If you can call me an academic,* and stares at Shelley in flushed, flustered embarrassment.

Her reply is perfect: "I like you, Louie," she says.

He is encouraged to add, "Speaking of crazy thinking, there's something you ought to know. About me. Something I should've mentioned much earlier." Then halts in amusement. It's a peculiar thing to say to somebody you met just yesterday. "Anyway, I'm bipolar. Or that's how I was diagnosed ten years ago. There's no history of it in my family, incidentally. Though my father did drop a couple hints that my mother, my real mother, might have been—unstable?"

"She died?"

"Elvira. When I was two. I don't remember her, and dad rarely spoke of her. I've wondered about that, why he spoke of her so rarely. And why he married my stepmother, who's not really a bad person. But she's this large *presence,* I mean psychologically, and also physically, and I've wondered whether she was a way for him, for my father, to block out the past.

"Actually," Louie goes on, "I have my theories about bipolarism. Actually, I'm wondering about misdiagnosis, or maybe it's something I've outgrown? Because I went off my lithium a couple of weeks ago, and I think I'm doing okay. Am I doing okay?"

"You're doing *fine,* Louie."

"I don't seem crazy to you?"

For a second or two uncertainty rumples Shelley's round, ingenuous features, but when her face clears, it clears comprehensively. She says, "Much less crazy than me. Here's me on my honeymoon, having lunch with a man I met yesterday."

"And here's me on your honeymoon, having lunch with a woman I met yesterday."

So far, throughout this very pleasant and thrilling day, there has been an assortment of little touchings—nudgings, tappings, upper-arm squeezes, hip grazings—but nothing direct and decisive. Now Shelley reaches across the table and, firmly, takes his hand. Physically picking up, perhaps, from where they left off in last night's taxi.

AFTER LUNCH HE LEADS HER BACK TO HEFFERS BOOKS, which to Louie's relief looks mostly unchanged. Then toward the river. They stop on a stone bridge and lean out over the water. "Look! Are those gondolas?" Shelley inquires.

Somehow her sounding doubly mistaken—she pronounces the word *gonDOHlas*—compels him again to take her hand; such inexperience begs protection. "Punts," Louie says.

"Like in the movies," Shelley says.

"Like in life," Louie continues. "Punts have been around forever. They were real things, useful things. All this was fens. You know, swampland."

"I didn't really know what England would be like."

"But what's it like? I'm trying to figure that out myself."

"I don't know, but not what I thought."

"What you're saying is, you need more traveling."

"I don't know, Louie. I can't imagine doing what you're doing."

"Which is?"

"Going round the world. By yourself."

Though she's praising him, Shelley's words release across the landscape a big, blotting shadow; some scheming black cloud, quick for all its magnitude, has come skidding between Louie and the sun. He says, knowledgeably, "Well, you have to wait till the time's right." He adds, "And I meet people on the way. Look, I met you, didn't I?"

"Do you think it's weird we're here?"

"I do. But look at it in a certain light, it's weird being anywhere, *anyone's* being anywhere. I mean, it's weird that Cambridge exists. Weird that *Homo sapiens* won the gene lottery and took over the planet."

"If you met me in a bar, d'you think we'd have anything to talk about?"

"I'm not very good at talking to any strange woman in a bar."

"Louie, that's not what I mean!" With her free hand—the one he isn't holding—Shelley models a fist and slugs him in the upper arm, a sweet blow delivering a concussive message of their having achieved, in twenty-four hours, a healthy bantering give-and-take relationship. He's to be teased for his pedantic locutions. And he likes being teased in this way. "I mean you and *me,* Louie. In a bar. In *Bal*timore. Talking. Would we be able to communicate?"

"Probably not very well," Louie concedes.

"And yet here we are! Talking. Talking just fine. Aren't we talking just fine?"

"We're talking just fine, Shell-gal."

"We're standing on a bridge in *England,* beside all these ancient *buildings,* and you and I are talking just fine. How can you tell me this isn't weird?"

And aren't they saying the same thing? Haven't they already reached high common ground? Through the upper reaches of Louie's chest a gratitude almost as light winged as love goes whirring. His lungs expand, and he takes Shelley's other hand—the one that freshly punched his upper arm—and with both of her hands bound up, he leans forward and kisses her plump lips decisively, while beneath their joined heads a storied river flickers and flows. For a moment the two of them are standing on a bridge over the Cam, kissing.

And these are transportive kisses. The two of them are on a bridge in *England,* but they're also in a fire-warmed lair, or den, inveigled, locked away from all strangers' eyes, nakedly wrapped in animal skins, and when they kiss, jawbones lock. And when the kiss breaks, adhesively, the impress of Shelley's lips on his lips lingers, tingles, tickles. The sensation accompanies him across the bridge and onto the other bank. "These are called the Backs," buzzing-lipped Louie says. "You know, the backs of the colleges."

He has been worrying that, after so much foregrounded magnificence, this walk might appear distant and anticlimactic. But the views are breathtaking. The two of them hold hands. (Her hand is the same size as his—or bigger.) Slowly the light is clarifying as the day progresses. Again, he's reminded of Constable: the celebrated, majestic painting of King's College that must have been executed right here. Trinity and King's and Clare, tower and spire and chimney intercept and distribute the sunlight equally. Is there, anywhere in the world, a more striking panorama of the pure, aspirant nature of university life? (What would its gowned dons make of the prefab modules of Ann Arbor College?) It's a view that inspires Shelley Pfister, who completed only three semesters at Towson State, to loftier diction: "Louie, this is so deeply awesome. Don't you just feel—the elevation of it all?"

Though she assured him, at the long-ago outset of their day, that her sandals were "super comfy," her feet have blistered. Louie discovers this only when they finally settle into the return train. She pops off her sandals. There's a painful-looking red patch on her right heel, with a pearl-pale oval rising in the middle. But Shelley seems admirably indifferent to it. This wouldn't have been true of either Florence or Lizzie, who for all their dissimilarities shared a tendency to fuss over trifling discomforts. Shelley's big plump bare feet with their bubble-gum-pink toenails have a childish look mirrored by her face's simple grateful neediness as she nestles her head on his shoulder. She crosses her shapely ankles. She's sound asleep by the time the train pulls into King's Cross.

She wakes, too, like a child, out of mysterious soundings, with a thorough disorientation that rapidly shifts into bright-eyed alertness. "We're home," she says.

"Back in London," Louie says.

"And what's next, Louie?" *Plan my whole day . . .*

"Next, we get a cab and climb out when we spot a pharmacy selling Band-Aids. And then I'll take you to dinner."

Though it's after nine, night has not fully fallen over London by the time the two of them wind up on a park bench in Soho Square, with Louie holding a paper bag containing "plasters." He'd forgotten the English term. There's a motley crowd in the park—dog walkers, old folks, desiccated-looking drunks, luckless parents of sleepless children—but the two of them find an empty bench. Shelley slips off her right sandal and plops in his lap her bare foot, musky with sweat. She takes it for granted that Louie will apply her Band-Aid, and this juvenile assumption pleases him. Over the years he has rarely found himself in a parental role. In childhood, Annabelle often played supervisory Mother to Louie's hapless Son. But Louie, back then, hadn't had anyone to oversee except Ordie, the family's unimaginative Welsh terrier, who resisted games of make-believe. (The name was short for

Ordinary—another of the *pater*'s little witticisms that Louie smiles at to this day.)

An inch of liquid remains in Louie's water bottle, as if he'd reserved some for first aid. He wets the sleeve of his shirt and swabs her wounded ankle, then dries her skin with the other sleeve. The plaster goes on with a pleasingly snug stretchiness. Louie kisses his fingertips and applies them to the bandaged wound. "All better?"

"All better."

Shelley shifts, seeking to remove the foot, but Louie holds on tight. He likes the ample weighted sweetly odorous expanse of it in his lap. "It stays so light here!" she cries. "I can't believe it's still light," she says.

"It's marvelous light."

"Yes," she sighs, sounding distracted and faraway. When she echoes him, it's as if she has misheard him: "Yes, magical light."

"We're quite far north. Significantly north."

"Louie, can you *believe* the light?"

Here in the dusk glow, in this modest green enclave in the heart of this vast gray city, her words levitate; the exclaimed syllables hover just over their heads. "We're actually a good ways north of Quebec," Louie reports. "We're on a latitude with the southern edge of Hudson Bay."

"That right?" Shelley says, and adds, wholly missing the point: "I've never been there." The point is that the southern rim of Hudson Bay is a location any American would likely consider extreme north—hundreds of miles above the southern shore of Lake Superior, say, which is Louie's own northernmost foray in the Americas. "It belongs to the polar bears," Louie replies.

"And we're in London, England," Shelley finishes. "*It* belongs to us."

"I like that," Louie says, and finds he does. Yes. *It* belongs to us.

After some wandering through Soho, whose pubs have overspilled into the streets, mostly in the form of clamorously tattooed men in T-shirts downing pints of beer on the narrow sidewalks, the two of them drift across Shaftesbury and soon find themselves before an Indonesian restaurant called Catamaran. Beside the entrance stands a chalkboard sign whose unqualified claim charms Louie: ONLY AUTHENTIC RIJSTTAFEL. "Do you like Indonesian food?"

"I've never had it, but I'm sure I do."

Shelley's expression is at once cheery, modest, and assessive. She's asking whether he understands her whimsical, self-disparaging sense of humor. He does. The two of them have achieved, with remarkable swiftness and accommodation, all sorts of linkages opening onto other linkages.

"Rijsttafel," Louie says as he imagines a Dutchman might pronounce it, with a rolled *r* and an *a* so soft and low in the throat as almost to become a long *o*. It's nearly the only word Louie knows in Dutch, and it pleases the professor to offer it: "It means rice table."

Louie harbors a veteran prejudice against Asian cooks, who even more than Europeans will use sauces to conceal nasty and unpredictable surprises; if you don't watch them, they'll serve you ingredients for which there aren't even legitimate English names. Still, he has had a number of likable curries in his life, and he loves both coconut cake and mango ice cream. In addition, there's the delicious irony that Shelley seems to regard him as some sort of gastronomic adventurer. He finds himself saying, "Let's go in."

The restaurant turns out to be big and dark and reasonably quiet. "Pretty," Shelley says. "Really pretty."

Louie looks around approvingly. Catamaran has the sort of low, recessed lighting he prefers. In the middle of the large room stands a broad bar whose base, a sort of dado/palisade, is lined with vertically halved green bamboo trunks. High above the bar hangs a spotlit model—maybe eight feet long—of a primitive sailing craft. "That explains the restaurant's name," Louie says. It's a kind of doubled, lashed-together canoe. Within it, a number of doll-sized figures—shirtless, black haired, brown skinned—hunch over their paddles. "It's called a catamaran."

For the first time, pupil looks at professor a little skeptically. "But that's not a regular catamaran," Shelley says.

"What do you mean?" Louie says.

"Frank's uncle had a catamaran. With this gigantic huge loud motor. Nothing like that."

"Well, no doubt it's the same design." Admittedly, Louie knows nothing of boats, navigation. He amplifies: "The same design principles."

The menu, too, affirms his ignorance—so many peculiar words and unfamiliar ingredients. He feels a little internal sharp-pronged poke of panic at the thought that soon, for the first time, he'll be in Asia. *Mee bakso, siomay, gado gado, kelapa muda* . . . It isn't merely that these menu terms are alien. But the words look so highly contrived and artificial, like some schoolkid's rendering of the babble an Asian island people might be expected to produce. *Mee bakso?* Louie decisively claps his menu shut. "We're both going to have rijsttafel," he announces. "That way we get a little everything. And beer. I'd recommend beer with this sort of food."

"I'm having a Duskcutter."

"And what in hell's a Duskcutter?" Louie says.

"It's the house-preferred cocktail."

"And I'm having one, too."

When eventually the drinks arrive, not even the restaurant's lenient lighting can make them look anything but disturbingly eccentric—unearthly.

"I don't know what would make any drink this color," Louie says. "Other than lapis lazuli." They're an icy, jolting blue.

And again Shelley volunteers an unexpected knowledge nugget: "It's usually curaçao makes them blue."

"How do you know these things?"

"I don't know—maybe too much time spent in bars?" Shelley's gusher of a laugh, far more proud than apologetic, likewise discomposes Louie.

"I would think curaçao would be something you'd drink in a Caribbean restaurant," he observes, still clinging to the rational notion that some basic familiarity with geography—with the whereabouts of human knowledge and experience—ought to assist in such discussions. But even as, playing the pedagogue, he offers up his little datum, he recognizes how nugatory it is. California, the Caribbean, the Pacific, the Indian Ocean, the Virgin Islands—these days such places are interchangeable and contiguous. For it's all becoming a single exclusive promenade of sandy beach, overseen by Donald Trump and Sterling Gall. And either you're one of the executive elite, strolling along the beach, or you're not . . .

Food is slow to arrive but keeps coming when it starts coming. Everything is awesome, and amazing. Their quite attractive, dark-skinned, lank-haired, presumably Indonesian waitress offers extensive, ranging commentaries over each dish. So far as he knows, Louie's hearing has not yet begun to go (unlike his vision), but he can isolate few meaningful syllables. The restaurant, growing crowded, floats on a surf of contented chatter. Louie makes a point of not inquiring what's in his cocktail, but when Shelley orders a second, he follows suit.

The waitress's comments being unintelligible, Shelley eagerly opens her menu and begins playing matchup with the long catalog of rijsttafel components. "Now *these* are shrimp crackers, right? . . . I bet this is chili relish . . . These have *got* to be egg rolls . . . I'm guessing this is a beef-and-potato fritter. Now this one we know for sure: this is white rice . . ." Louie meanwhile has grown somewhat distracted by a guy at the bar. Louie has decided, for the purpose of intensifying the guy's unlikability, that he's a hedge-fund manager in the City. Perched languorously, lankily, on his barstool, apparently drinking Scotch, he's disturbingly good-looking. This is what Louie keeps reading and keeps hoping isn't true: that London, no less than New York, is overrun by these people, whom Louie used to call yuppies but doesn't really have a word for anymore, ordering up their thirty-bucks-a-shot single malts, and *Oh, yes, another bottle of the Chez Parvenu . . .* What makes this particular hedge-fund manager all the more irritating is that he's wearing such a well-cut, splendid suit. In the restaurant's dim ruddy light the suit is slate gray with the faintest thrumming hint, all but subliminal, perhaps essentially imaginary, of a cerulean under-glow. Louie would feel much better about life if the guy were wearing some thuggish pinstriped sharkskin. Meanwhile, over the hedge-fund manager's head, over the heads of all the boisterous topers at the bar, the hunched, workaday homunculi go on plowing their unseen and illimitable sea. It may be that the Duskcutters are stronger than Louie initially perceived.

"You taste coconut? I think this has got to be the yellow rice cooked in coconut milk."

"You're leaving tomorrow. I wish you weren't leaving tomorrow," Louie says.

There's something bracing in the speed and fullness of Shelley's shift of attention, from the food outspread before her to Louie's face. "Where did you go on your honeymoons, Louie?" his Miss Bright Eyes inquires.

"Well, Florence and I hardly had one. We flew out to LA, planning some big drive up the West Coast. But it got shortened because she got this really nasty stomach bug. It was nobody's fault, though in retrospect it seems prophetic. Being with me made her sick. But Lizzie? Well, we came here."

"Here?"

"To London."

"To London? To *London*?" Shelley's wide eyes widen. "Louie, you mentioned being here with her, but not it was your *honey*moon!"

"I didn't?" He hadn't? "Well, it was."

"So you've had *two* London honeymoons."

"Two?"

"Counting the one we're on now, d-darling."

Louie appreciates Shelley all the better for her near stammer over the endearment. She goes on: "You do know you made all the difference? Now I can go home and honestly tell everybody I had this seriously fabulous time in England. And I won't be lying! I can tell them everything I saw, and ate, the paintings, the food, shepherd's pie, the colleges just like castles, shrimp crackers, Leonardo da Vinci, yellow coconut rice . . ."

Louie fears she'll take offense, missing the humor in what he longs to say. He says it anyway: "Hey, Shell-gal, here's a plan. You get engaged again? Your fiancé begs off? Just call me. We'll meet here. It'll be my third, your second, London honeymoon."

Her laughter is sincere and easygoing. He needn't have fretted. Shelley likes banter—and, yes, she's an artful flirt. "Oh, but I've already decided our next one. Paris! You'll meet me in Paris, Louie?"

"Course we'll meet in Paris, kid."

"And then *you* choose our next honeymoon. Maybe Rome?"

"Not Rome," Louie declares. "No, not Rome."

"It'll be like a movie. Meeting only for honeymoons. But what should the movie be called?"

"How about *Shelley's Honeymoons*?"

This launches her on a tide of giggly, giddy hilarity. "*Shelley's Honeymoons,* I love it! Starring *me*—Shelley! I'll play Shelley! I'm good at that! I'm a natural! But what about you, Louie? Who's gonna play you? Or do you wanna play yourself?"

Louie pauses, and the rowers overhead likewise pause in their rowing, waiting on him. He senses one of those acute conversational opportunities where a true wit would scintillate: a chance to utter something apothegmatic and profound about himself, about twists of fate, about identity. Oh, to be Oscar Wilde! But he can come up with nothing better than "It's probably the only role I play convincingly."

His tone is doleful and down in the mouth, but Shelley Pfister won't have it. She's full of curaçao, nothing but blue skies, and she's going to josh him right out of it. She takes his hand and lifts their interlocked fingers to her lips, kisses the face of his thumbnail, licks it maybe, and says, "No mopers or party poopers permitted on the set of *Shelley's Honeymoons!*"

And she makes good on her mock injunction. She cajoles, she teases, she furrows her brow in simulated censure, and in just a few minutes Louie has fully entered into the occasion's celebratory spirit: their last honeymoon meal in London. And he's eating in a way he never does, heedlessly, with reckless indifference to those slippery and squishy surprises which Pacific-island strangers may be preparing for him.

"Do you think this is the stir-fried noodles in sweet soy sauce?"

"Got to be," Louie says.

"And these are *definitely* chicken skewers."

"Though they look like pork."

He's finding this woman novel and attractive, and when was the last time someone new infiltrated his life and took his hand? Louie has to venture far back, out of his forties and into his late thirties, his midthirties . . . He thinks of something he'd like to say, were it not perhaps inappropriate: *You know, the last time I held hands with somebody new and attractive, I wasn't much older than you.* He says, "You know, the last time I held hands with somebody new and attractive, I wasn't much older than you."

"You're so romantic, Louie."

"I guess."

"And such a good guy."

"I wouldn't go that far."

Shelley's glance is keen. He has made a number of these vague allusions, and maybe he's priming for a confession. Which maybe Shelley has come to understand. She poses it as a demand: "Okay, give me the dark side, Louie."

"Dark side?"

"Wudja do to Florence, huh? To make her act that way? Make her run off with the devil?"

Louie ponders for a breath or two. In regard to Florence, Shelley has adopted his language and imagery. But she also has been doing some sisterhood-inspired pondering on her own.

Louie says, "You know, I honestly think I wasn't so bad to her. I mean, I was faithful. Insensitive? Okay. Unsupportive? All right. Grumpy? Sure. Condescending? No doubt. But faithful."

"And what about Lizzie, then? Wudja do to *her*?"

"Her I was just terrible. Really terrible."

"Tell me." Shelley squeezes his hand.

"Well, I was terrible. I had an affair. With a student."

"A former student?"

"I wish I could say so. But actually, it was a current student."

"Couldn't you have gotten yourself fired?"

"Absolutely," Louie says. "And in retrospect, I think that's what I was after. I think I had this romantic, absurd, self-important vision that if I just got fired I'd start writing the books I was meant to write. I've never published anything really . . ."

"Don't feel bad. Even if you had, I would'na read it." More of Shelley's appealing self-mockery. Louie smiles his insufficiently white smile—its own form of self-mockery.

"There is that," he says.

And this *that* is a sizable *that.* In recent years Louie has drawn perverse comfort from the notion that his entire field of scholarship, as its pitifully narrow audience attests, is mostly bogus. In art history, there may be technical questions of genuine interest and probative value *(Who painted this? When was it done?),* but in the broad domain of evaluation (*His ludic wit informs and is informed by a tradition of . . .* Or: *She unerringly uncenters our received expectations of . . .*), it's usually embellishments of an empty exercise; it's an elaborate live-music-with-speeches birthday celebration whose guest of honor has gone missing; it's a vigorously gymnastic form of well-groomed cheerleading enacted on the sidelines while the muddy contest takes place between indistinguishably muddy opponents; it's crap. If the truth be told, these days much of his pleasure in museum going lies in seeking out absurd curatorial assertions. They often interest him more than the art itself. At the Tate recently, Louie discovered that some numb-skull had hung up a mirror as a painting, and this was merely a yawn. But a curator had observed, "That's why this work is genius—art and reality are one," which did make Louie guffaw. Here is (unlike Louie) a successful writer—making a living composing stuff like that. And presumably picking up girls on the strength of such cultural insights, if girls were what the writer was after. Boys, if boys.

Back when he was still contemplating a doctoral thesis on John

Singer Sargent, Louie once had the experience of determining that a sentence he'd just effortfully constructed was utter, irredeemable rubbish. He was sitting in a carrel on the third floor of the grad library, looking toward the clock tower as every inch of campus filled with snow, and the fresh beauty and verve of those large, lacy flakes—explosions of confetti celebrating nothing more or less than the ebullition of flight—were a wonderful encouragement. *Push it,* those flakes urged. *Push the insight, Louie.*

He did. Louie sat and pondered as the snowfall romped and all but sang through the tall volumes of awestruck air. He saw that he'd written a sentence that was utter rubbish, but did his insight have a broader application? The true critic is audacious. *Push it.* His recognition of self-generated waste and failure brought a whirring excitement to his temples. He drove on. Rather than nervousness, Louie felt a reckless exhilaration at the further revelation that the paragraph containing the worthless sentence was itself quite worthless. And perhaps—perhaps—the chapter enclosing the paragraph might now, in a great golden shower of truthfulness, reveal itself as rubbish, and indeed his entire thesis . . . A few months later, he shifted from Sargent to Frederic Church.

"And Lizzie found out?"

"Worse than that. Much worse than that."

Of all the rooms in his soul, this is perhaps the one Louie is most reluctant to open. He would rather talk to Shelley about *anything*—his teenage masturbatory fantasies, or some of the crazy stunts he pulled right before his bipolarism was diagnosed, or even about adult-onset foveomacular vitelliform dystrophy. And yet he continues with his confession. In less than two full days, they've come an extraordinary distance, he and Shelley.

"The student's name was Annie. And it went on for nearly a year. Actually, *more* than a year. (I lied about the actual length until I guess I've come to believe my lie.) Anyway, Annie's father had died two years before, and it's tempting to conclude I was a father substitute, though I'm not sure I buy into that."

"I had a thing for one of my teachers. A serious thing."

"I mean she had these pictures of her father around her apartment, and the guy was *gigantic*. Six foot five, or something. No, being with Annie left me feeling much more like a student again, an undergrad, than being her dad."

"I kept taking his picture. Secretly. On my phone. Nothing ever happened, though."

"She lived off campus, and she had a roommate, this real nutcase named Chloe, and Chloe was just totally, wildly promiscuous. She'd go out drinking and bring guys back. Maybe nobody new for four months, and then three different guys the same week! Later on, when I was diagnosed manic-depressive, it occurred to me maybe this was Chloe's problem. You see where this is going."

"I hope not, Louie."

"I became sort of obsessed with Chloe."

"Uh-oh."

"It wasn't she was so all-out attractive, though she *was* attractive, in this dirty-barefoot-street-urchin sort of way. No. It was the freedom of it, the impulsiveness of it, the what-the-hell quality. It was this crazy suspicion that maybe you'd been confined your whole life without suspecting you were confined, and now you'll burst out and discover true liberty. So Annie goes off for the weekend, flying to Memphis for her uncle's funeral, and what do I do?"

"You *didn't*, Louie? When she's off at her uncle's *funeral*?"

"I did, but this gets worse. Hold on."

Louie is discovering, to his surprise, some genuine relief appended to this process of unburdening himself. He has never before told a woman these details—not even Florence. He has confided in a couple of male pals over the years, but even with them, and their broad fraternal allowance for the coarsest of masculine motives, he hadn't experienced this fine fluency, this satisfying blend of psychological acuity and abandoned spiritual abasement. It may be he's approaching for the first time in his life a state of absolute conversational license, where no admission is unsayable.

"So over the weekend I go to bed with Chloe, a couple of times—more than a couple, actually. Really quite a few, actually. And Annie gets home and the two roommates have this tearful reunion over tacos and margaritas, and of course *everything's* confessed. And the next thing I know? Annie has called my wife. She called Lizzie."

"And tells her what?"

Louie pauses only a moment. "Exactly. All of it. Lizzie's hearing I'm sleeping with not one but two different students. And the next thing I know, I'm out on my ear."

"And I don't blame her! Jesus, Louie, what the hell'ja expect?"

"I don't know what I expected, but hold on. This gets worse. Or weirder. Now it's a few weeks later, I'm on my own, it's Thanksgiving vacation, Annie's back home with her family in this little crazy town called Ontonagon, which is *way* the hell up in Michigan's Upper Peninsula. And I decide on a surprise visit. I'll drive up and tell her I'm in love with her and I want to spend my life with her. Do you know how far it is from Ann Arbor to Ontonagon? It's over five hundred miles, it's a ten-hour drive, you could probably cross Montana in less time, but ten hours later, I'm on their family doorstep. On Thanksgiving Day."

"Oh, *Louie.*"

"And these are very, very nice people! Good midwesterners, good Michigan folks, Dad's been dead a couple of years, but Mom is lovely and hospitable, there's a spinster aunt, a deaf grandmother, and Cliff, Annie's brother, who's even bigger than the old man ever was, I swear he's six-seven or something. You've seen those movies where a grizzly bear stands up? Sort of rises and—whoa—just keeps on rising? Then you've seen Cliff. And the next thing I know I'm sitting in their family room with a beer stuck in my hand and a piece of mince pie in front of me. I'm talking about what classes I teach. And then Annie's out of the room with her mom, some kind of crisis, the sound of tears, uh-oh, all sorts of muffled upheaval. *Uh-oh.* The aunt leaves the room, and Cliff leaves the room, and I'm talking curriculum and prerequisites and distribution requirements with the deaf grandmother, and I don't at *all* like the wailing sounds coming from the next room. And the next thing I know I'm standing on the front porch and Cliff's telling me if I'm not off the property in two minutes, he's going to first pound me into the ground like a fence post, then call the police. He's very strict about sequence: first pound me into the ground like a fence post, *then* call the police."

"So you drive back?"

"So I drive back, but I'm not sure that's really the end of the story, Shell. A couple of weeks later, acting bipolar I suppose, I decide I can't bear my job, I can't bear my life, I write out a long letter of resignation to the department chairman, outlining in absolutely lunatic fashion every complaint I'd amassed over the years, and I slip it under his office door. Six single-spaced typed pages. Six! Including the fact that I don't like his political neckties, which are not witty or illuminating. Or the way the department kitchen smells when he microwaves his ghastly Weight Watchers lunches. I mean, I leave out *nothing*."

"They're pretty disgusting. The only one that's even semi-edible—"

But Louie isn't about to be sidetracked. "I go home, that night I go to bed, I wake up at two feeling saner than I have in a long time, and what do I do? I go back into the department building, I find the chairman's office is locked, I try fishing my resignation letter out from under the door with a coat hanger, but I can't. Did I mention I brought a coat hanger with me? And then I break down the door. Did I mention I'd brought a crowbar with me? And I suppose that's why I still have my job."

"You honestly broke in with a crowbar?"

"But it's sort of worse than that. I mean there was something really terrifying about it. People talk about muscle memory, but this is nerve memory. I swear to God, I still feel it in my nerve endings, in my arms and shoulders, the *crack* when the frame of the door gave way. It's like all these little firecrackers, ladyfingers, going off inside me." Louie's shudder is unexpected and unfeigned.

"It makes a great dramatic end to the story—*I broke into the chairman's office with a crowbar*—but that was hardly the end. How could it be? It gets weirder, because naturally this is a news story. The chairman of the Art History Department at Ann Arbor College, Leo Mattoon, has his office broken into? Who would do such a thing? And why? It's the lead story in the college newspaper. It's *huge*. It's a huge story in the now-defunct *Ann Arbor News*. It brings in the college police. It brings in the Ann Arbor police. We have departmental *meetings* about the break-in, everyone's opinions are canvassed, and I'm terrified about fingerprints, I'm terrified about the beating of my telltale heart. I won't merely get fired. I'll get *jailed*! Want to know something, Shelley? You're the only one in the world who knows this story."

"Wow," Shelley says.

"Not Lizzie, not Florence. God forbid not my sister, Annabelle. Not my shrinks. Even now, you could probably get me fired if you wanted to."

"But why would I want to, Louie?"

Looking for a more satisfying response than *Wow,* Louie rephrases: "You're the only person in the world who has heard this story."

Shelley does in fact repeat her *Wow*. But then their gazes lock, and Louie no longer feels shortchanged, for she understands what he means to give her. What more precious gift than a well-shaped virgin story, reserved over the years for the proper recipient?

The story is actually richer—weirder—even than this, but Shelley would need some familiarity with academic politics to appreciate its piquant gruesomeness. Crazy Leo Mattoon—who in late middle age had grown a long flaccid ponytail and embraced video installation art and whose favorite word in the language was *subversive*—viewed the break-in as a dark validation of his intellectual potency.

Doubtless, he'd rattled the hidden powers that be, the true puppet masters of society's status quo, and he questioned the wisdom of calling in the Ann Arbor constabulary—for who would police the police? It might well be an FBI or a CIA break-in, seeking ways to silence Leo Mattoon, to intimidate Leo Mattoon, and he threatened to hire, at departmental expense, a team of private investigators. And Mattoon claimed that the thief had rifled the papers on his desk and confiscated notes for an essay he'd been shaping about images in Big Tobacco's magazine advertising in the Eisenhower era. No telling, really, who might have wanted to silence *that*.

Shelley says, "Louie, I have this voucher to redeem."

"Voucher?"

"It's for champagne. A bottle comes with the Honeymoon Suite. It's included in the price. Louie, will you go back to the hotel? We could drink it in the bar . . ."

"I've already had two strong drinks," Louie reminds her. "And some beer."

"I just couldn't ask them to pop it open when I'm sitting there alone. Can you imagine anything sadder? It comes with the Honeymoon Suite."

"Well sure," Louie says. "We'll drink champagne in the Penthouse Tavern of the Excelsior Palace. And then you'll put me in a grocery cart and wheel me out. I've had so much to eat. And drink."

"I'll be happy to wheel you around," Shelley says.

But before any departure can be effected there is more food to face: the twice-cooked egg, the baby shrimps, the jackfruit-and-coconut pancake, the glutinous rice cake. Even Shelley seems to be slowing down.

"I'm so glad you told me all about the Crowbar Incident," she says.

"Shelley, I still feel it! In the nerve endings in my arms. Little firecrackers, *pop, pop, pop*! I go on feeling it just the way *they* go on feeling it." Louie uses his temporarily empty fork to point to the catamaran— to the miniature brown manikins, bowed with eternal exertion, racing toward harbor with an approaching typhoon at their backs. He's discouraged to see that the yuppie in the gray suit has been joined by his extremely attractive, lean, leggy blonde girlfriend, who is wearing blue jeans and a sky-blue scarf—or, an even-less-bearable alternative, that the yuppie has managed tonight to pick up such a woman. Louie deliberately shifts his intense gaze to what is a perfect tropical complement to an iceberg: a cube of breaded, golden tofu (which he has no intention of eating), adrift in a tropical harbor of ruby sauce. A Frederic Church painting for the twenty-first century.

"Louie, am I really the only one who knows that story?"

Louie's feeling distracted, pulled in every direction, but once again her brown-eyed gaze retrieves him. "You, Shelley Pfister," Louie intones, "on the first of what I hope will be numerous honeymoons we shall share, are the only person who knows that I, Louie Hake, am a dangerous and unconvicted criminal . . ."

In the taxicab over to her hotel, Shelley's once more on the verge of tears. She calls out, abruptly, "Oh, Louie, isn't it all so sad?" and Louie declares (with a slippery sensation of having uttered something like this before, after she said something like this before), "It is, Shelley, except it isn't." And then quite naturally and logically, as if this were some old folk remedy for stanching a woman's tears, he reaches across and seizes her sizable breast. Through lacy fabric, lightly, tentatively, lightly, his fingers tease out her nipple, though the actual phenomenon might equally be described as one wherein her nipple finds his fingertips. Once again, they kiss all the way to the ushered, uniformed entrance of the Excelsior.

"Congratulations!" is what greets Louie when their bottle of champagne, lying in what is surely an American-sized (Trump-sized) ice bucket, is ceremonially presented. Somehow he fails to make the obvious deduction. He looks toward Shelley, who winks at him. Oh. The waiter is assuming (or pretending to assume) they're newlyweds.

The waiter is large and fair and freckled. He has a boyish face, but his strawberry-blond hair, severely combed straight back from his broad forehead, has begun to thin over his temples, and the corners of his eyes are scored by crow's-feet. A little short of amusement tonight, he's making the most of this opportunity to plant roguish insinuations. "For the tender young bride," he says, filling Shelley's glass. He pauses and pretends to ponder. "And for the ea-ger gentleman"—filling Louie's glass.

It's good to be back here, twenty-four hours later. After all the unpronounceable food, the champagne feels cleansing—sobering. Here's a view of the same office buildings he saw last night, when one glass of wine turned into two. But of course it's now a different zodiac—each evening's pattern of lights being as alike and dissimilar as snowflakes. Different lives under pressure, under deadline. New complications with the Singapore account, new snafus with the Billingsgate merger . . . It strikes him as not merely sad but somehow delinquent and alarming and blinkered that, while astronomers studiously chart the heavens, nobody is out there chronicling *these* constellations, the true night skies of the city. History is getting lost. The lights reveal a chronicle of everyday lives— of living being lived. Somewhere, a firm record ought to be archived, for what goes unrecorded is worse than lost; it's as though it never happened. *Rome never gets built.* We are recordkeepers, first and foremost, or we're nothing. Surely this is what God would do—maintain a record of *everything*—and Louie feels his head make a sort of drunken lurch. It takes a moment to get his footing again.

Shelley says, "Oh, I can't believe I'm going back: Hampden, Uncle Garvin's shop, and the dieting, oh God the dieting."

"You're going back tomorrow," Louie says.

"But that's the thing about you, Louie. *You're* not going back. You're going *forward.*"

"Is that the thing about me? Forward motion?"

"Is it okay if I say about you what I think, that I think you're one of the most fascinating men I ever met?"

It ought to be stirring—Shelley so patently means to elevate him. But who are her fascinating men? Presumably, the cream of Hampden's happy-hour crowd.

Louie makes a conscious effort to think more graciously; if he isn't careful, he sometimes turns lofty and grand, handily forgetting that he's a highly replaceable professor at what may be the silliest college in Michigan. He says, "It's okay only if you'll let me say about you that you're one of the most appealing women I've ever met." But is he being—in that awful pseudo-generous way so common to academics—

patronizing? Retaining a measure of superiority while pretending to mingle and merge? "Oh God," he says, and his voice abruptly breaks toward a sob, "you know what? I'm going to hold on to this. It's a vow. Twenty years' time, I'll still be treasuring the evening I drank a bottle of champagne with young Shelley Pfister on her London honeymoon."

"You know," Shelley says, "a girl never forgets her honeymoon." Such a marvelous coquette, really. She holds his gaze while turning and dipping her head in a sly, adjudicative fashion that signals piqued interest, and a burgeoning respect, and a discerning judgment at last tipped in your favor—everything a man could ask for in a woman. Or so it seems to Louie, who is acknowledging anew the effects of champagne after a very long day.

"I think I'm going to miss the Excelsior," Louie says. "And its creator and overseer, Sterling Gall, I'll miss him, too."

"Now, don't you start, sweetie . . ."

"I do like sitting here."

"You should see the room. It's a real suite."

"Big?"

"Not huge, but *big*. The *bed's* big."

Her boldness is unexpected—and altogether thrilling. There is no mistaking the intensity in her dark eyes. But Shelley is bolder still. She converts innuendo and double entendre into a naked proposition: "Plenty of room for two, Louie."

And so at last they have stripped bare this moment, the one for which all their maneuvering now stands revealed as mere preamble.

It has been present from the outset: this tantalizing possibility. Back when she was all but a stranger, sitting in Simon and Paul's Deli with a Thousand Island stain on her blouse, Louie was fantasizing about taking to bed this young woman on her solitary honeymoon.

But if the impulse and the inkling have been prickling him from the outset, Louie hasn't yet fixed on a distinct course of action. Even while opening his mouth to answer, he isn't certain of his reply.

"I'm thinking," Louie says.

He says, "Thinking where I am right now. Where you are now,

Shell. Just yesterday I wrote Lizzie a letter basically proposing we try once more to work things out. And in the taxi over here, you were almost crying over Frank. And all the alcohol. I'm just thinking I'd hate to feel I'd—" He halts on the brink of *taken advantage of you.* Is such a concern even relevant these days? Or is it antiquated and probably sexist and certainly condescending to be thinking in these terms? Shelley's a grown woman. He's a grown man. Is he taking advantage of her if he follows up on her initiative, accepting her generous offer of a bouncing romp in bed—an escapade of love?

Thoughts are racing as words falter in his throat. He has yearned to be seen as gallant—decent and helpful and considerate—but wouldn't he be undoing all the accumulated goodwill, and exposing the calculated male baseness of his motives, if he acknowledged some underlying scheme of seduction? And yet—why in the world would this be *base*? Why not flattering and life affirming? Why not warm and reciprocal? What stubborn repression is he the victim of?

Louie takes a new line. "I'm just thinking maybe it's best to err on the side of—" He lets this one, too, fall away. Shelley is examining him steadily. Meanwhile, he's warming his hand in the nest of her hand. "I'm wondering if part of this weirdness I'm feeling? Whether it's because London's where I first honeymooned? Isn't it possible, Shelley, we're just rebounding? Off other people? In a way that isn't ultimately—. On the other hand, is thinking this way a failure to give ourselves, you and me, the credit of our own reality?"

"I know exactly what you mean." Shelley sighs, but how *can* she know, when he's being so laughably inarticulate? "I'm sure you're right, Louie. It was just feeling it was such a *waste,* the bed being so big and all, eight pillows, so adorable, in different sizes, and everything so romantic. Think of it: my first Honeymoon Suite . . ."

It appears he has officially declined her proposition without fully saying so, or intending to. And Shelley seems pleased—grossly relieved, in fact—and happier than ever with him. "You're such a gentleman, Louie."

"Well—"

"Not every guy is, you know . . ."

And now it grows acutely evident, as her young, zaftig body swiftly withdraws from his lonely forty-three-year-old body, that the one thing Louie doesn't wish to be is a gentleman. No, he wants to be one of those aggressive bastards who push and push and push until they get everything they want.

Shelley's immensely relieved—she hadn't been utterly sold on the idea. Wasn't hers an offer made out of gratitude? Feeling she owed it to him, given all the kindnesses he'd shown her? And surely he doesn't wish to sleep with Shelley as something *owed*. No, he wants to sleep with her out of upwelling passion. What about rapture, ecstasy, catharsis? Wasn't it all getting lost? Lost in the too many complexities, the too many worries, and the tangled strings of past failures? Why in hell can't he believe in himself? In its deepest reverberations, the loss of Shelley has a conclusive, an eschatological, ring; here's one more appetite he will take unslaked to his deathbed. *My first Honeymoon Suite.*

What's the solution, Louie, but a stripped, primordial joy—the limbs denuded at last of all the mind's caking mud? Naked unthinkingness is surely the one true solution: life celebrating itself as it might have been celebrated this very evening, with disrobed abandon, in a suite in London's Excelsior Palace . . . His head is spinning. And it seems Louie has talked his way out of his sole opportunity of salvation.

He says, "It isn't impossible we'll meet again."

"You could come to Baltimore!" Shelley suggests brightly. "This place I know has the most amazing crab cakes!"

"Or you could come to Ann Arbor."

"Can you fly there?"

"Course you can. You fly to Detroit."

Shelley pauses only a second. "I'd like to do that. I need more travel. Maybe you've inspired me, Louie." She seems to understand, in her emotionally agile and personable way, that it has become her fitting task to offer praise and reassurances to her singular dinner date, the hesitant, likable, doubt-riddled art professor Louie Hake on his intrepid round-the-world tour. She tells him again, as they make their downward progress through the champagne bottle, what a "lifesaver" he is, how many experiences—unforgettable experiences—he has opened.

Focusing on everything just now sacrificed, Louie turns morose and monosyllabic, while reminding himself that nothing memorable has been lost—only postponed. But it's all happening too rapidly, this morning departure of hers. They review the details: flight out of Heathrow at eleven-thirty, which means limo service—arranged by poor Mrs. Hornebeck—from the hotel at eight, which means a wake-up call at seven. Once more he entertains the possibility of a brief meeting in the morning—but despite two Duskcutters and some beer and a half bottle of champagne, he possesses the lucidity of mind to recognize this as a *lousy* idea. He'd only feel worse: a rendezvous originating from different hotels, rather than a hand-in-hand emergence from the hushed, plush, pillowy, perfumed lair of a young woman's first Honeymoon Suite . . .

In the elevator's long descent from penthouse to lobby, the two of them find themselves alone. Shelley—bless her, Lord bless her—doesn't hold back. She steps right up and gives him a long, clinging, appealingly sloppy kiss. The inside of her mouth tastes dazzlingly sweet. Sometimes, on very hot summer days, you'll bite into a plum and you have to close your eyes, stop breathing, shut things down, because otherwise the flooding sweetness would wholly undo you. It's like that. His left hand lifts automatically, like an appendage under hypnosis, and clasps her breast, which yields with agreeable compliance. She means to do right by him. He breaks from the kiss to say, or at least he intends to say, *Sorry I'm such a fool* . . . But he fails here, too; he issues a sort of weird sibilant grunting noise instead. Meanwhile Shelley, who from their first serendipitous encounter has excelled him in dexterity, knows exactly how to negotiate these tremulous, unsettled final moments: "You're totally first class, Louie," she says.

IT MAY BE THAT IN THE *REAL* MIDDLE OF THE NIGHT NO MEANingful time or place exists. It's a zone belonging to H. G. Wells's nameless Time Traveller, who beached up on a shore of an etiolated Earth, beneath a cooling red Sun, though he was also simultaneously seated back at home, in Victorian London, feasting by gaslight on mutton and champagne. Simultaneity holds dominion. Time is elastic. Time is unplaceable. The champagne glasses clink in a London dining room, but on the icy shore of what was once England there is merely desolateness and the solitary contemplating of desolateness. Meanwhile, in what felt to Louie like the middle of the night, he was roused and awakened, in his room at the Mulder Arms, by a jet overhead.

In his dozing, he positively identified its muffled shredding roar as the sound of Shelley's plane. Shredding pages—the pages of the chapter called "The Daily Retreat." She was putting an ocean between the two of them. But though the sky is still black, Big Ben now begins to tick. Time has resumed (while a vanished woman, indignantly, demands of the skull-sized alarm clock in her hand, *Are you deaf? Are you deaf?*), and Shelley's plane won't leave for hours yet, and a spiteful hangover has Louie the Little Head in its grasp.

It was a game the two of them used to play—he and Lizzie—born one unrecorded night in some dreamlike condition where impulses have no traceable causes. The game was called Big Head, Little Head. One spouse would call out a name—Moses Hurd (their Orthodox Jewish landlord), or Suzanne Pickman (Louie's fellow grad student), or Jake-o (the cashier at their local convenience store), or Hillary Clinton—and the other would immediately have to make a judgment, a determination: either Big Head or Little Head. The judgment had nothing to do with the subject's intelligence or force of personality; it was all about skull circumference. The beauty of the game—its sole beauty—was that there was no middle ground: the entire populace of the planet was either a Big Head or a Little Head. Sometimes fierce disputes would arise ("Tom Cruise is no Big Head!"), but mostly the two concurred. Both Lizzie and Louie (despite his voluminous curls) were Little Heads.

Louie is drifting in a half sleep as he recalls playing Big Head, Little Head with Lizzie, as he laments the starry passing of Shelley's flight.

Louie shifts position, from his left side to his right, and his mind also shifts position, from left brain to right, or vice versa. (He has never been able to keep straight which hemisphere purportedly governs which functions.) In any case, he has begun thinking more analytically, or psychoanalytically. He now must unflinchingly confront the question of why he balked at Shelley's proposition. Did it actually have anything to do with gentlemanliness, with gallantry? Or everything to do with cowardice? Was Louie the Little Head scared of competing with the man who once swam across the sprawling Massapick? Was it possible she'd frightened him off with all her giggly allusions to Frank's hypermasculinity? Had he been intimidated, at the end of the day, by the prospect of having his sexual performance refereed by a woman recently engaged to a "total machine"?

Louie tells himself that nothing's lost—that when he finally returns home nothing would be easier than a flight to Shelley's Baltimore. From there, he could arrange another day trip, this one to DC and the museums on the Mall . . . But it seems something precious *has* been lost, irretrievably. Seems he has again allowed fear of impulsiveness—of his manicky side—to rob him of the pungent spices of life. *I'm trying not to close myself off to adventure.* He doesn't need Frank's unmanning presence to prove himself constitutionally a coward.

Or is it so simple? After all, the lowly art professor who once took a crowbar to his chairman's office door has good cause to spurn mad impulses. As he knows better than most people, the allure of genuine craziness proportionately diminishes the closer you approach. All his students are forever boasting about being crazy. His colleagues, too. (Proudly: "I did this crazy thing . . .") But most have no inkling of what it means to slip over the threshold.

Still, the jury keeps coming back with the same verdict: guilty of cowardice. Wasn't the Journey of His Life meant to be a Road to Adventure? Back into sleep he slides, he who has a rendezvous with the ends of the earth, the end of Earth. Once more, a plane's engine signals. Once more, the woman is leaving him. And once more, she's leaving you, Louie, and once more he rises and falls, like a body suspended in a tide, an open burial, the sea ceaselessly burying itself before the dawn.

LOUIE WAKES, HEAVY OF SOUL BUT ALSO REMOTE OF SOUL, heavy of body and all too fixedly fastened to his body, which is voicing numerous complaints. His throat is parched, his stomach perforated and acidified. His head aches altogether, but especially at the nape of the neck, where his brain perches on a lifeguard's tall slender throne whose wooden legs are of uneven lengths. It's threatening to tip.

The deficiencies of the Mulder Arms daily grow more evident. Prominent among them is a bathroom mirror mounted squarely over the toilet. Why does this *ever* happen in hotels? From an interior designer's perspective, the only conceivable point to such mirrors is the facilitation of a dialogue between a man and his penis. The two of them—disconsolate Louie and disconsolate penis—have little enough to say to each other this morning, as he urinates spasmodically into the bowl. One of them feels sheepish; the other, slighted. It would have been wise to make some schedule for his day, some routine to follow mindlessly. At the moment, he lacks the mental energy to fashion one. It's after eight. Shelley has departed for the airport.

While hunching under the drumming showerhead, Louie decides, for the first time this trip, to forgo shaving. Predictably, an internal voice commences nagging and admonishing. His response is mute and indirect and surly: he dons yesterday's stained and wrinkled shirt. *So there . . .*

Louie heads downstairs for his traditional English breakfast. Morning after morning, with an avocado-green plate obstinately lodged before him, he has located the charm buried within the nastiness. But today's breakfast seems purely, spitefully nasty. What nightmare beyond telling must it be to slave in the Mulder kitchen, daily serving up an eternal marriage of flabby toast and pooling grease?

Unshaved, ill fed, wearing yesterday's shirt, Louie meanders from the hotel. Over his head assorted revelations and reevaluations are breaking, perhaps chief of which is that he has been dim and mulish in thinking London is essentially the same city first visited with Lizzie in 1994. He has taken consolation in the Mulder Arms, even while it has grown steadily apparent that the place isn't—as he has pretended—clueless and incompetent. Rather, it's a coldly cynical establishment. It's peddling a false bill of goods, passing off indolent, unprincipled greed as feckless, makeshift charm.

Day after day, all over the city, he has been turning a blind eye to modifications of every stripe, both good and bad. The city is so much slicker, finer, faster, than it used to be. Everyone was *right,* the rumors were *accurate:* better food, better service, better transportation . . . And in some ways the city is also far, far crappier, as the intermittent waves of stench keep reminding him. Perhaps it's all the drinking out on the streets, the unspoken cost of a beer culture rather than a wine culture like Rome's, but no other city he has ever known smells so pervasively and pungently of piss. The street life of London moves to the raw, ceaseless background music of a voluminous bladder chorus, issuing out of any space even vaguely resembling a shelter—shrubs, phone booths, construction scaffolding, building entryways . . . What is he going to do today? Maybe a play? It occurs to Louie that he could find a matinee, perhaps a comedy, and then occurs that he couldn't. Today's Friday, and the theaters probably aren't offering matinees. By default, or by gravitational pull, eventually he winds up at the entrance of the British Museum. He marches in. Despite its admirable policy of free admission—an increasing rarity in the art historian's world—he soon ascertains that this visit is probably a mistake.

Louie winds up scrutinizing a row of Assyrian friezes. These, unlike so many of the Elgin Marbles, have weathered the years well. Many are devoted to royal lion hunts, and the transformation, over and over, of the king of beasts into a hapless porcupine, body bristling with javelins, is banal and depressing. To an art historian, the lions naturally recall Saint Sebastian, though they have none of Sebastian's rarefied aplomb in the face of torture. Actually, they're more like living insects pinned to a board, writhing in hellish agony. One of the lions has caught a spear through his eye sockets, and you can almost hear, ricocheting down the millennia, the blinded beast's outraged roaring.

In an adjoining room Louie comes across a diagram of a Greek temple. Somewhat defiantly, he poses a challenge to himself: How many of its component parts can he identify? Not many. He has never shone at this sort of exercise. Architectural terms, some of them extremely rudimentary, typically fly out of his brain. He can never keep straight, for instance, the defining differences among Doric, Ionic, and Corinthian columns, though this is material you might find on an Intro to Architecture midterm. (He worries occasionally about being called out for intellectual fraudulence, though his students at AAC are ill equipped to do so. One of them, just this past semester, inquired whether Spain, like Italy, is an island.)

But as he stands before the diagram's ungainly nomenclature—metope, triglyph, echinus, stylobate—a larger insight clarifies: there's something inherently pretentious about any "text-based collection" like this. So much writing on the wall. These days, *nobody* wants to read the writing on the wall. Too demanding. Too much hassle. Too much strain on our ever-more-limited attention spans. His students are right. It's all insufferably pretentious and obnoxious. Years ago, in some now-forgotten museum, Louie stood before a dusty potsherd—something you'd never stoop to examine if you passed it in an alley—whose caption called it a "delicious specimen of Etruscan orientalization." Okay, someone was having him on. But while it's harder to spot at the British Museum, someone is still having him on: showing off, while ostensibly instructing and enlightening. What poses as high-minded is actually overweening. The British Museum may well constitute the world's most intricate and colossal personal insult.

It's a horrible, horrible thought, but Louie must confront it even so: his students are right. His students at AAC recoil from demanding museums almost as violently as they recoil from demanding books, and they are right, and the rest of us must graciously concede defeat.

We've been persnickety and exacting but, hey, *no worries.* The victors are hospitable, and our differences are incidental, since most intellectual distinctions are fussy—anal. Counter though the notion runs to every humane impulse inside him, yes, awful and terrifying as it is to concede, he must concede it: his students aren't idiots. They're onto something . . . Louie shakes his aching head; he honestly isn't doing all that well.

Shuffling from room to room, hands pocketed, head bowed, he's feeling routed. Probably best to beat a retreat to a coffee shop. Only inertia is propelling him through the galleries.

Or perhaps it's not inertia at all.

Perhaps it's fate.

Perhaps, when he least expects guidance, somebody somewhere's looking out for his welfare.

Something unusual and uplifting happens to Louie as he stands before a striking photograph of a cathedral.

It's a peculiar and yet familiar-looking Gothic edifice constructed from a handsome coppery-brown stone, and Louie wonders why it's so familiar. Is it someplace he has actually visited? He steps closer. There's something queer about the stone, the perspective, the way the light arrays on its slender, ambitiously tall spire and many flying buttresses . . .

Queer indeed: for this holy site is a place Louie has never visited, no one alive has visited. Or you might say nobody in human history has visited.

The photograph is a digital reconstruction of Old Saint Paul's Cathedral, whose roof collapsed in the Great Fire of London of 1666. Some three and a half centuries later, an anonymous computer wizard extinguishes the flames and restores the roof. The medieval masterwork, rescued from holocaust, airborne on its stone wings, soars across the centuries and flutters down like a butterfly onto its contemporary perch: the computer artist has fitted it into a modern urban backdrop.

Louie stares and stares. Deep within him something stirs, and then his head starts to swim, through a murky current of images and memories. For a few moments, he's completely immersed, and all but blinded. But when he crawls ashore, he is standing in Ely Cathedral, twenty years ago.

Twenty years ago, one foreign blue morning, two kids, Louie and Lizzie Hake, younger even than the very young Shelley Pfister, took a train from London to Ely. Clouds were flying in that wild, unanchored way they display only in foreign countries. Louie was a grad student at U of M. Lizzie was working for its development office. They were honeymooning Michiganders let loose in the British Isles. This was their first day trip from London. Cambridge beckoned. Oxford beckoned. But grad student Louie was keenest first to see Ely's much-praised cathedral, whose photographs had long spoken to him.

It turned out to be the perfect choice. The cathedral revealed itself as far more beautiful even than Louie had dared hope. As they rode the clattering train back to London, Louie kept explaining and extolling. *Lizzie, dear Lizzie, it might well be the most beautiful structure on the planet* . . .

But even on that giddy train, Louie had refrained from communicating to his new wife exactly what had unfolded inside the cathedral. He had no way to start. Something deeply strange, something all but inexpressible, had taken place there.

It was a phenomenon he'd heard about and read about and often wondered about.

There was in the language an established phrase reserved for this phenomenon—*out-of-body experience*—which indicated it was an occurrence of some frequency: yes, this was something that consistently happened to people.

But never before had it happened to *him:* for a brief interval, Louie had felt literally—physically—transported outside the dimensions of his body. It was one of perhaps only two truly spiritual moments in his life. (The other occurred when he was a mere nine years old, sitting on the back porch beside his father, one midsummer dusk, waiting for nothing in particular.)

This time, too, a concentrate of spectacular colors had alighted from above. Strolling in Ely Cathedral one July afternoon in 1994, Louie had paused in happy, radiant bemusement at the spectacle of the light descending transversely, right to left, from a stained-glass window onto the floor of the nave. He watched the colored lights dance. The blue light in particular looked unearthly and unreal. It looked like a spill of powder, which might be scattered with the toe of his shoe. But when he provisionally inserted his toe into the light, it didn't scatter; it simply assimilated his foot. He stared and stared, and what happened next was surpassingly mild. Something within that dance of light tugged at his chest, with fingers pliant and gentle as milkweed, beseeching his heart to join the dancing, and for a few moments his heart had done nothing else: for a few moments, Louie Hake had watched his heart, still tethered to but outside his body, dancing on the stone floor of the nave in England's Ely Cathedral.

Louie back then, in 1994, had been no less an agnostic than he is today—disheveled, uncombed, and riveted to a digital simulacrum of a long-lost cathedral on this June morning in 2014. But back then, no less than now, he accepted as a given the quiddity of his soul. And it alters a person—to experience such things. (Perhaps the world is most meaningfully divided between those who have had such an experience and those who haven't.) He was nine years old when an Extraterrestrial materialized, and he required maybe fifteen years and the commencement of graduate study before grasping that on that day he'd beheld a species of Annunciation, worthy of Bellini or Raphael: a seraphic creature with jeweled wings had descended on him personally.

Typically, Louie has no patience with conventional mysticism; he would prefer to read even Marxist art criticism than accounts of some novitiate's progress on the road to enlightenment. But there's no disputing that even something as no-nonsense as Life will occasionally drop an angel upon your naked knee, or set your heart beating on a stone floor.

And if something like this happens, naturally you will wait your entire life for an encore; naturally you must remain in readiness. So, *that's* what he was meant to do with his day today: undertake a second pilgrimage to Ely. Louie wanders slowly, but now with purpose and intent, to the museum's exit. He's in no hurry.

After only a few blocks he stops in a bakery called Assingham's, where he sits down over a chocolate croissant and a cup of coffee. On its own, neither is satisfactory (the former much too sweet; the latter, bitter), but he enjoys a little game of immediately following croissant with coffee, seeking an agreeable sweet-bitter balance. "It's a good game," he thinks aloud, as if Shelley were here to hear. He wanders another half-dozen blocks and finds an Internet café. He opens his email. Many messages, but only one matters. It's from Lizzie.

Dear Louie,

How sweet of you to remember my mismatched feet! You're absolutely right that the difference tormented me. Such an absurd torment!

It isn't an issue for me anymore, though. And this raises another issue: my faith. My faith has changed everything.

This wasn't something that came quickly. It came slowly and quietly, and maybe all the more powerful for being slow and quiet. I mean my faith. It began to grow after my second marriage failed. I took Christ into my life, Louie, and this has made all the difference.

After Justin and I split, I was a lost soul. For many months, my life no longer mattered. I don't mean I was about to do anything rash, but I had no meaningful purpose in the universe. And that's when it came on me, slow and quiet: my faith.

And then a very, very funny thing happened. I decided to test God, which I see now is a very naïve and dumb idea. But I did. I guess I was much more histrionic back then. So I demanded that He give me some personal signal. (I was just as egotistical as that!) I was acting like some petulant teenager, saying to her parents, *prove* that you love me. It was completely immature, and He had every reason to ignore me. But do you know what? He didn't. Not Him.

I decided to ask for something very small and private. No one would ever need to know what. And you know what I asked Him? I asked Him to make my feet the same size. And you know what He did? He did.

They're the same size now, Louie, and I don't need to buy two pairs of shoes to make one pair! This has been confirmed, by the way, in more than one shoe store. I've had my feet officially measured, and they come out the same size. You know how He did it? He made my left foot grow a half-size larger and my right foot grow a half-size smaller.

Louie can't help but grin, and grimace, and pinch his nostrils, hard. It would be so easy, and so much fun, to ridicule the poor girl unmercifully: *Dear Lizzie, You petition God for a miracle, and after weighing the options (Nuclear disarmament? Universal literacy? A cure for malaria?), you ask that He make your feet the same size*? But he won't—Louie isn't going to make fun. If Lizzie's letter is uncovering her vulnerable, goofy side, he'll welcome it. For this is a vulnerable, naked goofiness that he, better than anyone else in the world, understands and appreciates. Cherishes, in fact. And because Lizzie (unlike Florence) can laugh at herself, he can laugh with her.

Louie, there were empty spaces in my life that I didn't even know were empty. And yet I was trying to fill them. Do you want to know something? I'm hoping that this wild-sounding journey of yours has similar motivations.

And could he himself have expressed it so well? Spiritually, Lizzie's moving beside him. Big things are moving, winds shifting, firmaments clarifying, as has only recently become evident. But she with her feminine intuition took it all in, right off the bat. She understands his *empty spaces*.

> I love what you had to say about empathy. I wrote it down
> in my journal. ("for in the whole history of civilization, what
> achievement is more impressive than human empathy?") You
> are a beautiful writer, Louie.

Well, yes—and he'll accept that! Yes, a *beautiful writer,* and therefore naturally looking for an appreciative audience. A *beautiful writer,* unlike some men he could mention. A *beautiful writer,* provided he has Lizoliz for his muse. But the next paragraph stops him dead flat dead.

> I'm still with Mitch, who shares my faith and helps me deepen
> my faith. (I think in a previous email, maybe a year or so ago,
> I told you about Mitch.) Two years now we've been together.
> In fact, I want to tell you something about us almost nobody
> knows yet, not even my parents yet. We're engaged! We're
> planning to marry at Christmas time. Needless to say, it will
> be a small affair (third time around).
>     Louie, I'm so glad you wrote. I've been wanting to say for
> some time, I really have tried to forgive you. My therapist is
> a member of our Church (actually, it's all less insular, or even
> incestuous, than it sounds!), which I think has helped me find
> the path of forgiveness.
>     Be well, Louie.
>
>                                                   Love,
>                                                   Lizzie

Louie peers and peers at the woman's name. He has been asked to assimilate a truly monumental news item, and he will do just that, but not before taking a few moments to scrutinize the six letters encoding his former wife's existence. He has never before noticed how her name contains, in its rough bilateral symmetry, a kind of face in the middle—those two outside observant *i*'s, those two inner humming nasal *z*'s. It's as though her signature is gazing out at him; he's being observed.

And he's heading to Ely.

Damn it, he's heading to Ely Cathedral, and whatever announcement his dear Lizzie has chosen to make is merely distraction and obstruction: something to surmount. He considers plucking an Ativan tablet from his wallet. But he doesn't need it. A firm sense of purpose ushers Louie to King's Cross and bundles him onto a train. Most of the ride will be a repeat journey, overlapping yesterday's route to Cambridge. And hard to believe only yesterday he had a substantial and cheerful Shelley beside him, sharing her laugh and looking to him to bandage her blisters.

Louie's feeling all right. His Lizzie will be all right—or better than all right. The lovely girl with the mismatched feet is gone (the girl once known as Lizoliz—she's gone), and that's fine with her, and will be fine with him.

As the train carries him forward, though, Louie experiences odd physical symptoms or manifestations—his body's acting up a bit. If he closes his eyes, it's as though some feathery organ beneath his sternum is reaching across the front of his lungs, to link with something high in his right shoulder blade. And his lower ribs are sending probes toward his sacrum. He's re-networking, it appears, and that's fine, that's healthy.

Meanwhile, perhaps he isn't exhibiting all the clarity of thought he has been thinking he's thinking. The famous Constable painting of King's College, recalled so fondly yesterday? It doesn't exist, at least as he envisioned. He'd confused King's with Constable's view of Salisbury Cathedral. A wholly different shape, wholly different location.

Louie begins to lose heart on disembarking from the train. He'd forgotten the long walk from the station. He'd pictured himself emerging hard into the embrace of the cathedral's arched entryway.

Louie has crossed only a couple of blocks, and he's on a busy street lined with auto-repair shops, when he's approached by an obvious boozehound. On this warm, overcast midsummer day the man is wrapped in ragged layer upon layer, as though it were midwinter. He shuffles, dragging one foot. To Louie's surprise, he holds out an empty palm. He's panhandling—something Louie has hardly seen in England. What he mutters sounds like "Give a good gain . . ."

Louie, who customarily ignores panhandlers, gets past him by means of a shrug and a downcast look of befuddled generosity. He has marched another block before it occurs to him that a refusal to give alms on one's pilgrimage to a medieval church may be unpropitious.

He swings around. The ragged little figure is already a hundred yards off, lurching from side to side as if trudging into a tremendous headwind, an arctic blast. But the day is unnaturally still.

In Lizzie's last email—the one before the one today—she dropped hints of a religious awakening. He overlooked them. Clearly, she wants him not merely to understand but to respect and admire her spiritual odyssey, and yet hasn't his darling Lizoliz made this impossible? Louie recalls his wayward shrink, Dr. Douglas, peering sternly at his patients while from his office walls Darwin and Kafka and Gandhi look down: eight imposing eyes in all. Beneath that human pantheon, it had been excruciating, really, to chronicle sordid Florence's shenanigans with sordid Daryl. Even in the midst of the maelstrom, Louie sensed it: how absurd and picayune and hackneyed were the fatal shortcomings of his romantic life. He'd once had a student refer in class to a "gravitas deficiency," which sounded like a lampoon medical condition. (The painter under examination was Pieter Brueghel!) But when seated in Dr. Douglas's office, discussing Daryl and Florence, there was indeed a gravitas deficiency. And the painful truth was that a gravitas deficiency can be all but paralyzing.

How, then, would Louie nowadays recount to the same eight-eyed jury that he has been yearning to reconcile with a woman whose faith was secured when the Lord inflated her left foot by half a shoe size and shrunk her right foot by an equal measure? Oh, forgive me, Darwin! Forgive me, Kafka!

Even so, here he is, on a pilgrimage to Ely Cathedral, where he once underwent a spiritual or mystical interlude. What he earnestly would ask of the Lord (if he believed in the Lord) would be to be spared the Lord's presence. Let me live my own life . . .

Louie keeps walking. The two squared-off unmatching spires of the cathedral are in view from the train station, but he loses them as he heads up Broad Street. He cuts through a park. Once more, the spires break into view, and Louie feels almost absurdly refortified. Reconciled to a hike, he deliberately elongates his path, swinging wide with a plan of coming upon the cathedral from the front. He's seeking a return of self-confidence. Somewhere along the way, these last days or years, he mislaid his self-confidence, and who ever accomplished anything of genuine merit without first embracing a belief in himself? In terms of earthly success, a belief in God may be useful, but a belief in oneself is indispensable.

In the metallic gray light the spires are revealed as the uplifted arms of a horseshoe magnet. They're beautiful, and the image seems wonderfully apposite: down the broad, open English centuries, countless pilgrims like him have been drawn magnetically to the horseshoe's arms. Louie feels pretty sure he is no fool, and he's fully mindful of the pitfalls in trafficking in the unavoidable clichés of spiritual pilgrimage. Still, in his case Life has conspired, time and again, to plunge him into bathos and farce, and any progress he's likely to make must be wrested from cliché. One wife praying for matching feet? The other wife burning up the bedsheets with the director of the Iowa-based *Impertinence of Being Earnest*?

The admission charge to the cathedral brings Louie crashingly back to earth. Sixteen pounds? Is he really forking over something like thirty dollars for the "total experience"—a phrase fitter for Disneyland or a strip club than a cathedral? (In this case, it includes admission to the stained-glass museum and a ground-floor tour.)

It's a new feeling—to be pickpocketed by a church. The alms he withheld from the panhandler have been extracted nonetheless.

Once past the admission booth, Louie's first sensation is of dazed dismay. He has been expecting feelings of homecoming. Yet everything appears unfamiliar. The spacious interior doesn't match his more intimate, sumptuous recollections, themselves perhaps conditioned by Italy. Led here blindfolded, he couldn't have identified which cathedral he was in.

Louie takes his time. The stained glass is muted, given the overcast skies outside, but even so he wanders up the north aisle, saving the brighter passage for later. If he has forgotten much, his taste is nonetheless vindicated: this place is tranquil and cool and beautiful. More than beautiful. Even in semidarkness. Especially in semidarkness.

Louie drifts here and there, purposefully purposeless. He'll be less slapdash later on. These first few minutes are a brisk reconnaissance. He takes in some statues, the modern Saint Etheldreda, with her timelessly vacant eyes, and the modern weird blue Virgin, the color of a Duskcutter, whose upraised arms evoke a swimmer about to plunge into a pool, and the ultramodern *Christ and Mary Magdalene,* one part Giacometti and one part Spielberg's E.T., which suggests that even on Mars the fallen woman is not allowed to touch the Messiah. Louie peers at the stained glass in Saint George's Chapel, the ceiling paintings in the nave, and a queer sculpted Green Man less camouflaged than consumed by foliage.

In the limpid light of Lady Chapel, whose medieval stained-glass windows were pulverized by the Puritans, Louie sits on a folding chair and opens up *The Boorish American's Guide.* The book includes a few day trips from London. To Louie's surprise, the ever-arch John Chapman Dwyer abandons all cynicism and jadedness:

> The place is gorgeous, absolutely God-bless-us-all gorgeous. I have my problems with religious edifices, and perhaps this is the moment to say I will NEVER FORGIVE Sister Antoinette's cruelty toward me forty years ago when I fell under her bloodthirsty hands as a poor Wisconsin choirboy enrolled in his first Catholic school. But Ely is holy ground.

And hasn't Louie perhaps known it all along—known that his select companion, his opinionated, acerbic, sesquipedalian, weirdly erudite, continually misinformed cicerone is in fact another flatland midwestern boy, who probably also used to sit on the peeling back stoop beside his father while the recessing sun drifted toward the unimaginable Rockies?

The site is right. The light is right. The stone is ideal stone. Spend an honest hour here and you'll never have another minute's difficulty seeing that the Tate Modern is WRONG, that the Salisbury Wing of the National Gallery is WRONG, that The Hayward Gallery is WRONG, that our beloved city has lost its bearings.

Louie acknowledges in himself a weakness, a special partiality, for outspoken, outrageous, aggressively one-sided writers. He's a sucker for the polemicist and pitchman; he revels in a boldness he himself rarely wields on the page, envying those with the effrontery to be continually affronted. Forever undeterred, *The Boorish American* goes on positing one erroneous judgment after another, and Louie is grateful. But now Louie feels something else toward Dwyer: an unexpected warmth. He'd like to meet him on a train and take him out to dinner.

Louie loves this church, inclusively, with a passion capacious enough to embrace even the stained-glass window of an airplane, circa World War II. Or the monument to a seventeenth-century bishop, Peter Gunning, whose stone effigy reclines on one elbow like a glutted Roman at an orgiastic feast, though the expression on his marble features is one of ecclesiastical censure and renunciation. Louie is wandering down the south choir aisle when the light shifts and a new dimension unseals itself.

A break in the clouds, and all at once the sun consummates its own, its interplanetary, pilgrimage: it alights at last upon the complex, variegated, porous but solid surface of the earth. All around Louie, the stained-glass windows, those dark chrysalides, steadily eclose and come flutteringly alive. They might have been born this very afternoon.

Louie feels compensated, yet calm. He recalls a surprising voice—Shelley's. It seems a remark of hers has been echoing and echoing in his head. Something she said as they sat in Soho Square, her big bandaged bare foot in his hands. They were reveling in a sun still abroad, still up and about, though it was past nine. Framed as a question, uttered as an exclamation, "Louie, can you *believe* the light?" is what Shelley asked.

Hers was the voice of the poet. And his? Summoning knowledge, that false prophet, he'd replied in the voice of the pedant, evoking latitudes and the southern shore of Hudson Bay.

Fortunately, her words outlasted his dark tutelage. *Can you* believe *the light?* (If Louie has any genius within him, surely it lies in his occasional ability to overlook his logic, his sophistry, his precious, pathetic learning. Why did he come to England? He came to meet Shelley. Their encounter was a supreme success. (He came to meet the woman who held the necessary clue to a solution he already suspected but couldn't formulate. He didn't come to England for its architecture. Nor to hear his native language spoken. Nor to connect with his past. (It was all about venturing outwardly inward, about being guided toward brighter territories, loftier latitudes.)))

Is he standing now near the very spot where he loitered on his first honeymoon, twenty years ago, attending to a summons he didn't know how to answer? Perhaps. In any event, he has received today a message formulated expressly for him, the man with the imperiled eyes, a message borne intact some ninety-three million miles, and this time he has the means, the gravitas, to respond. Until this moment, he has misconceived his purpose. The travails encountered thus far in his Journey, the bewilderments and disappointments, the false starts and swerving reversals—these were nothing but a preliminary foray, designed to assist him in identifying his rightful pilgrimage. And now he's got it. He can begin. Traveling northward. The light. North. Gravitating toward the light.

.  .  .

TWO DAYS LATER, LOUIE IN THE LATE AFTERNOON FINDS HIM-self in an English travel agency near Russell Square. It's called Go Away. None of that English quaintness here.

Yet it's an old-fashioned travel agency, in the crucial sense that there are people to consult who might perhaps assist you with your travel plans. Go Away is basically a pair of unaired rooms smelling acridly of fresh paint, though Louie can see no trace of its having been applied. The larger room contains four mismatched desks, three of them manned at the moment. Off to the side, there's a little lounge with a few mismatched chairs, but nobody sits there. Why sit when you can queue? Some half-a-dozen customers stand in wait for the next available agent.

A vast, yellowed, charmingly out-of-date world map presides over the lounge. Zimbabwe returns as Rhodesia. Tibet's sovereignty is as yet inviolate. There is still a teardrop-shaped nation with a perfect name, Ceylon—whose six letters once assumed a mirroring teardrop shape in Louie's mind, with a perfect, lachrymose dab of glitter in the hanging tail of the *y*.

This is one of those maps making no provision for the curvature of the earth. The world is a rectangular sheet, growing more and more distorted and inflated the farther you adventure north or south of the equator. Louie's destination—Iceland—is a pumpkin-orange oblong. It's a lovely color, linked to the number 7. It looks immense, an island of a magnitude with Texas, but in reality it's the size of Kentucky. Louie has done some online research. Iceland has 320,000 inhabitants. Lots of empty space, then, for a visiting contemplative.

He was a little disappointed to discover that the entire island lies just below the Arctic Circle. It would have been satisfying, on this ren-egade journey, to penetrate that icy invisible border, expressed on the map as a dotted line—as a string of mental barbed wire. But his brief research has reassured him of superabundances of sunlight, even on the wrong, the south, side of the planet's uppermost ring.

These days, so close to the solstice, the whole top portion of the globe spins in a froth of light. Louie's plans for Iceland are fluid, though he does intend to sit outdoors and read a newspaper at midnight. Newspapers all over the world are dying, and the next generation of readers—his students—will get their news online. Well, in Iceland, anyway, Louie will absorb his news in rustling paper form, in tribute to a medium that has given him (as it gave his armchair-dominating father, happily snapping the *Detroit News* each night on arriving home from work) countless hours of pleasure.

If you follow the logic of a map like this, distortion turns infinite at the North Pole and the South Pole. Object and image part ways; the farther north you go, the less real the world becomes. Greenland towers over the map's upper reaches. Greenland isn't a color like the other colors, or it's all of their colors: it's white. Greenland—the planet's remote refrigerated warehouse, where the glaciers are piled up and stored, where polar bears serve as the night watchmen—looks substantially larger than South America, and Frederic Church's Amazon rainforest is dwindled to a quaint little glade.

There they are: Turkey (a faded piney green) and India (a faded lavender) and Japan (a faded sky blue), all boasting their claims and appeals. How lovely it is, the ever-shifting Journey is, when you examine it in just this way. England is offering him one more unexpected treasure: a map which, in being so old-fashioned and out of date, tenders the promise that you could travel not merely through space but through time, the mind untethered by a map turned magical with the unfading promise of Elsewhere.

Queuing is all right with Louie, who is in no hurry. The problem isn't the waiting but the pair of lovebirds standing before him. Louie ought to look in some other direction, but he can't peel his eyes away. Minute by minute, they drive him crazier.

They're good-looking, and young—maybe late twenties—and they can't keep their hands off each other. Boyfriend dyes his hair. Not because it's gray, which surely it isn't, but because dyeing your hair is one of the things men in his world do. Along the sides, he has short—almost buzz-cut—chestnut-colored hair. On top, his hair's long and curly and a pale wheat blond. The sleeves of his black shirt are too short. He's tallish—maybe six feet—and skinny, though Louie is cheered to observe the modest overhang of a potbelly above his beltless waist.

Girlfriend's pretty—or close enough to prettiness that her natural vivacity shortfalls the difference. She's in constant movement—jiggling, swaying, tapping her feet upon the plum-colored linoleum. She's maybe ten pounds overweight—you might simply call her voluptuous. She's wearing very tight blue jeans she'll surely have to dispose of soon. Not merely frayed, they present to the world a crossword puzzle of open holes. So tight are the jeans, at each hole the flesh bulges slightly outward, as if pressing eagerly for the freedom of nakedness.

One of the holes, a large one, lies at the back of her tan upper thigh. This hole exposes a red-and-violet tattoo of a serpent snugly wrapped around a pole, cartoonishly mounting upward, famished and open-mouthed, toward the beetling jut of her right buttock.

Boyfriend and snake are in territorial competition, actually, with Boyfriend going at her bottom from above. When Boyfriend and Girlfriend kiss, which they do frequently, he slips his fingers an inch or two down the top of the back of her jeans. The lovebirds are heading to Copenhagen. And when they're not kissing, they're conducting an argument.

"You're thinking it's all pot, but it's not," she tells him. Or so Louie determines after a moment. What he first hears is "You think it's all paught, but it's naught." *Paught* and *naught* ought to belong to a posh accent, but hers is anything but. Even Louie, hopeless in sorting out British speech, feels confident of this. "You're thinking it's all Amsterdam," she goes on. "But it's a completely different country, isn't it, Denmark? They probably speak their own language."

"Look, there's got to be smoke," Boyfriend says. "Don't you be fretting: you'll get your smoke."

The two of them are growing impatient. They've been summoned to one of the desks, but the agent has suddenly begun typing—seemingly endlessly.

"You can't even decide which way you say it," Girlfriend resumes. "With you, sometimes it's *Copen-HAH-gun,* and sometimes *Copen-HAY-gun.*"

Without looking up from her typewriter, the woman agent says, "I don't know for certain, but I vote for *Copen*-HAH-*gun.*"

At this point, invitingly, the exchange seems to have crossed over into that public realm where a knowledgeable voice—a professorial voice—might feel entitled to speak. "Actually," Louie volunteers, "I think we can say it however we want. Because we're wrong no matter what. In Danish, it isn't even a *p* but a *b. Co-ben . . .*"

A pause ensues, during which Louie fears he looks like an interloper. But after a collective examination of him, the surrounding faces relax into a cordial acceptance. Everyone's bored stiff, and he evidently represents a happy, perhaps comic, distraction: the visiting egghead.

Boyfriend says, "I vote with the Yank. It's any way you want."

Girlfriend lifts a playful fist and swats Boyfriend's chest. "Course you vote for *him*. You just don't want to be *wrong*."

Then Boyfriend says something startling. He says, "I vote with the professor."

Is this a random stab of a guess, or has Louie's occupation been diagnosed with quick, unnerving accuracy? It's all the more disturbing given Louie's own difficulties with British accent and gesture.

"I'm off to Iceland myself," Louie confides.

Girlfriend takes it up. "Now *that's* an idea." Again she forms a loose fist and knock-knocks on her boyfriend's chest as if it were a sagging door. "We go back to Iceland."

"The two of *you* have been there?"

The pinched tone of Louie's question comes out all wrong. Boyfriend and Girlfriend peer narrowly at him. Louie is aware that disappointment may have been visible on his face.

"Only in a manner of speaking," Boyfriend replies, and the couple laughs, and Boyfriend coughs. For such a young man, he has a real geezer's splintery smoker's cough. "It's hit the bottle nonstop is Iceland. It's hit the bottle right out of the airport duty-free."

"They're the best partyers in all Europe," Girlfriend factually declares. "Better than the Spaniards."

"Oh, *much* better than the Spaniards," Boyfriend confirms. "It's no comparison."

"Better even than the Dutch," she goes on.

"Well, now, I'm not sure about the Dutch," Boyfriend replies. He deliberates. Clearly, he doesn't wish to make an irresponsible assessment, to be injudicious or unjust toward any nationality.

Louie feels a clarification is in order. "I want to see the landscape. What did you two think of the landscape?"

"You like the moon?" Girlfriend asks. "It's the moon."

"Nothing wrong with the moon," Boyfriend adds. "Nothing wrong with sipping a little vodka in a crater on the moon."

"I want to see all the sunlight," Louie goes on. "I'm told you can read a newspaper standing out in the street at midnight."

Boyfriend looks dubious. "You're looking for light? Man, I wouldn't pick Iceland. Not a whole lot of light up there."

Again his girlfriend strikes him in the chest. "We went in *January*! All the dark? It's just the opposite now!"

A pause.

"It flips," Louie explains.

Another pause. Boyfriend lowers his voice an octave, thickening his speech to a growl. To Louie's ears, it sounds like someone with an ignorant accent putting on an ignorant accent. "Hey now, you calling me stu-pid, girrrl?"

"Call yourself what you want," she replies. He laughs, coughs—that dogged smoker's cough—then leans forward for a kiss. She pauses, in mock indecision, then steps forward eagerly. The girl's thigh-serpent— that old mischief-maker—quivers and resettles. Lips join and crisply smack, and Boyfriend's fingers slip an inch or two down the torrid backside of her jeans.

"Can I help you?" Their travel agent has finished typing at last. She motions to the two of them to sit down . . .

It's only a minute or two before another agent is free. This is a middle-aged woman who looks pummeled with exhaustion—as though no task on earth could be more wearying than sitting in one spot and arranging other people's far-flung journeys. She's weeks and weeks behind in the dyeing of her auburn hair. The whites of her eyes are threaded with minute red veins.

Louie has dropped into a seat beside her. She's an utterly inauspicious presence, but sometimes we don't select our audience. We're flexible. He releases the bright remark that flared up within him only a few moments ago. Ostensibly apologetic, in truth it shimmers with a giddy amour propre, with a winning faith in his own spontaneous and chancy resourcefulness. "Hello, I have for you what may be a difficult request: I want you to arrange my one-way trip to Greenland."

# PART THREE

# Qaqqatnakkarsimasut

*while here's a darker flower,*
   *an exotic bloom that takes you*
*to a land of melting deserts*
   *where the third dream wakes you.*

YOU MIGHT NOT IMMEDIATELY SUSPECT IT, BUT SOME-times the most difficult leg in a person's getting to Greenland lies in clarifying to his elder sibling the proposed benefits of the trip. So Louie now discovered. Poor Annabelle did some hard swallowing over his detour to London, but nothing like this. She was close to hysterical when, standing in a phone booth off Tottenham Court Road, he reached her by phone. She didn't know, quite, where Greenland was. And wasn't it completely uninhabited? All right, but if it was Eskimos he was searching for, why not Canada? Didn't Windsor lie right across the Detroit River?

Such questions were fairly easy to parry, once he'd pacified Annabelle somewhat, but others were harder to negotiate, especially those involving finances and future travels. Was he still planning to catch up with his original itinerary—Turkey, India, Japan? If so—when? And if not, what portion of his various tickets just might be refundable?

Money. The financial aspects of his peculiar situation wouldn't bear scrutiny, though indeed they did give Louie pause. Money: the stubborn goddamn dollars and cents, all those painstakingly machine-tabulated sums awaiting him on ballooning credit card statements back home, those to-the-penny figures that mostly peeved him but occasionally in the middle of the night terrified him . . . Wild, impulsive spending was a common symptom of manic behavior, true. His decision to visit Greenland was spur-of-the-moment, true. And *had* he done the math? No, not exactly. What *would* this outlandish diversion cost him? He wasn't sure, exactly. What would any sensible cost-benefit analysis reveal? And exactly which notable architectural sites did he hope to view in Greenland? Igloo villages? Turf houses? Corrugated-aluminum sheds? In Googling "Greenland Architecture," Louie had come quickly upon the word *laughable*. Twice.

He was facing all sorts of accusations—from Annabelle, from a pair of wives, from a chorus of departmental voices. But if anybody would only take the time to listen, he had mostly solid defenses and rebuttals. Yes, of course his finances were one significant aspect of his life—to be duly weighed in the bobbing balance of any important decision. But what lay upon the other side of the scale was no *aspect*. What lay over there, on that other side, was his *life*—and how does a person weigh an aspect of his life against his *life*? First, by acknowledging the issue's complexity. Second, by suspending judgment. People need to hear him out.

Maybe you do pass up Istanbul's Blue Mosque, and who's to calculate the magnitude of such a forfeiture? It could be momentous—Louie willingly concedes this. But likewise who's to calculate the compensation when, in exchange, you substitute a vast herd of icebergs convening for the summer solstice? What financial value is to be placed upon a glimpse of some mountainous emerald iceberg brooding over an uninhabited bay under a midnight sun? Ask Frederic Church, who back in 1859—more than a hundred fifty years ago—underwent such trouble and expense, and danger, too, in order to see his vision. *See your vision*—not a bad motto.

"What about my refrigerator?" Annabelle calls frantically into the phone. Her dismay reverberates across a choppy ocean, from her sad house in sad Livonia, Michigan, to the London phone booth where toiling Louie would placate her. He hasn't been sleeping well, which perhaps accounts for his brain's slipping a cog, leaving him momentarily wondering whether she's alluding to the ancient quip about selling refrigerators to the Eskimos.

Then icy truth breaks over Louie's culpable head. Of course. Annabelle's refrigerator: that kitchen appliance of record. So far on his travels, despite his sterling intentions, and his handsome new Italian leather portfolio, he has failed to maintain a journal. Which means that Annabelle's festooned refrigerator, all those choice paper scraps secured by her whimsical, beloved magnets, provides the sole significant annals of the Journey of His Life. She has created a mural-like artwork not so far removed, in spirit, from the friezes at the British Museum. It's easy to laugh, but Annabelle takes her creations seriously, and her panicky dismay mustn't be dismissed. However long it takes, however expensive the calls, she must be talked round.

A very touching exchange revisits him: the evening, about a month ago (though it seems much longer), when Annabelle so proudly, bashfully unveiled her reconceived refrigerator. Tears tactfully ignored by the two of them glittered in her eyes. This wasn't creativity that any art historian, other than Louie, might appreciate. It fell between two stools, two schools. It certainly wasn't sophisticated. And it also lacked the tunnel-vision fierceness of that branch of folk art known as visionary art; Annabelle was quirky, but eminently sane. Still, her fridge creation demonstrated both sincerity (unlike the "hard honesty" in so much contemporary art) and excitement (as opposed to pumped-up, fashionable anxiety). Annabelle was temperamentally no traveler, but Louie's Journey had inspired her, for the first time in her forty-five years, to venture imaginatively round the world: Turkish mosques, Indian holy rivers, Japanese mountain shrines . . . Unless he now recognizes, and atones for, his guilt, he's a very guilty man.

One after another, apologies bubble from his lips, as well as fervent talk, intoxicating talk: the beauty of Greenland, the incomparable beauty of austere angling northern sunlight, the splendors of Frederic Church's icebergs (those arctic visions that navigated their way into a canvas-backed harbor where nothing would ever dissolve them again). When Church conceived his arctic paintings, my dear Annabelle, his hold on the future was assured. His work in the Hudson River School guaranteed him a seat in the pantheon, to say nothing of *Niagara* and *Heart of the Andes*. Even so, he journeyed strictly northward. On to Newfoundland, Labrador. Think of it. Just think. Wearing crappy, inadequate nineteenth-century clothes, eating crappy, inadequate nineteenth-century food, nursed by crappy, inadequate nineteenth-century medicines, sleeping on crappy, inadequate nineteenth-century bedding, Church struggled to pay fair artistic tribute to icebergs whose monumentality transformed his high-masted schooner into a plaything. Endlessly seasick, cold, sleepless, with wind-chapped fingers, while his vessel pitched beneath him, he sketched and painted. This was something new, something innovative at the deserted top of the world. Heretofore, up there it was nothing but a vast, open-air float-and-melt, with nobody artistically schooled enough, and materially well enough equipped, to subject the icebergs to concepts of transcendent artistic justice . . . You might ask whether an iceberg actually floats and melts if nobody's there to paint it.

Not all of this got said; even with Annabelle, Louie wasn't the teacher he ought to be. Some of it hung back in his incomplete sentences; some was strongly presaged but finally inexpressible. Still, Louie felt himself convincing himself, and much of Greenland's raw poetry did pass through that narrow funnel that divides and distances any two people, however intimately conjoined they think themselves. Annabelle began to come round, which was essential. There was no proceeding unless Annabelle came round.

And that's what he satisfyingly accomplished, in calls from London telephone booths, in the various winsome, bright, funny, affectionate emails he sent winging her way. His brain had taken an agile and dynamic turn; it didn't seem unreasonable to conjecture that he'd actually gotten smarter. Annabelle, your little brother's heading off to *Greenland,* of all places. Isn't this exciting? More than that: a splendid development? Support him—congratulate him, savor the journey with him. And then, dear sister Annabelle, fellow art lover, my own highly painstaking contemporary kitchen artist, may you joyously rededicate yourself to the revising, the reinventing of your refrigerator.

But getting to Greenland presented no simple task. Even if the would-be pilgrim *does* manage to talk his elder sister round, formidable obstacles arise. There's the issue, for instance, of what to do as departure nears if you start coming down with some vague and hardly life-threatening but nonetheless acute ailment. Let's say you're served tandoori chicken in an Indian takeout in Russell Square and the rice tastes *funny*—but you eat it anyway. And the next morning you wake up feeling not quite yourself, but without the immediate signs—the abdominal queasiness, the plunging diarrhea—of simple food poisoning. No, you wake up feeling bad *all over:* your joints ache, and your body, hoarding its toxins, is hot but not sweaty. If that's what's happening as departure nears, how do you proceed?

In Louie's case, you move forward. In Louie's case, you confront full on the issue of whether it's psychosomatic, or even prophetic: Is your body rebelling, or maybe forewarning you about the folly of your plans? His head is wheeling. Or reeling. And it scarcely matters if it's psychosomatic, since the effects are genuine. There are *bugs* in the body—no less real, if invisible, than the ants parading across your kitchen counter in Ann Arbor. No less real than the flies compactly wrestling (like Samson wedged between the pillars of the temple) with the wires of the Ann Arbor bedroom screens.

So, Louie's somewhat sick. Or more than somewhat. Summer flu? Lyme disease? (He read somewhere that nowadays summer flu screams Lyme disease.) Fortunately, the illness brings sensations of floating detachment, his body merely some troublesome piece of luggage—a listing suitcase with one wheel broken. You make do. Louie finds himself on a flight to Iceland, with an overnight stay in Reykjavík's Hotel Bubbi. He'll fly then to Qaqqatkivisut, Greenland. Qaqqatkivisut? The first flight of his life to a destination he has no clue how to pronounce.

Iceland lies underneath a national mantle of rain. Louie studies the terrain as his bus winds from Keflavík Airport to surprisingly distant Reykjavík; apparently the journey may take more than an hour. Low visibility, but through the bus's rain-bespattered windows Louie discerns a gray land as incisively fissured as the moon. Unearthly is what it is, just as promised. And ancient looking. Rain has been falling steadily here since the twilight of the Cretaceous, when a few relict dinosaurs petered out and the land was left to the trolls; this is no country for people. He's ailing. His body is *aching,* and he's not thinking clearly. He needs to rest. He is progressing toward landscapes of perpetual sunlight, at least theoretically, but overall this is the darkest destination in the Journey of His Life. The nameless couple in the London travel agency—Boyfriend of the snakelike ponytail, Girlfriend of the serpent mounting the backside of her tan, plump, shamelessly exposed upper thigh—trumpeted an Iceland where the party begins at the airport, bottles fresh from the duty-free popped open. But the atmosphere on *this* bus is subdued and sedate. The passengers are phlegmatic Icelanders intermittently muttering low monosyllables. Their conversation? Presumably, somebody saying, in judgment, *Rain.* And somebody else, after according the matter due deliberation, replying, *Rain.*

Louie reclines into his new and much-too-expensive olive-green down jacket, purchased in an "outdoor store" (indoors) near Piccadilly Circus. He'd feared a shortage of suitable clothing stores in Iceland, and none at all in Greenland, where if you're feeling cold you slap another sealskin over your shoulders. Of course he's fully prepared— eager—to laugh at his laughable ignorance. The down jacket was a brand he didn't know: Yankee Ingenuity. Only after hauling it back to the Mulder Arms did he discover it was manufactured in China.

He has much too much luggage. This would be true even if he were feeling hopeful and energetic. Now, given his body's pitiful state, the task of further transporting his luggage seems insurmountable. But when he disembarks in Reykjavík, at the bus station, he has the good fortune to find as cabbie a fair-haired ox. He's young—can't be much over twenty—and he maneuvers Louie's suitcases like empty stage props. Does he know the Hotel Bubbi? "Sure thing."

Sure thing? As oxen go, this one winds up being preposterously idiomatic and articulate, much more than Louie himself, who's ready to hand over not merely his luggage but his lecturing duties at AAC. The cabbie cheerfully explains that he is "not so much overall in favor" of American culture, whose "worldwide domination is unfortunate, arguably." But with exceptions. He reveres Bill Evans. Does Louie know Bill Evans? "Jazz pianist," Louie says. "Sure thing. A real classic."

And he worships the actress Margaret Sullavan—is Louie acquainted with Miss Sullavan?

"Sure thing. Another real classic," Louie says. But while the name's familiar—Louie certainly has seen some of her films—he cannot at the moment, given his burning body and smoky head, spring any to mind. The cab streams along a drenched street of hefty blocky concrete houses, dark hulkers under a dark sky. How much has it cost him, so far, to venture to this sunless Land of the Midnight Sun?

"It is the movie *The Shop Around the Corner* that is the profound wonder," the cabbie elucidates. "Yes? Directed by Ernst Lubitsch. Who had the famous touch. In 1940, a war year, though America had not yet entered the fray. With James Stewart playing a young Hungarian male salesperson. Of course it is absurd and ridiculous. But it is comic genius."

Addled though he may be, Louie congratulates himself on identifying how this young man's marvelous facility with English enhances itself through an avoidance of contractions. "That is right," Louie says. "That is so true. It is an absolute classic."

"The true comic genius. Everyone once said that my mother exactly resembled the actress Margaret Sullavan. The resemblance was visual and vocal also. My mother died at the age of forty-three only, of ALS. You know it?"

"Amnio . . . amyo . . . amyo-something lateral sclerosis," Louie says, not exactly proud of his performance, but certainly he could have come off worse. He adds, somewhat hesitantly, "Your mother was exactly my age." And adds, still more hesitantly, "My mother died when I was two." And adds: "She had a Nordic name: Elvira." And adds, intimately: "Her nickname was Elvie."

"Amyotrophic lateral sclerosis. My friends have proposed that I am so fond of the actress Margaret Sullavan because she exactly resembles my mother. But that fails to make into consideration one thing. This is comic genius."

"There's no arguing with genius," Louie says. Even in his muzzy state, the words carry a fatuous echo, which causes him, fatuously, to append a warning: "Or if you do, watch out. Watch out."

Louie explains that unfortunately he isn't feeling well, and therefore believes he might require assistance with his bags at the hotel, unfortunately. This is no easy thing to ask, given Louie's pride in self-sufficiency, and he feels compelled to speculate on causes of illness. He mentions the tandoori chicken, while in fairness supplementarily pointing out having consumed, earlier that same day, a dicey rice pudding . . .

But when they reach the Hotel Bubbi, all such talk seems excessively, even prissily, detailed. The blond ox, Louie's bulging bags securely in hand, blazes his way to the doe-eyed receptionist. This deer looks even younger than the ox. Their exchange is hasty. The cabbie disappears into the elevator, and Louie's still huddled at the check-out counter, sorting out forms and payment, when the cabbie returns, empty-handed. Actually, not empty-handed: he deposits a key in Louie's palm. "Bags in your room," he announces. Louie suddenly feels flustered—unequal to the thin stack of Icelandic kronur in his pocket. He doesn't remember the conversion rate. So he extends an American five-dollar bill, but the kid openhandedly shrugs it off. He says, "And Margaret Sullavan in *The Shopworn Angel*. That is the comic performance of great genius."

"I'll watch it," Louie promises. And it seems never in his life has he offered a more heartfelt promise.

"And Bill Evans playing the song 'Some Other Time.' It does not get any better."

"Exactly. Precisely," Louie says. "I'm listening," he calls after this cabbie who has turned out to be a lifesaver. Lifesaver? But the ox has plunged out into the rain.

"Some Other Time"? What time is it? Louie has read about an arctic sun that progresses more sideways than up and down, resiliently bouncing off the horizon and leaping up again. And in a land of perpetual sunlight, what does Time matter when skies portend only mist and rain? He's jet lagged, maybe. Sick, certainly. Louie finds his way to a room furnished from some Ikea catalog of twenty years ago, when the Swedish company was getting started in the States, or first impressing a young Louie Hake recently convinced that his professional life lay in fine arts. Clean lines, blond wood, a passion for functionality over ornamentation. Back then, it had taken Louie a while to comprehend that much as he admired this aesthetic, he didn't adore it. He was a Motor City boy, after all, blessed with a father who lovingly instructed his young son in the finer points of a golden age of automotive design: elongated fins, plump pregnant-looking curves, two-tone paint jobs, spirited outcroppings of chrome. Somewhere between Ikea and the Charles Dickens house—isn't that where we want to live?

As its sole concession to decoration, the room offers a large oil painting. Sunflowers. An original canvas. The signature contains only one name: Einar. An Icelander. The painter has conveyed much of the harshness and brutality, and none of the harsh and brutal beauty, of Van Gogh's incandescent sunflowers.

Louie's friend the cabbie, who revered an actress whose name at the moment escapes Louie, the loquacious, charming shopgirl in that movie with Jimmy Stewart, has deposited carry-on and both suitcases neatly beside the bed's foot. The suitcases can remain unopened. Groaning, aching, Louie hoists the carry-on onto the bed, unzips it. He has some NyQuil, or its dubious English equivalent, whose capsules, punitively large, might challenge a horse's gullet. (He once read about a horse that swallowed, whole, a child's tennis shoe. But now he can't remember: Did it live?) He selects one pill, removes toothbrush and toothpaste from toiletry bag, and on the bathroom sink lines up all three. He requires nothing else. It's presumably dinnertime, but there's no way he can negotiate an Icelandic restaurant.

Having zipped his Yankee Ingenuity parka tight to his throat, Louie shuffles down to the hotel lobby and into the street.

Why shouldn't any movement hurt—why should we expect pain-lessly to haul around forty-plus-year-old bodies across the jagged stone face of the planet? Why shouldn't infirmity be the norm, good health the exception? His hotel lies in the shadow of Hallgrímskirkja, the city's best-known building. It's a vast, surpassingly ugly Lutheran church, even more malproportioned than tourist pamphlets suggest. He walks down a hill through drizzly fog until he reaches a bakery. The golden odor of bread. The only food of human invention he really craves.

Big bright lights, and the place smelling wonderful. It's the rich-est palette on earth, Louie now conclusively recognizes, those autumn hues of harvested grain put to the oven, kernel and germ and refining fire . . . "Do you speak English," he asks the skinny, intensely freckled red-haired girl behind the counter.

"Of course," she says. Just as though he'd asked whether she ever drank water, or breathed air.

"I *love* your bakery." Saying this brings, farcically, a blush to Louie's cheeks, as though he'd declared, *I love your eyes* or *I love your jeans*. His head is swimming. He tries a new, a professorial tone: "Now tell me, of all the breads you sell, which is your personal favorite? Personally."

The sound tripping from the girl's mouth could not be more remote if she were conversing in Martian or Venusian: welcome to Icelandic.

"What you just said," Louie says. "That's great. But which one's that?"

"*Fjallabrauð?* Mountain bread." She points.

"I would like, please, a loaf of the good mountain bread."

"That is not one we slice. It is extremely—dense."

"Density," Louie snugly returns, "is exactly what in today's travels I happen to be seeking."

The loaf's unexpected weight under Louie's arm is wonderfully bolstering. He has come away with something substantial. And warm. Surely recovered health is at hand. For the moment, trudging through both a literal and a mental fog, Louie feels fully compensated by life.

Another moment, and he realizes bread alone isn't sufficient. Peanut butter. The cleanest, keenest wish he can isolate is an appetite for peanut butter.

And surely his is a doomed wish . . . In London once, years ago, Lizzie identified a sudden raging desire for a PB&J. The jelly, of course, was available in bewildering abundance, but the peanut butter was another matter. The two of them combed the streets in a quest that ended up with their purchasing a leaden substance, nominally peanut butter, which was gray in pallor and grainy in texture; it shredded the bread. If that was London, what are his chances in Reykjavík?

And yet—and yet . . . Louie has walked but a block or two, through raindrops so small they create no impact on striking, when something called a *heilsuhúsið* looms out of a sodden Icelandic oblivion. Oh. Whole House—like Whole Foods. Inside, a person can purchase water-chilled blocks of tofu and vitamin $B_{12}$ supplements and Cajun-spiced dried mango slices and frozen meatless "mock sausage." And peanut butter. No, the plural—nut butters: peanut, almond, cashew. Smooth or chunky or super chunky. Organic or "conventional." After much glazed contemplation, Louie settles on a glass jar of Country Auntie Franny's Guaranteed Always Organic Super Chunk Peanut Butter. Does he have a fever? His forehead feels hot, but perhaps only because his hand is cold.

What keeps him moving slowly but steadily along, through the gelid rain, is a hopeful sensation of being uniquely in possession of the world's choicest plunder: mountain bread under one arm, dear Auntie Franny's finest under the other. Into the hotel lobby—"Hello," "Hallo"—and into the gleaming lap of the waiting elevator.

In his room, perched at the foot of his bed, his new olive-green Yankee Ingenuity parka draping his shoulders, Louie belatedly discovers he has no utensils. Will this stop him? Hell, no. Will he go downstairs to borrow a knife? Hell, no. He rips a heel off his loaf, which in its mountainous denseness doesn't tear easily. Using right index finger as palette knife, Louie erects a knoll in the center of left palm. He has struck gold—gold in the Icelandic mountains. With slow almost painterly self-possession, Louie utilizes that same right index finger to deposit, stroke by stroke, a smooth tawny membrane over the bread's tors and craters.

These last few days of illness, he hasn't been seeing clearly, but as he hunches over his creation, fixed within the sharp-edged cone of the bedside lamp, everything finds a focus preternaturally acute. It deserves notice as a landscape, his ragged hunk of bread—a remote, aberrational terrain of juts and crags and pitfalls—and the golden peanut butter boasts a broad array of trace pigments you wouldn't detect unless you looked very, very closely: lavender and rose and apple green and persimmon orange. And Louie knows this is a moment he shall not forget. It's the one he will forever summon as the vividest sight he beheld in Iceland: a lovingly, painstakingly hand-slathered heel of bread.

ONE OF THE COMPLICATIONS IN VOYAGING TO GREENLAND IS that arrival may not seem like arrival. Greenland may feel remarkably like wherever you departed from.

Say you're to fly out of the tiny Reykjavík city airport, where you gaze out onto a parking lot shrouded in pale gray mist. The crowd of cars extends almost to the terminal doors, as if clamoring to get in and fly away. You wait and wait. Finally, you're led outdoors, through rain cold as ice shavings, clumping along with a sense of clogged and muddled purpose, your body aching and febrile, stepping into a tight propeller plane that holds, at most, thirty seats. The flight attendant isn't concerned with welcoming her passengers; she is preoccupied, worrisomely, with weight distribution—getting passengers and carry-ons arranged so as not to imbalance and tip the aircraft.

The balance holds. After a couple of hours, dozing to the loud chop of the invisible propellers, you disembark in Greenland, in a pale gray mist, under rain cold as ice shavings. What has changed? Perhaps the only change is you feel sicker. And the taxicab that brought you to your Reykjavík hotel was a Mercedes. This one's a battered Honda. So far, that's the major difference.

Somehow Louie and his bags find their way to the Hotel Royale, and after painful delays requiring too much standing, hotel guest and luggage are settled in their room. The novel interest of this particular illness—its sensation of securing a new vantage on life—has long worn off, even if the illness hasn't. How he gets from point to point scarcely matters. What matters is that ultimately there are blankets, and a big bed that is actually two twin beds shoved together, and a snowily white toilet, and bread and water and peanut butter.

Time, too, scarcely matters. Louie dimly recalls a barbershop magazine article about leap seconds, periodically inserted into the worldwide calendar to align us with the colossal peregrinations of the sun and stars. *Someone* is keeping track, right down to cosmological fractions of a second, which means he doesn't need to. It's striking, really, how many things a person needn't attend to.

His jeans are sagging at the waist. He can't seem to rouse any appetite. He still has his jar of peanut butter, and a broad hulk of mountain bread, and also a whole other loaf of mountain bread, steadily growing denser and harder. (The loaves demanded lots of room in his overstuffed suitcase, but a man has to eat, and he'd worried about finding nothing edible in Greenland. So he'd jettisoned some tan linen shorts and a herringbone linen shirt, both presumably perfect for steamy India. Well, when he arrives in New Delhi, new clothing should be cheap.)

Dinner at the Hotel Royale is available from six to nine. Somehow he came away from the receptionist with a folded-up menu in his pocket. He could feast tonight on halibut and stewed carrots for 195 Danish kroner. Or ham steak and stewed carrots for 180 kroner. Or musk-ox steak accompanied by stewed carrots for 210 kroner. He's content with mountain bread and peanut butter. The water from the bathroom tap runs cold as glacial melt.

He sleeps deep—almost too long to call it a nap. Still feeling quite ill, Louie seeks consolation in the notion of feeling ill in a new way. His brain, right behind his forehead, has begun to throb, big decisive throbbings, though bearable. It's 9:10. At night, presumably. In which case dinner is no longer served, but he doesn't honestly want dinner. Still, he wants *something*. He shuffles down to the lobby and asks the cute pimply plump blonde teenager behind the counter, who has braces on her teeth and an unfortunate drooping pair of silver rings threaded through each reddened and swollen-looking nostril, whether he might get a cup of tea. He'd be content to carry it upstairs, but she's determined to seat him in the little dining hall, whose big windows survey an enveloping gray mist. Red-and-white checkerboard tablecloths, overlain with clear sheets of plastic. Under the plastic, despite the plastic, his tablecloth bears the stains of tomato sauce and coffee.

A polar-bear skin sprawls on the wall.

The thing is *huge*. It looks much bigger than a bearskin. It looks like the hide of some creature that might dine exclusively on polar bears.

A waitress comes over and, like virtually everyone in his new Nordic world, she's young. She must be an Eskimo, though if Louie were not in Greenland, he'd have called her Asian. Of course the Eskimo DNA is essentially Asian, and his brain isn't functioning lucidly.

Louie thinks of Eskimos as low and squat of build, but this girl is of average height, and thin. The thinness perhaps makes her appear taller than she is. She's informally attired, to say the least. She's wearing as shirt or blouse what looks like thermal underwear, though it bears a rectangular unpunctuated motto upon its chest: I ♥ LA. The sleeves are too short and it's tight across the bust. The material is porous, and through it Louie traces out a lacy cobalt-blue bra.

She looks louche and a little crass, but on the other hand Louie is hardly the same dapper fellow he was in Rome, in his silk-blend tweedy sport coat and Bacco Bucci loafers. He hasn't changed his powder-blue Oxford shirt in a couple of days. He hasn't shaved since—since Shelley's departure. It's been a while since he bathed.

Though he requested only tea, the girl sets a plate before him. To his surprise, she also provides a cloth napkin—a crisp, starchy cloth napkin.

The order of tea, when eventually it arrives, consists of a heavy-duty red thermos of hot water, a heavy-duty white porcelain mug, and a Tetley bag. The same brand provided, morning after morning, at the Mulder Arms. Some things never change. But some things do, and to be served tea by an Eskimo girl is one of them. Is the preferred term in Greenland *Inuit*? Or is that local to Canada? Louie says, "Do you live here in"—he takes a wild stab at the name—"Qaqqatkivisut?"

She corrects the pronunciation: "Qaqqatkivisut."

"Do you live here?"

She peers with an expression of heightened attention—as though his were a truly absorbing question. But she does not signal a reply.

It seems any attempt at meaningful conversation is over, for when Louie looks to pay his bill, it's the sore-nosed pimply Danish girl who makes the transaction.

Yet the following night, after a gray and bedridden day, his Eskimo girl returns to ailing Louie. He dreams of her. She appears just for him, leaning against a black refrigerator in a shadowy kitchen whose windows stand open on this balmy and special summer afternoon. He knows her in part by her cobalt-blue bra, for that's all she wears above the waist. Below the waist, it's alluringly baggy egg-yolk-yellow gym shorts. A chain of complicated and precarious events, having engineered the two of them here, now melts tracelessly away. Where did everything go? How did the two of them get here? These are questions pointing to a question as richly dense as any he knows, but one never quite formulable when awake: *How do the dreams begin?* He has arrived at that state where, having shucked most of his faltering external self, his questions are as valid as anything that anyone—Darwin, Kafka, Gandhi, Freud—might ask. Do the figures in a dream emerge full-blown, like actors stepping from the wings onto a theater stage? Or are they like figures in a painting—a scumble of diffident colors, a murky emergence of shapes, logs becoming limbs, and finally a miraculous quickening as pigments somehow learn to breathe and see and think and speak? Louie knows this kitchen, having been here before. But he has never done what he's fixing to do.

No sensation of touch in Louie's experience, forty-three years of fingers extending for this or that tactile gratification, can match the humming, charged comeback of these motions, as one of his hands slides across the girl's shoulder blades and the other hand across her slim lower back. She is so warm. Fresh from a tennis court, body sweating evenly, open every pore. She returns his embrace. The balls of their fingertips might literally be balls, so smoothly do they roll across flesh. No friction. Her flesh invites this rolling, revels in it. Each of her delicate, prominent rib bones sings, sings like a tuning fork. Cobalt blue is the color of her brassiere, a hue whose intensity the sky has sought to equal since our earth began rolling, without ever getting there, quite. The loveliest day anyone has witnessed is an exquisite falling short.

Blue for the art historian: always the true mystery hue, the unattainable perch on the prism. The shock and promise of unearthed lumps of lapis lazuli, aglitter with microscopic flecks of pyrite, carted upon a camel's back from mythical Afghanistan. The introduction of ultramarine into the Mediterranean painter's palette, arriving in time to burnish the canvases of Michelangelo and Titian. The blue of Mary's robe, rarest and most expensive pigment in the paint box, as well as the blue in the spray gun, waiting to settle upon the plumped Renoirish flank of a '57 Bel Air. Louie holds it all there, between his itching fingertips, the clasp of her bra, its lace sere as an onionskin envelope poised above the rectangular black maw of the mailbox, the penned confession of your worldly hopes, your prayers transforming into postage. All at your fingertips. You release the envelope, you unclasp the bra with one hand, while the other hand slips its way beneath the lavish elastic enclosure of the yellow shorts, shattering their yolk—and the result is literally so breathtaking that you awake gasping, lungs rasping in primitive need. Louie wakes, for a few seconds scrambling toward the knowledge that he's in Greenland, and has been sick.

Meanwhile, elsewhere, elsewhere, all in a rush (with his own extinction so close at hand), he's sliding down an endlessly long slippery industrial drain. He's bound within a tube of innumerable circles whose distant terminus glitters kaleidoscopically. The light keeps shifting. Already he cannot recall, though everything ought still to be so fresh, the solid furnishings of the kitchen of his dream. His breath slows into wavelets of blue, and eggy yellow, and a humming hand glowing even yet: his hand is a pumpkiny orange, the hue of lucky 7.

He is awake enough to awake; asleep enough to sleep. Louie snugly slips his hand into his crotch, basking in the color's embers. His breathing slows. Louie sleeps.

But in the morning, the dream's still inside him. His tingling right hand isn't completely his right hand—as though, in the tumbling voyage from one world into the next, he'd constricted its circulation. And the glow has turned partly into a hum; his hand hums. His body pulls his hand backward, his hand pulls his body forward, or vice versa; Louie's still feeling traces of a swaying flu, and in order to limit his pitching in the shower, he plants both palms flat on the tile wall. Though he's in Greenland, there are copious floods of hot water, and the steam's white clouds embrace him.

He's beginning to feel somewhat better. At long last, he's improving, though the weather, perpetually gray and foggy, isn't. Sometimes the mist and fog open a little, sometimes a little more than a little, but there are few vistas.

And Qaqqatkivisut is a dump—a chilly dump. Generally we speak metaphorically when calling a town a dump. But Qaqqatkivisut is a literal dump. Apparently, whenever anybody in town wearies of anything, or finds it outworn, he drops it at his feet and shuffles away. Torn plastic shopping bags, windshield wipers, broken street signs bearing unpronounceable names, cigarette butts by the tens of thousands, rusted bicycle baskets, dented beer cans, brown whiskey bottles, clear gin bottles, AAA batteries, an inexplicable tube of sunscreen—everything was evidently jettisoned at the precise point where its usefulness or interest gave out.

Louie has read that Qaqqatkivisut lies not so far from one of the most active calving glaciers in the Northern Hemisphere. Here and there, through the mist, a stray and forlorn low gray lump squats on the gray, resigned waters of the harbor: Louie's first icebergs.

They're more than disappointing, frankly. If, back in grad-school days, his thesis on Church never advanced very far, he did arrive at a fine title: "'Marvelously Sensitive to a Steady Gaze': The Landscapes of Frederic Church." Its quotation came from the Reverend Louis L. Noble, who accompanied Church on his 1859 expedition to the frozen waters of Labrador. Icebergs were, according to Reverend Noble, the most magical objects in God's creation.

But not these lusterless gray SUV-sized bergs floating in Qaqqat-kivisut Harbor. To the pilgrim come from afar, they're an unwelcome reminder of a painful truth: travel's promises are habitually empty. *Elsewhere* turns out to be no better than *here*, or not as good as *here*—and *here* was never any good. The icebergs feel like a betrayal.

More than he sees it, he smells the cold sea, which, hour after hour, whispers to itself, foggily. Sea and sky are a true, unadulterated gray holding no hues but black and white. The town is a collection of hut-sized houses in blazing fluorescent colors, and some larger houses, rusty, with black tar-paper roofs, all perched on the rim of a bay, surrounded by brown snow-seamed hills. Since his arrival in Qaqqatkivi-sut, he hasn't glimpsed a single tree.

Nor a squirrel. And not many birds. What he has seen in abundance are sled dogs, chained to penitential gray boulders. Mostly they sleep, these scattered prisoners, though night and day, at intervals known only to the canine calendar, they set up a congress of howls to wake the dead.

Other than a couple of improvised hotel restaurants, the town appears to have only three places offering a real meal: a Chinese dive called Happy Lucky, a Thai dive called Thai Time, and a run-down café called Rue de Rivoli, which serves up the largest orders of French fries that Louie has ever seen presented to a single person.

Taxis overrun the town, which initially surprises him. But it turns out that from end to end Qaqqatkivisut's paved roads extend only some four or five miles. With nowhere to go, why would anybody trouble himself with the expense and bother of owning a car? If you need to reach the town's one decent-sized grocery store, or you're looking to visit the town's one bank or one "unisexed" hair salon, you cab in.

Lots of drinking's done in Qaqqatkivisut. This isn't a conclusion you come to by reading a magazine article. No, you see people staggering. Louie might as well be back in Soho. Maybe it's mostly the tourists, those stragglers to Greenland who have met a gray wet wall. Maybe things are different if and when the weather ever lifts. But whatever time of day it is (and the timelessness probably helps explain the inebriation), people are seen staggering.

Most townsfolk are Eskimos—Inuit. Before his arrival in Greenland, Louie's visual sense of the Inuit was dominated by photographs of smile-seized faces in fur-fringed parkas. But the people of Qaqqatkivisut are somber folks, wearing precisely what you'd see people wearing if you stood in front of a Home Depot in Michigan: oversize sweatpants, oversize blue jeans, fluorescent sneakers, oversize athletic jerseys, baseball caps . . .

The children, though, who apparently haven't been informed they're the tragic heirs to a dying way of life, seem wholly happy. Inuit kids. Kicking a soccer ball in a boulder-strewn vacant lot. Or spiraling through the streets on big-tired bicycles. Or inexpertly puffing cigarettes in front of the grocery store, where, to Louie's amazement, no fresh fish is for sale. (Louie doesn't much care for fresh fish, but he'd thought a Greenlandic fish counter might be painterly and picturesque—a chance to commune with the shade of William Merritt Chase.)

Louie keeps returning to the hotel dining room, seeking another glimpse of his Inuit waitress, but each time it's someone else, who, being someone else, scarcely matters. It's an illogical hope, but a natural one, that at their next encounter her face will register some of the consequences and implications of his dream. They've shared an intimate exchange, and it seems only fitting that she acknowledge complicity.

In the hotel lobby he does meet up with a very appealing American kid named Kevin, a grad student from Duke researching glacial movements. Kevin's off to the central ice sheet, which, so he informs Louie, overlays some eighty percent of Greenland. North to south, it's longer than the distance from Montreal to Miami. Really? Louie asks. Yes, and it's unbroken. Kevin is part of a scientific team camping out for weeks on end, hundreds of miles from the nearest permanent habitation. The only way to get where they're going is by helicopter . . .

"But what about polar bears?"

"We take a rifle." Kevin grins. "But really not much risk of polar bears where we're going. It's too remote, too desolate. There's not enough food to sustain them."

Too remote for polar bears! What could be more welcoming? Louie could listen all night to such talk. Oh, he has a hundred questions! But unfortunately they've chatted for only a few minutes when Kevin's ride pulls up, and suddenly the kid's gone, without leaving behind even a last name. Feeling just a trifle self-pitying, perhaps, Louie retreats to the hotel dining room for tea.

The tea comes with a mini-container of long-life milk. It seems long-life milk diffuses differently. (Or is he seeing milk for the first time?) Louie studies as he pours. The milk plunges straight to the bottom of the clear mug, then quickly, flowerlike, blossoms upward, outward. As its white petals open, Louie consciously realizes, at last, what he has wordlessly known for a while now:

The kitchen of his dream? He's been there before. Unforgettably. It's where, a quarter century ago, still just a college kid, Louie Hake Jr. kissed Mrs. Gantry—the unreckonably exotic Veronique.

Mrs. Gantry has been in his mind—perhaps more than he knows. Didn't he rattle on and on about her in Rome to that sweet inquisitive gentleman, the other Louie, the Philadelphia dentist? The two of them enjoyed such wonderful talks, such thoughtful conversation, beautifully pitched between openness and manly restraint, though Louie did perhaps confide too much, especially about Florence. (Those conversations seem so long ago; it feels to Louie as though he has not merely experienced a lot but has actually changed a lot since then.)

And he told the other Louie about Lizzie, too—all his regrets and second thoughts and unresolved feelings. But didn't he turn, in the end, to Veronique—to that incomparable distant moment when, in her limeade-lit kitchen, she stood closer than proprieties would propose, gazing at him with a steadiness suggesting an imploring need? And timid Louie Hake Jr. handsomely stepped forward and, addressing her need, kissed her. Again and again.

You have to know how to read your dreams. It isn't the lovely young waitress in the blue brassiere he's longing for— darkly inveigling though she might appear in the flesh. He's coveting a return to an actual afternoon when, after giving a tennis lesson on a puddled court, under a rain-rinsed deep blue Michigan sky, he followed his student home. She was a married woman, and he just a kid. But she accorded him such a flattering, dizzying respect: he was her teacher, after all.

"It's a crazy long shot," Louie mutters aloud.

He goes on: "But I have to know . . ."

Isn't it true you sometimes have to venture farther and farther out to reach the center of things? You voyage to Greenland in order to reach Fallen Hills. Yes, he does need to know.

Would it be possible to track down Veronique on the Internet? He has no idea where she lives, what she does. Is she still in the States? The last thing he knew, she was heading with her doctor husband to Omaha. And feeling unhappy about it.

Louie has steadfastly avoided all computers in Greenland. But they are readily available, or so he has been told. The Hotel Royale offers a "business center."

Which turns out to be a converted supply closet, equipped with a single ancient boxy Hewlett Packard. What is his time on the computer costing him? He doesn't want to know. He's dealing in Danish kroner, a currency of playfully colorful bills. None of it's real. Again he's online. It's only right—it must be done—that he check his email first.

There are ninety-seven messages, half from Annabelle. Or thereabouts. He's not sure he can bear it. But he does in fact open each of Annabelle's letters, serially, and reads at least the first paragraph.

Annabelle's sounding nervous, she's sounding frantic. Is he still in Iceland? Is he feeling well? How is he feeling? Has he been in touch with doctors back home? Do they have real doctors in Iceland and has he consulted them? Greenland? Louie, *Greenland*? Where is he? Where is he?

She has done some Internet research. Does Louie know that in the seventies a Michigan man from Kalamazoo tumbled down a crevice in Greenland and his body wasn't recovered for three years? Louie types a rapid response:

Dear Annabelle,
   Was the Kalamazoo guy who tumbled down the crevasse alive when they found him? If so, I'll bet he was pretty hungry . . .

Louie laughs gaily as he pushes Send. Feeling punchy, he forces himself to calm down enough to write a PS:

Annabelle,
   Well, I'm safely in Greenland and no crevasse in sight. The major dangers here are surely psychological; in the hotel lobby they were piping in Neil Diamond singing "Kentucky Woman" when I arrived. Could anything be more ominous than that?
   Annabelle, you must stop fretting! I'm fine. If you think about it, everything I'm doing has to do with my earlier research. You'll remember that I almost wrote my doctoral thesis on Frederic Church, and I always took a *special* interest in his arctic paintings. This is my chance to see what he saw firsthand. That's all. This is basic research.
   Not that I'm seeing much at the moment. We're "socked in." Everything's overcast. That's Okay. I had some kind of flu bug, as of course you heard, but it's passing.

Greenland is extremely sophisticated. You can use a Visa card anywhere.

And they have extremely superb medical care.

Louie pauses to scrutinize his last sentence. Having made a preposterous assertion for which he has absolutely no empirical backing, he finds that its attractiveness beckons and he expatiates:

The country of Greenland is basically run by Denmark, which is universally regarded as having the best medical care in all of Europe. Which is to say the best medical care in the whole world. (Google the longevity tables.) I'm feeling closely monitored.

Closely monitored? Who is he trying to kid? There's nobody to check whether he eats anything, or stays up for forty-eight straight hours, or comes down for dinner in the hotel dining room wearing pajamas, or drinks a fifth of Scotch a day. And yet he isn't being fully dishonest. For he's watching himself more attentively than he can ever remember doing.

Something very interesting is happening—developing. It's going on inside him, fortunately. He is recovering; he's slipping into another phase. The seemingly impossible search for Veronique Gantry locates her in a few keystrokes. Louie is reasonably adroit with computer research, yet old enough to marvel at how rapidly an impossibly nebulous goal turns securely tactile. He'd envisioned the search for Veronique as elaborate and roundabout—the sort of quest you'd hire a detective for—but within moments he has not only made a positive identification but has produced her actual photograph.

She isn't on Facebook. But she's in Tulsa. She's a single mother of twin boys, who are fourteen. They're athletic. She's working in the office of the Payton Avenue Presbyterian Church in downtown Tulsa. They have a website. They have an "About Us" where employees describe themselves. He's struck by how idiomatic her English is. Then suspects it's *too* idiomatic and she had assistance. (He recalls her English as halting—but this was twenty-plus years ago.) She says: "As a single mom, I have worked six years as liaison between the Church and the Congregation. In this time my duties include everything from delivering an Easter ham to a family with mother with TWO broken legs to helping an indigent woman find counseling for alcohol and gambling addictions. My great pride and joy is my twin boys, Gus and Trevor, who are both seven and a half inch taller than me! And I mustn't forget their 'baby sister,' Sheila, a golden retriever puppy who will eat everyone's shoes if you don't watch."

She's divorced, clearly. Easy to compose the scenario. Louie dimly remembers her husband, Dr. Gantry, a tall, balding, big-shouldered and athletic SOB. Who no doubt took up with a nurse. A blonde all-American nurse born and bred in Oklahoma. Leaving Veronique with two boys. Whom she raised herself. She was a woman adrift, and the church took her in.

But the photograph. There's a photo on the church website, and Louie, shuttered in the mausolean business center of the Hotel Royale, studies it for a long, long interval. At first the woman staring out from the computer screen disturbs him. Deeply. She's older, though this shouldn't surprise him. Most of us are, after a quarter of a century. But as the doctor's wife, Mrs. Gantry, she was such a girl—so schoolgirl-ishly earnest in trying to remember, as a ball came bouncing her way, to plant her feet and get the head of the racket back. And now she isn't a girl. She's a woman, whose face betrays destructive pinching lines around her mouth. She's standing under a tree in bloom. Probably a magnolia—big bold pink blossoms. The picture's a little out of focus. But she has thickened in the hips, no question. Slender—she'd had such slender hips. You could see the lithe muscles bulge in her thighs and her bottom as she stretched and crouched for a ball.

Yet the longer Louie contemplates his Veronique, the more suc-cessfully he recovers that winsome fine-boned creature who, in her kitchen, stood surprisingly close one summer afternoon after a tennis lesson. The eyes have grown harder, giving her a still-more-unapproachable look, but softer, too; they are the same eyes. He knows them. They were always tough to read, but once, trusting in their warmth and receptivity, he pulled off the boldest act of his life—or boldest until embarking on his Journey. Even now he trusts those eyes. The separated halves of an unlikely couple contemplate each other, the Vietnamese single mother standing under a magnolia in Tulsa, Oklahoma, and the much-off-course pilgrim Louie Hake in Qaqqatkivisut, Greenland, who hasn't shaved for days, who lives mostly on peanut butter and mountain bread, and between the two of them a shiver of understanding flashes.

Nights have been rough, his illness reasserting its hold on his head and chest. Eventually, his Internet explorations for the moment complete, Louie wanders up to his room and takes two NyQuil, or whatever they are. The girl of his dream is still with him, in her blue brassiere, but her gaze has altered. Into her pupils has gathered an invincible wisdom, and she is no child as she offers herself to him.

Louie wakes in the morning feeling a little better. The weather, too—a little better. The gray of the skies has broken enough to reveal portions of the surrounding, snowy hills. In his frigid, soupy tennis shoes he makes his way out of town, on a paved road that soon becomes big-pebbled gravel. There are no clear property lines in town, no fences (except around the tilted white crosses in the graveyard), and the odd gaudily painted shacklike houses seem randomly distributed over the rolling terrain. He is reconnoitering in search of distant glaciers. He doesn't see any, but he does see dozens and dozens of chained long-haired sled dogs, some white and some gray and some black, who eye him with that woeful attentiveness which the immobilized always show the freely ambulatory. The edge of a glacier is called a snout, Louie has recently learned, and these snouts can be filthy-looking things, having consumed tons and tons of grit in their tortuously slow journey to the sea. Glaciers are the world's sloppiest eaters—so someone wrote and Louie appreciatively read, and for a moment it seems it must have been the Boorish American, but our

Boorish American has nothing to say about Greenland. Louie has no guidebook. He's on his own at last.

He sleeps in the afternoon. Lately he has needed enormous amounts of sleep. The walls of his room are the precise pink of the peppermint-stick ice cream he'd order as a boy at Hercules's Drive-in. Annabelle's treat of choice was French vanilla, an artificial yellow almost as fierce as the color of mustard.

Louie that evening ventures to the austere bar of the Hotel Royale. He's feeling better and he orders a beer. Would he prefer Danish or Greenlandic? Greenlandic, definitely. It's his first sip of alcohol in many days—since, in fact, the night he and Shelley, after a couple of Duskcutters and some beer, polished off a bottle of champagne in the Penthouse Lounge of Sterling Gall's Excelsior Palace. Louie soon winds up in conversation with the somewhat-battered-looking, fair-haired, dirty-haired guy—Louie's own age or a little older—sitting two stools over.

"You're an American."

It's not the first time on this trip Louie has heard the statement posed as an accusation. The guy isn't facing Louie, though. He stares straight ahead, as if peering into the mirror over the bar—but there is no mirror over the bar.

"That's right," Louie concedes and smiles. He actually enjoys this role. It's satisfying, on his endless travels, to parry churlishness with a sunshiny Yankee cordiality: "My name is Louie Hake."

Louie's companion pauses, weightily, as if to assess whether Louie's contribution merits a reply. Then he says, "I'm Bendiks. Bendiks Overgaard."

"And that's a Danish name," Louie pronounces confidently.

"True enough." Bendiks sips from his drink. Still facing forward, which makes his request seem at once detached and oddly intimate, he says, "Tell me about yourself."

Now this is, after a moment's uncertainty, quite an appealing conversational turn. On his voyage Louie has gregariously introduced himself to various people in various venues—in airplanes, in airports, in taxis, bars, hotel lobbies, museums—and consistently Louie has been struck by their uninquisitiveness. Generally, the aspect of his explorations that people have found most interesting is what he himself regards as unremarkable: his decision to travel without phone or computer. Their incuriosity rankles him. He hypothesizes that if only he were to meet somebody doing what he's doing—roaming the world for gorgeous architectural sites—Louie would have plenty of questions for *him*. And while recognizing here the dangers of self-glorification, he nonetheless feels confident that if somehow he could meet himself, he would find himself genuinely fascinating.

So Louie bends to the task. It's funny how quickly a foreigner's mastery of your language can assert itself. Though Bendiks has spoken only a few sentences, Louie senses absolutely the man's superb English; Louie needn't abridge or simplify. Louie tells his faceless companion about teaching at AAC, for a change making the institution sound presentable. He tells him about being divorced and now separated from wife number two, though he spares the Dane most of the grisly details. He tells him about having started a pilgrimage in Rome, as stepping-stone to Istanbul, and how, abruptly waylaid, he detoured to London.

Bendiks interrupts: "And what brings you to the suicide capital of the world?"

"To the—? I'm sorry?"

"The suicide capital of the world. Greenland."

"Is it? Is it really?"

"Far and away . . ."

"More than Japan?" Louie asks.

"Japan? Japan doesn't even make the top ten."

"Not the top ten?" But this can't be right.

"They're overrated. As self-destroyers. Putting all their energies into ritual and vocabulary, rather than the actual grim business . . . Meanwhile, Greenland's rate is twice that of the nearest competitor: Guyana."

"Twice? Guyana?"

"And Greenlanders feel each suicide more, given their small numbers: less than sixty thousand people on the whole island."

This can't be right either. Louie ponders a moment. "What brings me to Greenland? I want to see icebergs," he declares. "One of the painters I studied in graduate school, a nineteenth-century American named Frederic Church, he painted Greenlandic icebergs he saw in the sea off Labrador."

The response, when it comes, is startling: "Not precisely. Basically, he sketched them. The finished oil paintings were done in New York. Often some years later."

Louie pauses. "You're an artist?" he asks, with the sudden plummeting dread this question must naturally inspire.

"Certainly not."

"You're an art historian," Louie says, with a different, but still-quite-familiar, dismay.

"Again, I am not."

Louie brightens considerably. "Well, tell me about yourself," he urges.

Bendiks still does not swing round. He continues to address the nonexistent mirror over the bar. It turns out he spent two years in Rochester, New York, in the early nineties, pursuing a PhD in physics. It was his first trip to the States. He'd had a vague notion that Rochester, New York, must strongly resemble New York, New York. It hadn't. Did the snow bother him? Louie asks.

Bendiks turns slightly: "What snow?"

He asks this with so straight a face that Louie's tempted to explain that Rochester is notorious for blizzards. He catches himself in time, though. Louie chuckles. He says, "So tell me why you abandoned your PhD."

"Did I? Abandon it? Or did the field expel me? I don't know. I can tell you I began to dislike the subject matter. Somewhat intensely."

"What did you dislike about it? I mean, if you can explain it to a nonmath person . . ."

"But I can't."

"A simplified version?"

"Honestly not possible."

"Okay," Louie says. And adds, "All right."

A pause opens, and is the conversation over? Perhaps.

But Bendiks reverses himself. He says quietly, almost apologetically, "I have the wrong temperament for the discipline. Or I have a temperament for physics, but in another era. I'm temporally maladjusted."

Louie ponders. "I can imagine," he says.

"Probably not. You've taken some physics?"

"Well," Louie begins. "I've—" he begins. "No."

"Perhaps I can introduce the subject."

And a little academic lecture ensues. Bendiks opens by saying, *It's all emptiness,* and waxes from that unpromising start. Louie, on his second half liter of beer, listens contentedly and respectfully to some fair portion of the discourse. There is something quite peculiar in how level voiced and evenly spaced is Bendiks's delivery, as though he's reading and not speaking: Descartes's "corpuscles," Newton's three laws of motion, Gilbert's magnetic earth . . . A colleague at AAC, Ricky Lyons, once explained to Louie that in science departments there was a well-understood descending "hierarchy of sanity": biologists were the least crazy, followed by chemists, mathematicians, computer scientists, and physicists at the raving bottom. Of course Ricky was a biologist.

It's all emptiness, Bendiks begins. But it wasn't always. Atoms once solid as billiard balls. Solid as your fist. Read your Lucretius. "But these days, it's emptiness. People always knew that what's above, outer space, was mostly empty. But it's all empty down below, too, and that's recent. Discovered in 1909, really. Think of the element lead, think of the most solid thing you can think of. And in 1909, we learn that a lead atom is basically miles and miles of air. With all the air removed."

Louie could listen all night, perched on a barstool as though it were a classroom chair. He has always preferred being a student to being a teacher. An old excitement has gratefully awakened, an unquenchable personal dream: his hope that ignorance will at last be lifted from him. Has Louie had the good fortune, here in Greenland, right off the bat, to stumble upon a genuine Danish existentialist? Talk about going to the source . . .

"Exactly," Louie intones. "Air without the air."

Again, Bendiks turns slightly. "Do you mind more classroom talk?"

"I *like* classroom talk."

"All right. Well, I thought I was okay with that emptiness. After all, from my perspective, the year 1909 was long ago. Initially, I thought what bothered me was point particles—you know, lacking spatial extension, zero dimensional. But carrying a charge. And yet if they have a charge and no extension, then the combination of quantum theory and relativity would lead one to conclude that the charge has to be infinite. Clearly an absurdity. So we go about renormalizing, a process of removing infinities by progressive approximation."

"Removing infinities," Louie agrees. "Right."

"And we do this finer and finer, limited only by computing power and boredom. Today we are down to eighteen places."

"Eighteen. That's amazing."

"Amazing much more than you can imagine. Still, it's all hocus-pocus. All a cheat. Initially, I thought *that* was what bothered me: it was all a cheat. But over time, I began to see that what bothered me was more basic; it went back further: I mean, that initial post-1909 emptiness. You see, I'm temporally maladjusted."

"I do sometimes feel I'm not fully in the modern world," Louie says. "On this trip of mine, you know I brought no phone or computer?"

"It's not the same thing at all," Bendiks counters. "Not at all."

"Right," Louie agrees.

"All right, if the nucleus of a uranium atom had a one-centimeter diameter, about the size of a cherry, do you have any idea how far out its furthest electron would lie?"

"I haven't the faintest idea."

"Guess."

"I haven't the faintest idea . . ."

"Guess," Bendiks insists, as though Louie were merely uncooperative rather than hopelessly clueless. Five yards? A quarter mile? The distance from the earth to the moon?

"A long way, I'm sure."

"A long way? Well, it's a long way if you think of a thousand meters as a long way. The approximate ratio is a hundred thousand to one."

"A hundred thousand to one. Now that's amazing," Louie says.

Bendiks's hefty drink is Irish whiskey. Louie is now a committed devotee of Greenlandic beer. Sometimes it takes a while to figure out your true preferences.

Bendiks elaborates: "I should have been a physicist in the age of Lucretius. I would have done just fine in Newton's cosmos, where I would have made highly significant discoveries. But some people are not suited, temperamentally, to live in deserts."

"But isn't Greenland itself actually a kind—"

Bendiks overrides the objection: "Too much empty space? It oppresses them."

THERE'S A CHANGE IN LOUIE'S HEALTH. NOT IN HIS BODY— which continues to feel achy and logy and sometimes downright awful. Rather, in his skeptical mind—where he keeps receiving reports that bodily recovery is near.

Maybe it isn't. Maybe illness is no more likely to lift than Greenland's mist and fog. He'll lie forever in his peppermint-stick tomb. How long has he been sick? Only six days? Well, there's another way to look at it.

He's been sick in three countries. He picked up this bug in England, two days before departure. But could it really be that only a week ago he was a footloose agent in a metropolis of buses and subways, restaurants and museums and clothing stores where a man might purchase a pair of Spanish walking shoes or an Italian silk tie?

The last time he had the flu—the real flu—recovery took two weeks. And when he complained to his doctor, Dr. Framingham, he was told, "Two weeks is about right." In which case, Louie hasn't yet hit the halfway point. He *will* be sick forever.

Huddled in his imported Yankee Ingenuity parka, Louie wanders out in the nominal middle of the day and buys a seven-ounce bag of Uncle Tio's Mesquite Mix Potato Parings, for nine dollars, which comes to something like twenty dollars a pound, and also buys, in a junk shop, a worn paperback called *The Norse Atlantic Saga: Being the Norse Voyages of Discovery to Iceland, Greenland, and America.* He spends most of the day reading and sleeping. (Mostly sleeping.) He's been making steady progress with *Great Expectations,* though its plot, as he approaches the conclusion, increasingly oppresses him. He isn't oppressed, as someone else might be, by Miss Havisham and all her rat-riddled wedding finery. That's all in good fun. No, what oppresses Louie are the complex difficulties Magwitch has in fleeing London. Could it honestly have been so difficult, back then, simply to vanish? In nineteenth-century England, surely, a man could disappear—get off the grid, make himself scarce, slide off the map. But in *Great Expectations* the Thames is closely, rigorously monitored. It's as if Magwitch is a tiny data point in a world already regimenting its tiniest data. As if, *already,* the rudiments are in place for an authoritarian society where everybody's under constant surveillance.

At the moment, it's the sweetest dream he can think of: the notion that Louie Hake, leaving computer and phone behind, has truly managed to elude his overseers. Who they are he isn't quite certain, but he wants—craves—release from his overseers. True freedom must mean just that: freedom from overseers. Surely, even in the twenty-first century, a man can fully escape, slide off into terra incognita. *I'm nobody's data point!* he proudly longs to declare, tucked away in a little Greenlandic fishing town well above the Arctic Circle—where, just today, he has left an electronic credit card trail that any decent high-school hacker could trace in a flash: a cappuccino, a bottle of Cool Lemon Bittersweet, a Snickers bar, a couple of local beers.

Louie returns to the "business center" and writes Annabelle an email. Actually, he writes four emails, though really a single letter disguised as four. (Four letters should go some ways to redressing the imbalance between his correspondence output and hers.) He proposes she take a badly needed vacation. "You really do sound overly anxious and a little overwrought, my dear." He adds, for clarification: "Good health begins with mental health, which is good." And adds, for reassurance: "One's deepest needs are the hardest to identify" and "Distance is liberating" and "Freedom means freedom from freedom." He also does some fact-checking and confirms that Bendiks's unlikely statistics are accurate: Greenland *does* have the world's highest suicide rate, more than twice Guyana's, and Japan fails to break the top ten. And there are fewer than sixty thousand Greenlanders. On a fall day during football season in Ann Arbor, the U of M stadium houses twice as many people as reside in a country whose borders exceed the distance from Miami to Montreal. Well, what do you know? Ours is a strange planet.

He turns to *The Norse Atlantic Saga* and soon arrives at the conclusion that its author, whose name is Gwyn Jones, is a superb stylist. Louie admires the vocabulary, which must be incorporated elsewhere, somewhere, in some choice place: *denudation, incursus, concubinage, retardive*. Louie admires the graceful and old-fashioned phrasing: "these sea-girt and mountain-shackled lands," "as tendentiously as wrongly," "such mind-cargo is rarely lost to human memory." Sentence by sentence a conviction of artistry grows, and with it an unexpected urge at emulation, as Louie aspires as he hasn't dared aspire in years: he really *could* write his book on the American Impressionists. Or on something—anything. Just a book, in a world in which everybody except him has written one. A book with his name at the bottom, Louis Hake. He already has arrived at a dedication perfect for any volume of art history: "To the late Mr. Paint, Louie Hake Sr., who brought color to his son's world."

Yet the further Louie reads, the more *The Norse Atlantic Saga* likewise oppresses him. Louie is initially cheered to discover that in one sense Greenland really is the center of the world: the omphalos, if he has the right word. It was from here that *Homo sapiens,* a millennium ago, came full circle. From here that, so to speak, we met ourselves, when the Greenlandic Vikings, setting out for the New World, met up with the people they called Skraelings, ancestors of the modern Canadian Indian.

We'd done it: the branch of humanity that had funneled out of the Horn of Africa into Europe tens of thousands of years ago, and the branch that had spilled across Asia and over the Bering Strait and across the tundra expanses of what would become Canada, at long last were reconnected. By Viking Greenlanders. It was a consummation "thirty generations in the making."

And what did we do next, our fair-haired Vikings and our dark-skinned Skraelings? Slaughtered each other. Louie-the-dentist long ago, back in Rome, shuddered at an Italian landscape watered in blood. But you leave steamy Italy for temperate England, and you leave temperate England for shivering Greenland, and it's the same old story: blood and bludgeon, brothers at war.

From their treeless Greenlandic homesteads, the Vikings pushed on to the crowning and inexhaustible forests of the New World. And were defeated. The first Europeans to discover the New World lost it again. Shamefully, they retreated home to Greenland, where the last Viking settlements disappeared in the fifteenth century. When the New World was next discovered, it was from a southerly embarkation, and a new cycle of rout and rapine would commence . . .

Louie returns that evening to the hotel bar. He's relieved to spot Bendiks's lean and glum visage, suspended over another hefty whiskey. This time, conversation is harder to start. "A hundred thousand times," Louie begins.

"Mm?"

"The distance from nucleus to electrons," Louie clarifies, but Bendiks looks bored. Eventually, though, Louie hits upon the right prompts.

He says, "It seems you're something of a philosopher."

"Not a word I'm fond of."

"Theologian, then."

"Worse. Worse yet." Bendiks pauses, sips his drink. His thin upper lip lifts in disdain. "At Rochester, I roomed with an ex-law student. A strange chap. He'd dropped out, temporarily. He was worried, you see."

The sound of *chap* rings pretentiously in Louie's midwestern ear. But this isn't Bendiks's first Briticism, and, to be fair, why should he speak like a midwesterner? England is much closer to Denmark than Michigan is.

"He's constantly worrying: Was he starting to think like a lawyer? He wanted success in law school. And a good job. Oh, he wanted all the benefits. The perks. But this constant worrying: Was he starting to *think like a lawyer*? He viewed it as a mental infection. I remember wondering, Why take up a discipline if you don't want it influencing your thinking?

"But then something strange. You know what? I caught my own infection. Mine was *thinking like a physicist.* I've met many physicists, maybe some of them better than me, who could put physics utterly aside. But some of us can't. We can't partition. This glass?" He held up his whiskey. "Most of the time, you have to think of it as a mere glass. Something that conveniently holds whiskey. And sometimes, as a physicist, you have to think of it as this vast and tiny thing, unbelievably vast and tiny—so many atoms the brain can't contain the numbers. You have to be okay with that. Your brain must *live* in this place where your brain can't contain the numbers."

Louie's having trouble following, not so much the man's ideas but his intensity. Louie's happily back into the Greenlandic brew. Does it matter if the glass is half empty or half full? The important thing is—you have a glass! And what do the atoms matter, so long as they're behaving—so long as they not committing fission (fusion?)? A second beer has gone straight to his head. He's in need of company. And all the better if it's somebody who doesn't call on him to say much.

"And what if you can't stop thinking about what it really *is*? What if the glass is no longer a glass—but always this unimaginable, this uncontainable number? You see, it's the *opposite* of mysticism, of theology. It's being un-. . . unstoppably factual. Philosophizing? Religious mystics? It's all too easy for *them* to discard reality. Because they never grappled with it to start with. They went right to the easy stuff, like love and the soul."

"Those things are matters of faith," Louie observes.

"Faith? *Faith?* But don't you understand? How there's no responsible discussion of faith until you've done the numbers? The Bible keeps talking about faith the size of a mustard seed. You know how big a mustard seed is?"

"Not exactly." Louie feels compelled to add: "But very small."

"Very *small*? A mustard seed is *huge*! A huge assemblage! I've done the math. The number of molecules in a mustard seed? Roughly one followed by nineteen zeroes. That's more than all the grains of sand on the Earth, incidentally. Do you see what God is doing when he asks you to take an intangible thing—faith—and turn it into something you can see? Do you see how *unreasonable* God is?"

Surely these numbers are not correct. And yet Louie has an uneasy feeling that they might be, and suddenly feels quite glad that he will never think like a physicist.

"But what if you can't stop grappling with the hard stuff, and it *oppresses* you? Oppressed by this weird huge zoo of subatomic particles. This weird huge zoo of creatures so bizarre they ought to be imaginary, but they're the realest thing there is. And what if you can't stop thinking about the zoo?"

"I can imagine."

"You can't."

Louie gently shakes off the blow. "It's true, I can't," he says. "Zoos. I don't think I think that way," he says, drawing some pleasure, anyway, from his gift for elliptical phrasing.

"I began thinking of it as a country: Soobatowmia."

"Soobatowmia?"

Bendiks modifies pronunciation slightly: "Sub-atomia. The strangest place of all. This teeming, empty zoo."

And Louie recognizes his old friend: the standby universe, the unheralded one that underlies his—everyone's—existence. "Subatomia," he says, thankfully. He goes on: "I look at the glass and I say, It's clear glass. Or it's colored glass."

"Don't talk to me about color. Don't get me started."

"All right . . ."

Could he maybe eat something? Attempt a real meal? When did he last eat a real meal? Hot food? He's been subsisting mostly on Snickers bars (which, unlike Coke and saltines and Lay's potato chips, really do taste in Greenland the way they're supposed to), and peanut butter slathered on mountain bread, the mountain steadily growing harder and denser, harder and denser, like some sort of mysterious molecular phenomenon.

Bendiks is talking about alternative realities—or, more accurately, urging Louie *not* to talk about alternative realities. "We're talking about what atoms *are,*" he says. "What this bar *is.*" And he brings his fist down upon the bar's pale wood, not slamming it but meeting it solidly—if an essentially empty object can be met solidly. "What this glass is." And with a sucking sound among the upended ice cubes, he empties his half-full but always-empty glass.

Meanwhile, Louie is steadily razing his amber tower of Green-landic beer. He's recovering.

"Am I sounding like a theologian?" Bendiks begins, and he goes on for a while, concluding almost sheepishly: "I don't see how you can be a serious physicist and not be something of a theologian." Ben-diks is probably making perfect sense. You can never escape questions of causation. Or maybe he's saying causation is the first thing you have to renounce. Whatever he's saying, there's a message behind the words, and it is poignant. Unlike Louie, Bendiks is a born teacher. And—ironically—while Louie is fated to spend his life in overenrolled classrooms, hapless Bendiks is left to scrounge up his students in deso-late airports and doctors' waiting rooms and empty Greenlandic bar-rooms.

"Well," Louie offers, "if you can say this wooden counter is made of so many atoms of such and such a size, can't you also say the sky is blue?"

Dumb question, apparently. Bendiks expatiates at some length, siphoning the two of them through the gigantic, narrowing tubes of progressively more powerful microscopes, until at last they are bobbing in that waterless sea where what exists exists on a scale of a single micron—the domain in which color first inheres. Below this, to speak of color is meaningless. Again, Louie doesn't quite follow. Is Bendiks declaring that objects are real, colors an illusion? Intuitively, this runs fiercely counter to Louie's own perception of the universe, where color is primal: color was there, and particles emerged to find it. Though maybe his perception's nothing but an old, helpful illusion, by which great paintings get made . . .

Louie fails to catch Bendiks's eye. The man's gaze jumps and jitters, alighting everywhere but upon his audience. His rust-colored hair is short, maybe half an inch long, and all of a uniform length. There's something peculiar about his hairline, which has a jagged, almost serrated look; if his hair is receding, it's doing so in fits and starts. The effect is of something ripped or slashed. Indeed, everything about him suggests rips or slashes: his nose carries a queer sharp hitch, just below the bridge, and his clothes—a faded pair of jeans, a flannel shirt whose pocket holds a pack of raggedly torn open cigarettes—are in tatters. Bendiks has taken up a new phrase: *a hunger for responsiveness.* It's the natural response to the physical world's indifference to your wishes, whether at the level of neutrinos and muons or pulsars and blue giants. But how, Louie wants to know, is this any different from everyday life? Louie says, "Driving down a road, go ahead, pray all you want to, but will your prayers make a traffic light hold its green signal one hundredth of a second longer?"

His sentence is a fine and complex construction, and Louie pauses for an acknowledgment of such.

"But it *is* different," Bendiks peevishly insists. "In the art historian's world, your prayers—or let's call them wishes—can count for something."

A pause. Louie doesn't know what to say. He says, "How is physics any different?"

"In physics, your wishes count for nothing. You can move things, but you can't change anything. But in art history? You can change things."

In his steady, unrattled way, Bendiks has found a new conversational track, and Louie's grateful. Conversation's in no danger of halting. Louie's starved for conversation.

Then the subject veers, and Louie's being asked to produce the name of an eminent art critic of an earlier generation.

"Well, I don't know," Louie says. "Maybe Harold Rosenberg? Meyer Schapiro?"

Bendiks waves the men aside. "It doesn't matter. But let's assume they had the vision to recognize a great Danish painter. You know Hammershøi?"

"Vilhelm Hammershøi. Yes, yes. Turn of the century. Danish. Quite a good painter."

Bendiks finally fully turns, to lower upon Louie an expression of pitying disparagement. "Much better than good." Again he seems uncertain whether to bother to continue. He sips and says, "Now if you were Schapiro, or Rosenthal, and you had much better taste than I assume they had, you could do something about Hammershøi. You could move the electrons around. You could say, '*Here* is a painter who makes'"—and he produces his names with proud nonchalance—"'Chaim Soutine or Paul Delvaux or Ellsworth Kelly look like amateurs.' You could bring notice."

"Well, those three painters, you're talking about *wildly* different eras and styles. I think this is a question of apples and—"

Another look of disdain. "You could move things forward," Bendiks repeats. "Move Hammershøi's reputation forward, though he'll get there eventually. It's like Vermeer. How long did he have to wait—"

Louie can't help himself. "Again, you're jumping all over the place. This is absurd. And there were so few Vermeer canvases, scattered across Europe."

"You can shift the particles. Your universe has play. Mine has unpredictability, but that's not play."

A morose or even sullen silence opens. Louie says, "You live in Copenhagen?"

"In Copenhagen?" Now it is Bendiks's turn to look befuddled. "But I live *here.*"

"Here in Qaqqatkivisut?" Louie says.

"No, I don't mean *here,*" Bendiks replies in another outburst. "Not in Qaqqatkivisut. I mean here in Greenland. I wouldn't live *here,* in this ungodly armpit of the world. Who would? Can you imagine living *here?*"

"No, I couldn't," Louie is able to offer honestly. He's pretty sure Qaqqatkivisut is the most godforsaken place he has ever visited.

"Whatever gave you the idea I live *here?*"

"Well, where *do* you live?" Louie counters.

The sound emerging from Bendiks's throat is impossible to visualize: "Qaqqatnakkarsimasut."

"Beg pardon?"

"Qaqqatnakkarsimasut. North. Thirty kilometers north. Sometimes they're called the Twin Towns. Live in Qaqqatkivisut? I wouldn't live *here.* My God, what must you think of me, that you'd think I'd live *here?*"

"Is the town you live in so very different?"

Again, one of Louie's questions stirs Bendiks to the verge of outrage. "Well, Qaqqatnakkarsimasut's an armpit, too. But Qaqqatnakkarsimasut isn't Qaqqatkivisut, now is it?"

Louie feels glad to be able to answer with some confidence. "They don't sound the same," he replies.

"What are you paying? What are you paying a night to stay at this Hotel Royale?" Bendiks sounds almost petulant.

"I haven't totally figured it out," Louie softly replies. Bendiks has unwittingly hit a tender spot; though Louie has been in Greenland for some days, he still hasn't figured out the exact value of the kroner. "I think it's roughly maybe around a hundred and ninety dollars? That's breakfast included."

"You come up to my place." Again Bendiks is looking Louie directly in the face and, again, Louis is wishing he wouldn't. "I own a bar, it's called the Rotten Egg. I've got a couple rooms, I sometimes take in guests. Sort of a B and B. You come up to the Rotten Egg. Your Greenland B and B. A hundred sixty bucks a night. Meals included. You'll eat exactly what I eat. Better still? All your Scotch and beer you want to drink—it's on the house."

"I'm not usually much of a—"

"On me."

Louie has two thoughts, occurring in such rapid succession as to be all but one. The first is that this proposal is absolutely insane. Who in the world, while ailing and aching with some undiagnosed bug, would volunteer to head to a Greenlandic town he's never heard of, to stay at a place called the Rotten Egg, everything to be supervised by somebody who has, in the brief time Louie has sat here, consumed three double Scotches? The second is that he's going to accept Bendiks's offer—yes, and accept it eagerly. Isn't this the fitting culmination of everything? Hasn't he been patiently, steadfastly awaiting an invitation to dine and drink and board at the Rotten Egg?

"BUT IS THERE AN INTERNET CONNECTION? A BUSINESS CENTER?" Louie offers the inquiry less from actual concern about lost lines of communication with the outside world than from a need to reassure himself he isn't behaving altogether recklessly. He'd like to suppose he hasn't completely forgotten how to plan for contingencies.

Even so, the sputtering boat he's about to board—which belongs to a *chap*, a friend of Bendiks's—is as gray and sullen and woebegone as any rivercraft that ever plied the Styx.

Bendiks exhales a cloud of cigarette smoke. "Yes. Sure. Internet. Business center."

Louie is off to Qaqqatnakkarsimasut. He likes the sound of that. The sky is an unfavorable dark gray, but the sky is always dark gray. Maybe he hasn't been near death, but certainly he's been sick enough to feel himself emerging into an altered world. The cloud cover will or won't ever lift, but he's off to Qaqqatnakkarsimasut. As anyone must who aims to evaluate the respective merits of the Twin Towns.

Louie's still sick, but he's exploring sickness of a new stripe, where he can lucidly survey its earlier phases. He has been lurching. He has impulsively agreed to go to Qaqqatnakkarsimasut. Once more he has packed his too-voluminous suitcases. He has settled his bill at the Hotel Royale. He has agreed to hand himself over, body and soul, to a temporally maladjusted Danish Greenlander—is this what's called a Faustian bargain? And only now, at the last minute, does he think to ask whether he's severing every tie with the only world he knows.

And Louie has boarded the boat. Presumably, he would have boarded it in any case, whether losing the Internet—the world—or not.

Gray sky—perpetually gray sky. Flecks of rain. A dark gray boat. A few icebergs dot Qaqqatkivisut's harbor, but these are gray, too, and much smaller than his perhaps feverish envisioning. There's nothing here to take down the *Titanic*. Maybe the *Good Ship Lollipop*.

It's one of the prerogatives that Louie seizes upon as a midwesterner: no one should expect him to understand the first thing about navigation, seamanship, tides, knots, landlessness. One side is starboard and the other isn't. One end is the stern and the other isn't. On the coast of Greenland there's apparently never, ever a moment when the country's defining feature, its vast and invisible central ice sheet, isn't sneaking under your down parka and nuzzling up against your chest. The temperature isn't so cold, but he's shivering. And still a little ill. Always still a little ill.

He huddles inside the boat's cabin, whose plastic windows are dirty, further reducing visibility. He's handed a mug of steaming liquid, which he assumes must be coffee but may be hot chocolate. Bitter, anyway. He huddles on a bench, wrapped in Yankee Ingenuity. A submerged engine putters him away.

When, eventually, he first glimpses his room at the Rotten Egg, he feels a sharp, stabbing qualm. There isn't even a bed. Just a mattress—no doubt filthy—on the floor. Everything's musty and cigarette smoky. The room's one window looks out on the corrugated aluminum wall of a warehouse, or maybe a residence with fewer windows even than the Rotten Egg. There is no closet. There isn't even a mirror. (What exactly had he expected, at a place called the Rotten Egg?) Louie is prepared to welcome crappiness provided it is picturesque—like Van Gogh's famous bedroom in Arles, with its buckling floor and tilted wall hangings. But no famous artist will ever paint *Bedroom in Qaqqatnakkarsimasut*.

And yet—Louie feels instantly cheered, even heartwarmed, by the appearance of Bendiks's two children, whose improbably British-sounding names are Martin and Fiona. They are blond and blue eyed, with luxurious dark eyelashes and lips so nearly red as to look, for a moment, artificially enhanced. Theirs is the blush of perfect health. They are surpassingly beautiful, and obviously we all need to raise our children above the Arctic Circle. Indeed, Louie feels certain he's never seen a fairer brother and sister.

Martin is the elder by a couple of years. He turns out to be thirteen. Both children are soft voiced, with truly superb if sometimes mumbled English. And they are immensely, if gently, solicitous. Martin leads Louie to a room that is a makeshift restaurant or bar—whatever it is, it's makeshift—and gestures him to a seat with a flourish of real elegance and soon brings him tea and soup. Louie's sorry to see it's split pea with ham, one of those thick broths that too easily conceal squishy bits. But it winds up being bitless and delicious—just the thing he has been craving.

He almost spits out his first sip of tea—something wrong with it. Then he realizes it's spiked with whiskey. He leaves the rest of the cup untouched. He isn't interested.

Martin brings a second helping of soup and two cellophane-wrapped packages of oyster crackers. These, too, are extraordinarily satisfying.

Louie takes his time, spooning steadily, and does not halt until this second bowl is empty. It turns out that, while he was eating, the beautiful little girl, Fiona, has been busy in his room. While nobody could make it look anything but bare-bones, she has done her pretty best to prettify it. (As it happens, a tan corduroy bedspread drapes over the low mattress, reminding Louie of his childhood bedspread; the thing has a surprisingly homey and enticing look.) New pillows have been added. She has brought in a standing lamp with a burgundy-colored shade. Its light is comforting.

Louie lowers himself gratefully onto the tan bedspread, sprawling on his side. The soup is purring contentedly, like a cat, inside him.

"Are you rather tired?" the little girl, Fiona, asks.

The unexpected phrasing amuses him. "Rather," he replies.

Shyly, adorably, Fiona extends to her prostrate foreign guest a worn paisley silk handkerchief. For her size, the girl has large (if slender) hands, which, as with a puppy's big feet, portend future growth. She isn't only a beautiful little girl; she will be an elegant and beautiful woman.

Inside the handkerchief is a motley collection of trinkets/treasures. She wants to share with exotic Louie her modest bag of exotic delights.

There is a tiny hand-painted plaster giraffe, no more than two inches tall. Giraffes are oddities everywhere. But to a native of Qaqqatnakkarsimasut, this gentle tropical herbivore might have dropped from the dark side of the moon. One of its front legs is sharply broken, leaving a snow-white scar.

There are two marbles, one an intense translucent jade green and the other a clouded gray-black. There is a large wishbone belonging to another queer and alien creature—a turkey. There is a key-chain ornament, a paint-peeled plastic Buddha the pink of pink bubble gum, whom Louie momentarily mistakes for a putto. There is a thin wooden bookmark on which a border of tulips has been painted. It bears a pregnant motto, written in flowery cursive with old-fashioned dangling squirls: THE TALE TAKES MANY A TURN.

This offering of her treasures seems so precious, so trusting and intimate, that Louie feels called upon to reciprocate. But how? And then, for all his exhaustion and illness and disorientation, he's visited by inspiration: his neckties. He unspools from his suitcase, as the girl watches, a dozen gleaming, glorious strips of silk, and then *he* watches *her*: her eyes spellbound, her ivory hand stroking each in turn. The plot, often, is revealed only with time, and these moments of enchanted show-and-tell are, it turns out, the reason why, back in Ann Arbor, he packed an extravagant dozen neckties.

He asks once more to hold the three-legged giraffe. Minutely, he studies the otherworldly creature, whose hide is a lemon yellow daubed with ocher mottles. Laterally, he studies the other otherworldly creature, the one gazing intently at the object in his hand. The girl's eyelashes—well, they themselves might ornament a giraffe. They are a wonder: a black, long, luxuriant fringe . . . Like the red of her lips, they seem artificial, but this is prodigal Nature's own artifice; Fiona is Nature's child.

"So pretty," Louie says, of the giraffe, and is amused, and also just a touch embarrassed, to see a flush of blood creep up her flawless cheek, just as though he'd been speaking of his diminutive new chambermaid.

IN WHAT MUST BE MORNING, FOR WHAT THAT'S WORTH, Louie is led to the same table—a folding card table—where he was served soup last night. Preposterously, appealingly, smiling Martin refers to this room as "the salon" and suggests that Louie "relax a bit." (The language the two children speak is like nothing Louie has ever heard from children anywhere.) Martin brings him scrambled eggs and rye bread and two pats of butter in silver packets. There's a cup of Tetley tea. And beside his teacup there is—Louie confirms by smell—an invitation to vice. It's a small tumbler, an inch of brown liquid waiting in ambush.

"Whiskey?" Louie inquires. He almost laughs.

Martin smiles benignly.

"In the morning?"

"Beautiful morning," Martin chants, and a still-broader, still-more-benign smile dawns.

It's all so irresistibly, deliciously improbable that Louie tips the whiskey into his tea, sips, beams at the beaming Martin. "All good," he declares.

And the thirteen-year-old boy (oh, how fiercely Louie wishes some friend were here to confirm the weirdness of it all!) actually replies, as Jeeves might, "Indeed, sir."

It turns out there *is* Wi-Fi, linked to an old Dell desktop tucked away in what doubles as a pantry. Bendiks, solemnly ragging his new guest, has dubbed the room the "business center." The children, equally solemn, have adopted the term. They are a family of straight faces. The computer has a sticky keyboard. But the Wi-Fi connection is good, which amazes Louie, though it shouldn't. When you think about it, it makes sense. You can't buy fresh fish in the main grocery of this Greenlandic fishing town, but you can buy, in its freezer case, Corporal Major Goldbrick Fitzhugh's Extra Crisp Fish Fingers, and you've got a nice stable link to the Internet. The future may not be as dire as everyone supposes.

He writes Annabelle. "Dear Sister," he begins, and has he ever begun a letter with this salutation? Isn't it the truest way to address her?

> I have come to the town of Qaqqatnakkarsimasut, where
> I believe I will settle for some time. I am working hard on
> my book about 19th century American landscape painting.
> I am staying at a restaurant/bar/B&B called the Rotten Egg,
> where, to my amazement, I was served a shot of whiskey this
> morning.
>
> It is an unusual spot. It's run by a boozy chain-smoker
> who has been tutoring me in Danish philosophy and sub-
> atomic physics. There is no mirror in my bedroom. And no

mirror in the bathroom. Well, maybe it's a sign that I ought to look inward? Could it be in Greenland you locate the exterior space necessary to view your interior?

He prattles on. He'd go on at still-greater length if the keyboard weren't so sticky and jumpy, the letter *o* in particular. He has to make many corrections: *Rtten Egg* and *sht f whiskey* and *yur in terir*.

Bendiks keeps an old cat, a white longhaired Persian named Casper. When Louie asked its name of soft-voiced Fiona, he misheard it as Gasper, which he took for another of Bendiks's unsmiling witticisms; the creature suffers from allergies, or hair balls, wheezing and choking with a desperation alarming to nobody in the house except Louie. Casper, incurably sociable, craves endless caressing, an appetite Louie would satisfy more happily if Casper didn't smell so bad.

Actually, the whole Rotten Egg smells like a rotten egg. Not really, but the place *is* foul and funky. Not just cigarette smoke, but unwashed laundry and unwashed dishes and cat hair and dust of many years' standing.

At lunch, there's another tot of whiskey beside his plate and Louie, falling into a when-in-Rome spirit, slips it readily into his tea. (It is easier, it turns out, to follow a when-in-Rome spirit when not in Rome.) He is presented with a bologna and cheese sandwich on white bread and a bowl of canned corn. The chef at the Rotten Egg (is Fiona the chef?) has no way of knowing it, but this particular combination was a childhood lunch favorite, though back then he didn't supplement it with two shots of whiskey. Outdoors, nearby, enclosed in a mist, icy gray wavelets are breaking on icy gray boulders. Louie feels more content than he's felt in quite some time.

Apparently, the setting out of shots of breakfast whiskey, and lunch whiskey, is pro forma for the Rotten Egg's resident pair of angels, who accommodate their devilish father in this fashion. How could they understand that Louie feels defiantly sinful sipping whiskey as a breakfast beverage? It seems the children bring Bendiks drink at every meal, and between meals. Though Bendiks never appears really, totally drunk, maybe he is never really, totally sober. Perhaps he regularly achieves a precisely modulated mental state, soothing to a temporally displaced physicist, where external objects posit just the right degree of firm and graspable reality.

Nothing in Bendiks's world is more mysterious than his championing of Qaqqatnakkarsimasut over Qaqqatkivisut. To Louie's eyes, the Twin Towns truly are twins. Qaqqatnakkarsimasut, like Qaqqatkivisut, has one decent-sized grocery store, and generous strewings of garbage in its vacant lots, and compact polychromatic houses and chained sled dogs and squadrons of taxicabs and cheery Inuit kids daredeviling around on clunky bicycles. Although there are only a handful of restaurants, in Qaqqatnakkarsimasut, too, there's a Thai place, called not Thai Time but Thai Day.

Qaqqatnakkarsimasut *does* have a café, if you'd call it that, the Café Rock Hip Hope, which sells native crafts: heart-shaped earrings made of narwhal horn and plastic polar-bear salt-and-pepper shakers and tiny costumes to convert your Coca-Cola bottle into an Inuit doll. He does purchase for Annabelle two refrigerator magnets (a map of Greenland, a confused-looking polar bear cub), but doesn't get around to mailing them.

Like Qaqqatkivisut, Qaqqatnakkarsimasut has a harbor sheltering dozens of fishing boats. And as in Qaqqatkivisut, the boats in Qaqqatnakkarsimasut boast cosmopolitan names. Though mostly Danish or Inuit, some are in English (*Markland, Olympia*) and one is in Spanish (*El Gitano Malo*—the *Ill Gotten*).

On his fourth evening at the Rotten Egg, Louie sits up late talking with Bendiks. They've known each other far too briefly for repetitive conversation, but Louie has already heard much of what Bendiks has to say tonight. At Rochester he roomed with a chap who worried about "thinking like a lawyer," he doesn't approve of the term *philosopher*, he'd've made a powerful ally to Lucretius. Etc. Was the repetitiveness the result of drink? Or just that natural indifference to one's audience so commonplace in academia?

Then the conversation turns quite interesting. "My adviser at Rochester, Gerry Gulbenkian, referred to me as 'a type.' You've heard of Gerry Gulbenkian?"

Louie harbors perhaps more than his share of your typical academic's reluctance to admit ignorance on any topic, however remote from his stated specialty. But it does appear safe to concede unfamiliarity with an Armenian physicist based at the University of Rochester. "I don't think so," Louie says. "Perhaps."

"No matter. But he said I was a type. I was, quote, uninnovative. And a, quote, type. An uninnovative student of physics who, predictably, believes he would have made great breakthroughs in another era. And I said to him, 'I'm nobody's type. I'm Bendiks Overgaard of Helsingør, Denmark, and I have my own view of the world.'"

"As for *that*," Louie begins excitedly, "that's exactly what I've been saying about myself. You have to flip it, you know? Mutatis mutandis. I'm Louie Hake and I have my very own view of the world."

But Bendiks Overgaard will have none of it. "It's not the same thing at all," he says, and the abruptly extended promise of some deeper linkage is severed by the brisk, side-to-side slicing motion of Bendiks's lean skull.

Who is Bendiks? No saying how he came into ownership of his run-down house, one of the older and larger structures in Qaqqatnakkarsimasut. The mystery doesn't stop Louie from playfully speculating. Bendiks is some exiled minor Danish royalty. Bendiks (whose veiny arms are imposingly muscled) murdered the house's previous owner in ruthless Viking fashion. Bendiks inherited it from his beautiful Danish wife, who died giving birth to their beautiful daughter.

What Louie can say confidently is that Bendiks didn't acquire the house through any applied business acumen.

Bendiks described his place as a sort of B and B, but Louie is the only guest. He also described it as a sort of bar, but there doesn't seem to be any menu. True, in the salon there's a barlike counter and three actual barstools, as well as a motley jumble of chairs and sofas and two folding card tables. True, too, there are sometimes two or three or four or five guests sitting inside it, munching crackers and potato chips, drinking beer and whiskey fetched by Martin or Fiona. But these drinkers seem less like customers than friends, and Louie has witnessed no form of payment.

Louie himself, on the other hand, pays steadily at a hundred sixty dollars a day. He doesn't much mind the money (though it adds up to more than a thousand dollars a week), but the Rotten Egg may be the only establishment in Greenland not honoring Visa cards, and his cash supply is limited. He does feel satisfied with the no-frills food, which both Martin and Fiona have somehow been taught to deliver with an extremely cute bow that is almost a curtsy.

"This weather is highly un*u*sual," Bendiks keeps repeating. The grayness never breaks. Bendiks utters *unusual* with so pronounced a middle *u* that Louie begins to hear it as *un-you-sual*. It's as if he, Louie, is being held accountable, culpable—as if his arrival hexed the heavens.

The world outside, like the heavens above, has become unreal, and it is this unreality, as much as anything, that permits Louie to begin a day with shots of whiskey. His occasional forays into the littered, dripping town of Qaqqatnakkarsimasut only confirm his sense of an exterior unreality. Now and then he wanders over to the Café Rock Hip Hope for a Coke and a chance to survey the solemn, sorry "native crafts."

On the other hand, the Vikings were once undeniably real, and his reading of *The Norse Atlantic Saga* carries profound satisfactions. Behind his bedroom's closed door, lying closer than usual to the earth's stony surface, on a mattress without box springs, Louie declaims incantatory sentence after sentence. How neatly it's phrased: "Who first saw Iceland, and whether god-impelled, mirage-led, wind-whipt and storm-belted, or on a tin-and-amber course laid north to roll back trade horizons, we do not know." Or: "a crumbling cellerage of unveri-fiable tradition." Or: "thrown out by men with more bone in their fist than he." He wasn't exaggerating as much as you might suppose when informing Annabelle of the progress he's making on his book. He's honing his writing skills.

Perhaps it's this melding of the two conditions (doubts about the world's reality and inklings of advances in his self-expression) that incites him to do what he's been fantasizing about for some time: composing a just-for-fun, never-to-be-mailed, far-flung, free-flowing email to Veronique. He lets himself go:

Dear Veronique,

I suspect you may be surprised to hear from me, and even more surprised when I tell you that I am in Greenland! But it's where I am.

I am a professor of art history and I have come to Greenland to work on my book about American landscape painting.

I have often wondered if you have wondered what became of me. Did you? Did you ever think I would be art professor? Did I never mention, back in the summer of 1990, in Fallen Hills, Michigan, when I was your tennis instructor, that I was interested in art? I'm not sure I did.

Maybe you thought I would become professional tennis player! Alas, I am a lowly professor instead. I teach in Ann Arbor.

My life has had twists and turns and I suspect yours has too. These include a divorce and I wonder if you can imagine what that is like. Maybe I do not need to go into that right now, though of course I would like to hear your life's adventures.

I see that you are living in Tulsa, Oklahoma. I remember from that summer of 1990 that you were moving there, and you were not so happy about that.

I have never been to Tulsa, Oklahoma but I suppose you have never been to Qaqqatnakkarsimasut, Greenland, and it is certainly true that the tale takes many a turn, as they say! Sometimes things go forward in unexpected directions, but sometimes they loop backward, and we wind up where we once were, on a tennis court, or maybe two people in a kitchen one summer day, only appreciating things more, with more passionate feeling, and things have changed but they are also the same. The heart is a mystery.

I think often of that summer of 1990 and though it was more than twenty years ago, certain aspects of that summer remain very vivid in my mind! I have changed of course, but in other ways I am much the same person. I even look mostly the same, I think, though I'm probably fifteen pounds heavier. (I still have all my hair, though it is turning a little gray at the temples.) (I think my hair amused you. I remember once you patted my head after a tennis lesson.)

"You write someone a letter?"

It's little Fiona, close by, close to his shoulder, though he didn't hear the door to the business center open and close. In her graceful way, she moves stealthily.

"A letter. Yes. But I do not send." Louie smiles at her. With him seated like this, and the girl standing, she and he are precisely at eye level.

She's carrying two glasses. One holds a hefty shot of whiskey. The other holds ice.

"You will not send it?"

"No, no. It is crazy. Crazy letter."

One of the peculiarities of his conversations with the girl (he has realized with some amusement) is that she speaks in fuller sentences than he does. Though her command of his language is marvelous, he often addresses her as though she speaks brokenly. He's the professor, and yet he winds up speaking pidgin English.

"But you do not send it?" Fiona repeats.

"Crazy letter," Louie repeats, and his eye falls upon (of all things!) his absurd references to his hair.

"If you do not send it"—again a pause—"she will be sad."

Louie plops an ice cube into the whiskey and sips, though in truth he's not in need of additional drink.

Fiona's words please him, inspirit him. "You think so?" Louie says. "She will be sad?" he asks. And how clever the girl is, to ascertain it's a woman he's writing!

"She will be sad."

"She wants to hear from me? You think so?" Louie says.

"I think so. Yes."

"She wants to hear from me?"

"She will be sad," Fiona chants and then, surprisingly, her slender ivory adult-sized hand alights on his and imparts a gentle and yet firm nudge, toward the Send button.

Quite large forces are suddenly deployed in this tiny room, obeying their own peremptory prompts and demands. Louie's hand slides as if under the spell of a Ouija board. He hardly has time to throw down one more clattery gulp of whiskey before his trigger-happy thumb (just as he's realizing—too late!—he has failed to attach a valediction and his name) strikes Send.

MARTIN HAS TAKEN TO WEARING ONE OF LOUIE'S NECKTIES. He'd asked to see them, having heard about them from his sister, and he, too, was wonder-struck. When he held one to his throat, Louie proposed he try it on.

This was a tie Louie was particularly fond of: gold and olive green and terra-cotta. The gold shapes were (or perhaps were not—it was a design of exquisite abstraction and subtlety) silhouetted lions. Unfortunately, Martin seemed to believe Louie had intended it as a gift, and Louie so far hasn't had the heart to ask for its return. If he *has* parted with it, he can't altogether regret the loss. There's something so deeply charming in seeing the beautiful Greenlandic lad so beautifully bedizened. Martin wears the tie constantly.

Louie has never done this before—spent an entire day in various degrees of inebriation. Let alone follow such a day with another. It would all be more alarming if the world were completely real, but even speaking of days is an illusion, since there is no real light, no real dark. The heavens have gone to sleep and everything's misty gray. Sometimes a lighter, fuzzier, foggier gray. Sometimes a darker, thicker, rainier gray. And behind it all, the sea whispering and sighing, morosely. Under such strange and slumberous circumstances, he'd be a fool to behave as though ordinary codes of behavior obtain. He sleeps more than perhaps he's ever slept, suspended in a lethargy far larger than he is, but he's also subject to sudden onrushing energies, careening out into the sloped, rubbly streets of Qaqqatnakkarsimasut, peering sharply, almost accusatorily into the seemingly sun-tanned, planar faces of its Inuit inhabitants. *What are you doing here?* he wants to ask them. *Explain yourselves.*

At other times he reads about the Vikings who inhabited this coast, indeed this very harbor. He reads: "What was the world-picture, the *imago mundi* of the Norsemen?" (He asks: "What is the world-picture, the *imago mundi* of Louie Hake?") Surely they envisioned this country as a way station, a stepping-stone. They saw their visions. They were fated for other, farther, fairer, finer shorelines, a *mundi (mundo?)* where immense trees would grant everyone a soaring roof beam, and wild grapes would fatten on the vine.

What Louie doesn't do is loiter in the business center. The place holds painful associations ever since, at Fiona's artful urging, he mailed Veronique his insane letter. To Greenland, too—to impossibly distant Greenland—Louie Hake has brought a familiar, stubborn, dislodging notion of places that must be avoided: places of shame.

He regrets the craziness of his letter all the more because, love weaving a sort of spell, Veronique returns to him more vividly by the day. Things come back he might have thought he'd forgotten, rendering her increasingly more precious. She wore a sky-blue headband. She loved strong cheese, to the amazement of her Vietnamese relatives. She knew the lyrics to the opening jingle for *The Beverly Hillbillies*. She loved snow and ice.

He's still a little sick. Always a little sick. But sick now in a new way. His insides are rebelling. He of the efficient and dependable bowels has begun, at irregular intervals, to excrete explosive loads bearing inhuman stenches. It mortifies him to use the bathroom even at the Rotten Egg—the odors linger so. Louie keeps reading in *The Norse Atlantic Saga* about outlawry, crimes so egregious that the malefactor must be cast outside any human confederacy. Louie knows what this means, since he's no longer fit company even for the Rotten Egg. His body means to outlaw him.

MAYBE IT'S THE EXCEPTIONAL PURITY OF THE ARCTIC AIR, but Louie is keenly aware of the nasty assortment of little stinks floating ceaselessly through Qaqqatnakkarsimasut. The acrid diesel breath of the trucks. The pinching reek of cigarettes on the street. Warring whiffs of chemicals wafting off the many construction sites. The backyard drying racks of leathery-looking fish that may be rotting rather than drying in this sodden weather. The angry tang of burned rubber. The sour emanations of insufficiently bagged trash. The fact is, Louie could walk the streets of his own inner city Detroit with less offense to his nostrils.

Offenses to the nose, offenses to the eye. A literary critic might posit that the supreme irony of this, the so-called Journey of His Life, is that a pilgrimage intended to discover the world's architectural marvels has deposited him in the ugliest town he's ever seen.

No, that's not true. He's seen worse, not least in some of Detroit's ravaged neighborhoods. But those other places were degraded by poverty and crime, which doesn't apply to Qaqqatnakkarsimasut, where nobody's begging in the street and people aren't peering over their shoulders for potential muggers. The ugliness seems, as much as anything, a matter of choice and preference. My neighbor has painted his house a blinding fuchsia? I'll paint mine magenta! He's decorated his house with some bald automobile tires? I'll festoon mine with a cap-sized broken-legged table!

But there's a bigger irony still, which is that Louie can't regret a single step. The tale takes many a turn. He'll get back on track. And when he does, his travels will be all the richer for his strange, soggy, boozy sojourn in Qaqqatnakkarsimasut.

The Taj Mahal? Ginkakuji Temple? He's coming around to accepting the improbable notion that these sites are best understood (perhaps only to be understood) by the person who grasps the humble ambitions motivating the streets of Qaqqatnakkarsimasut. History begins here, where *Homo sapiens* rounded the globe at last.

He's preparing for another leap, and this one may take time. He needs to catch up on sleep. No matter how much sleep he gets, he needs more. Of course it makes no sense to be catching up on sleep where there's no night, but the Journey has always sprung choice incongruities.

After lunch one day (a very midwestern, tasty, maize-fueled lunch: a bowl of canned corn, topped with butter and salt and pepper, and a bowl of cornflakes, topped with raisins), Louie dozes off into a singular dream. A child once more, he's riding in the backseat of a car. His father's driving. Just the two of them, traveling. Louie finds a corkscrew in his hands, which he rotates and rotates until popping a clean hole in the car's floor. Somehow the hole is much larger than you'd expect, given the corkscrew's fine nib: the hole is the size of a dime. And through the dime-sized hole, peeping Louie can watch the floor of the road roll by as Father drives along. He sets to work making another hole. And another.

The car halts. The door swings open beside Louie, and Louie feels him looming there: Daddy, glaring down at his son. What has the boy done? What on earth has the boy done this time?

Frantically Louie would cover up the damage with his fingers, but hands are too small, holes too numerous. Louis is huddled on the floor, culpable, shocked, wormily squirming.

Then what happens? A deep breath. What does the Father say to the Son who has punched holes in the floor of his car? The Father pauses, pauses in that fair-minded, measure-taking way of his. And with the wry, doleful, thoroughly tolerant male mildness that has always been Louie's prime protection in life, the Father says: "Well, well. You know, Son, it's an interesting spot from which to see the road."

After the dream, for a couple of hours, for the whole next day in fact, Louie feels literally blessed. The dead among us accept their own responsibilities, and they will return to us, who require their wisdom. Aren't we all yearning to see the road in a new way? What looks like a setback, a small act of destruction, may be anything but.

The road takes many a turn, and Louie *does* have to wonder what will befall the world's unlikeliest aristocrat, he of the rare blood and mysterious provenance, little thirteen-year-old Martin Overgaard of Qaqqatnakkarsimasut, Greenland. Prince Martin of the leonine cravat. Into what boardrooms or ballrooms will his patrician features admit him? And the girl, Fiona—whom will she marry? An Englishman, probably, but the tale might be richer if she shucked her arctic heritage and wound up in some Mediterranean palazzo. Or—better still—found a home in the heartland of America. The tale might turn in all sorts of backtracking and lovely ways . . . "You have been to America before?" Louie asks the children. He's sitting in the salon, voyaging with *The Norse Atlantic Saga.* He has been sailing slowly. Sometimes he'll discover, halfway down a page, that he has read these paragraphs before. Both children are on the floor. Martin is stroking Casper. Fiona is coloring in a book called *Victorian Costume and Finery.*

"Never!" they echo back, excitedly, freshly, just as though he has never before posed this inquiry.

"You will take me with you," Fiona cries with that queer funny disarming directness of hers. So unflinching and imploring is her gaze, Louie can't fully meet it; his own eyes wobble.

"I will come as your au pair," she continues.

"I have no children," Louie protests.

"Maybe?" the little girl answers.

THE MYSTERY OF THE CHILDREN'S BEAUTIFUL AND FLOWERY English was quickly solved. There are three rooms upstairs: Bendiks's room, the bedroom the children share, and a small dingy room with a small TV and a large collection of DVDs. It holds a domineering, squat armchair upholstered in pine-green velour and a tiny desk and desk chair. The children mostly curl up on the pink-and-gray cat-hairy faux-Oriental rug. In addition to some DVDs in Danish, there is *What About Bob?* and *Groundhog Day,* but mostly what there are are BBC period pieces. There's a Charles Dickens Collection and a Complete Collection of Jane Austen and the Anthony Trollope Collection—all evidently viewed innumerable times. The children are born Anglophiles. Which also explains the Briticisms and archaisms coloring their fey and fanciful speech. Louie would swear he once heard the little girl utter an imploring *prithee.* Not *pretty please* but *prithee please.* Was it any wonder the child was utterly irresistible?

Louie sits down one night, or afternoon, or morning, and watches *Great Expectations.* He hadn't expected to meet Pip again so soon, and he much enjoys—seated in the ugly but actually quite-comfortable green armchair, sipping a tumbler of whiskey that props itself handily on the chair's extensive arms—pointing out to the children, in perhaps too professorial a tone, the architecture of the story. In truth, brother and sister seem to know the tale better than Louie does. In his defense, it's a long time ago, or seems so, since he proudly hauled back to the Mulder Arms a copy of *Great Expectations.*

At Martin's urging, the three of them watch *A Handful of Dust,* based on a novel Louie has never read by Evelyn Waugh. Weirdly, Dickens has a role in this one, too, though he arrives late in the plot, through the machinations of Alec Guinness, a madman ensconced in the Amazonian jungle. Our poor aristocratic hero, Tony Last, tumbles into the jungle as a result of his wife's scandalous affair. *You see, chil-*

*dren,* Louie is tempted to say, *sometimes a cuckolded husband beaches up in strange and remote places.* In truth, let's be honest, he has much to teach them!

As for Tony Last, he winds up incarcerated in Guinness's household, compelled for his food and lodging—it's all too absurd—to read Dickens aloud to Guinness every day into eternity. Well, if the parallels are there, Louie will let somebody else descry them. What he sees most clearly are the differences. If spurned Tony Last and spurned Louie Hake have each retreated to the ends of the earth, one to encounter the Man Who Loved Dickens and the other to encounter the Dickens Collection—this may be as far as the similarities extend. Tony was held in the jungle against his will. Louie on the other hand has chosen Qaqqatnakkarsimasut over every other site on earth. He has sought the suicide capital of the planet in order to regain stability and mental health. It's where he wants to be, where he belongs: watching, day after day, beside his eccentric lovely rarefied adopted children, the unhurried unfolding of novels he has never read by Dickens, Austen, Trollope.

LOUIE'S PRESENCE IS ALREADY ALTERING THE VERNACULAR of the house. The room with the computer is now the business center. Casper has become Gasper. And the room with the TV is the DVD den. Fiona in particular savors the animalistic resonance of *den.* She'll take Louie's hand and, staring up with her wonderful unnerving straightness of gaze, whisperingly plead, "Louie, let's go to the *den.*" Fine with Louie, who mostly has avoided the business center since mailing off his demented plea to lovely Veronique. Letters from Annabelle must be steadily amassing. He won't think about them. He has considered, mostly jokingly, informing Annabelle that some research scientists have invited him to their campsite on the interior ice sheet. And adding in a PS that she's not to worry about predators, since the landscape's too fierce for polar bears.

Will Veronique reply? Probably not. In all likelihood she'll sensibly conclude that Louie's letter is too manic and odd to merit an answer. Okay. Okay, but it doesn't seem utterly implausible that she, too, may still be attaching tender sentiments to that summer of 1990, and she, too, glimpses there a purity of feeling since mislaid. Is that so crazy?

And so long as Louie doesn't check email, this hope exists. And he needs hope. Does Veronique continue to think of him? The possibility tantalizes Louie as he reclines in the armchair, sipping whiskey, again watching a cobwebby, almost mummified Miss Havisham inform little Estella that men, without exception, are a woman's downfall and must be tyrannized lest they tyrannize you.

The little Estella in the film (Jean Simmons) is indeed a charmer, but not so priceless a beauty as the child, curled on the floor, playing her understudy, mouthing the words as Estella recites them.

Sometimes, seated in his monarchical green armchair, Fiona and Martin on the floor before him, Louie recounts childhood anecdotes. They listen raptly, as who would not? For he's a visitor sprung from those most exotic of all global coordinates: Fallen Hills, Michigan.

One afternoon—shyly, sweetly—Fiona presents him with a gift. It's a drawing. It is her own vision: a stick figure, with blue legs and short arms and an enormous explosion of wiry hair, standing on the lip of an enormous hole or chasm. Louie takes a few seconds to evaluate. Could it be? Excitement unsteadies his voice: "Is that *me*?"

The girl doesn't speak. This is a big moment. Solemnly, magnanimously, the artist nods. Her heartbreaking eyelashes snap.

"Okay," Louie says, "that's me. But what's the hole in front of me?"

Fiona pauses. Her wounded tone makes clear that he should have required no assistance. "Those are the Fallen Hills, Louie."

"Of course. Of course, dear," Louie soothes. "Obviously. You know," he vows, "I'll keep this drawing on my refrigerator."

And adds: "You have a gift for art, Fiona, as well as language."

And adds: "I'll keep it on my refrigerator at home. When I go home. You'll find it there when you visit me at home."

Home?

Later, Louie sits up into the night with Bendiks. Louie hears again about how Bendiks lived in Rochester with a strange chap who worried . . . How a blinkered world consistently undervalues Danish accomplishments . . . How he would have made a trailblazing physicist in the age of Newton . . . But none of this is what Louie longs to hear. He's fixated on learning about the children's no-doubt-beautiful mother.

Louie has let his imagination run amok. Here, in the world's suicide capital, the poor woman did herself in. Or having turned her back on her family, she's now an international fashion model living with her Milanese boyfriend in Greenwich Village. She's a high priestess in a mountainside cult in Oaxaca. She's a heroin addict in Amsterdam, in need of a good midwestern man's guidance. Clearly, the children balk at speaking of her. And Louie, though he can be a stubborn and forceful interrogator, hesitates to nudge either child.

"Does your mother live in Greenland?" he asked Fiona once, in the den. They'd just finished *Jane Eyre*. The Rotten Egg offers two different versions. This was the one in black and white starring Orson Welles and Joan Fontaine. Louie had forgotten, and was horrified at the end to discover, that poor Rochester was blinded in the fire that incinerated his mad wife. But in a voice-over coda, Louie learned that Rochester's vision was sufficiently restored (the power of love, presumably) for him to see his son and heir.

"Greenland?" Blink, blink. Those gorgeous eyelashes. But Fiona's blue eyes were strangely vacant.

"Does your mother live in Greenland?"

A pause. "Denmark. She is in Denmark."

"Do you visit her there?"

Another pause. "Visit?"

Louie had been thinking the two of them were thoroughly alone, but Martin materialized in the doorway. "Look, Sister," he called. "I have cut my thumb on the stupid scissors." He held up his hand, and indeed down the ball of his slender white thumb a blazing drop of blood trickled. "Will you help me?"

And of course the girl was off—the conversation broken.

But the two men are drinking whiskey. Louie keeps alluding to the children's mother, as Bendiks feints and dodges. Or has other things to discuss. As he explains it, he's in an eschatological mood tonight. The world is probably coming to an end.

The world indeed may be ending, and if so, the people of Greenland, whose crystalline environs are liquefying and trickling away beneath their very feet, will be the first to know. One afternoon, one midnight, Louie sat up for sleepless hours reading on the Internet about Greenland's collapsing ice shelves. These days, concerned Pakistani and Indian scientists have been studying this coast, monitoring and calculating, proceeding on the assumption that what happens in these rarefied latitudes, above the Arctic Circle, has terrifying implications for the monsoons in the Indian Ocean. Which includes the Seychelles: the very isles of Paradise will be drowned.

It's the butterfly effect: an insect flaps its wings in the Andes and a hurricane pummels the Caribbean. Everything's ethereally connected—perhaps too connected, and our world may indeed be arriving at an end. There's no earthly reason to suppose things don't end. Most things do. Nearly everything does. Of species on the planet, ninety-nine point nine, nine, etc. percent have gone extinct. More extinctions each year. Nonexistence is the norm: our daily death.

But if the world's indeed ending, Louie plans before the close to crack the mystery of the vanished mother. After a while, after God knows how many evasions and how much whiskey, Louie says, "Tell me about the children's mother."

"The children's mother?"

"Yes. What is *her* story?" Try evading *that* one, Bendiks.

"Actually, she is not well."

"Where is she?"

"Actually, she is in Denmark. She lives with her parents."

"She is not well?"

"Actually, she is mad. Irretrievably. Paranoid schizophrenia, if you believe in such diagnoses. I prefer *mad,* as the more accurate term." A pause, and Bendiks does something he rarely does: he looks his interlocutor square in the eye. Perhaps it's just as well he does this so rarely. The aggressive bite in his gaze, underneath that weird, choppily receding, corrugated hairline of his, is unnerving.

Bendiks continues: "Not mad as in raving. You talk to her, she sounds saner than you or me. Like many insane people, she's fond of public libraries. She goes every day. But I was once told she was a potential danger to the children. I was told she must not be left alone with them."

Instantly, the blur of alcohol vanishes throughout Louie's body, and his senses are whip-crackingly sharp. An airy, icy chill fans out across his back. The horror of it can't be absorbed at once. Oh, the human heart, the heart! A danger to *those* children?

"I'm so sorry," Louie says, which is perhaps the wrong thing to say. Bendiks's gaze burns unabated.

"I have been drinking lots of your whiskey," Louie volunteers, as both apology and bond.

"You drink what you need to drink," Bendiks returns gravely. Both men understand that the other topic has been dropped. Slowly, a great tension relaxes. "Sometimes whiskey is antidotal."

"Antidotal?" When Bendiks fails to elaborate, Louie says, "Where does it come from? The whiskey?"

"Denmark."

"Denmark? Danish whiskey?"

Louie is simulating wonder, but in fact he already knows this. According to the label, he has been drinking Irish Scotch whiskey from Denmark.

It's surprising, or maybe it isn't, but Bendiks is a Danish chauvinist. Købke and Hammershøi are much greater painters than any of the Impressionists—as good as Turner or Ingres or Chardin. (Many strange fish wind up in Bendiks's far-flung nets.) And Carl Nielsen is one of the great composers. His Fourth Symphony, "The Inextinguishable," can stand beside Beethoven or Mahler's best. And in no other country does anyone produce such superb pickled herring. (Sometimes Louie speculates that most of Bendiks's conversations are elaborations on some mirthless strain of Danish humor. The closest Louie has seen Bendiks come to laughter was in describing how, one April Fools' Day, teaching an undergrad Physics-for-Poets class at Rochester, he announced that an integer was recently discovered lying between 27 and 28, and watched his students excitedly record this breakthrough. There might have been a moment, in recounting the story, when a smile played upon Bendiks's lips.)

Sometimes Louie has to question exactly what role, what purpose, he's playing in Bendiks's life. Things shift hourly. Sometimes Bendiks is solicitous: *Is the food all right?* And *You must be patient with the weather—this is quite unyousual.* Other times, Bendiks is curt, or simply disappears altogether.

Louie has been in Qaqqatnakkarsimasut more than a week—although, as he keeps reminding himself, days are an arbitrary measure. Here it is always day; here it is never day, and in the past week he hasn't glimpsed sunlight. All highly unyousual.

What hasn't shifted is Bendiks's collecting the rent each day. Bendiks is not so caught up in his river of booze that he loses sight of this simple accounting. Louie's formidable stack of hundred-dollar bills is dwindling.

Louie has been in Qaqqatnakkarsimasut more than a week—not long. But there's a way—not just a way, a reality—in which this stay is longer than his stay in the Ann Arbor apartment into which he parachuted back in February. *This* stay is realer. *Here,* Louie does what he was always meant to do: shuffle around the Rotten Egg in his slightly food-stained sweatpants (his slovenliness somehow cosmically atoned for by Martin's crisp ever-present necktie), sipping tea, sometimes drinking whiskey, petting that old malodorous extortionist, Gasper, reading about the Vikings, conversing with those enchanted golden children whose absurd, anachronistic English allows for a graciousness that Louie the professional talker (for what is a professor, if not a professional talker?) has rarely attained. *Prithee, please?*

In Italy once, some time ago, in a run-down bar on an utterly run-down day, Louie glimpsed a mural of a man gazing out over Umbrian valleys. Its artist had a glimpse of paradise, a world wherein your very existence entitled you to wine and a hammock, but the artist failed to grasp true Paradise—the broader concept, whose far-flung outposts just might include a mist-enfolded, fusty, and dilapidated wreck of a house harboring under the shadow of a monstrous unseen glacier.

Harbors are unaccountable things. Outside the house, a world of menace seethes. A world melting, boiling over. Cleverly concocting poisons, inventing sharper blades. A world where, if a bomb goes off in a home for handicapped orphans, competing underground organizations will each claim responsibility. A world where mothers are lost, perhaps forever. *Irretrievably* was Bendiks's word, describing the children's mother. It's all madness. But such madnesses lie far, far away from Qaqqatnakkarsimasut, where there's distance and ice enough to last one man's lifetime, surely.

You might think that in speaking so frankly Bendiks had assumed a position of vulnerability. Nothing like. Clearly, he isn't intending to draw any closer. And Louie unexpectedly feels a lack, an outward yearning. Oh, for that miraculous find, somewhere on the planet: a true friend, somebody whose thoughts quicken to meet your thoughts. True friends must be rarer and harder to come by than true lovers. The spirit's needs are odder, and harder to voice, than the body's. Aren't we all missing something? He's looking for someone with whom to speak of Florence, of Lizzie, of a lifelong failure at scholarship, of a failure with women, of Dad's swallowed-down disappointments, of an enthralling girl/older woman who once embraced him, perspiring body to body, in her kitchen. And also of AOFMD and the threat that the light of the world might be stolen from you, irretrievably.

TONIGHT BENDIKS IS IN AN ESCHATOLOGICAL MOOD. WELL and good, indeed the world may be ending. At Republican Party conferences, doubts may still linger over whether the climate is altering—

and the question ultimately be shelved, deemed far too speculative for profitable discussion—but this isn't the case in Greenland, where lives and livelihoods are melting away. Louie wishes he could recall in better detail some of his recent damning Internet research—the shifting currents, the dwindling ice sheet, the dying fish, the dying seals. But Bendiks has the details in hand. He likes data, is comfortable with data. "The icebergs just off the glacier here? Just north of here? Sometimes they would reach a hundred meters tall. Nowadays, you're lucky if they're fifty. Icebergs are the cathedrals of our oceans. And what's happening to our cathedrals? Sinking. Shrinking. Our cathedrals are disappearing. It's 'La Cathedrale Engloutie.'"

Louie nods, but Bendiks, in that irritatingly pugnacious and exacting way he has, says, "So, you know 'La Cathédrale Engloutie'?"

And only when Louie, feeling cramped, is finally forced to shift from knowing nods into an expression of humble befuddlement does Bendiks reply: "Debussy."

Well. This is the first moment when Louie experiences a genuine dislike of Bendiks. Until now, he has known wariness, and disappointment, and sometimes an unfocused distaste, but nothing so pure as dislike. There's an irreducible cruelty to the man. And why *would* anybody's hair recede in Bendiks's sharp, serrated way unless he was at bottom nasty and aggressive and untrustworthy?

"Look ahead," Bendiks says. "All quite terrifying if you have the gift of extrapolation."

"Extrapolation," Louie echoes.

"Such a beautiful word. In fact, the most beautiful word in the English language: *extrapolate.*"

"I suppose so," Louie says.

"What is it about you? So quick to agree?"

"You prefer I disagree?"

Bendiks rattles on: "Louie, say you have some data. Say you acquired some knowledge. Now, extrapolate. You're going to push it, and *get somewhere.* That's what the word is saying. Get smarter, extend your mind. The mind will travel where it hasn't gone and will do so rigorously. Will do so *responsibly.* What's more beautiful than that?"

"Push it," Louie echoes, again with a confusing sense of parroting someone not present.

Louie sips from his drink. He wishes Bendiks would slow down the observations—maybe shut up altogether. On the other hand, Bendiks has been nothing but generous with food and whiskey and beer. Always topping up Louie's glass. The food hasn't been anything to write home about, but Louie has been perfectly content with its good no-frills simplicity: lots of boiled potatoes, and hash-brown potatoes, and mashed potatoes, and spaghetti with Paul Newman's spaghetti sauce, and yogurt and Kellogg's cornflakes and bologna sandwiches and cheese sandwiches. Food doesn't seem to count for much in Bendiks's life, who appears to subsist on pickled herring and dark rye bread. Evidently it's not the worst diet for one's health. Though you couldn't say Bendiks looks robust—his lean face has various dents, in which pockets of grayness gather—he looks healthier than any man who drinks as much whiskey and coffee as he does, smokes as many cigarettes as he does, ought to. Stomach's lean, veiny forearms ridged with muscle. And his little eyes, sharp as brads, couldn't be brighter.

"You know what Gulbenkian said? He was—"

"He was your academic adviser at Rochester."

"He once told me I don't really think like a physicist. What it was was, he felt threatened by me."

"I'm not surprised," Louie says.

"Going on about my doing a, quote, unsatisfactory job. Going on about my, quote, irregularities and about, quote, computational errors."

"My sense of the academic mind—"

"And that's why my funding was cut off . . ."

All at once, a stunning reappraisal is called for—not an unwelcome reappraisal. And it's as though Louie's question is uttered before he has fully formed the thought: "You mean you flunked out?"

"In this case, the so-called facts hardly reflect reality." Bendiks's lean head lifts on his lean neck. "The explanations were empty."

"Well, it's all emptiness," Louie agrees, echoing a familiar Bendiks line.

But Bendiks replies: "And Gulbenkian once explaining to me, as if I'm some sort of half-wit, that there's no such thing as emptiness, atomically speaking. As if I didn't understand *that*!"

"Right," Louie says.

Bendiks is in an eschatological mood tonight and Louie relinquishes all traces of anger. Why sweat little affronts and resentments at world's end? Bendiks goes into something of a rant: The globe is going straight to hell faster than anyone could have predicted. We're raping the planet in a stunning mixture of finite calculation and infinite greed. (Louie nods in acknowledgment of the fine phrasing.) Bendiks goes on: It's essentially a European invention, historically speaking, Max Weber got some of it correct, and this particular deadly blending of the finite and the infinite is European in spirit, and the world would be far, far better off if everyone died out but the Inuit. Not that much good can be said of *them,* sentimentalized beyond recognition and, what's worse, having themselves bought into the sentimentality. Admit it, people everywhere are a bad, bad bargain.

"Everybody dying off?" Louie volunteers into an abrupt pause. "Funny, but I guess I've been living all my life with that notion. These people down the street, four houses down, the Larkins, they built a bomb shelter. They kept to themselves, no kids, Mr. Larkin was a chiropractor, and she was this very skinny woman with a big double chin and this enormous backyard raspberry patch." Raspberries and a bomb shelter. What did Mrs. Larkin do with all her berries? Louie can't remember eating a single one. Did Mrs. Larkin jelly them and store them up against doomsday?

A memory arises. The *pater,* perched on the back stoop one summer evening, beside his son and namesake, remarking in that sweet and gentle timbre of his, "If the Russians came and bombed us, Louie, I wouldn't want to survive it."

Oh, but little Louie would! To choose not to survive? Not be alive *at all*? His father's words stung him—they howled of a terrible desertion, burned with a terrible betrayal. The boy wouldn't, couldn't, accept going down so easily. After all, how bad could the end of the world *be*?

Another memory, somewhat later, a similarly reflective nightfall. The boy's father remarked of the Larkins, whose shelter little Louie so passionately envied and resented, "A childless couple and a dead world—what would they be living for?" And a plan was hatched in little Louie's ingenious brain, a survival plan to be confided to nobody except Annabelle: when the air-raid sirens blew, announcing the end of our world, securely hand in hand the two of them would scurry down to the Larkins' house, who would lodge them in the shelter before the unimaginable detonation. Then simply wait and wait—until the Hake children emerged as the Adam and Eve of a new planet.

"Were you ever inside it?"

"Mm?"

"Inside the bomb shelter?"

"Yes . . ."

It isn't like Louie to lie in this particular fashion—flagrantly, gainlessly. The lie has something to do with having been shown up about Debussy—in being out-cultured by a man from Qaqqatnakkarsimasut. But now, having committed himself, Louie fires to the task. "They had a stereo in the shelter and an extensive collection of classical music, Tchaikovsky, Mendelssohn, Satie. And this big library, the Harvard Classics, though neither was much of a reader. But I guess they supposed that after the world went up in flames, they would develop an interest in Charles Dickens, and Montaigne, and Aristophanes."

Bendiks draws deeply on a cigarette. "I have a bomb shelter . . ."

"You have a bomb shelter?"

"Yes."

"You have a bomb shelter?"

"Yes." Bendiks exhales a grand cloud of smoke.

"A bomb shelter? In Qaqqatnakkarsimasut?"

"Uh-huh."

"Could I see it?" Louie asks.

Bendiks does not answer, but he nods ever so slightly.

When Louie rises to his feet, he finds he's swaying a little. The effect is enhanced by watching Bendiks. In the short passage down the hallway, Bendiks's hands keep lifting to touch the walls.

There's a door opposite the entrance to the kitchen. Louie has seen it before, but never really wondered what lay beyond it. Bendiks draws a clanking set of keys from his pants pocket. Much to Louie's surprise, the door is double locked, in a house where nothing is locked.

"Here it is," Bendiks says. "My bomb shelter."

Louie follows Bendiks, though there's scarcely standing room for two. It isn't much more than a closet. It's musty, and empty except for a couple of cardboard boxes. These contain whiskey bottles—Bendiks's Irish Scotch Danish whiskey.

"I find this sight highly reassuring," Bendiks says.

Here, under a naked dangling lightbulb, is an image and a revelation that Louie Hake, surely, will be recounting to someone, somewhere, some years from now. There are maybe two dozen bottles. The story might be better, Louie initially concludes, if there were only four or five bottles. Or four or five hundred. But no. And in a way, this is just right.

In fact, it's *perfect*. Can it be that Bendiks, with that tirelessly mathematical mind of his, fails to grasp that, given his daily consumption, he hasn't squirreled away spirits enough to last through the duration of Noah's rainfall, let alone some inextinguishable rain of radioactivity?

"That's something," Louie says.

"Highly reassuring," Bendiks says.

As he follows Bendiks back to the salon, it occurs to Louie that the man may or may not have a wife in Denmark who suffers from paranoid schizophrenia. Bendiks's personal disclosures cannot be trusted. But one thing is certain. The fellow Louie has selected to serve as his landlord and companion and guide is himself some species of genuine madman.

. . .

LOUIE HAS GROWN A BEARD. GIVEN THE NOTABLE SHORTAGE
of mirrors in the Rotten Egg, he comes slowly to this realization. The
beard is both a surprise and not a surprise. On the one hand, he wasn't
sure he *could* grow one. A beard. On the other, in recent days he has
developed a pleasing habit of running a ruminative hand through his
ever-thickening whiskers.

Growing a beard was never an express intention, but he has
neglected shaving since the morning of the day when he last saw Shelley. Afterward, there was a stretch when he went around pointedly
disheveled, and then he got eternally sick and lacked the energy to
shave.

The revelation about the beard arrives by way of a mirror in the
deserted Café Rock Hip Hope, where Louie ventures through an afternoon drizzle for a Coke and a change of scene.

In a mirror across the room he catches sight of a bearded seated
man—and the man? The man is him! Louie approaches it obliquely, as
though to study the bulletin board beside it.

It's a round mirror, less than a foot across, on whose pinewood
frame various silhouetted animals—bears, fish, seals, whales—
ceaselessly circle. The stick-figure animals are charred into the wood.
The mirror is for sale. Native crafts. Louie stoops and peers at himself. Under his breath he says, "Now tell me honestly, would you say
that that's a bearded man? Tell me true, wouldn't you say that that's a
bearded *man*?"

He's encouraged to have overcome the worrisome sparse patches
between chin and sideburns. And discouraged to see how much of the
beard is gray, especially around his chin. Were he to grow a goatee,
any observant person would probably call it gray, and this hardly
seems fair. (Though he dislikes goatees, surely in his youthful forties
he's entitled to grow at least one brown one.) Still, there was the sheer
enchanting fibrous reality of the thing—to look at, to stroke, to fondle.

"Would you say that that's a gentleman with a beard?" he whisperingly inquires. He replies, "You would certainly say, *There* is a gentleman with a beard."

And here's the potential for humor. He opens another mental email to Annabelle: *Sorry not to have written, but I've been so busy growing my beard.*

He shudders to think of how many demanding, imperative emails have amassed in his AAC account. He hasn't visited it in days, partly because he doesn't want to go there for any cause, and partly because he fears a reply, or none, from Veronique.

He misses the Inuit waitress in the assertive cobalt-blue bra. He misses Veronique and, indeed, he has missed her for decades. Though he's not particularly sad, though in fact he's happier than in quite some while, in Greenland he has been prone to unpredictable flushings of tears. His eyes will suddenly well over, not in sadness but in some less classifiable emotion. Isn't there a poem that begins, "Tears, idle tears, I don't know what they mean"? He should've taken more English classes. So long ago. Here he is now, with no access to a library, in the Café Rock Hip Hope, a gray-bearded American embarrassedly wiping tears from his cheeks.

He has roused himself from his room at the Rotten Egg and ventured out into the drizzle partly because he's upset about events at lunch.

Fiona was bringing soup (cream of tomato) and crackers. As she set it before him, with that neat little curtsy of hers, the edge of the saucer clipped the table's edge and some soup overspilled the bowl. And then to Louie's horror—and more than that, to Louie's disbelief—his little innocent angel uttered the f-word. He couldn't quite believe his ears. She'd spoken so softly—surely he'd misheard. And yet, Louie would have sworn she'd released the f-word! Then padded back into the kitchen. But not before dropping him another curtsy. Oh prithee, please.

·  ·  ·

IT'S NOT TILL LATE THAT AFTERNOON THAT HE FINDS THE gumption to open his email. He has 177 unread messages. He has left the world, but people keep calling to him anyway. He can't bear to open a single one of Annabelle's endless string. The mere subject headings detach his hands from his body, so they jump and twitch of their own accord. "LOUIE WHERE ARE U?" and "WHAT'S HAPPENING??" and "I NEED TO KNOW!!!" But doesn't she understand that he has been incommunicado as a member of a research group of glaciologists encamped in tents on the central ice sheet, carrying out precise measurements with highly sensitive instruments that may foretell the end of the earth? He should've sent her that message. Or perhaps he did? (He has dispatched some pretty peculiar messages from Greenland.)

There's a note from that pretty ex-student of his, Claire Cheever, who must have graduated three years ago. (Or four? Or five?) She writes from Chicago that she's unhappy with her job in marketing for Side-Real, which manufactures residential vinyl siding, and she's wondering about grad school. In art. She remembers him and his class so fondly! And in April she went to Italy where "the Boticellis in the Ufizzi were awesome." *Dear Claire,* he types, in his head. *You should not consider grad school because, if I remember right, you are incapable of constructing even a five-paragraph essay that follows a single coherent line of thought. You not only can't spell but can't be bothered to use Spell Check. You have a gimpy vocabulary. PS Does the CEO of Side-Real have a son of marriageable age?* He types, in his computer:

> I am of course sympathetic with the frustration you must
> be feeling at Side-Real, dear Claire. Unfortunately, I think
> your generation has had a particularly tough time of it,
> given the problems in the economy and a rightward political
> turn that has led to the defunding (and delegitimizing) of
> the humanities in education and elsewhere. As for those
> Botticellis in the Uffizi (note spellings) I'm quite fond not
> merely of the most famous ones, The Birth of Venus and
> Primavera, but also the Annunciation, where Mary and

Gabriel mirror each other through marvelous diaphanous effects. Such paintings are a tonic reminder that there is more to life even than vinyl siding.

But Louie quits typing. In his present state of mind, this second letter is no more dispatchable than the first.

There are messages from Turkish Airlines, on which he was once scheduled to fly from Istanbul to New Delhi (or was it from Shangri-la to Xanadu?) and of course these he won't open. There's a message from crazy Leo Mattoon, his department chair, which normally Louie might be tempted not to open but which he opens because he doesn't want to think about Turkish Airlines. Mattoon doesn't use capitals, presumably not wishing to be caught privileging one member of the alphabet over another:

hey louie, i've been thinking about your 4 masterpieces course for spring. i think you might want to rethink use of word masterpieces which smells musty maybe? and it occurs to me that all 4 are centuries old (or millennia old like the pantheon) and mayhaps you might proffer a more modern example. there's a great deal of very exciting stuff going on now especially in developing countries and if you were to position yourself

Louie deletes the email.

Then he comes upon a byline more nerve-racking even than Turkish Airlines. Ldouglas. That's Lawrence Douglas. To see the therapist's name on the screen, invading Louie's in-box, is to evoke not only the man's exacting gaze but the gazes as well of Darwin and Kafka and Gandhi. The eyes have him covered. His overseers. Louie's damned at once from a psychological, biological, artistic, and humanitarian point of view. The subject heading is as alarming as it could possibly be: "I am Concerned about you."

Why? And how would Dr. Douglas know to be concerned—or

Concerned—when Louie hasn't seen him in months? Doc Douglas was last heard of in Florida, playing tennis with a fetching young thing in matching lime-green shorts and halter top, which was flabbergasting but less so than his attending a midnight showing of *The Incredible Hulk* on the night of his cardio incident.

Louie gives way to real resentment. What *right* does Lawrence Douglas have, after completing his tennis match, and throwing a companionable hand over his perspiring partner's bare shoulder, and wiping his face with a hand towel, and sipping a cold gin and tonic with a bobbing crescent of lime, to express Concern about how Louie Hake's holding up in his tumbledown room at the Rotten Egg?

Still, Louie cannot make himself delete the letter unread. Nor can he make himself open it. The letter sits there. Waiting to detonate?

Louie asks it again: What *right* does Lawrence Douglas have to show Concern? It's one of the things Louie most likes and admires about Bendiks. Though he has occasionally displayed something like hostly solicitude, Bendiks has never embraced the pretense of harboring any personal warmth toward Louie. That's the kind of friend Louie can appreciate, somebody who doesn't particularly care for you, for anyone. In truth, if we're honest, we frankly don't give a damn what happens to each other, and Bendiks—bless him—is a rare honest man.

But back to email . . . The Friends of the Earth want Louie's opinion. So does Amnesty and the Democratic National Committee. And so does the Sierra Club and MoveOn and Oxfam. All are organizations to which Louie has made small donations. And all want his opinion. They all wish him to take a brief survey, an instant poll. And after the survey or poll there's to be a fund-raising plea, for the survey or poll is just a fund-raising ploy. Nobody wants his opinion.

Click, click, click. Goodbye to gender justice. Goodbye to human rights and honeybees and coral reefs and halting the diabolical Koch brothers and dignity for the impoverished. He deletes messages by the dozen. He almost deletes unopened a letter from vegantry, which in his haste he absorbs dyslexically: *Try vegan.* There's no subject heading.

It's from Veronique. Ve-Gantry.

A vast silence opens, though there is no sound in the room. Once more she stands before him, in her heat, in the flowing candor of her sweat. Louie clicks his way into the woman's letter with a flourish of his baby finger.

Veronique's message consists of only two sentences. There is no salutation and no valediction or signature.

Short as the sentences are, they convince Louie that her English hasn't significantly improved over the last twenty-four years. This is the woman who once so memorably remarked, "I am depressing when it rains." Clearly she received enormous help with her "About Us" portrait for the Payton Avenue Church of Tulsa, Oklahoma.

The two sentences are: "You are the wrong person. Please if you do not write."

Surely she meant to say, *You have the wrong person.*

But in the starkly bereft world that Louie has freshly entered, he recognizes that her phrasing crystallizes its own poetry and rightness.

"Louie, you are the wrong person," he declares, drains his glass of whiskey, and sets it down with a small yet oddly triumphant thump.

Louie bustles into the bathroom, crisply snaps the door shut. There is no mirror, but Louie has discovered that he can make out at least a distorted and partial image on the top of the water tap, on which he locates the blanched visage of the bearded man who has just now entered and carefully secured the door. He remarks to this man, rather loudly, "It's quite simple, really. You are the wrong person." And laughs more extravagantly still.

The laughter echoes, and dies, and Louie is left questioning whether little Martin and little Fiona have happened to overhear. And if so, whether they wondered what on earth the wandering pilgrim from Fallen Hills was privately laughing about so loudly in the bathroom.

THERE'S POETRY AND JUSTICE AS WELL IN THAT OTHER SENtence of Veronique's: *Please if you do not write.* Though Veronique has no way of knowing how faithfully he has been fulfilling her injunction, in fact he has been steadily not writing since finishing grad school. Which only goes to show that, as a man, as a potential partner, he's more Veronique's type, more reasonable and compromising and thoughtful, than perhaps she realizes.

It's a courtesy he has lately been extending to various women. He has not written to Florence, to tell her he was in England not so long ago, and in Iceland, and is now in Greenland, which means they are both holidaying—she in the Virgin Islands, he in Qaqqatnakkarsimasut—along a stretch of Atlantic coast. So far as Florence knows, he voyages pluckily on, to Turkey, to India, to Japan. Does she think of him on that other, mislaid, nonexistent journey, marching ambitiously toward the Taj Mahal, and if so, does she experience any qualms? Does she wonder what it would feel like to meander hand in hand with Louie Hake along Kyoto's Higashiyama range toward the venerable preserve of Ginkakuji Temple?

*Is* she still in the Virgins? Still screwing Satan? Poor Florence. But oh, Lord, what use is his pity? For such a woman, what does pity count when arriving from somebody taking shelter in the Rotten Egg?

Nor has he again written Lizzie, who is striding toward a third marriage on those two feet that the good Lord (a craftsman who stands behind his work) adjusted on her appeal, rendering them a matching shoe size. Louie for the life of him can't at the moment recall Lizzie's fiancé's name. Louie has no need for anyone's pity, but there's comfort in knowing that if he *were* to request it of Lizzie, she would extend pity to her old beau and lover and spouse and partner, who once took her for picnics on the sunny shores of Lake Michigan, and who has somehow wound up in Qaqqatnakkarsimasut, pondering where to head next.

For he can't stay forever at the Rotten Egg. It isn't merely the money. It's the sensation of being pulled at, importuned, imposed upon. Even if he avoids the Internet, the Internet is there, and available, and its availability vitiates everything. It spoils life. Though it has been something of a joke, spun out in imaginary letters to Annabelle, he has in actual fact been wondering about traveling to some scientific research outpost, reachable exclusively by helicopter. Only a few other people, and no animals, no plants, just ice—could anything be more perfect? Though he didn't catch the kid's last name, he'd bonded with that Duke grad student Kevin, who could be tracked down. Louie might carry equipment, or perhaps he could cook. It would doubtless be cooking with few ingredients, which is his sort of *cucino*.

Louie needs to clarify his thinking. He needs to clear his head, which oscillates between frantic bouts of worry and an almost invincible languor. He needs to drink less whiskey.

For the hell of it, Louie Googles "alcohol poisoning." A glass of whiskey glows beside him. To his huge surprise, he gets only nineteen hits. But maybe this isn't so surprising. And is quite damning of humanity, in fact. Isn't it fundamental human nature to be in denial and constant evasion—ignoring, if at all possible, the harsh realities that threaten us all?

Then he sees that the keyboard's sticky *o* has been spreading mischief and he has mistyped *g* for *l*: *agchl pisning*. He retypes the entry correctly and is surprised and a little overwhelmed to get three million ten thousand hits. But maybe this isn't so surprising, and is quite damning. Isn't it fundamental human nature to gather such overwhelming amounts of information that it all winds up being useless?

He has to vacate the Rotten Egg, partly because the children are making him uneasy, especially the boy. Martin's closer to puberty than Louie originally thought, and as sometimes happens when a boy's crossing that threshold, something nasty and aggressive is emerging. Recently, the three of them were watching *Upstairs, Downstairs* in the den, Louie in the armchair and the kids curled on the floor, and Fiona got up to fetch some cookies and accidentally trod on Martin's foot. And what popped out of the boy's mouth in a low mutter? The c-word: "Stupid c . . ." "Martin!" Louie cried, and for one split second Martin showed his guest an altogether new face.

It was shocking, really, the boy's new face: an expression of raw and feral defiance. Just for a moment. A single flash. The very next moment, with amazing suddenness, the boy's fair features exuded ami-ability and civility once more. And, again, Louie had to wonder if he'd misheard. But he'd seen what he'd seen. It was an ugly, ugly look: the snarl of the beast within.

Everything was piling up. The children's language (and Fiona mustn't be given a pass here!) was shocking. And on the same day when Louie received his first and final letter from Veronique ("Please if you do not write") he stumbled upon an obscene drawing in the back of Hemingway's *Green Hills of Africa*. Over the years the Rotten Egg has opened its doors to pilgrims from all over, and a little infor-mal lending library of abandoned books has assembled. Some are in Danish, some in English. Two are in French, and one in some unplace-able Asian language. (It waited on the shelf, with the patience of Miss Havisham, for the improbable arrival of another reader.) Admittedly, anyone could have fashioned the drawing. But Louie, studying it quite closely, detected not merely a crude mind but a childish hand—which narrowed the pool considerably.

The drawing consisted of two human bodies, caught from the waist down. On one, an erect and monstrous phallus stood. The other torso, supine, legs spread, was proffering a dripping and furry vagina, the pubic hair penned so furiously that it scored the paper.

What was the point in confronting Martin? The boy would not only deny it but deny it while assuming his artful, impregnable look of innocence. So slick—the kid was so damned slick! Thus it would be *Louie* who would come off as the deviating and lascivious one. And this was how it was arranged. That was how they'd arranged it—so Louie must either appear a little unhinged or be silenced altogether. But Louie knew what he knew. He'd seen on the boy's features that other sort of look—an animal snarl that was all but audible.

Louie's catching on, belatedly. It's all an arrangement, with Louie detecting sly winking exchanges between brother and sister. Far more is being communicated than is said. Living in an all but private world, the two children have evolved and perfected a private language. Any visitor has to *expect* uncanny activities when traveling above the Arctic Circle, where the sun doesn't shine for weeks at a time. Only a fool would look for psychological normalcy in the suicide capital of the world. Louie feels increasingly sure of it: for all the children's courtly politeness, all those mock curtsies and by-your-leaves, they were trafficking in cruel and inhuman mockery.

Everything drew itself with sharper outlines when Louie recalled Henry James's *The Turn of the Screw*, assigned in one of his too-few English courses at Kalamazoo. In *The Turn of the Screw*, too, you meet a pair of beautiful children with very English names—though Louie at the moment can't pull up either one. And there, too, you meet a web of communication extending into the paranormal.

The three of them were sitting in the den.

"Louie has promised to take me to America," Fiona chanted sweetly.

"He has promised to take me, too," Martin echoed. "I am going to study the art of painting. But Fiona, what will you do there, in America?"

"I will be an au pair to his children."

"And what about his wife? Won't *she* take care of the children?"

"No. Poor thing. She's going to die young. Of diphtheria."

And perfect Fiona, she of the luxuriant black eyelashes and unshadowed blue eyes, who might have stirred that master portraitist John Singer Sargent to immoral longings and immortal undertakings, lowered on Louie a survivor's look of victorious commiseration.


IF THUS FAR HIS PLANS TO JOIN A SCIENTIFIC EXPEDITION on the ice sheet have failed to pan out, perhaps because he has done nothing to further them, the ice sheet's isolated conditions can be simulated through a voluntary withdrawal from the Internet. Louie says goodbye to email. If someone needs to reach him, they can reach him, maybe, by posting a regular old-fashioned letter, care of the Rotten Egg. But why would anybody need to reach him?

He reads about the Vikings, who proposed to raise cattle on Greenland's icy ledge of rock. Sometimes alone, sometimes with the children, he watches DVDs: *Wuthering Heights* and some of both *Middlemarch* and *Brideshead Revisited.* Outside, the weather is gray and misty and cold, and often windy. He watches some of *Upstairs, Downstairs,* which is in black and white and is hard to follow, partly because of the accents, partly because the sound is muddy, partly because Martin keeps refilling his glass.

The accents remind Louie of that greasy-haired Scot in the lovely patisserie near South Ken: "I agree with everything you're saying, only it's the opposite, love." But though Louie ably recounts the story, and actually does a creditable job of pulling off a Scottish accent, neither child laughs. They don't see what's so funny, and the plain and unignorable truth is that neither one, for all their charm and intelligence, has a ghost of a sense of humor.

It's just one of many ways in which there's something uncanny and alien about the two of them. Louie has triumphantly seized on *The Turn of the Screw* as a delicious stroke, providing future fodder for hilarious traveler's anecdotes: *I was in Greenland, near the glacier, and I took up residence in this utter wreck of a faux-Victorian household that held two satanically beautiful children . . .* But he's coming around to seeing that James's novella in truth offers clarification.

Clearer and clearer it grows that there's a game underneath their game. So mutually attuned are the children—in their specialness, in their beauty, in their isolation—that they're able, soundlessly, to signal, to intrigue, to complicate, and to plot. A rich discourse lies in their sighs and glances and even coughs and sneezes: a private language, leaving them free to formulate rites and games. These rites and games are mischievous, silly, even perhaps a trifle malicious, incorporating into their structure one fascinating but ingenuous guest, the American art professor, Louie Hake.

Here's Fiona: *Louie is going to take me to America as his au pair.*

Here's Martin: *Louie will take me to America to learn the art of painting.* (Of course that *would* be the ambition of our little Danish/

English/Greenlandic squire of the manse, who is secretly a porno-graphic graffiti artist. Scheming his way through life, Martin will require some suitable, gentlemanly avocation, and he's looking to Louie to provide a cover.)

That's what's going on on one level. But there are designs under-neath such designs, and it is these Louie begins to decipher. They are seeking to catch him up in something, weave him like a helpless buzz-ing fly into a web subtle as spider's silk, but he has the great advantage of being onto them. They do not know he knows. And they couldn't begin to see the humor in it all at all. *Humor* is another word for per-spective, which of course they lack. But Louie hasn't lost perspective.

Louie's from Michigan. It's the Wolverine State, though its dwin-dled swamps and forests no longer harbor wolverines. But Louie for years had a photo of a snarling wolverine on his AAC bulletin board—posted because the furry creature, almost risible in its transmission of unreasoning rage and hostility, had seemed a perfect mascot for Aca-demia. And Louie, just recently, has glimpsed that snarling face anew, and Louie isn't going to forget it. Nor forget the eruptive obscenity of Martin's drawing, Martin's mind.

Louie puzzles it out afresh. Isn't it possible that the children's mother, who supposedly represents a danger to the children, is not truly mad? Maybe she's a victim? After all, she's not in any asylum—she lives with her parents. She goes daily to the public library. Isn't it pos-sible that while her wits may indeed have come undone at one point, this was partly the result of sensing something genuinely, unspeakably disturbing about her two unusual children?

But if the children are in league, obviously the girl is less an accom-plice than a subordinate. She's too young to be anything else and—yes—still too innocent, despite the dark proximity of a depraved elder brother. Oh, make no mistake, Martin's the ringleader. In Fiona's eyes, it still looks like a mere game. And perhaps a fateful battle is taking shape, for Louie understands, to his cost, what the little girl cannot possibly compass: the depths and depravity of male evil. This is ferocity limited only by what you think you can get away with. This is ferocity that would exuberantly tear your heart from your chest, Aztec-style, before a rapt audience. This is ferocity that would gleefully slash open your bowels, wolverine-style, if the opportunity arose. And though it's impossible to imagine what preventive steps might be required, Louie is beginning to envision circumstances arising where, in some act of heroism forced upon him, he will be duty bound to protect and rescue the poor girl.

BENDIKS IS WAKING HIM, SHAKING HIM BY THE SHOULDER. THIS has never happened before.

"Sun's out."

"Mmm?" And Louie's head is aching.

"Sun's out."

Something is out, or up. In Louie's room there's a bizarre glow, everywhere.

"You're wanting icebergs? We will go see icebergs. We'll go to the glacier."

Yes . . .

Sunlight—overexcited, puppylike, bounding and bouncing every-where at once—transfigures the bathroom, too. It's a new room. Lou-ie's toothpaste glitters with microscopic diamonds that will grind and polish his teeth to a perfect luster, whitening his smile at last.

Fiona is bustling around with those attuned white hands of hers, bringing him a cup of tea, a shot of whiskey, a bowl of cornflakes. Louie ignores the whiskey but eagerly sips the tea, munches through his cornflakes. He's surprisingly hungry this morning. Though the windows in the salon are small, this room likewise is rejuvenated, and greater illumination can only heighten the child's beauty. Sargent? It would take a Botticelli to do the girl justice.

Louie and Bendiks promenade in silence through the streets of Qaqqatnakkarsimasut. They are meeting "some chaps" down at the harbor. The sun is blinding, blissful. Between them, each contrib-uting an arm to the task, they are transporting a cooler. It is laden with beer, whiskey, graham crackers, Ritz crackers, and four tuna fish sandwiches. "Louie, I made them the way you like them," Fiona near whispered in the doorway, standing quite close, as though confiding an intimacy. And she actually pressed his hand, the precious darling. "Not too much mayonnaise and lots of sweet pickle relish."

Qaqqatnakkarsimasut is an ugly town? Yes, of course it is, and the blazing sun only highlights the clutter and litter: the shattered bottles and dented aluminum cans, cigarette butts and plastic trash bags, odd lengths of mysterious plastic tubing and stray boards of abandoned projects. But in the sunlight the houses seem far more excusable— the fuchsia and magenta and purple and cobalt-blue dwellings coming together to create Qaqqatnakkarsimasut: the one true Qaqqatnakkarsimasutian town. Colors become sounds, and the houses upraise to the heavens open whoops of gladness, spirited celebrations of our patient sun, our own dear solar system. How nicely, cozily, the universe is assembled! Everything must be seen anew.

It turns out there are six other chaps, most of whom Louie recognizes from their visits to the Rotten Egg. Three are clearly Inuit, and three are harder to place. Louie is about to climb aboard a boat. He hasn't boarded a boat since the night—longer ago than mere days can measure—when Bendiks lured him from Qaqqatkivisut to Qaqqatnakkarsimasut, from the Hotel Royale to the Rotten Egg.

The accommodating chaps have been awaiting their arrival. No sooner are Louie and Bendiks and the cooler aboard than the boat— with more ease than you might suppose in transferring from one geographical medium to another—puts to sea. Just like that. The sound of the engine, shudder after shudder, resides between a *putt-putt* and a *thump-thump*. Louie is leaving Qaqqatnakkarsimasut. And all over town, as if to mark his departure, the sled dogs set up a howling.

Bendiks refers to the boat as a "trawler." All right: trawler, then. It's maybe twenty feet long. It's made mostly of wood in need of paint. Its name is—oddly, happily—Italian. *Scompaiono—The Companion.* The trawler trails a churning white wake like a crowd of uplifted fists, water rising and falling and rising once more: triumph, defeat, triumph.

Louie knows as much about boats as he knows about horses—or hormonology. In the center of the trawler stands a snug elevated cabin, housing the pilot. Everyone else—the crew—remains on the deck, behind. It's quite warm, or the unprecedented sun fosters delicious illusions of warmth. Louie unzips his Yankee Ingenuity parka, and the gentle, fluttery, enormous wings of this new phenomenon alight upon him: arctic sun.

Louie smiles to think he's far, far north of the southern edge of Hudson's Bay. North of Hudson's Bay altogether. Oh, what an insufferable pedant he was that night with Shelley, in a little park in Soho, dutifully explaining that London lay on a latitude with the southern edge of Hudson's Bay. And admirable Shelley? Saying all that needed to be said: *Louie, can you believe the light?*

Louie believes the light. The sun is yellow and the sea is blue, and the yellow sun enters the blue sea, and all sorts of wonderful, complicated, unexpected, twinkly things transpire as the light breathes through its new marine medium. Downward, downward the glints travel, just as far as they can go, excursions of photons, if that's what they are, into an ocean deep and blue and so cold as to steal your heart away. (It does not bear thinking about, how briefly a man—a man named Louie Hake, say—would survive if dropped into that element.) (So, don't think about it, Louie. Set your heart elsewhere.)

Their doughty trawler arrives at a juncture where Qaqqatnakkarsimasut is a lovely pocket of jewels, an open, tiered box of crayons, and after that a threshold is reached, and breached, and the town grows smaller still, and duller, and they're really at sea. Qaqqatnakkarsimasut is a bright dot wedged into an endless run of bare brown-gray hills outstretched on either side, north and south.

In Greenland finally Louie has glimpsed his first icebergs: low gray sullen masses loitering in a deadbeat harbor. But if those were icebergs, he needs a new word for what he's witnessing now, a parade of tall pristine whiter-than-white hills upheld by a blue firmament. So much larger, but that's only the start. These icebergs are radiant beings. They are of this world and beyond this world. They are light.

Not just full of light but light—as near weightless as meringues, as spun sugar, spun cotton. Closer kin to clouds than to ice. The little trawler is headed toward the glacier.

Louie has been told the glacier's name, but like so much instruction in Greenland, it has rolled out of memory. In fact, he relishes the phrase's unspecified, primordial sound: *headed toward the glacier.* As if there were but one. The ur-, the alpha, glacier.

"How far's the glacier?" Louie asks Bendiks.

"As the crow flies? Not far."

"But we're not going as the crow flies?"

"We will wander. We will be out most of the day. We're celebrating." The hand perched on Bendiks's knee holds a whiskey bottle.

"Celebrating?"

"It's Sunday."

"Is it?" Louie says.

"Or Tuesday."

"I was thinking more like that. Like Tuesday."

"We are celebrating the return of the sun at last."

"It has been quite unyousual weather," Louie observes.

"Drink?" Bendiks waggles the whiskey bottle.

"Maybe later."

Louie has no need for inebriants. The air's inebriating. The light is inebriating, rebounding off the sea in configurations quicker than thought. The receptive flanks of the icebergs signal each to each, like chess pieces. Louie once read a grandmaster explaining that a peripheral pawn's movement changes the value of every piece on the board. Ten? Twenty? How many icebergs can he count if he swings his head completely around? And all linked somehow—linked in a unified bobbing concourse of northernness and salt sea and sun.

There is no color on earth, it turns out, more lovely than the soft blue hue huddling and flourishing in the sanctuary just underneath the edges of some but not all of the icebergs. Louie has long suspected Frederic Church of exaggeration—taking painterly license with his iceberg pigments. But no. Church was seeking merely, pure-heartedly, to do justice. He was following an artist's compact that said, *If this world offers such beauty, it shall be my task, the best I can, to replicate it.*

Bubbles of pure filtered bliss keep pop-popping in Louie's bloodstream, up and down each limb. He's all but airborne. By nature, this sort of ecstatic state cannot last, and yet this one lingers and lingers. Every day, every day without knowing it, his soul has been praying for arctic sun and sea, and now, having been given them, he'll ride them in a state of apportioned rapture. He saw a silent movie once where a man rode a cake of ice down the slopes of a golf course, mutely guffawing the whole way, steering his ice cake as surely as their little trawler threads through its blue-and-white labyrinth.

They are heading to the glacier. Around them, the white maze of icebergs thickens, growing taller.

"More than a hundred thousand years old."

"Mm?" Louie says.

"Deep in the ice cores on the ice sheet, the snow can be more than a hundred thousand years old. A thousand centuries. Of course these icebergs are much younger."

But Louie ignores Bendiks's final qualification. The image is too beautiful not to be pervasively true. One-hundred-thousand-year-old icebergs! While these crystal sculptures were being compacted, mastodons lumbered through the Loire Valley, camels moseyed across Wyoming. And in Greenland a dusting of snow was commencing a sea journey that would consummate in a thousand centuries.

"How tall do the icebergs get?" Louie asks.

"Maybe a hundred meters." Bendiks is right at home; he enjoys talking numbers. "In 2011, one broke off that was ninety-seven square miles. Bigger than four Manhattans."

"Four Manhattans," Louie marvels. "It's a frightening thought," he goes on. "Surely one Manhattan's quite enough, thanks." Louie laughs bobbingly, and redoubles his laughter when Bendiks fails to join him. A hundred meters, nearly a hundred square miles, a thousand centuries, a hundred thousand years—Louie is floating through a blizzard of zeroes.

Most of the icebergs are blindingly white, but the juddering boat comes upon a true *ice*berg. It isn't grainy the way the snow icebergs are. It's smooth and transparent as a cube in a cocktail. It's of a modest size, maybe thirty feet tall, though Louie has indeed entered a reordered world if blocks of ice standing thirty feet tall are modestly proportioned.

But that's not what's most remarkable. What's most remarkable is how intimately this iceberg mimics a Henry Moore sculpture.

Come closer.

Come closer, bring your little trawler closer. The ice rings you round. Enter the enclosure, and the resemblance only deepens. The engine thumps, its wake a crowd of pumping white fists, and the iceberg—the reclining body of an epicene colossus—becomes more Moore than Moore. Truly the likeness is astonishing. (It's enough to make you subscribe to that immemorial notion that nothing in art is created—merely rediscovered, found anew. Since the beginning of time the glacier has been fashioning Moores, indifferent to any copyists who might emerge to observe them. (And into the sea, casually, the glacier dumps its refuse Moores. And the sea, though cold enough to kill a man in minutes, is too warm for the Moores: it burns them up. (Come closer, enter the enclosure. The glacier is pitching one gigantic Moore after another into a smelting furnace, liquefying and recycling: the sculptures are to be fashioned anew. (And no escaping the revelation that this particular Moore, glimpsed one blazing day in July of 2014 by Louis Hake Jr., age forty-three, is more beautiful than any mere Moore. A thing of purer materials, purified inspiration.))))

Clouds are scattered across the sky, but they keep missing the sun. Or you might say the sun steers through its own field of bergs, artfully avoiding collision.

Louie in his Yankee Ingenuity is plenty warm, which is a good thing, for they're headed due north. When Qaqqatnakkarsimasut disappeared, it disappeared utterly. Now it might be a mile behind them, might lie remote as Miami. The shore is a far succession of dark basaltic hills, veined with snow, on which no sign of life resides other than the muddy olive green of what must be lichens and moss. Not a tree, not a shrub. Above the land's brink, white gulls spiral and spiral, like-wise seeking signs of life. There were gulls in Rome. They have been following him. Or he them. Black birds, too, are spiraling.

"Cormorants," Bendiks says. "Drink?"

"Maybe later."

"We're celebrating."

Louie is. Usually when he reaches this degree of pleasure and excit-ability he needs to shift into action: go somewhere, purchase some-thing, maybe make love (if someone's around to make love to). But now he's content effectively to lie back, though he is standing up, let-ting everything wash over. Protracted minutes. The boating party will be out for much of the day. Or out until sundown (where the sun never does go down). Time all but stops.

Behind the pilot's cabin, standing in its lee (if that's the nauti-cal term), Louie drops his head back and shutters his eyes. The boat rumbles in its bones, and his own bones rumble with it. Against his eyelids the sun inspires a seething dance of fluorescent oranges and greens, the internal counterpart of the dance unfolding on the sea's surface. The dance on the sea mixes melting lozenges of lavender-tinged beige with melting lozenges of lemon brushed with robin's-egg blue. The Impressionists are universally too much loved, and Louie is always sniping at them in his classroom, but you could argue that they, especially Manet, were the first painters to see the sea: all those big improbable dollops of color disporting on the surface, the shades all wrong if you stop and look, but the paintings a confirmation of the notion that in looking you must never stop. The true sea painting is kinetic, and you fail the painting unless you're kinetic, too. A second later, this particular sea sector is a different place, the painting a dif-ferent painting.

Louie yearns to start over. Start grad school over and this time do it right. He recently watched *Oliver Twist,* and he, like Oliver, is say-ing, "Please, sir, I want some more." Not some more gruel, but some more life, a new start. There's no earthly reason he can't complete his book on American landscape painting, or can't write a groundbreaking essay about those overexplicated Impressionists. If he often has trouble marshaling his thoughts, he nonetheless sees freshly—sees things not everybody sees.

Though they've been on board less than two hours, he's hungry. He takes a tuna sandwich from the cooler, vowing to eat only half. But the humble creation is perfect: tuna and finely minced onion and not too much mayo (but not too little mayo) and a generous blending of sweet pickle relish, all enfolded in soft white bread. Fiona, his dear little factotum, who will turn eighteen the year Louie turns a youthful fifty, has even found a crunchy leaf of the only variety of lettuce Louie truly loves: iceberg, of course. Louie is staring out toward the shore. Trimmed with snow, brown bare hill follows brown bare hill, north, north. Mile after mile, and not a house, not a tree, not even a bush. It's a prospect of pure desolation in delicious contrast with the bounty and industry and collective human ingenuity embodied by the sandwich in his hand. In the sun, the iceberg leaf is a delectable pale green with hints of gold within, and the bits of pickle are another delectable pale green with hints of gold, though the two greens are not quite the same green, even if they embrace the same gold. Nothing he has partaken of since his arrival in Greenland equals it.

Though he likes to think of himself as a mostly gregarious guy, if not a hale fellow well met, Louie has made no effort to get to know anyone in Qaqqatnakkarsimasut other than the three inhabitants of the Rotten Egg. He has been ill, and this journey to the glacier represents convalescence. Health is the true friend he seeks. He has met most, maybe all, of his fellow passengers, who at one point or another have sat in the salon drinking with Bendiks, but Louie recalls none of their names. He has failed utterly to reach out, man to man. Now, to make amends, he grins fondly at each in turn, points at his sandwich and grins, points at this or that iceberg and grins. Sunny grins relay round the boat. Friendships blossom. They're a good lot, these hearty chaps, and they don't seem to hold Louie's former surliness against him.

Everyone is drinking but Louie.

Louie needs no drink. He has gone into rehab; the sun is his detoxifier. Honestly he requires nothing but sunlight and a deserted coastline and a blue sea that you'd swear was warm—so warm is the color—were it not for the panoramic icebergs suspended within it.

And what have we here? They are approaching the most extraordinary iceberg of all. Not the tallest or broadest, but the most singularly shaped. It is an animal—the largest animal ever beheld. It dips down at one end, as though crouching, and triumphantly swells upward at the other. It is a couchant lion. It is a sphinx, though bigger and subtler than anything ever erected, by thousands of nameless and dehydrated slaves, back in the Fourth Dynasty. It's a wolf howling at a vanished moon. It's a Chinese New Year's dragon parade float, ushering in a zodiac of unprecedented health and prosperity. Or (as seen from a boat whose wake is a throng of white fists) the beast's upraised head is the vastest protesting fist in all creation. It is the blazing white zenith of Stalinist sculpture—a proletarian triumph so complete that the age-old tyranny of aesthetics itself is overthrown.

The string of not-quite-discovered similes leaves Louie restless. He rubs his palms fiercely together, as though they itch. "I'll write in my travel journal," he says aloud.

He has written very little there, actually. He has proceeded in fits and starts. He scribbled some twenty pages in a Kensington café on his way to the Natural History Museum. But that was basically a letter to his lost Lizoliz. What he wants to record now is a credo.

Louie writes in bullet points. You might argue that he has always written in bullet points, and this has been his problem: he has trouble connecting the dots. Or you could say those dots are his icebergs, and he is ready now to thread his way among them.

Louie writes:

· The traveler comes to Greenland mostly to see what the country throws away. All sorts of things, but the item of greatest interest is icebergs. They're big and intricate as cathedrals and the country casually dumps them into the water every day.

· Today I saw an iceberg that looked more like Henry Moore than Henry Moore does. [There's a better way to phrase this; maybe come upon it later?] It was a recumbent figure. A nude, I'm tempted to say—an androgynous nude. (What is that better synonym for androgynous? Begins with an *e.*) It had that air of outward-gazing curiosity Moore gives so many of his figures. So that when you're approaching them, saying What exactly is that?, they're saying What exactly are you? [Better—pretty good in fact.]

· You might not guess it, but sometimes the hardest thing in getting to Greenland is convincing your big sister about the value of your trip. [Phrasing could be better.]

· It may be the most beautiful blue in nature, the blue that gathers underneath a sunlit iceberg, though maybe some of its beauty lies in how close it comes to something tawdry—the blue of mouthwash, of toilet-bowl cleaner, of Duskcutters, of jellybeans that have abandoned any pretense that their flavors are extracted from actual fruits.

· Sometimes it's amazing what we don't see, even if it's right in front of our eyes. But equally amazing is what we <u>do</u> see, though maybe we don't realize we do. Many lifetimes ago (actually maybe a month ago) I was sitting in my apartment in Ann Arbor, having breakfast alone, maybe feeling sorry for myself. I was eating a bowl of Rice Chex and I looked at the cardboard half-gallon milk container and I realized that I can judge with real accuracy how full a milk container is by the extent to which the cardboard bows ever so slightly with its contents. The more contents, the more it bows. We're talking here about a tiny, tiny shift, in the scale of millimeters, but it was as if I could see right through the opaque cardboard to the milk within. I <u>knew</u> what was there, exactly how <u>much</u> milk, behind the veil of the container. The moment was antidotal. In it, I appreciated the miracle of sight as much as I appreciate it when I'm standing beside an iceberg more painstakingly fashioned than Orvieto's Duomo.

· I read somewhere about a man who could identify classical LPs across the room by the shimmers of light their grooves threw off.

Even different recordings of the same piece. You could cover up the record label and he could identify which version of Beethoven's Fifth Symphony it was by the microscopic variations in the grooves. You think, What a bizarre talent. It wasn't the result of training or cultivation—he just realized one day this bizarre ability was hard-wired into him. He might never even have known he had it. That's what's so haunting. He had to be born in an age of LPs to recognize this strange God-given talent, a kind of bar-code decoder in his brain allowing him to make extremely fine distinctions involving extremely fine gradations. And of course you have to wonder, How many people are born with a similar ability to read the world's obscurest bar codes, only they never identify their talent?

Louie senses he's onto something genuine at last. He pauses a few moments and then writes:

· Like icebergs we all take the light in. But what then? How richly do you glow? Isn't that the real question: How richly do you glow?

"You're not celebrating." Bendiks.

"I'm celebrating." Louie. "I'm celebrating with words. And I'm passing through a narrow ocean passageway between two vast icebergs that could grind and crush our little boat if they had a mind to, only they don't have a mind to. This is why I came to Greenland. I've never been happier."

But Louie is happier still as their little trawler slips alongside a much-lower iceberg, maybe only twenty or thirty feet high, but long—long like a football field, long like the quadrangle at Ann Arbor College that is the school's one glory, long like those city blocks in Detroit where buildings have been razed and the horizons beckon. Here, too, is a city, yet a thriving one. This iceberg is a floating plateau or tableland. It is horizontal in character and outlook, like (Louie feels himself addressing a classroom of AAC undergrads) all the best work of Frank Lloyd Wright. (We'll ignore how that great man, who was also a pitiful megalomaniac, made plans for a mile-high building.) Yes, here, too, is a city, like Orvieto on top of its plateau: blocks, neighborhoods. Roadways and roundabouts. Causeways, esplanades. Push it now, push yourself: truly consider its creation and re-creation, over the centuries, all so painstaking, all accomplished to the creaking pulse of the glaciers' retardive music. Upon this floating island everything is compact, Manhattan-style. And everything white, the synesthete's delight, the marriage of all colors. White marketplaces, white offices, white graveyards, white temples, white greenways. See your vision, Louie. The buried civic dreams of Nineveh and Babylon. Akkad. Ur. It's the best dream there is, perhaps, or the best dream he himself is capable of: the fair-proportioned community, the packed, negotiated, collective genius of home. Pediments and archways and peristyles swinging past, balconets and balustrades; ashlar and cladding; metope, triglyph, echinus, stylobate; post and beam, the invention of the arch, the airborne arch spun on a fixed axis to originate the dome. And all of it celestial white, the White Everlasting. And all of it dissolving. Into a burning salt sea older than the hills.

TWO, OR THREE, OR FIVE HOURS LATER, HAVING WOLFED down more than his share of the tuna sandwiches (three of the four) and having sipped a little whiskey, Louie comes upon the strangest sight of all. It materializes as they return to harbor. There's a taxi waiting where they dock, though nothing strange about that. But the person inside the taxi, who as the trawler reaches its berth steps out of the taxi into brilliant sunshine, is somebody he knows.

It's somebody he knows and yet doesn't know, for when things are as strange as this, even the most familiar sights and objects and people may appear alien.

There's a strange popping sensation when this sizable figure steps out of the taxi. It's like the way Louie sometimes feels on a plane, when he'll swallow and his ears pop—his head pops—and abruptly every sound alters: the engine's roar, the voices around him, the voices over the PA system. He has relieved the pressure on his eardrums and no sound can remain the same.

It's just like that: his eyes pop, relieving a pressure, his entire head pops, and nothing's the same. For the briefest of moments, he knows he knows the figure clambering out of the black taxicab into the queer glaring sun, but it could be anybody. It could be Florence, having abandoned Satan and the Virgins in her belated pursuit of him, or it could be dear Lizoliz, in her blue Keds with red laces. It could even be girlish Veronique, warm and fine and slick with sweat.

This is just like a dream, and then the dream wakes him. It's Annabelle.

It's Annabelle, and when he baby-steps down the wooden gangway onto solid ground, stony ground, forward she comes bounding and throws her arms fast around him. "Louie! Louie! Louie!" she cries, as if he isn't returning from a day's excursion—as if he is miraculously reconstituted from the domain of the dead.

"You're all *right*!" she cries. "Look at me, look at me, *look* at me! Oh my God your face, Louie! A beard! This isn't you at all!"

This isn't you.

"Not you at all! And your lovely hair! When did you last get a haircut? Or even brush it? Tell me you're all right, Louie! Tell me you're all right."

"I'm perfectly all right," Louie replies. "I've been monitoring everything very carefully."

"And your body! Look at you—*look* at you! You're wasting away! For heaven's sake, you must weigh *nothing*."

He is gathering his wits, and this time his reply is perfect: "I am steadily becoming a concentrate of myself."

"Greenland!" Annabelle cries. "Louie, you made me chase you down in *Greenland*!"

"I'm here working on my book," Louie points out. "Distance is clarifying. Antidotal. And I'm making progress. Today, in particular, making real progress. Please understand, finding the right work space, the balance of external and internal, is a mysterious process, as any true artist will tell you. I needed to flip it."

"Look at you! A beard! Your hair! But you're all right? Tell me you're all right! You weigh nothing! And I've done nothing but worry!"

"Yes. Yes, of course I'm all right, Annabelle."

"Why didn't you *write* me? Why did you stop *writing*?"

"I've been needing to concentrate. In order to write."

"But you're all right. Thank God, thank God, it's my little brother and he's all right . . ."

The other passengers dissolve away. It's what bystanders tend to do in Annabelle's presence: dissolve away. It's as if only the two of them remain. They might be a pair of children stepping out from the Larkins' bomb shelter, into the afterglow.

Annabelle rattles on—so many words. She's been so worried. She's been beside herself. He has no idea. They climb into the taxi, though the Rotten Egg is easy walking distance. "I can see it. I can see you're all right, Louie," Annabelle declares as the clattering black taxi winds up a trashed stone hill toward the Rotten Egg. "You need rest, of course, and care and supervision, and lots of decent decent food, but you're all right, really."

"I'm making genuine progress at last," Louie points out.

"I'm sure you are."

It's quite confusing. Louie's prepared to introduce his sister to all the ramshackle charms and eccentricities of the Rotten Egg, but she explains that she has already been there. It was the first place she stopped after her journey by boat from Qaqqatkivisut. "Honestly, Louie, honestly! The Rotten *Egg*?" she cries—her voice grown even shriller inside the taxi. "And the air in that place—my God! It's unbreathable! No wonder you're sick."

"I wouldn't say I'm sick precisely," Louie says. "The air? I guess it's all the smoking Bendiks does."

Now they're climbing out of the taxi. Annabelle is paying by credit card. She's catching on to how things work in Qaqqatnakkarsimasut.

Hold on to your money. Send the bills back to far-fetched America, where they're less likely to bother you. Or track you down.

"The *Rotten* Egg? What were you *thinking*? Couldn't you tell just by the sign?"

"The sign?" Louie echoes.

"The *sign*, Louie." Annabelle points upward, maybe eight feet above the door.

The sign isn't large—maybe a foot and a half square—and quite weathered, so maybe it's not so surprising that Louie steadily missed it day after day as he trudged in and out through the fog and rain. And yet it *is* surprising, and disturbing, actually; it's hard to believe he has been so unobservant.

It's a tribute or a parody, Louie supposes, of a traditional English pub sign. Another of Bendiks's mordant little strokes. At the top of the sign, the twelve letters of THE ROTTEN EGG are in a Gothic script. Below is an egg, plump at the bottom and tapering toward the top. And on the surface of the crudely painted and badly faded egg, you can discern the bulge of South America on the bottom left and the bigger bulge of Africa on the bottom right, and above them the raggedy outline of Europe, a faded brown dollop of Iceland, and the foreshortened gray-white splotch of Greenland, whose big arrowhead shape once, as glimpsed on an outdated map in a travel agency in Soho, pierced Louie's heart. The Rotten Egg? The rotten egg is our own Earth.

Annabelle not only has already been here, she has set things in a whirlwind of motion. She has been in Louie's room and sorted through his suitcases and the various items on the floor. She has done a wash. She has done more than one wash. Even as the two of them arrive, his clothes are spinning in the dryer.

"Louie, where on earth is your herringbone linen shirt?"

"My herringbone linen shirt?"

"The one I bought you. For your trip. You said you packed it. You said it would be perfect for India."

"Ah, India . . ." Louie says. "You know I ate some bad tandoori chicken. I think it was the chicken—"

"And what are you doing with that old bread? I honestly thought it was a rock. I honestly thought it was a *rock*."

"Well, I did quit eating it a while ago."

"The Rotten *Egg*! Louie, honestly now. Honestly . . ."

"There is a logic here."

Now the two of them are sitting in the salon. Fiona has brought bowls of corn on which little pillows of butter comfortably repose. Also she sets beside Louie a tumbler with an inch or so of liquid. "What's that?" Annabelle asks sharply. She holds it up to her sensitive nose. "Take that away," she orders.

Louie spoons up his corn. It's all overwhelming, but it's also quite fascinating. A collision of two worlds, here, in Greenland, where wonderful precedent exists for worlds in collision.

Fascinating, too, is Annabelle's force—the field of force that surrounds her, that she marshals. Never before has he perceived so clearly this invisible field of force. His own sister. As if she had to materialize in Greenland to come fully into her unstoppable own. Really, she is something.

"Are we flying out today?" Louie asks. In fairness, he would like to be informed of what is happening.

"*Today?* There are no more flights out *today*. Honestly, you can't believe what a burden you put on me, getting to whatever this place is called."

"Qaqqatnakkarsimasut." He has been practicing the sound. Surely no native of the town could rattle off the syllables with much more fluency.

"If you say so. Honestly, Louie, honestly."

"Well, it's good we're not leaving today. I'll need a little time. To put things in order. In fact—well, I don't want to hold you up, my dear. That wouldn't be fair. Maybe you'd want to leave first, Annabelle? Maybe I could join you later?"

"Hold me up? Leave first? *Listen* to you! Do you hear yourself? Out of the question, Louie. *Out.* You don't honestly think I'd leave you *here* do you? Not when you're this way."

"I'm not sure which way you mean."

"But you're *all right*. Knowing you the way I do, knowing your *face* the way I do, I can tell everything. Behind that beard you can't hide a thing, and my little brother's all right. Or you're going to be all right."

And all at once, tears well and spill from the woman's eyes. Louie feels an urge to reach across and take her hands, which is what he customarily does in a restaurant or bar when a woman across the table succumbs to tears. But Louie overrides the urge. Displays of that sort aren't the way he and Annabelle communicate.

"I'm making progress," Louie offers.

"But you're out of here."

"Out of here?"

"You've spent your last night in the Rotten Egg, I'm happy to say."

"I have?"

"I've booked us two rooms at the Polar Nights Hotel. Just up the road. It's no Econo Lodge, but it's perfectly all right."

"That's okay," Louie says. "That's okay if it's no Econo Lodge."

Martin approaches and wonders whether the two of them "require anything."

"Yeah," Annabelle says. "I'd like a Coca-Cola. You have Coca-Cola? You know Coca-Cola?"

Martin would be delighted to bring the two of them Coca-Colas.

Of all the sweeping and dramatic changes that Annabelle's presence has immediately wrought, none is more striking than the wholesale transformation of the children. Louie in recent days has been spinning the Rotten Egg through *The Turn of the Screw*, partly in fun and partly in the gathering suspicion that the book has something informative to say about the beautiful siblings' clairvoyant closeness. But none of these suspicions can stand up to Annabelle's arrival. The supernatural withers and fades in the presence of her stolid, midwestern commonsensicality. Both of these awesomely bright and eloquent children stare at her in a kind of dumbstruck awe. And as Martin sets the Cokes before them, Louie observes, at the base of one artful ivory nostril, a burgeoning red pimple. He's merely a boy, after all. A boy approaching the befuddling and humbling mortifications of puberty. Nothing is less aristocratic than a pimple.

"Quite a handsome young lad," Louie observes to his sister after Martin disappears.

Annabelle shakes her head sagely. "All the girls? Ooh, they're going to have to watch out for *him*. He's a born Romeo, that one is. Up to whatever he pleases. A born Romeo."

But where is Bendiks? Bendiks has vanished, which is only appropriate, since the world he inhabits and the world Annabelle inhabits are antipodal. And she has established an impregnable beachhead here, in Bendiks's sanctuary. Bendiks is forever talking about reality—molecules, magnetic fields, the universe that is nothing but air with all the air removed—but in reality, reality itself cannot stand up to the undeniable substantiality of Ms. Annabelle Hake, spooning up canned corn and drinking a Coca-Cola.

"And the girl," Louie continues. "Fiona. She'll break hearts herself."

"Oh, now *she's* something else, Louie. Calling me *madame*. Not madam, *madame*. And those sly, slide-y eyes. I trust *her* no further than I could throw her."

"But I think she's very dear. Very *sweet*," Louie protests. He must defend his easily misunderstood Fiona, who day after day has watched out for him with those ardent blue eyes and busy slender white hands. She, too—the surpassingly lovely au pair to his nonexistent children, to the child within him—is drifting away, like a fading song, a lullaby.

"Sweet?" Annabelle echoes, and sips from her Coca-Cola. "That one's rehearsing to be a man-eater, Louie."

"Annabelle, surely . . . I mean, I mean she's just a—"

"You can trust me on that. I know them when I see them. Gobble, gobble. Man-eaters."

All the butter has melted on his bowl of corn. Gone. Or invisible—one more invisible presence.

"So you're in Qaqqatnakkarsimasut," Louie says.

"I'm in whatever-the-heck," Annabelle says. "Whatevertheheckville. You can't believe what all it took me to get here. You sent me on some wild-goose chase, Louie Hake."

"But Annabelle Hake is in Qaqqatnakkarsimasut."

Annabelle laughs, the first time he has heard her laughter since her arrival. No one else on earth knows her bright hiccupy laughter as he does. Throughout her life, no one else so often has made her laugh, made her hiccup. "Yes," she says, "Annabelle Hake is in What-evertheheckville, Greenland. And you really are going to be all right, Louie. You're sounding more and more like yourself. Up to all your old clever tricks. Remember how often she used to say it: *The boy wants watching?*"

*She* is their distant stepmother, out in Arizona, caring for her brothers—her true family.

"That old dance of yours, Louie," Annabelle goes on. "Making it impossible for anybody to stay angry with you. Acting now just as though your coming to Greenland was all done for my benefit. You want watching, Louie. Somehow turning all your hijinks and mis-deeds into these oh-so-considerate actions."

"I thought of Dad today," Louie says. "How much he would have enjoyed seeing all the colors in the icebergs."

*"Dad,"* Annabelle says and sighs contentedly, as if she has summed him up perfectly—as though the search for him were now accom-plished, rather than freshly begun.

"You see, Annabelle," Louie goes on, "you and I were born at just the right time. Nobody from Michigan in Dad's generation would have thought of coming to Greenland. And a generation from now, it's going to be too sad for words, melting away to a point where not even the Republicans will be denying it. But you and I, Annabelle, we've arrived at the magical melting point."

Louie as they sip their Cokes is struck by the size of Annabelle's head. Perhaps Danes and Inuit tend to have relatively small heads, but Louie feels prepared to testify that Annabelle's skull has increased by at least one hat size since he saw her last. Of course, his own head's still reeling.

"Are we leaving tomorrow?"

"Louie Hake, you honestly don't have *any idea,* do you? Of all the troubles you've put me through? What do you think this godforsaken town is, Las Vegas? With a flight out every twenty minutes? If you *knew* the difficulties you gave me in getting out here, in arranging our flights back . . . We fly out of the other Q town in three days."

"The other Q town?"

"The other town that begins with *Q.*"

"Qaqqatkivisut." Louie adds, "It's a bit of a pit."

"So you come and settle in the Rotten Egg instead?"

She laughs once more, although this time the laughter isn't fully genuine. He has worried her.

"You must admit this unyousual establishment has atmosphere."

Louie waves his arms around, to take in the salon, the business center, the DVD den, the boozer's bomb shelter, and poor stinking Gasper, who in all of his nine lives will never once leave town. "More even than an Econo Lodge."

Annabelle shakes her head censoriously, but at bottom she's too elated for censure, too elated to be here and find him okay. His old dance is working.

"If you know how worried everybody was . . ."

"Everybody?"

"Dr. Douglas, for one."

"Dr. Douglas? That old skirt-chaser? So he took time off from chasing his tennis babes to show his Concern?"

Another shaking of her head, although this time the censure looks more genuine. "Louie, you really do need *rest.*"

"Rest? That's all I've been doing," Louie protests. And protests again: "Though I've been working hard. I've been working very, very hard on my book."

"When we get back, Louie, I want you to move in with me. I won't take no for an answer."

"I'm going to move to *Livonia*?"

"Just until you get things settled."

"What is there to settle?" Louie asks.

"I've come too far. I won't take no for an answer."

"No, I suppose you won't," Louie says after a moment.

He smiles to show he means no offense, and in her reciprocating smile, in which her upper teeth emerge and clamp down on her lower lip, Louie glimpses once more the buried child in his middle-aged big sister. All the years for a moment recede, and there she is, his companion in arms—just a kid, biting her lip. As they always have, they are playing together, here in Greenland: strategizing against the world.

"So we're not leaving for three days?" he asks.

"That's right." Big sister Annabelle is positively aglow. "If there's no other choice, well, heck, we'll just make the best of it. There's an Inuit settlement that we can go visit, and a sled-dog display, and some meet-your-local-craftsman thing at the Polar Hotel tomorrow night."

"Meet your local craftsman?"

"With things for sale. Does that sound good?"

"Well—. Sure thing. I bought you some magnets."

"Magnets?"

"For the fridge."

"The fridge?"

Her thoughts are far removed from her kitchen in Livonia. She says: "Louie, you have to understand this is the most exciting thing I've ever done! My first time across an ocean, and where do I end up? No one'll believe it back at the shelter." The animal shelter. "Annabelle's back from *Greenland*! We have three whole days, Louie, and I mean to make the most of them. Though I am going to have to speak to somebody about how they treat their dogs here."

"They're sled dogs. Annabelle, the Inuit have been dealing with their dogs since the beginning of—"

"I do need to speak to someone about it."

Fairness, justice—these must be his paramount concern, and these are in fact complicated ideals. Contrary realities are competing, and hers, above all, must be respected. Louie understands her bubbling excitement and empathizes with it. Above all, he must be fair. Annabelle, too, is making her way. If you think about it, about the women he knows, Annabelle has done such a bold and improbable and noble thing in venturing alone to Qaqqatnakkarsimasut. His bold, brave big sister, come to fetch him home.

"That's right. It's your journey," Louie pronounces. "You're on your journey."

Annabelle takes his hand on the tabletop, meshing their fingers up to the knucklebones. "It's our journey, Louie," she replies. "And it's going to be wonderful."

## LULLABY FOR L

The first of your dreams discovers
   a Mediterranean rose,
beckoning you toward its center
   as the warm petals close.

The second rose is English;
   its old garden is a place
where stalks have been cut back,
   grey autumn shows its face,

while here's a darker flower,
   an exotic bloom that takes you
to a land of melting deserts
   where the third dream wakes you.

# ACKNOWLEDGMENTS

Writers will often harbor unrealized ambitions, with debt clearance prominent among them. In my own case, indebtedness seems only to deepen over time.

Thanks are owed to two of my oldest friends, Rick Lyon and John Chapman, who offered helpful queries, and occasional protests, about earlier drafts. I'm grateful to Dr. Marjorie Block for dental instruction. And grateful to Arthur Higbee and Alice Houston, who provided me with creative shelter on two continents.

Whenever something I'm working on leads to scientific questions—with this novel, questions about physics—I drag them over to Kannan Jagannathan of Amherst College, who over the years has shown a strikingly cheery and unflappable patience with a slow but stubborn pupil.

Perhaps the deepest debt of all belongs to my remarkable editor, Ann Close, who through four decades has stuck beside me with vinelike fidelity.

## THE ART STUDENT'S WAR

The year is 1943. Bianca Paradiso is a pretty and ambitious eighteen-year-old studying to be an artist while her bustling, thriving hometown turns from mass-producing automobiles to rolling out fighter planes and tanks. For Bianca, national and personal conflicts begin to merge when she is asked to draw portraits of the wounded young soldiers who are filling local hospitals. Suddenly, she must confront lives maimed at their outset as well as her own romantic yearnings, and she must do so at a time when another war—a war within her own family—is erupting.

Fiction

## A FEW CORRECTIONS

According to his obituary, Wesley Sultan led a quiet, respectable, and unremarkable life. Our narrator, however, is about to discover that nothing could be further from the truth. As he travels from the bleak Michigan winter to the steamy streets of Miami to the idyllic French countryside, in search of those who knew Wesley best, he gradually reconstructs the life of an exceptionally handsome, ambitious, and deceptive man to whom women were everything. As the margins of the obituary fill with handwritten corrections, as details emerge and facts are revised, our mysterious narrator—whose interest in his quarry is far from random—has no choice but to confront the truth of his own life as well.

Fiction

## THE FRIENDS OF FREELAND

Freeland—happily isolated and stubbornly independent—is in trouble. The sins of the rest of the world have begun to wash up on its shores in the form of drugs, restless youth, and a polluted, fished-out ocean. To add to the complications, when Hannibal, who has promised to step down as president, decides to run again, the opposition imports three "electoral consultants" from the United States. While Hannibal is Fate's adored, Eggert, his shrewd, devious sidekick and adviser, travels perpetually under a cloud. Orphaned early, he must make his way by his wits. We follow him from his youth as he adventures Down Below (any place south of Freeland), collecting women, lovers, children, restlessly churning out fifty books in his search for love and admiration, returning home at last to raise a family and to serve his friend in his political hour of need. This stunning, magical book brims with pleasures: delicious satire as the independent-minded natives meet the U.S.-trained "spin doctors"; a vibrant comic-strip vitality; and an edgy poignancy. Readers who journey to Freeland will find it both a land of wonders and an ideal place from which to view the world they've left behind.

Fiction

VINTAGE BOOKS
Available wherever books are sold.
www.vintagebooks.com

Printed in the United States
by Baker & Taylor Publisher Services